A Test O

"Anyone who has ever struggled in a mother-daughter relationship will identify with Karen Ball's *A Test of Faith*. The story is as real as the evening newspaper. It was as if I was reading about my own mother, my own daughter, and perhaps more profoundly, reading about myself."
—DEBBIE MACOMBER, *New York Times* bestselling author

"As a mother of daughters, I was quickly drawn into the world of Anne and Faith. I laughed and I cried throughout *A Test of Faith*. And at the end, I thanked God for my own mother and daughters. Thank you, Karen Ball, for this beautiful and memorable story."
—ROBIN LEE HATCHER, bestselling author of *Beyond the Shadows*

"With fierce reverence, Karen Ball takes hold of truth with both hands and lovingly molds it into a life-changing story that readers will treasure."
—ROBIN JONES GUNN, bestselling author of the Sisterchicks™ novels

"A story this honest could only come from the deepest, most tender places in a writer's heart. Karen Ball is a highly skilled author who has gifted us with a gripping, heartfelt tale of the times."
—KAREN KINGSBURY, bestselling author of *One Tuesday Morning*, *Oceans Apart*, and the Redemption series

The Breaking Point

"*The Breaking Point* is compelling and strikingly honest. This story touches the heart and gives hope for struggling marriages. Karen Ball writes with clarity, depth, and power. It's a pleasure to recommend this engaging and memorable book."
—RANDY ALCORN, bestselling author of *Safely Home*

"*The Breaking Point* is must-reading for any couple seeking God's ideal in this wonderful covenant we know as marriage."
—ANGELA ELWELL HUNT, author of *The Debt*

"Gut-wrenching in its honesty and passion, *The Breaking Point* packs a powerful message of obedience and God's healing."
—BRANDILYN COLLINS, bestselling author of *Color the Sidewalk for Me* and *Eyes of Elisha*

"An honest, heartfelt novel about the craggy recesses of marriage—where God does some of His best work. Karen Ball's writing is emotionally gripping and full of insight."
—JAMES SCOTT BELL, bestselling author of *Breach of Promise*

"In *The Breaking Point*, Karen Ball exposes the painful, honest truth of marriage: It's hard work. This story of lives out of control, love misplaced, and the wounds we often give each other in the name of righteous direction is carefully balanced with God's love, hope, and ministry of reconciliation. I highly recommend this book."
—TRACIE PETERSON, bestselling author of the Desert Rose series and *Eyes of the Heart*

Novels by Karen Ball

A Test of Faith

The Breaking Point

"Bride on the Run"
in the 3 Weddings and a Giggle anthology

A Test of Faith

[A Novel]

Karen Ball

Multnomah® Publishers *Sisters, Oregon*

This book is a work of fiction. The characters, incidents, and dialogues are products of the author's imagination and are not to be construed as real. Any resemblance to actual events or persons, living or dead, is entirely coincidental.

A TEST OF FAITH
Published by Multnomah Publishers, Inc.

International Standard Book Number: 1-59052-265-6

Cover image by Liz Von Hoene/Getty Images

Printed in the United States of America

For information:
Multnomah Publishers, Inc.
Post Office Box 1720, Sisters, Oregon 97759

04 05 06 07 08 09 10 — 10 9 8 7 6 5 4 3 2 1 0

For my mom, Paula Sapp.
Mom, yours was a life of true faith and love.
You lived out your devotion to God every day,
sharing His love and kindness with everyone around you,
rejoicing in His blessings of family and friends.
You showed me that all the eloquent talk in the world doesn't
measure up to one simple act of love. And though you're gone,
people still talk about the way you made others feel special,
about your gentle spirit and your wonderful, sweet smile.
You were the best mother any daughter could ask for.
I miss you every day, and I'm so grateful
God shared you with me.
We'll be together again one day, in eternity.
What a grand reunion that will be!
You loved to hear me sing "Shepherd of Love," and I enjoyed
singing it, because it made you smile. And it made you cry.
No wonder, then, when I needed a special song for the mother
and daughter in this book to share, I knew right away which
song it would be. And every time I write about that song,
I'll sing it for you.

And for Julee, Heather, Caitlin, and Alyssa.
The sister and daughters I never had. I love you.

Acknowledgments

Many thanks to my physician, Susan Derry, and her wonderful nurse, Joanne, who always answered my medical questions—some of which I'm sure seemed quite odd—with patience and humor.

Thanks, also, to Heather, Caitlin, and Alyssa, who brainstormed ways to make young Faith real and shared them with great enthusiasm. You girls are wonderful!

My eternal gratitude to my church family. You upheld us, prayed with us, supplied us with meals for months, and cried with us as we walked the path with Mom in her last days. We couldn't have made it without you. And my true devotion to the wonderful women who've been part of my life for as long as I can remember—Anita, Marge, Pat, Therese, Verva, Betty, and Maxine—who reminded me on that first Mother's Day, the day after Mom's memorial service, that I still have spiritual moms. I love each one of you.

Finally, special hugs to The Coffee Crew—Linda, Sarah, Jennifer, Lori, Sandy, Deb, Andi, Connie, Max, and Patti—the original Yada Yada Sisters. (Though we gave ourselves that name years ago, it still fits us perfectly!) Your humor, faith, and wisdom have been an anchor for me through the toughest of times; your care has upheld me when I couldn't stand on my own. Thank you, dear friends, for all of that—and for letting me use you in this book! Shows you're not only good friends, but really, really good sports!

Part One

"A mother is the truest friend we have, when trials, heavy and sudden, fall upon us; when adversity takes the place of prosperity; when friends who rejoice with us in our sunshine, desert us; when troubles thicken around us, still will she cling to us, and endeavor by her kind precepts and counsels to dissipate the clouds of darkness, and cause peace to return to our hearts."

Washington Irving

"Listen! A farmer went out to plant some seed. As he scattered it across his field, some fell on a footpath, and the birds came and ate it. Other seed fell on shallow soil with underlying rock. The plant sprang up quickly, but it soon wilted beneath the hot sun and died because the roots had no nourishment in the shallow soil. Other seed fell among thorns that shot up and choked out the tender blades so that it produced no grain. Still other seed fell on fertile soil and produced a crop that was thirty, sixty, and even a hundred times as much as had been planted."

Then [Jesus] said, "Anyone who is willing to hear should listen and understand."

Mark 4:3–9, NIV

"Therefore this is what the Lord Almighty says:
'See, I will refine and test them.'"

Jeremiah 9:7, NIV

The Farmer

"Listen! A farmer went out to plant some seed..."

MARK 4:3

one

"If it was going to be easy to raise kids, it never would have started with something called labor."

Barbara Johnson

IT WAS TIME.

Anne savored the moment. Pain didn't matter. Fear was nonexistent. All she felt was joy. Deep, overwhelming joy. She couldn't stop the grin that spread across her features.

But then, she didn't want to.

She'd waited so long. Despite the doctor's dire warnings, she'd known this was right. Known it was God's call to her. And so she prayed, begged, threw herself at God's feet. And now…

"Jared." She meant to whisper his name, but it came out in a sharp groan.

His eyes opened, and he sat up in the bed. "What? Where?"

Anne's grin broadened at the rapid, caught-in-the-headlights blink of his eyes as he fought his way through the fog of deep sleep. With his hair askew and the imprint of the wrinkled pillow on his cheek, he looked like a little boy waking from a nap. His fists clutched the bedsheets, crumpling them into tight balls.

He was adorable.

Jared reached out to flick on the bedroom light, rubbing the remnants of sleep from his eyes with one solid fist.

A flush of utter happiness washed over Anne. It wouldn't be long before she'd see a little boy with those same eyes…or a little girl with that same tousled, sandy hair.

Their child.

All the years of waiting, the visits to doctors, the requests for prayer. All the hopes and dreams they'd shared, given up, then reclaimed every time Anne thought she might be pregnant. All the disappointments, the sense of failure and empty longing as other women had baby after baby, as though it were the easiest thing in the world. It was all over.

She was having a baby.

Another stab of pain gripped her, and she sucked in a breath. She was having a baby, all right. And she was having it now!

"Honey—" Anne grasped Jared's arm—"it's happening."

That brought his eyes wide open, and he was up and out of the bed in a heartbeat. In Jared's typical prepare-for-every-contingency manner, he'd slept in his trousers. His shirt, socks, and shoes lay waiting near the bed, perfectly positioned for getting dressed should the baby decide to make its appearance during the night.

Last night Anne hadn't been able to resist teasing him. "Your child wouldn't dream of doing anything unexpected, dear."

"*Your* child—" came his laughing response—"wouldn't dream of doing anything else!"

Apparently Jared had been right.

As Anne pushed herself to the edge of the bed, Jared perched on the mattress to pull on his socks and shoes. He glanced at her over his shoulder. "Are you okay? Is the baby okay?"

Anne's laughter was only slightly strained as she patted his muscled arm. "We're both fine. It's—" Words lodged in her throat as a contraction cut through her. When it finally eased, she drew in a deep breath and managed a smile. "I think your son is in a hurry to meet you."

A tender smile lifted his lips, and he held a hand out to pull her up. "More likely your daughter figures it's time to be the center of attention."

Anne let him enfold her, leaning against his solid frame as his arms came around her, holding her, sheltering her. She spread her palm over his heart, feeling the even beat. How could one man be so strong and yet so gentle? And how had she ever been so blessed that he should love her?

Anne didn't know, but she'd spend her whole life being grateful.

Another contraction hit, this one more extended. She buried her face in Jared's chest until it passed, then looked up and started at the grimace on his features. Glancing down she saw the handful of chest hair she'd been clutching.

It took all of her willpower to not laugh out loud. "Umm…sorry."

He eased her fingers free and rubbed his chest, the lopsided grin she loved so dearly peeking out at her.

"Not near as sorry as I am." His fingers entwined with hers as he lifted her hand to kiss her fingers. "But I forgive you. Now, what say we get you to the hospital and get this baby born?"

"I say—" this time she was the one who grimaced as her midsection convulsed—"*yes*."

He helped her waddle toward the door. "I thought you might."

"Aaahhhh!"

The scream escaped Anne despite her best intentions. She hadn't thought it possible, but the contraction seemed to double, and her hands dug into the sheets. Jared's strong arm slipped behind her. "Cleansing breath, hon. Remember?"

She nodded, teeth clenched, and sucked in a breath.

"Pant, Annie. Hee hee *hoo*…"

She tried to focus on her husband's coaching. He fed her another ice chip, then dabbed a cool cloth to her face.

I'm so tired, Lord. Please…please…make the pain stop.

Wetness trickled down her face, and Anne shook her head. What was she doing crying? This baby wasn't supposed to happen, wasn't supposed to be possible. Diagnosed with diabetes five years ago in her late twenties, the doctor had told her over and over that her disease would make becoming pregnant difficult, even dangerous.

"Your sugars are all over the map, Anne," he'd intoned on more occasions than she could number. "We're doing our best to regulate them, but your body isn't cooperating." This was always followed by him flipping her chart shut, the click a sound as final as a door closing in her face. "Add your age to that—"

"But Jared's doctor says he's a *perfect* age for having children, and he's only two years older than I am!"

The doctor shrugged. "What can I say? He's a man. But for you, I'm afraid pregnancy just isn't a safe option."

Anne had shed many tears over those words. Needless tears, because though the doctor dealt in medicine, God dealt in miracles. He not only planted in her the strong desire to have children, He touched her body, bringing her rebel sugars under control. He helped her manage her eating habits and get her body in shape. She and Jared took up jogging. She wasn't an athlete like he was, but she was determined. She *would* be healthy.

Then, when against all odds she finally became pregnant at the ripe old age of thirty-three, God helped her come through the difficult pregnancy so well that her doctor could only shake his head.

On her last visit, he set the chart down beside her on the examining table and patted her arm. "You're doing great, Anne. *Somebody* must be watching out for you."

Indeed, He was.

So how could she complain now about a few hours of labor? So what if she had to endure pain? God had given her a child.

"Hon?"

Anne turned to see Jared studying her. "Are you okay? You got so—quiet."

She mustered up a smile. "I was thinking how lucky I am."

Before he could respond, she was seized by searing pain. She squeezed her eyes closed, concentrating on what she'd learned in their childbirth classes. *Pant, pant, blow. Pant, pant, blow*… "Hee, hee—*hooohhhh*!"

"Can't you *do* something?"

Jared's firm question snapped her eyes open. "I'm *trying*!"

"We're doing everything we can, Mr. Bennett."

At the nurse's low words, Anne realized Jared hadn't been talking to her but to the nurse at her side.

As the contraction finally eased, Anne licked her dry lips and laid her head back against the pillow. If only she could sleep. Over the last twenty-four hours, she'd snatched a moment here and there, but the contractions never let up long enough for her to really rest.

"Maybe you could give her something. Some medication to ease the pain—"

"*No*." Anne wasn't sure they'd understood the word, coming out as it did on a groan. "No…medication."

"Annie—"

She shook her head at Jared. "No. I want to do this right, without drugs. I want…" She brushed a hand over her face. "God will bring us through this."

Her husband allowed himself a small frown, but Anne didn't have the energy to say any more.

Jared slanted a look at the nurse. "Is it normal for labor to go on this long? For her to be hurting so much?"

Through a growing haze, Anne pondered his questions. Odd, but suddenly the pain wasn't so bad. In fact, she hardly felt anything.

"She's having a baby, Mr. Bennett." Anne felt herself smile at the nurse's wry observation. "Pain is an unavoidable part of that process."

Jared's voice grew a tad testy. "I realize that, Nurse. But she's been in labor almost twenty-four hours. I'm concerned she can't take this much longer. *Look* at her. She's exhausted."

No arguments there. Good thing she was finally going to sleep. She must be. Why else would the room be growing so dark?

"I'm sorry, Mr. Bennett, but until the doctor—"

A shrill beeping sounded someplace in the distance,

piercing Anne's ears, setting her nerves on edge. She wanted to ask the nurse to turn the thing off so she could sleep, but her tongue wouldn't cooperate. She wanted to look for the woman, but her eyes were shut. When had she closed them?

It didn't really matter, though, because everyone else seemed to be speaking at once. A clutter of unfamiliar voices flew all around her.

"She's crashing!"

"The baby's heartbeat is dropping!"

"Get the doctor in here!"

"What's happening?"

The last voice Anne recognized. Jared. But she'd never heard him sound like that before. Alarmed.

Frightened.

"I'm sorry, Mr. Bennett. You'll have to go to the waiting room."

"Why?"

"We have to get your wife into surgery."

Another voice broke in behind Anne. "Come on! Move! We're losing them!"

Suddenly Anne was moving. She wanted to tell Jared not to worry, but it was as though everything—her arms and legs, her head, even the sheet over her—weighed a ton. They pulled her down...down...

She managed to pry her eyes open, spotting her husband just before they took her from the room. His face was so pale.

Don't worry, Jared. I'm fine...

Had she said it out loud? She wasn't certain. All she knew was that the darkness was growing stronger. And she was too tired to fight it.

With a sigh, she let her eyelids lower and surrendered, welcoming the inky blackness as it enfolded her, drawing her, at long last, into blessed, peaceful nothingness.

Two

"[God] saves us in our disasters, not from them."

ROBERT FARRAR CAPON

JARED PRESSED HIS ACHING EYES, GRATEFUL FOR THE darkness around him.

"God, please...let them be okay."

He was glad he was alone in the hospital chapel. Leaning his forehead on the pew in front of him, he drew in a shuddering sigh.

He couldn't get it out of his mind. His last sight of Annie. How pale she'd been. How she couldn't keep her eyes open. How the doctors and nurses had rushed around, alarm in their every feature and movement. And then those terrible words...

"Move it! We're losing them!"

No matter how he tried to block them out, they kept playing over and over in his mind until he thought he'd go mad.

It wasn't supposed to happen like this. They were having a baby, not facing some dire illness or surgery. They were supposed to be sitting together, staring down at the miracle they'd created.

The baby was a girl. Jared was sure of it. She'd be a tiny replica of Annie, and every time he looked at their little girl, he'd see his wife's beautiful moss green eyes and sweet smile.

His throat constricted. Would he ever see that beautiful smile again?

"Mr. Bennett?"

He started, then stood and faced the doorway. A nurse stood there, her eyes somber. "Mr. Bennett, we've been looking for you."

Jared was almost afraid to ask. "Is my wife…?" He couldn't make himself say what he feared. "Is she okay?" *Please…*

The nurse's expression didn't change. "You need to come with me."

Jared put a hand on the doorjamb, steadying himself. How was he going to survive without her? How could he face a moment, let alone a lifetime, without his Annie?

A touch on his arm startled him, and he looked to find the nurse peering at him. "Please, just come with me."

He followed her, focusing on her brisk stride, her sturdy shoes, the whiteness of her uniform—anything but what lay ahead.

The nurse came to a doorway and stopped, signaling him in. Jared hesitated.

I can't…I can't.

"Mr. Bennett, your wife—"

He put a hand out, halting her. He couldn't let her say it. Couldn't stand to hear the words. He shook his head and moved into the room.

Annie lay on the bed, the sheet pulled up to her chin. He drank in the sight of her, knowing it would have to last him forever. He walked forward.

She looked like she was asleep. If only that were true! If only she were lying there sleeping rather than dea—

"Jared?"

His breath caught in his throat, almost choking him. He stared. Rubbed his eyes. Stared again.

Annie's eyes—those beautiful, tender eyes—were open.

He lowered himself into the chair beside the bed, took her hands in his, and pressed them to his cheeks, covering them in kisses.

"Thank God!"

"Jared—" her words were slurred, as though she was heavily medicated—"I asked them to bring you here. I didn't want anyone else to tell you..."

The relief that had surged through him at the sight of her open eyes suddenly fled. The baby. *Oh dear heaven, I forgot about the baby.* Had they lost her?

"Jared, we have a daughter."

For the second time in a matter of minutes, relief so intense it was almost painful filled him. Annie reached to the opposite side of the bed. A bassinet stood there, and he could barely see the tiny bundle inside.

"Sweetheart, come meet your little girl."

Trembling, he walked around the bed and reached down to lift the sleeping infant with reverent care. His daughter. This was his daughter.

Cradling their child in the crook of his arm, he moved back to sit beside his wife. "Annie, she's beautiful."

No response. A quick look told him his wife was asleep, her breathing deep and even. Jared smiled. He touched a finger to his baby's cheek, marveling at the softness of her skin. Just then, she opened her eyes.

Jared blinked, and suddenly his eyes were awash again. He tried to speak, but nothing came out. He tried again and managed a raspy, "Well, hello there, little one." He grimaced, hoping the ragged sound of his voice didn't frighten her.

It didn't. She stretched and yawned again.

"Long day, huh?" He grinned and settled back in the chair. "Me, too. But everything's okay now because you're here." He glanced at the bed. "And since Mommy's sleeping, what say you and I get to know each other? Hmm?"

His baby blinked up at him with beautiful eyes. Annie's eyes. Emotion gripped Jared's throat in a velvet vise. "You're a beauty, you know that?"

Just like her mother. The first time Jared saw Annie, he was lost. Captured forever by the most beautiful woman he'd ever seen. Her auburn hair formed a soft cap of curls framing a lovely, heart-shaped face. Her sweet mouth and wonderful green eyes could make the sun shine on the darkest of days. It was no surprise to him that she was voted homecoming queen their senior year in college, and though she barely stood five-foot-four, her bearing was pure royalty.

He was pulled from his memories by a soft sound as the infant in his arms gurgled. She reached out and wrapped her tiny, perfect hand around Jared's finger. In that moment he knew, for the second time in his life…he was lost. Nothing would ever be the same.

Not ever.

Funny thing was, he didn't mind. Not one little bit.

Anne opened her eyes, blinking at the bright room. Where was she?

"Hi, there."

Gentle fingers brushed her cheek, and she turned her head. Jared. She gave a sleep-dazed sigh and took in the sight of him.

He looked terrible.

His hair looked as though someone had tried to style it with a demented weed whacker. His eyes were bloodshot, his face sagging from fatigue.

But he was smiling. A big, broad smile that made her want to smile, too. "What…?" The words caught in her dry throat, and Jared pressed a wet cloth to her lips. She smiled at him and tried again. "What happened to you?"

His tender laugh warmed her. "You, sweet girl. You happened to me."

"Hmm." She thought about that. "Looks like it hurt."

He lifted her hand and kissed the back of it. "Yeah, but it's a good pain." He pressed her hand to his stubble-roughened cheek. "You gave us a beautiful little girl, Annie."

A daughter. Anne hugged herself at the news. A little girl to love and guide and share the world with. She could hardly take it in.

"Our little Faith Adelle is finally here."

Faith Adelle. They'd chosen the name within days of finding out Anne was pregnant—Joshua Aaron, if it was a boy;

Faith Adelle if it was a girl. Faith, because God had answered their prayers; Adelle, to remind them to raise her to have a noble and kind spirit.

"She's okay, isn't she?" Anne knew the baby was fine, but she needed to hear it from him.

He chuckled, a glow of pure happiness lighting his features. "She's more than okay. She's wonderful."

"And she's eager to see her mommy again."

They both turned. A nurse stood in the doorway of the room.

She smiled at them, and Anne's focus shifted to the tiny bundle in the nurse's arms. Without another word, the woman came into the room and handed the bundle to Anne. "You did good, Mom."

Anne looked onto the delicate face, the long lashes sweeping down to caress plump, velvety cheeks. She reached out to touch the puckered mouth, then lifted one tiny baby fist to study the miniature fingers. "Look at all that hair!"

The nurse nodded. "Amazing, isn't it? Most babies are born bald as my grandfather, but this little one had enough hair we could even put a bow in it!"

She pushed the blanket back so Anne could see the little pink bow clipped to Faith's dark auburn hair. "The nurses all agree; she's one of the most adorable babies we've ever seen."

Just then, Faith's eyes opened and Anne found herself staring into her baby's eyes. Her baby. This was her baby!

Emotion flooded her heart until she thought it would overwhelm her. Speechless, she lifted the downy head to her cheek and felt the soft, wispy hair.

"She's amazing." Her hushed words brought smiles to Jared's and the nurse's faces.

"She is that." The nurse tucked the blanket under Faith's tiny chin. "And I'll tell you somethin', this little lady has a mind of her own. She wanted to be born, and she wasn't waiting for anything or anyone."

Anne cuddled her daughter against her and looked from Jared to the nurse. "What happened?"

The nurse eased into a nearby chair. "Your labor wasn't progressing; you remember that?"

Did she ever! Anne nodded.

"We were about to call the doctor to check things out when you and the baby decided it was time to get things over with. Now. You both went into distress."

Anne looked at Jared. "Distress?"

He took one of her hands, holding it like he'd never let go. "Your blood pressure dropped, Annie, and the baby's heartbeat slowed. I thought I was losing you both."

The memory of his frightened face came to her then. "Oh, Jared. I'm so sorry."

The nurse stood, patting Anne on the shoulder. "You gave us all a scare. We're still not quite sure what happened, but all's well that ends well, isn't that what they say?" She beamed down at Faith. "You and this little girl made it through in fine shape. God definitely had His hand on you both."

Anne couldn't hold back a smile. "Yes, He certainly did."

"And now it's time for you to spend a little time with your daughter, getting to know her." She nodded to Jared. "I need you to come with me to fill out a few more forms."

Jared nodded and stood to follow her. He leaned over, brushing a soft kiss across Anne's forehead. "I love you."

"I love you, too. Hurry back." She smiled, watching them leave the room, then looked back down at her baby and caught her breath.

Faith was looking right at her, and Anne had the sense of the whole earth shifting beneath her.

Her baby's wide, innocent eyes were the greatest source of wonder Anne had ever known. She'd thought about this moment for so long, but now that it was here, it was so much more than she could have imagined.

"Oh, Faith—" Anne kissed her daughter's sweet-smelling skin—"I've been waiting for you all my life."

It was true. Anne's earliest memories were of helping her mother care for her little brother. All she'd ever wanted was to be a wife and mother. To shower the same love and devotion on her own children that her mother had given her. And she'd always hoped for a daughter. A little one to talk with and play with, to teach about life and God, to show all the joys and wonders of being a little girl.

Anne looked again at her daughter's beautiful baby hair. Thank heaven Faith inherited her father's genes in the hair department. Anne had always bemoaned the fact that her hair was too fine to do much with. But Faith, she would have full, thick hair. Anne was sure of it.

And she was sure of something more. The nurse had been right. God had her little girl in His hands. He'd known Faith from before the time she was born, and He'd chosen to give this precious girl to them. That was an honor almost beyond comprehension.

And a responsibility.

The weight of that truth settled on Anne's shoulders like a heavy mantle, cloaking her with the powerful awareness that she would do whatever it took to ensure this little one grew up safe and strong, physically and spiritually. Anne tightened her hold on her daughter and met the infant's steady gaze.

"I'll take care of you, I promise."

"You mean *we'll* take care of her, don't you?"

Anne smiled up at Jared as he sat next to the bed. She leaned her forehead against his. "Of course. We'll take care of her."

Jared slid an arm around Anne. "You and me and God, Annie." He squeezed her. "What a time we're gonna have with this little girl."

Anne nestled against him, savoring his closeness and the feel of their daughter snuggled between them. *Amen, Lord.* She smiled. *Let it be so.*

Three

"If we could only know what was going on in a baby's mind."

JEAN PIAGET

ANNE WANTED TO SCREAM.

She clamped her lips together, holding back the frustration clawing at her, drawing her hands into tight fists.

What was *wrong* with her? Drawing in a breath of sheer determination, Anne went to the nursery and walked to the side of the crib. She would try one more time.

"Please, Faith..."

The baby looked up at Anne's whisper, and her tiny fists and feet bounced in the air. The colorful collection of Winnie-the-Pooh characters danced from the mobile hanging over Faith's crib, as though they, too, were delighted to see Anne. That was something, anyway. Anne knew Faith was always happy to see her, always excited when she came into the room. If only that were enough.

Steeling herself, Anne reached down to lift her baby from the crib. Keeping her movements slow and cautious, she drew Faith closer, closer...

So far, so good.

Easing her breath out on a sigh, Anne cradled Faith in her arms and cuddled her close. *Please, baby...*

She'd pleaded, cajoled—even prayed. But it only took a second for Anne to know it was all for naught. The moment she nestled her infant daughter against her, Faith stiffened. Anne knew what was coming. The same thing that had happened every time she tried to cuddle her little girl close. Whether here at home, at the church nursery, or at Bible study, the result was the same: Faith's little arms shot out and her fists planted themselves firmly against Anne's collarbone, pushing her mother away.

Just like they did now.

"Fine!" Anne choked on the angry word, her throat constricted with the hurt that wrapped itself around her like barbed wire. She laid Faith back in her crib. "Fine! Just...just—" Anne kicked out, sending one of Faith's stuffed animals flying—"*fine*!"

"Whoa, Annie!"

She spun around. Jared was in the doorway, holding the stuffed animal. His lopsided grin held a tinge of concern. "First time I've ever been nailed with an elephant."

"Ohhh..." Anne shook her head. "I'm sorry, Jared."

He came to stand beside her. "What's wrong, hon?"

Anne couldn't hold back the hurt any longer. "What's wrong with me? Babies love to cuddle with their mothers. It's the most natural thing in the world for every other baby!" She paced in front of the crib. "Am I some kind of monster?"

Jared couldn't have been more astonished if she'd sprouted wings and laid an egg on his shoe. "Of course not, Annie. You're a wonderful mother."

"Well, tell *her* that!" Anne knew how childish she sounded, but she couldn't help it. She rubbed her fist at the sudden tears running down her cheeks.

"Faith loves it when you sing to her, Annie. And when you read to her. She gets all giggly when you read that book of kids' bedtime Bible stories."

"I know, but she never wants me to hold her. That's not normal, Jared. And she won't nurse, either. Every time I try to feed her, she turns her head away. Or cries and makes angry little fists."

"The nurses warned us she was strong-willed, remember? That she had a definite mind of her own from day one."

When he reached out to stroke a soothing hand down her arm, Anne jerked away. His lips twitched. "Kind of like her mother."

Anne directed a glare at him. "Meaning?"

He wasn't the least bit put off by her temper. "Meaning when she's got a head of steam built up, nothing will placate her until she's good and ready to let it."

Anne started to shoot back a retort, then clamped her mouth tight. The man's logic was so irritating! Especially when he was right.

Like now.

She rubbed the back of her neck, trying to ease the tension. "She won't even let me cuddle her, Jared. She just pushes me away." She flung her arms out. "What kind of baby pushes her own mother away?"

Jared went to stroke Faith's brow, as though it were as furrowed as his own. "But Anne, Faith loves to cuddle. You've seen her at Bible study. She's fussy until I pick her up and walk her—"

"Exactly. She loves to cuddle with *you*. Which means the problem is with me." She all but spat the words out, and he turned to her, brows lifted.

Anne opened her mouth, then closed it. What was she doing? Why was she attacking Jared? It wasn't his fault their daughter adored him and hated her. It was hers. It had to be.

Jesus, You created women to be mothers, so what's wrong with me? Why doesn't my own baby love me?

She sank into the rocking chair next to the crib. Jared knelt in front of her, taking her hands.

"Annie..." He spoke her name as a caress, and all the fight went out of her—but not the hurt. That clawed at her heart, burrowing even deeper. "Honey, the nurse told you that some babies just don't take to nursing. We've been feeding her with the bottle, and that seems to be working well."

He was right, of course, but there was little comfort in that. "But nursing is supposed to be one of the most natural things in the world."

"Says who?"

"Says Allyson."

Jared groaned. "Annie, Allyson is a nut!"

"She's not a nut."

He held up his hands. "If you say so, but all that flower child babble sounds nutty to me. She walks around with flowers in her hair and enough beads to weigh down a freight train."

"But she's had three children—"

"Who she named Unity, Harmony, and Licorice!"

Anne ignored him. "And she says nursing is a wonderful part of being a mother, of bonding with a baby."

"Do all women nurse their babies?"

She frowned. There he went, being logical again. "No, of course not—"

"But they bond with their babies?"

Anne sighed. "Yes, of course."

"Then there you go." He gentled his tone. "Annie, hon, it's 1969. No one can say how things should or shouldn't be done. You need to figure out what works for you and Faith. That's what matters most."

But that was just it. Anne couldn't figure it out. And if she hadn't failed at nursing, then it meant Faith had no desire to bond.

Not with her.

Anne's lip quivered, and she leaned forward to bury her face in Jared's shoulder. "I'm a terrible mother."

His arms came around her. "Sweetheart, you're exhausted. You've been up almost every night with Faith, and she doesn't nap long enough for you to get rested."

Anne sniffled.

"Why don't you go take a nice, hot bath, then crawl into bed?"

"I have to feed the baby." She spoke the words into his shirt and felt him chuckle.

"I'll feed her. You try to get some sleep."

She straightened, then pushed through her weariness to extract a smile for her husband. "I must be the smartest woman in the world."

The sparkle in his eyes wrapped around her chilled heart, warming it. "And why is that?"

Anne leaned forward to press a soft kiss to his lips. "Because I married you."

"Then you are indeed a woman of great insight and wisdom."

Though Jared was laughing, his love came through loud and clear. And if he loved her so—undeniably and unequivocably—she couldn't be all bad.

He stood and pulled her to her feet as well, hugging her before he propelled her toward the door. "Go get some rest. And don't worry about the baby. We'll be fine."

She knew it was true. Her husband and daughter would be just fine without her. And that thought should be a comfort.

But it wasn't.

Instead, it did something Anne hadn't thought possible.

Made her feel more rejected than ever.

Anne woke with a start.

She sat up, blinking in the darkness, every sense alert. She'd heard something…

A quick look told her Jared wasn't beside her. Maybe he hadn't come to bed yet. She'd followed her husband's prescription and soaked in a nice, hot bath. She even added fragrant oils and bubbles. Lots of bubbles. Amazing how comforting being surrounded by bubbles could be.

By the time she slipped into bed, she was relaxed and yawning, though it had been barely 6 P.M. She managed to read two Psalms before her eyelids drifted shut. Giving up, she turned off the light with a sigh. It was always so encouraging to be reminded she wasn't the only one who struggled. Within moments of snuggling into the pillows, she dropped into a deep, dreamless sleep.

Now Anne glanced at the clock on her nightstand then frowned. Nearly midnight. Jared should be beside her, his soft snores providing a familiar cadence to the night.

She listened again. The sound was barely discernable, but

when Anne slipped from bed and cracked open the door, she recognized it immediately.

Faith was crying. Wailing, really. That shrill, gasping infant shriek that brought a mother running to provide comfort. Anne hurried down the hallway to the nursery door and pushed it open.

The darkened room was lit by the pale glow of a Winnie-the-Pooh nightlight and soft moonlight peeking in through the open blinds on the window. When Anne's sight adjusted to the dim lighting, she realized Jared was in the rocker next to Faith's crib. He rocked back and forth, his inconsolable daughter stiff against his chest. His large, work-roughened hands patted the baby's back.

"Come on, baby, hush…hush…it's okay."

Her husband's weary crooning brought a smile to Anne's face. If there was one thing she knew, and knew well, it was that struggle to maintain a soothing tone despite utter desperation. How many nights had she sat like that, trying to coax their little girl to sleep, to relax in her arms? More than she cared to count.

Strong-willed? Faith gave the term new meaning.

But instead of dejection at the thought, Anne just chuckled. Jared had been right—all she'd needed was some sleep. And now that she'd gotten some, things didn't seem nearly so hopeless.

She padded across the thick carpet and laid a hand on Jared's sagging shoulder. "Honey, let me take her."

Jared jumped slightly and turned to her. Regret seeped from his bloodshot eyes. "I'm sorry. I tried not to let her wake you."

Anne brushed a kiss across his lips, then slid her arms around the red-faced, anger-stiffened infant. "It's okay." She raised her voice to be heard over Faith. "I'm feeling bet—"

Pure astonishment trapped the word on Anne's lips. She and Jared stared at one another, eyes wide.

It was quiet.

No screams. No crying.

Just…silence.

As if following some precise choreography, Anne and Jared looked down at their suddenly soundless daughter. She lay there, cuddled in Anne's arms. The fingers of one little hand circled Anne's index finger. With one soul-deep sigh, Faith closed her eyes.

Within moments she was fast asleep.

Anne raised stunned eyes to Jared. He leaned back in the rocker, a smile easing its way across his features. "I guess she wanted her mommy."

A silly grin spread across her face, but she didn't care. "I guess so."

Jared pushed himself from the rocker. "I'm guessing you're not ready to put her in the crib."

Anne was still grinning. "Good guess."

He nodded as she lowered herself into the chair and started rocking. Jared put strong hands on her shoulders and kissed her hair. "Enjoy, hon."

Anne leaned her head against him for a moment. "Count on it."

She watched him leave the room, then looked down at her sleeping baby, taking in the long lashes resting on chubby cheeks, the tiny mouth puckered.

A hymn drifted into Anne's mind, and she started to hum it, then sing the words, soft and low. "*Shepherd of Love, you knew I had lost my way...*" She loved that song, cherished the image of a loving shepherd tenderly guiding a lost sheep back on the path, back to safety.

Rocking with gentle motion, she sang to Faith, letting the beautiful words wash over her as well. When Anne finished, she realized Faith's little fingers still held onto her as though they'd never let go.

But Anne knew better. As precious as this moment was, as much as it nurtured her battle-worn soul, it was most likely a temporary reprieve. So she focused on every detail, savoring, absorbing, consigning to memory the fact that, at long last, her daughter needed her. Wanted her.

Only her.

And no matter how brief this moment was, it was enough.

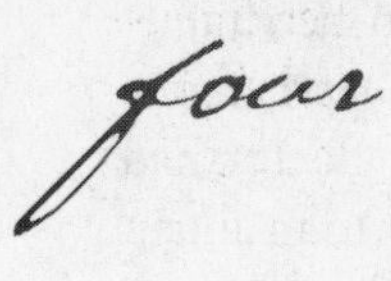

"What we see depends mainly on what we look for."

SIR JOHN LUBBOCK

FAITH WAS RELENTLESS.

"Again, Mommy."

"Sweetie, we've already played four games."

"Play again. Please?"

Anne started to refuse, to say she had things she had to do—vacuuming, dusting, dishes—but tears sparkled in her daughter's eyes, turning them an even deeper green. Faith might only be five years old, but if there was one thing she'd perfected, it was turning on the waterworks. Jared liked to tease, saying they had a budding Drama Queen on their hands.

Budding nothing. Faith had blown past budding and gone right to full bloom.

"Pleeeeaaaase, Mommy."

Patience...give me patience, Lord. Yes, five games of Chutes and Ladders was above and beyond the call. But her little girl was growing up so fast. Wasn't spending time with her more important than keeping her house spotless?

Your mother managed to do both.

Anne pushed the thought away. Her mother hadn't had to deal with diabetes. The disease had taken more of a toll on Anne in the last year. The worst part of it was how she kept gaining weight. No matter what she did, she simply could not get rid of fifteen wretched pounds that had taken up residence on her frame. For some that might not be such a terrible thing. But when one was just barely five-foot-four, it was horrid. Her doctor had warned her going on insulin would make it harder to maintain her weight. Well, he'd been right.

Of course, it has nothing to do with the way you eat, right?

Anne refused to listen to that irritating inner voice. So she snuck a few treats now and then. So what?

So, it's not helping. It's making you more and more tired.

Anne grimaced. As much as she hated to admit it, it was true. Yesterday had been especially bad. She'd given in to the lure of a plate of brownies, and before she realized it, she'd finished them off. The lethargy set in within the hour. She knew there was cleaning to be done, but she couldn't get herself off the couch to do it.

By the end of the day, it took all of her effort to get dinner ready and the table set just right. After dinner? Well, she'd gone to bed earlier than she could ever remember. She'd actually left last night's dirty dishes sit in the sink overnight.

Her mother would have been scandalized.

Though she'd purposely avoided baking anything to replace the brownies, today hadn't been much better. She felt like she was moving through molasses.

"Mommy?"

Anne pulled herself away from her morose thoughts and focused on Faith's pleading face. Housecleaning could wait. "Okay. One more."

Faith squealed and grabbed the game pieces, plunking them down at the starting place. Anne watched her daughter, taking in the way her little mouth pursed as she concentrated, the way her beautiful hair framed her pixie face. Anne loved her daughter's hair.

She fingered a lock of her own hair. She and Faith shared the same hair color, which was fine, because the color was the one thing Anne *liked* about her hair. Everyone else liked it, too, and often commented on how the rich auburn sometimes seemed to dance with golden highlights when the sun hit it just right.

But that was where any similarity ended.

Faith had what Anne had always wanted. Girl hair.

She'd said as much to Jared a few nights ago as they stretched out on the couch together after putting Faith to bed. Jared nestled Anne close and stroked her hair. "You know, Faith is a little carbon copy of you. She's got your eyes, your smile...she's even got your hair."

Anne grimaced and shook her head. "Hardly. Faith's got *girl* hair."

His chuckle was deep and resonant. "Well, I sure hope so."

"No, you goof—" Anne poked him in the ribs—"I mean, she's got that thick, silky long hair that bounces and looks...well, like a girl's hair is *supposed* to look. Like you see on girls on TV." She gave him a sideways glance. "Like those women on that new show."

He laughed. "Am I supposed to know what new show you're talking about?"

She swatted at him. "You know, the show you go gaga over. The one with those women detectives."

"Ah—" he waggled his brows—"*Charlie's Angels*?"

"That's it!" Anne settled back, triumphant. "Now *they* have girl hair."

Jared tightened his arms around her. "Don't you have...uh, girl hair?"

"Hardly." She leaned her head on his chest, pulling at a loose thread on one of his shirt buttons. "This stuff—" she let go of the thread and tugged at her hair, trying to ignore the fact that the texture of it wasn't much different than the thread—"is *not* girl hair. Girl hair isn't thin and straight. As for long, well you can forget about long. I have to keep it chopped short to look even close to decent."

When Jared's finger trailed down her face, she glanced up at him. The tender amusement painting his features stirred the embers of peace within her—embers nearly doused by yet another day of conflicts with a certain increasingly independent and opinionated child.

"You know, you look just like Faith with your lower lip sticking out like that."

Anne batted at his chest, and he caught her hand, lifting it to his lips. Then he leaned down to kiss the top of her head.

"I think your hair is perfect." He cupped her face with those strong, gentle hands. "Just like the rest of you."

Anne sighed anew at the memory. Whether she agreed or not, Anne hadn't been inclined to argue with him…not when Jared did such a good job of proving to her he meant it.

"Are you too hot, Mommy?"

Anne started and looked at her daughter. "Too hot? Why?"

"'Cuz your face is all red."

Sometimes her child was entirely too perceptive. She was about to comment on that fact when she heard the sound of a car pulling into the driveway.

"Daddy!"

The board game and pieces went flying as Faith jumped to her feet and ran to the front door. Alarm rang through Anne as she followed her daughter. It couldn't be that late, could it? One glance told her it was, and her heart sank.

What was *wrong* with her? How could she let the day slip away without getting her chores done? What would Jared think when he walked in the door and realized not only was the house a mess, but dinner wasn't ready?

Taking Faith's hand in hers, Anne pulled the front door open and stepped outside, forcing a lightness to her tone as she greeted her husband. "Hi, honey!"

"Well, hello there." He smiled as he slid from the car and closed the door. "Isn't this nice? My two best girls coming out to meet me."

Anne passed Faith's hand to him. "Jared, I hate to ask it, but would you be willing to run to the store for me? I…I forgot to pick up a loaf of bread for dinner." Well, it wasn't really a lie. She'd forgotten dinner altogether.

Jared hugged Faith and nodded. "Sure thing, hon."

"Can I go wif you, Daddy?" Faith leaned against his leg. "I missed you soooo much!"

The wry twist to Jared's lips told Anne he wasn't fooled.

They both knew Faith figured that if she went along, she'd be able to coax a treat out of her daddy.

"Sure, sweetie. You can come with me."

Anne made herself stand there as they piled into the car, then pulled out of the drive. She waved, then, when they were finally out of sight, raced into the house. She had twenty minutes, more or less, before they got back.

Dashing into the living room, she scooped up the board game and dumped it into a drawer. Then she grabbed the vacuum and gave the living room rug a quick once-over, then managed a hit-or-miss dusting with the dust rag. That done, she scurried into the kitchen to throw some soup in a pan, slice cheese for grilled cheese sandwiches, and make quick work of a head of lettuce and a plump tomato for a salad.

She'd just finished setting the table when she heard the car in the driveway again. She turned to head toward the front door and caught a glimpse of her reflection in the hallway mirror: Her hair was a disaster, her face was flushed, and her mascara was smudged.

Oh yeah, you're a regular Carol Brady, you are. The perfect wife and mother.

Swallowing back the shame that rose, hot and bitter, in her throat, Anne did her best to repair the damage her mad dash around the house had wrought. Exhaustion weighed her down, and for a moment she considered sitting on the floor and bursting into tears. But she shoved that self-pitying thought aside.

So she wasn't Carol Brady. Or her mother. Or any of the dozens of women who could keep it all together, managing house and home with ease. Fine. "At least I'm doing my best," she told her reflection. "That should count for something, shouldn't it?"

She turned away from the mirror, not giving herself—or that despicable, nagging inner voice—time to answer the question. Because she was afraid she knew what that answer would be.

Instead, she resolved to do better, starting now. She wasn't going to give in to the fatigue anymore. She would beat this stupid disease, lose the weight, get her energy back, and that was that.

Hadn't her mother always said, "You can do anything when you put your mind to it?" So that's what she would do. Put her mind, heart, and soul into being the best wife and mother possible.

Her family deserved nothing less.

Determination straightening her spine, she put a bright smile on her face and went to open the front door and welcome her family home.

It was early in the morning when Anne heard Faith's voice drift from the living room into the hallway.

"Read it again, Daddy."

Ah yes, it was Saturday.

Anne went to peer into the living room. What she saw lifted her lips in a warm smile.

Jared was sitting back in his recliner, Faith cuddled on his lap, his hands holding their favorite book, *Make Way for Ducklings*. Ever since Captain Kangaroo featured the book on his morning show, Faith loved to hear it read over and over. She never tired of it. Or of having her daddy read to her.

Even now, she leaned her head back against Jared's broad chest, one hand reaching up to pat her father's face as he read.

Jared's cheek rested against Faith's soft hair. Anne leaned against the doorway and couldn't hold back another smile as she listened to him changing his voice from one character to another.

Faith followed the story, clearly entranced. Jared was enjoying himself as much as Faith, and he never seemed to tire of this Saturday morning ritual, either. Without fail, right after Anne brushed Faith's hair—which was a trial, considering that Faith hated having it done and Anne often ran out of patience with trying to brush a fidgeting target—the little girl scooped up the book and padded to the kitchen to find her father. It was as though Faith had decided this was her reward for suffering through the dreaded hair brushing.

Anne held back a sigh. How well she recalled her own mother brushing her hair. She'd loved the feel of her mother's hands as she coaxed the tangles free, the way they'd talked and sung songs together. That was their special time together each morning, and Anne had been so sure it would be the same with Faith and her.

Guess again.

What Faith loved was the Saturday reading time with Jared. She slipped into the chair beside him at the kitchen table, book held against her chest, peering up at him, waiting for him to finish eating breakfast. Jared knew the moment he put down his fork, the question would come.

"Now, Daddy?"

Jared's smile was what drew Anne to him the first time they met. It was a purely male smile, no doubt about it. But it was more. His smile always held such tenderness and warmth. In that smile, Anne had seen the promise of so much—a man who would cherish her…a man who would stand between her and whatever might come against them…a man committed utterly to God and to loving her as truly as anyone could. A man who would thrive on being a husband and father.

Jared had fulfilled every promise she'd seen, and then some.

So every time he turned that smile to their daughter, as he did whenever she asked him to read to her, Anne knew what Faith saw there: unquestioning, unrelenting love.

Little wonder Faith adored her daddy's smile as much as Anne did.

Anne was sure this Saturday morning had been no different, except for one small fact: Faith had corralled her father *before* getting her hair brushed. Apparently, she'd figured to skip the suffering and jump right to the reward today.

"Again, Daddy?"

The question pulled Anne from her thoughts, and she looked up to see Faith gazing up at her father, her most persuasive expression on her face.

"I think—" Jared's low tone was clearly holding back

laughter—"you have another appointment."

Anne recognized her cue. "Come on, sweetie. Time to do your hair."

The look on her daughter's face as she eyed the hairbrush was far from enthusiastic.

"Come on, squirt." Jared closed the storybook and lifted Faith from his lap to the ground, giving her backside a pat. "Go with Mama."

Faith pouted, but she did as her father bid and followed Anne—albeit slowly—back upstairs to her room.

Once there, Anne rubbed Faith's back—a surefire way to calm her. "Okay, now, hold still, honey. It won't hurt so much if you don't pull away when I'm brushing."

The stiff set of Faith's shoulders spoke volumes. She wasn't buying it. Okay, time for a distraction.

"When I was little—" Anne started brushing again. *Slow and even strokes. Easy…easy…* "My mommy used to brush her long, beautiful hair every day."

"She had long hair?"

Anne nodded. "Just like yours. And she would put it in long, pretty braids with ribbons. Just like we fix your hai—"

"Braids are *stoo*pid."

Anne pressed her lips together. Yet another lovely trait her daughter was perfecting: that sullen, mutinous tone. *Patience…* That one word was becoming a mantra for her life. *A soft answer turns away wrath, right?*

"Hold still, honey. We're almost done."

Unfortunately, being still wasn't in Faith's makeup. The little girl fidgeted, dancing from one foot to the other, squirming like a worm frantic to escape the hook. "Pleeeease, Mommy, can't I go outside?"

"Fine!" Anne slammed the brush down on the dresser and grabbed one of Faith's hair bands. She handed the piece of plastic to Faith, shaking her head as her daughter shoved it on her head, barely breaking stride as she made for the hallway.

So much for our morning ritual.

Anne made her way down the stairs, then watched her daughter out the kitchen window. Faith's neighborhood friends were already waiting in the backyard. She jumped in the middle of them with a squeal, and they rolled and tumbled, all giggles and arms and legs. Without a pause, they jumped up and raced to the large evergreen in the yard, scrambling up the limbs like a pack of playful squirrels.

Of course, Faith was the first to reach the tree. And the first to grab a branch and launch herself upward. Anne saw her daughter's jeans catch on a branch and tear, but Faith didn't even seem to notice. No surprise there. Faith was more at home in torn jeans and scruffy tennies than anything else.

Anne shook her head and turned the burner on under the teakettle. Whatever happened to the little girl she'd always dreamed of? To the dresses and ribbons and lace?

A small laugh escaped Anne. Faith was as fond of dresses as she was of braids. And the last time Anne put a pretty bow in Faith's hair, it ended up on the dog as a makeshift leash.

"Whatcha thinking, Beautiful?"

Anne glanced at Jared over her shoulder, then turned back to the counter, reaching to lift a mug from the rack. "I don't know. I'm just wondering how a child I carried in my body can be so different from me."

The teakettle whistled, and Anne snapped the burner off, then poured the steaming water into her cup. She looked at Jared, but he shook his head.

"None for me, thanks."

She nodded, gathered up her tea bag and container of honey, and went to sit at the table. Jared joined her, silent, waiting. Anne tried to sort through her thoughts as she dipped the tea bag in the water, watching how the color changed with each dunk.

"Faith and I..." She sighed. "We don't seem to connect on anything. It's as though we're from two different planets."

Jared took her hand and held it, the solid feel of his touch a comfort beyond words. "You're different in some ways, hon. But you're the same in other ways."

She peered at him, holding back a snort. "Such as?"

"Well, you both love holding hands when we pray at mealtimes, singing silly songs, and parties and holidays." He weaved his fingers through hers. "I swear I've never seen two girls who love celebrating as much as Faith and you do."

Anne smiled at that. "I got that from my mother. She used to do such special things. It always made her so happy to surprise me..."

When she fell silent, Jared studied her. "What?"

Anne almost couldn't contain the sudden excitement that scurried through her. "Jared, that's it!"

He blinked. "What's it?"

It was perfect. Why hadn't she thought of it before? "It happened when I was about Faith's age."

"*What* did?"

Anne jumped up and threw her arms around her husband. "Oh, honey! You're a genius!"

With that, she gathered up her tea and started for her room to plan.

"Annie? Hon?"

She stopped and turned back to Jared.

"Will you let me know one of these days what I did that was so wonderful?"

The look on his face was so comical, Anne giggled. "I'm sorry, Jared. I got so excited."

"Yeah, I could tell."

She couldn't hold back a grin. "It'll be perfect."

"What will?"

"She'll love it."

Jared's brow furrowed. "Love...what?" He pushed back his chair and put a gentle hand on her arm. "Hon, before you get all excited, remember Faith doesn't always like the things you do."

"Yes, but—"

"She hated the frilly dress and hat you bought for her last Easter—"

"I know—"

"And the ballet class for tots was clearly a mistake."

Anne crossed her arms. "That instructor overreacted. Threatening to get a restraining order if we ever brought Faith back." She sniffed her disdain. "Faith's a creative child. Just because she thought it was more fun to pretend she was Bruce Lee than a flower…"

"She *did* knock down three of her fellow 'daisies,' hon."

"Yes, well—"

"And stomped on their little construction-paper petals."

Anne lifted her shoulders, conceding defeat. "Okay. So Faith wasn't ready for ballet. But I'm sure Faith will love this!"

"It's just…I don't want you to be disappointed, Annie."

Disappointed? No chance. She patted Jared's arm. "Not to worry. Not this time. I know she'll love it. What little girl wouldn't?"

"Maybe *our* little girl?"

Anne understood his need to say it, but she waved off his concern. "It'll be wonderful." She went up on tiptoe to kiss his cheek. "And you get to take all the credit!"

She turned and all but floated out the door. Nothing he said would discourage her. Not even the dubious reply he tossed after her.

"Or the blame."

five

"In a dark time, the eye begins to see."

THEODORE ROETHKE

EVERYTHING WAS READY. ANNE HAD BEEN WORKING on it for weeks, scanning magazines for the perfect setup. She'd finally found an article showing the first lady, Betty Ford herself, holding an event almost identical to what Anne wanted to do. If that wasn't proof it was a good idea, Anne would be a monkey's uncle. Er, aunt. Whatever.

It was the perfect time of year, too. Few places were as beautiful as Southern Oregon in the late spring. Flowers were bursting to life, filling the yard with color and the air with sweet fragrances. Anne had even called the time and weather number to check the forecast. Sunshine. Highs in the seventies. A light breeze. Perfect for sitting out on the patio, looking out at the mountains surrounding the valley where they lived.

It was as though everything, nature included, was falling in line to make this day as special as possible for Anne and her little girl.

The night before the big event, she had been like a kid on Christmas Eve. Instead of falling asleep the moment her head hit the pillow, Anne lay there, staring at the ceiling, savoring the anticipation, picturing the delight on her daughter's face.

On Faith's face or yours?

Anne frowned. Well, both, of course.

Do you really think Faith will be pleased? Isn't this more something you would like?

Anne rolled over and punched her pillow. That was ridiculous. What little girl wouldn't like what Anne had planned?

Your little girl.

This time she pulled the pillow over her head. She would not listen to this voice of doubt. Everything would work out the way she'd planned.

Early the next morning, Anne pushed away her fatigue and went to wake Faith with a kiss. "Mornin', sleepyhead." She sat on the edge of her daughter's bed. "Did you know today is a special day?"

Faith blinked up at her and yawned, stretching her child arms up over her head. "Is it Christmas?"

"No—"

She sat up. "My birthday?"

"No, honey."

Faith stood, now fully awake, and started bouncing on the bed. "Your birthday?"

"Faith!"

The little girl plopped back on the bed and fell silent. Anne drew a steadying breath.

"*Do not exasperate your children...*" Anne hesitated. That's what she'd done. She came in, woke Faith up, and got her all excited. And now she got irritated at Faith for reacting like any child would.

Anne looked at the smiling bears on Faith's bedspread. Why was it Anne could be so patient with others, but when it came to her own daughter, she seemed primed for frustration?

Sorry, Lord. Please, help me to do better.

"Mommy?"

Faith crawled over to sit next to her, and Anne drew her daughter close. "Yes, honey?"

"What's special about today?"

Anne smiled at her little girl's wide-eyed expression.

Emotions swelled in Anne's throat, and she had to swallow a couple of times before she could speak. How she loved this child! Yes, Faith might drive her to distraction at times, but Anne loved her more than she could ever express. "Well, we're going to do something special. Something my mommy did with me with I was your age."

"What?"

"It's a surprise, but I'll show you part of it." She went to pick up the gift she'd left outside the door. She hid it behind her back, then returned to sit on Faith's bed again. "Close your eyes and hold out your hands."

Faith complied, though the bouncing resumed. Anne pulled the gift from behind her back and let herself take another look at it. It was the most exquisite doll she'd ever seen. The porcelain face was perfection, with its deep blue eyes, rosy cheeks, and plump pink lips. Long blonde curls held back with a blue ribbon cascaded over the doll's shoulders. She was dressed in a beautiful deep blue dress adorned with tiny roses, lace, and ribbons. Her little feet sported patent leather shoes, complete with a shiny buckle.

Anne held the doll carefully and set her in Faith's outstretched hands. The little girl's bounces doubled.

"Can I look now?"

"Go ahead."

Faith's eyes popped open. Anne waited for the smile to fill her daughter's features.

And waited.

And waited.

Faith stared at the doll, then looked up at her mother. "Is it for you?"

For a moment, all the doubts that had nudged Anne last night surged back to haunt her. But she pushed them away and mustered up a smile. "No, honey, she's for you."

Faith looked at the doll. "Oh."

That one word spoke volumes.

"I don't want you to be disappointed, Annie."

She watched Faith stick out a finger to poke at the frilly dress, then pull on the long locks of golden hair. Anne swallowed. What was tightening her throat? Not disappointment. Never, in a million years, would she admit it was that.

She leaned forward to touch first the doll's cheek, then Faith's. "This isn't just any doll, sweetie. It's your own special tea-party doll."

Faith's brow furrowed. "Tea party?"

Anne infused her tone with excitement. "That's right. We're going to have a tea party. You and me and your new doll. With special cups and sandwiches like when I was little."

"Do we *have* to drink tea?"

Anne recognized the emotion choking her now. Frustration had an all-too-familiar flavor. "You'll like it."

"Can I have milk and honey in it?"

She sighed. "Yes, of course. It's all set. All you have to do is get dressed."

Faith set the doll down and slid from the bed, going to pick up her jeans from the floor.

"No, honey." Anne went to Faith's closet and lifted out the dress she'd put in there last night. A dress that matched the one the doll wore. She'd shopped for hours to find it. "This is a dress-up party. Here." She held out the dress, watching for the awe to fill Faith's features at the elegant garment.

Faith's nose crinkled as though she caught a whiff of some dead, rotted creature, and she looked up at her mother. Before her daughter could voice the objection Anne saw building, she knelt in front of Faith and held the dress up against her.

"You'll look like a princess, honey."

The "princess" glared down at the offending garment. "Don't wanna be a princess. Wanna be a tiger catcher."

Dread sat on Anne's chest, weighing it down, making it hard to breathe. *I was wrong. Oh, Lord, I was wrong…*

But she couldn't stop now. Surely, once they were sitting at the table having their tea, Faith would see what a special event this was. "Try it, okay? It's really going to be fun."

She did her best to keep her tone light, but even she could hear the hurt resonating behind the words. Faith shrugged and took the dress. Before she could change her mind, Anne helped her daughter slip out of her pajamas and into the folds of the dress. New socks and patent leather shoes followed.

It took all of Anne's patience, but she managed to ignore Faith's squirming and complaining as she dressed her daughter and brushed out her hair. A velvet ribbon in Faith's hair was the crowning glory.

Anne stood back and studied her little girl. Faith did, indeed, look like a princess. "Okay, now you wait here, honey, while I go get the camera!"

Faith didn't say anything, stubbed the black toe of her shoe into the carpet. Minutes later, Anne gave a deep sigh. Faith was beautiful. Dressed this way, with her glossy auburn hair cascading down her back, she was a vision suited to the cover of any magazine.

Or she would be, if not for her expression. The scowl creasing Faith's features was far more suited to a Most Wanted poster than to the cover of a magazine.

Unless, of course, it was a horror magazine.

"Please, Faith. One smile?"

"I wanna go outside and play."

"But we're almost ready for our t—"

"Wanna go outside, Mommy. Please?"

"Faith."

"Pleeeeaaaassssse?"

Anne surrendered. *If you can't fight 'em...* "Okay, Faith. Give me one smile. A *nice* one—" she hurried to add, knowing her child's propensity to ruin any picture with crossed eyes and a tongue hanging out of a goofy grin—"and you can go outside until the party is ready to start."

With that, Faith's scowl melted into a smile that was the very image of innocent beauty. Anne snapped the shot, breathing another sigh as her daughter bounded toward the door.

"Be careful of your dress, honey. You promise?"

Faith turned wide eyes back to her mother, giving one solemn nod.

A smile twitched at Anne's mouth. "Cross your heart?"

Faith's eyes sparkled. She loved the cross-my-heart rhyme—though her version was a bit different than most.

"Cross my heart 'n' hope to fly, stick a dweeble in my eye."

Anne held her laughter captive. Leave it to her little girl to rewrite an ages-old pledge. But Faith meant the words sincerely, and Anne didn't want her daughter to think she was making fun of her. "Okay, honey. Have fun."

In a heartbeat, the little girl scampered out of the room, down the stairs, and out the back door, her new doll tucked under her arm like a football.

Anne followed more slowly, shaking her head. "Mom, was I ever this much work?" She set the camera on the shelf and made her way to the kitchen. "If I was, I really wish you were still alive—" she lifted the teakettle and poured steaming water into the silver teapot—"so I could apologize."

She flicked the lid of the pot closed, the silvery *clang* ringing in her ears. She set the pot on the tray and added the creamer and a small silver bowl with tea bags. Lifting the tray, she carried it to the table, pausing a moment to take in the picture-perfect scene before her.

Her mother's Irish linen tablecloth flowed over the table in a wave of rose-embossed ivory. Delicate cloth napkins captured in rose napkin holders stood guard over the china plates and newly polished silver. A bouquet of fresh flowers sat in the middle of the table, a splash of playful color in the midst of elegance. A silver three-tiered tray held elegantly, decorated sugar cubes, tiny finger sandwiches, and an assortment of luscious cookies she'd bought from the gourmet shop. The mere sight of it all made Anne's mouth water.

Smiling, she set the tea tray in place, then stepped back. It was exactly how she remembered. Faith was going to have so much—

"Yeeeooowwwll!!!"

The piercing banshee screech sent Anne racing to the back door leading from the kitchen to the backyard. Something was clearly being tortured out there!

She pulled the door open and found herself engulfed in utter chaos. The screeching came from the neighbor's cat, Sweetums, an orange tabby the size of Pittsburgh. Sweetums was, without a doubt, the largest cat Anne had ever seen. "Filled out," his owners called him. Anne called the animal fat.

Sweetums usually lay like a blob in whatever spot of sunlight the owners put him in. Anne couldn't recall ever seeing the cat walk. Her neighbors carried him outside, then came to heft and carry him back inside.

Anne often wondered if Sweetums's poor legs even worked anymore.

Well, the answer was right in front of her. They not only worked, they worked well. All four of them. For they were whirling and clawing, doing their best to shred her daughter. Or they would be, if they could reach her. But Faith had the cat pinned to the ground under a fishing net, gripping the handle just out of reach of those claws, exerting just enough force to keep him from escaping.

She wasn't hurting the animal, of that Anne was certain. Faith adored animals, even to the point of weeping when she saw one dead at the side of the road. She'd never hurt an animal. Not physically, anyway. But the cat's wounded pride was evident in the furious feline's ever more ear-splitting shrieks.

"Faith! Let that cat go!"

Faith jumped at her mother's bellowed command. Sweetums took advantage of the distraction, flipped out from under the suddenly slack net, and streaked across the yard as though his life depended on it.

Anne stared after the creature, mouth agape. It was like watching Jell-O race through the grass. Amazing. Who knew that much bulk could move that fast?

"Mommy!"

Faith's disconsolate wail drew Anne's attention back to her daughter, and when she took in the sight before her—her little girl standing there, hands on her tiny hips—Anne almost swallowed her tongue. Faith was covered, head to toe, with dirt and mud. Her carefully arranged hair now looked like a ball of yarn had exploded on her head. Her arms and face were scratched, her dress torn, and the beautiful doll—the doll Anne had spent nearly two weeks tracking down—was on the ground, face-down in the mud, clearly a casualty of the battle with the cat.

Anne's breathing kicked into overdrive. "Faith! What on earth were you *doing*?"

Faith blinked, eyes wide. Her bottom lip popped out. "But Mommy, I'm a tiger catcher."

"Faith!"

Those little shoulders stiffened. "We were playing jungle, and Sweetums is the tiger—"

Like wisps of smoke from a campfire, anger wove its way through Anne's gut, spiraling into her chest, her face, tightening her jaw until she spoke between clenched teeth. "Faith Adelle, what did I tell you about being careful of your new dress?"

Silence met the question. Faith looked down at the ground, but it was plain to see there wasn't any remorse on her features. Just pure, unadulterated stubbornness.

Anne crossed her arms. Everything was ruined. She'd wanted this to be such a special moment. *Why, Lord? Why, this one time, couldn't Faith be good?*

She glared at her daughter. "Go to your room, Faith."

Her head came up. "But we're going to have a tea party—"

She pointed inside. "To…your…room."

Faith's chin jutted out. Shoulders high, she marched past Anne, the very image of a wounded princess. As she stomped by, Anne caught her muttered words.

"Don't care. Tiger catchers don't even *like* tea."

Hours later, Anne stood in the doorway to her daughter's room, watching the even lift and fall of Faith's small chest as she slept. Slow steps carried Anne to Faith's bed, and she eased down on the edge, careful not to wake her sleeping child.

She sat there, silent, watching…

Why, God? Why does anger last for a moment, while the regret it brings lasts for an eternity?

If only she'd kept her temper in check. If only she'd been able to take the unexpected in stride and not let it ruin everything.

Anne stroked Faith's soft hair, smoothing it away from her sleep-flushed cheek.

She'd wasted so much time and energy on anger today. She'd simmered all afternoon, waiting for Jared to come home so she could complain to someone. But the oddest thing happened. When she finished telling him her tale of woe, pacing back and forth the whole time she spoke, she turned, expecting to see sympathy on his face.

Instead, she caught her husband fighting laughter. "Sweetums…*ran*?"

Anne stared at him. "Well…yes." She blinked. "Sort of…I mean, it was kind of a *rolling* run."

Jared gave up the fight. A grin danced across his features even as his chuckle slid free.

Anne crossed her arms over her chest. She was *not* going to give in. She was angry, doggone it, and had every right to be! She arched her brows at him. "You certainly couldn't blame the poor creature. I thought Faith was going to squash him."

"I didn't think that monster's legs worked."

Anne couldn't help it. Her lips twitched. "I know."

"And Faith managed to pin him down? Good grief, he weighs almost as much as she does."

Her husband's humor was as infectious as a case of the measles. The anger Anne had nursed all day dissipated, leaving a swell of giggles in its place. She pushed at his arm. "Jared, be serious."

"I'm *always* serious."

She lowered herself into the chair beside him, giving him a sideways look. "Seriously demented, maybe."

His hand flew to his chest. "I'm wounded!"

"Hmm."

Leaning his elbows on the table, he rested his chin in his hands. "Come on, Annie. Admit it. You've never even seen the beast walk on his own."

She held her hands up. "Okay, okay, I admit it."

He sat back, nodding. "See there? Our little girl wasn't tormenting the critter; she was working a miracle on him!"

"Ohhh, *you*!"

Anne smiled anew at the exchange. Then her smile faded. She brushed Faith's bangs away from her forehead, blinking back sudden tears. *Why, Lord? Why can't I see things the way Jared does? Why can't I find the humor in life's little crises?*

When she thought about it later, after talking with Jared, after her hurt and anger had drained away—when she pictured Faith, determined face framed in a crown of wild hair, holding down that monster of a cat with a fishing net—she couldn't help but laugh.

Why do I let myself get so frustrated and so often over nothing? Nothing that matters, anyway.

Yes, the tea party had been ruined. But not by Faith's escapade. It had been ruined by Anne's anger. She was right to scold Faith. Though the little girl hadn't hurt Sweetums, it still wasn't right to snag the poor creature with the fishing net. And Faith had broken her promise to be careful of her dress. Still…

Anne could have cleaned Faith up and given her a time out. For that matter, she could have let Faith change into her beloved jeans and T-shirt for the party. What they wore didn't matter. It was being together, creating memories they could treasure that mattered. Not clothes or pretty hair.

The heavy sigh that escaped Anne seemed to come from someplace deep within her. If only she'd realized these things sooner.

Lord, please, help Faith know I love her. Because I do, Father. So very much.

As though sensing her mother's distress even in her sleep, Faith stirred beneath Anne's hand and turned to blink up at her with sleep-laden eyes. She reached out one small hand to pat Anne's cheek. The gesture brought tears to her eyes. Underneath all that bravado and stubbornness, her little girl had such a tender heart.

Protect that heart. Keep her close to You. Reach her, Lord…

Prayers flowed through Anne, and she cupped her hand over her daughter's, begging God to do what she had not—to love her daughter just as she was.

"Mommy?"

Anne smiled down at Faith. In the dim light from the hallway she could see Faith's green eyes were wide, eyes so full of wonder as she watched the world around her. "Yes, honey?"

"Will you sleep with me tonight?"

Warmth flooded Anne. *Thank You, Lord. Thanks for a child who forgives.* "Just for a little while, okay?"

"'Kay."

Faith scooted over as Anne slid under the covers and cuddled her close. Faith nestled against her. "Mommy?"

Anne leaned a cheek against Faith's hair, breathing in the sweet fragrance that was her daughter. "Yes, sweetie?"

"I'm sorry I ruined the party."

The tears were back, and Anne had to swallow several times before she could answer. "Oh, Faith, you didn't spoil the party. Mommy did, when she got angry." Anne shifted so she could meet Faith's sleepy gaze. "Honey, I'm sorry I got angry. That was wrong."

Faith studied Anne's face for a moment, then she nodded. "It's okay, Mommy. I forgive you."

Anne hugged her. "Tell you what. How about if we have a different party tomorrow. One with chocolate milk instead of tea?" So it wouldn't be exactly the same as it had been when Anne was a child. So what? Chocolate milk would be that much more special in a silver teacup. "And you can wear your jeans and tennies."

"Really?"

The delight Anne had hoped to see was finally there, in full radiance. "Really."

"I'd like that, Mommy. Lots."

Anne cradled Faith against her. "Then that's what we'll do." She felt Faith nod against her, and then one little hand came up to pat Anne's face again.

"I love you, Mommy..." Faith yawned, and her sleepy voice drifted off. "Bunches and bunches."

Memories to treasure. That's what Anne longed for, and that's what God gave her. Right here. And that, Anne closed her eyes on a smile, was better than the most elegant tea party in the world.

six

"Eternity was in that moment."

WILLIAM CONGREVE

IT WAS A GOOD DAY.

Laughter floated on the breeze, and the sound was music to Jared's ears.

He sat, perched on a large boulder, and watched as his wife and daughter scrambled over the trails and rocks a few yards away. Even from a distance, the exultation in Anne's tone was evident.

She loved coming here, to the Oregon coast. It was the one place lately that seemed to stir the child within her to life. She'd been struggling so with fatigue, with discouragement over her weight and health, that Jared had grown concerned. Last week had been the worst. Anne had finally gone to see her diabetes specialist to find out why she was having so much more trouble than she used to have. Jared hoped she'd come home with a game plan for feeling better.

Instead, she'd come home in tears.

The doctor offered no hope, she said. Just the same old rant: eat less, exercise more, lose weight.

"He says it like it's so easy!" She flopped onto the couch. "Well, I'd like to see *him* lose weight simply by deciding to do so."

That was when Jared made the suggestion. "Let's get away. Take Faith and go to the coast."

Anne looked at him through the wetness still shimmering in her eyes. "Oh, Jared, can we? It's such a long drive."

"No, it's not. A couple of hours at the most. Come on, we'll take it slow and easy. Just enjoy ourselves. And I've got some money set aside for something special, so we can stay overnight in a hotel. Go to a restaurant for dinner."

Annie's features lit up, and she launched herself into his arms. "You're so good to me! How'd I get so lucky as to marry you?"

"Hey, I've always said you deserve the very best!"

He'd been laughing when he said it, but he'd been serious, too. She did deserve the best. She deserved so much more than he was able to give her. His job as a programs director at the YMCA brought in enough money to pay bills, but not much more.

Keeping up with the kids kept him in shape, and that was good. But it kept him busy and away from home, too. Working six days a week made it hard to find "quality time" for his family, especially since he'd started taking small side jobs fixing things in people's homes so he could have some extra money to do special things for Anne and Faith. Things that brought those beautiful smiles blooming on their faces.

Smiles that seemed more and more rare. At least for Anne.

Jared lifted his face to the ocean spray, tasted the hint of salt on his lips, and breathed in the earthy fragrance that was the Oregon coast. There was something restorative about the coast. The rugged beauty spoke to his heart as much as it did Anne's. They'd both needed this trip. She, to get away from the constant struggles to keep up with her daily chores. And he needed it to hear her laugh.

He'd known, deep inside, that their marriage vows would be more than mere words. But he never imagined how connected they'd become over the years. They were like a single entity divided into two bodies. Complete only when they were together. And when she hurt, the way she had been lately, his heart nearly broke for her.

He knew she wasn't happy with the way she was. He'd told her over and over she was still beautiful, still desirable. And she was. One of those teasing, playful smiles from her, and his heart rapid-beat almost out of his chest. Still...

He looked out over the vast ocean, watching the waves rise and fall, break and recede on the shore. He listened to the solid pounding of the surf, loving the rhythm, the steady cadence that reminded him all was as it should be. If only he had that confidence with Annie, that she really was doing her best to take care of herself.

When she knew what the diabetes was doing to her, what was at risk, why did she still insist on eating things she shouldn't? It was as though the very things that could kill her called to her, wooing her, drawing her to embrace them even as they destroyed her body. It scared him. He didn't want to lose her.

He didn't say much about it, though. It hurt her too deeply when he seemed to be criticizing her.

"Hey, you lazy bum!"

The saucy challenge pulled him from his thoughts. Anne and Faith stood waving at him on top of one of the craggy rocks they'd been scaling. "What?"

"Why don't you come up here with us, you handsome devil?"

The breezed tossed Anne's curls and filled her cheeks with a rosy blush. Even from this distance, he could see the joy on her face. She'd told him tale after tale of her childhood, being a Girl Scout, following trail after trail with the surefootedness of a mountain goat.

"I was born to hike," she'd said once.

Looking at her now, he believed it.

"How about a walk on the beach, instead?" He looked toward the surf. "I'm guessing there's a sand dollar or two waiting for us."

"I get the first one!" Faith followed this declaration by scrambling down from the rock and running along the trail. "Race you!"

Annie was on her daughter's heels, and their laughter

floated around Jared, filling his ears and his soul.

Yes, this had been a good idea. And if he had to work nights and weekends to pay for it, he didn't care. All that mattered was his Annie was happy again.

Hours later, they pulled their lunch from the picnic basket, spreading a virtual feast out on the table before them. Their walk along the beach had yielded two sand dollars—one of which was whole and still had the seven "angels" inside it—a pocketful of rocks that Faith had found particularly beautiful, and a tiny dried-up starfish. These treasures were lined along the raised rock wall behind their table, drying in the sun.

"Look, Daddy! Look at the gulls!"

Jared turned to watch Faith rip pieces of bread apart and toss them in the air, where waiting gulls swooped down and caught them with aerobatic ease.

"Greedy things. They're going to be too fat to fly soon."

He grinned at Anne's laughing comment. "They're not near as greedy as the squirrels." He nodded toward the bushes covering the ground all around them.

Annie tossed a piece of bread toward the nearest bush, and three squirrels jumped out.

The gulls and the squirrels along with the picnic area that overlooked the beach were what made Harris Beach Jared's favorite day-trip location. The heavy brush covering the ground was alive with squirrels. They were careful enough not to come too close, but still provided ample entertainment as they begged for morsels of food. Faith called Harris Beach "Squirrel Beach," and Jared couldn't argue with her.

Anne came to slide her arms around his waist. "Thanks for suggesting this. It was a great idea."

He folded her into his embrace. Though they'd been married nearly twenty years, she never ceased to bring a smile to his face—and his heart. "That's the only kind of ideas I have." He rubbed his cheek against hers. "Great ones."

"Like marrying me, of course."

His grin widened. "Of course. Though you could hardly resist me, handsome man that I am."

Anne's laughter bubbled. "Oh yeah, that was it. I was so

captivated by tall, lanky guys with big ears."

"Who sat off in corners, singing to themselves. I know, I know." Jared gave her a swat on the behind.

"Daddy's spanking Mommy!"

At Faith's gleeful giggles, Anne pulled away, her cheeks reddening. "Faith, shhh!" She looked around. "People will stare."

Jared laughed and pulled Faith into a bear hug. "Yeah, squirt. Don't you know I want to keep your mommy all to my lanky self?"

Faith giggled even harder. "What's *lanky* mean, Daddy?"

"Tall and skinny."

The crease in Faith's forehead made both Jared and Anne laugh. "I used to be skinny, sweetie. When I was younger." He pulled a muscleman pose. "Now I'm all filled out."

"Now you're *just* right." Faith grabbed one bicep and pushed off of the table to dangle from it.

Jared kept his arm flexed. For all that she was seven now, she was so slim and light that he didn't have to strain to hold her in the air. "You think so?"

Faith nodded, clearly sincere.

"Come on, you monkey." Anne caught Faith and lifted her to the bench of the table. "Time to eat."

The three of them sat and held hands.

"Do you want to pray, Faith?"

"Yes, Daddy."

They all bowed their heads, and Faith kicked her heels against the picnic bench, starting her prayer in slow, thoughtful words. "Thank You, dear God, for this day. Thank You for this food." Then, as though thinking up things to be thankful for had fueled her excitement, the rest of the prayer poured out on one breath: "Thank You for the gulls and the squirrels and the sand dollars and Mommy and Daddy and the squirrels and the starfish and the rocks and the ocean and the flowers and the squirrels and the pretty rocks and…and…"

Jared wasn't sure how he managed to hold back his laughter, but he did. He peeked out of one eye and saw his little girl chewing her lip, thinking hard so she didn't forget anything.

"Amen?" Anne suggested.

Faith nodded. "Amen!" She let go of their hands and grabbed up a sandwich. "Yum, Mommy! You cook good."

"Yeah, Mom." Jared bit into a peanut-butter-and-jelly sandwich. "You cook good."

"Keep it up and that's all I'll cook for the next week." But the grin on his wife's face belied the threat, and Jared just smacked his lips.

"Jared!" Anne almost choked on her laughter.

He shrugged. "I'm savoring every luscious bite." He caught her hand and tugged her close for a peanut-buttery kiss. She buried her face in his neck for a moment, and he realized he'd only been half kidding.

He was savoring something. Every precious moment of this day. Every smile from his wife and daughter. Every tinkle of laughter that rose on the wind. And the sweetness of these things fed his soul, filling him to overflowing.

Yes, it was a good day. A blessed day. And he'd never, ever forget it.

Sunlight streamed in the kitchen window, dancing across the room to caress Anne's face as she sat at the table, lancet at the ready.

She steeled herself for the prick, grimacing as the tiny needle did its work. Darn her sugars! They'd behaved so well while they were at the coast. She let herself believe they were finally getting under control. But since they came home, she was right back where she'd been before their wonderful get-away.

Out of control.

Amazing how much ground one could lose in seven years. She thought often about how pleased the doctor had been with her during her pregnancy. Lately, anytime she saw him, he looked at her with that grave expression.

Well, what was she supposed to do? It was as though her body was on strike. Nothing she did seemed to help.

She squeezed a drop of blood onto the test strip, then counted off the sixty-second wait. If only she could figure out why her sugars had suddenly gone out of control, fluctuating from sky-high to basement-low. She was feeling the effects of it, too. Sluggish one day, irritable and jumpy the next. It was enough to dread getting out of bed in the mornings.

Even her doctor couldn't explain it. After her last bout of dangerously low sugars, he'd given her a thorough checkup, then shrugged. "Diabetes is a disease with a mind of its own sometimes."

Anne's teeth clenched at the memory. A lot of help that was. No wonder they called it *practicing* medicine.

Of course, though he couldn't explain or cure the problem, he could add to it. Which he did by telling her to check her blood more often.

So now she got to prick her poor fingers to within an inch of their little lives.

"Mommy?"

Anne turned from the sink where she'd gone to wash the drop of blood from the test strip so she could read it. Faith stood there, worry evident in every angle of her seven-year-old face.

"What's wrong, sweetie?" Anne tried to split her focus between Faith and reading the test strip. If she didn't read it now, she'd have to prick another finger for more blood.

The color showed up. Darn! She'd have to adjust her dose of insulin again.

She tossed the strip in the trash and knelt so she was on eye level with her daughter. Faith's lower lip trembled. "Mommy…does it hurt?"

Anne brushed back her daughter's soft, auburn hair. "Does what hurt?"

The little girl's glance shot to the table, where Anne's needle waited. Understanding dawned. She held her hand out to Faith, bringing her into the circle of her arms.

"Let me show you something." Anne took the cap off the needle and held it so Faith could see it, fighting a smile when her little girl leaned away from the offending device. "See? It's a really, really thin needle. I don't even feel it when it goes in."

Faith leaned forward, her somber face intent. "Really?"

Anne nodded. "Really." She slid Faith to the floor, showing her how she filled the needle with insulin. Faith watched, eyes round, but when Anne was ready to give herself the shot, Faith put her hand on Anne's arm.

"Wait, Mommy."

"It's okay, honey—"

Faith shook her head. "Not yet." She moved to lean against Anne's leg. "I wanna pray first."

Anne looked down at her daughter. *Oh, Faith...my precious girl.* "Okay, sweetie."

"Fold your hands and close your eyes, Mommy, like when we pray at bedtime or when you pray for me when I get hurt."

Anne obeyed, bending her head until her forehead touched against Faith's.

"Dear God—" Faith's sweet voice was full of trust—"help Mommy. Help the shot not hurt. Amen."

"Amen," Anne echoed around the emotion clogging her throat. She met Faith's solemn gaze. "Now?"

Faith nodded, and Anne gave herself the shot, then held the syringe up. "See? The needle's so thin I don't even bleed."

Faith's mouth opened in a little *O*. "It really doesn't hurt?"

Anne knelt beside her. "Not even a little."

When Faith's small hand took hold of hers and lifted the bruised fingers, Anne held back a grimace.

"I bet *that* hurts, huh?"

She wouldn't lie to her daughter, no matter how much she wanted to. "Yes, honey, that does hurt."

Faith kissed each of her mother's sore fingers. Then she let go of Anne's hand, and a smile lit her sweet face. "All better?"

Anne caught her in a hug. "Better than better—" she rested her cheek against her daughter's head—"the very best of all."

On the Hard Path

"As he scattered it across his field,
some seed fell on...the hard path....
Then the evil one comes and snatches
the seed away from their hearts."

MATTHEW 13: 4, 19

seven

"Rebellious, the storms it wooeth,
as if the storms could give repose."
Mikhael Lermontov

IT WAS A BEAUTIFUL SEPTEMBER DAY, THE KIND OF day where the wind caressed your cheeks while the fall sun splayed its warmth across your shoulders.

It never ceased to amaze Anne how warm this time of year could be in the Rogue Valley. The scorching heat of August—when temperatures averaging mid- to high-nineties could climb as high as 115!—had only recently started to cool to the mid-eighties. The days were growing shorter, bit by bit. And early morning held a slight bite of cool that, though it never lasted past 9 A.M., was nonetheless a solid reminder that winter was coming.

Anne looked down at her daughter, walking so straight and proud at her side. Where had the years gone? One moment Faith was a tiny infant and now? Now she was eight years old, on her way to her first day of third grade, raring to take the world by storm.

Happily for Anne, the school was mere blocks away from their home. She and Jared had determined early on that they would make going to school something positive, even fun. For months prior to Faith's first day at Lincoln Elementary, Anne and her husband told Faith how lucky she was to be going to school.

True to form, Faith bounced in her chair, barely contained excitement in her every move as she listened to how wonderful it would be. Night after night, she climbed into Jared's lap before bedtime, leaned her head against his chest, and pleaded on a yawn, "Tell me again, Daddy. Tell me about school."

With a smile at Anne, Jared would launch into tales of all Faith would do and learn, of how much she would enjoy the teachers and other children. Faith's smile was pure anticipation as she drifted off to sleep.

Faith sailed through her first two years of school. She'd been a favorite with her teachers, who sang her praises at parent-teacher conferences. Creative. Personable. Bright. Outgoing. All words Anne heard to describe her daughter.

Now, it was time for third grade. Jared had taken the morning off so he could be there to share in the excitement.

That morning, they barely got their exuberant daughter to sit still for breakfast. She and Jared kept breaking into song and then into laughter. Faith loved singing choruses and praise songs with her father, and their voices blended with a pure beauty that stole Anne's breath at times.

She joined in from time to time at Faith's insistence, though she enjoyed listening. By the time breakfast was over, Faith was all but dancing as they gathered her things together and headed out the door. Anne walked beside Jared, her hand nestled in his, and watched Faith skipping ahead, listening to her clear, sweet voice sing out, "*This is the day, this is the day, that the Lord has made…*"

It almost broke Anne's heart.

Of course she was happy Faith was so excited about going to school. But that happiness couldn't erase what lay within—the painful awareness that with each passing year, Faith was taking steps away from her.

Her daughter stopped suddenly and pointed. "Mom! Dad! Look! My school!"

How Anne longed to share the excitement ringing in her daughter's voice. Instead, she had to fight the driving urge to run forward, pull her baby into her arms, beg her not to grow up…grow away. But even if it had been physically possible, there was no way on earth anyone would stop Faith from plunging headlong into this new adventure.

A bit different from your first day of school, eh?

As different as midnight from noonday. Anne could still remember how hard it had been all through grade school. On the first day of school, from first grade through fourth, Anne clung to her mother, weeping, begging to go home. She remembered staring at the large, imposing building, how she'd been surrounded by adults she didn't know and children she hadn't seen for months. The very thought of staying in that place had terrified her.

"Holy cow! Lookit all the new kids for me to play with!"

Faith's rapturous tone tugged Anne's lips into a smile as she followed the direction of her daughter's gaze. Children scampered across the playground, laughter ringing in the air around them.

"You're going to have a great time this year, kiddo."

Anne had no doubt Jared was right. Faith would be in the middle of everything in no time. People were drawn to her. Even as an infant, total strangers had remarked on how beautiful and engaging Faith was, how her tinkling laughter could draw a smile from the sourest soul. No surprise, then, that Anne's baby girl had grown into a little social butterfly whose ease among strangers never ceased to amaze her own mother.

Anne slipped her hands into her jacket pockets as they walked past the children and went to Faith's classroom.

"Welcome, Faith!" Her teacher was a lovely older woman with a soft crown of salt-and-pepper curls. Soft brown eyes sparkled from behind her glasses, and the tiny crinkles peeking out from the corners of her eyes bore clear testimony to the woman's penchant for smiling. "I'm Mrs. Rice. And I'm so glad to have you with us."

Mrs. Rice winked at Anne and Jared as she showed them around the room. "And this—" the woman's sweet, weathered face smiled down at Faith—"is your desk."

Faith's mouth opened in a gasp of pure delight, and she

smoothed her hands over the wood top, then slid onto the seat as though she'd sat there a hundred times before.

Anne studied her daughter's glowing features. What was it like to feel at home no matter where you were? To look forward to, rather than dread, being in new places, meeting new people? Anne hadn't a clue, any more than she could fathom how someone who sprang from within her—someone formed from the very fiber of her being, whom she'd nurtured with her own blood and body—could share so little in common with her.

That's a good thing, though. You wouldn't want Faith to go through all you did because you were so shy, would you?

No, of course not. And yet, Anne couldn't help feeling a bit left behind by her outgoing, spotlight-loving little girl. *Well, fine. Let Faith take the spotlight. You can cheer her on from the wings.*

Indeed, she could. And she did. All the time. It felt as though she'd been doing so from the moment Faith was born. Still…

Anne allowed herself a small sigh. She couldn't deny it. Deep inside, she wished Faith were more like her. Not to limit the child, but so they could relate better.

Or so you could be sure she really needs you?

Before she could ponder that startling question, a small hand slipped into hers. She glanced down to find Faith gazing up at her with those deep emerald eyes.

"Mommy?"

Anne squeezed her daughter's hand. "Yes, sweetie?"

"I wish you could come to school with me."

"Why, honey?"

"Because I miss you."

Anne looked up to meet Mrs. Rice's gentle smile. "You know, Faith, your mom's already been to school. Now it's your turn."

There was a slight crease on Faith's brow, and she leaned against Anne. "I know. I wish…you could stay with me."

The uncharacteristic tremor in her child's voice rendered Anne speechless. She knelt and gathered her little girl in her arms, burying her face in the fragrant softness of her hair. *I'm sorry, Lord, I forgot...even butterflies need someplace firm to land between flights.*

"Oh, honey, don't worry. You're going to have so much fun you won't even notice I'm not here." She leaned back and met her daughter's somber gaze. "And then at the end of the day, I'll come get you, we can walk home together, and you can tell me all about your day."

Faith pulled back. "You'll come every day?"

Anne nodded.

"Promise? You won't forget?"

"I won't forget. I promise." Anne smiled up at Jared, and his answering grin told her he knew, as Anne did, that only one thing would dispel the glimmer of doubt still lurking in Faith's eyes. Anne looked back at their daughter. "Cross my heart and hope to fly..."

Faith giggled. "Stick a dweeble in your eye?"

Anne hugged Faith again. "Ten dweebles at least, sweetie, if I ever forget you."

School was the best. Faith loved going to school. She loved walking there with her mom each morning and loved the way her mom always hugged her and told her the same thing: "You be a good girl today." Faith liked being a good girl. 'Cuz it made Mommy smile.

This morning Mom gave her a big hug, then waved as Faith ran onto the playground to meet her friends. And her teacher. Faith loved the teachers and the playground and the desks and the pictures on the walls and even the sound of the chalk as Mrs. Rice wrote words on the blackboard. School was her most favorite place of all.

Well, *almost* favorite. Her really *most* favorite was home, with Mom and Daddy.

"Hi, Faith."

She turned to see who was calling her and smiled. Winola Gregory was sitting on a swing, waving at her. Swinging was Faith's favorite thing to do. It was so neat to feel like she was flying. She hoped the bell didn't ring for a long time. It was lots of fun on the playground.

Especially with Winnie. Faith saw Winnie all the time, both at school and in Sunday School. Winnie was really quiet, and her short, yellowish hair kind of stuck out funny, and she had big black glasses that made her look like a big ol' owl with giant brown eyes. But she was nice. And she knew funny jokes.

Faith and Winnie had been friends since first grade, when a big rubber ball that Faith kicked smacked Winne in the head. Winnie was hanging upside down on the jungle gym at the time, and she dropped to the ground with a yelp and a plop. Faith went to help her up and say sorry.

But Winnie just gave her a shy smile. "That's okay. You jus' scared me a little."

From that point on, Faith knew Winnie would be her best friend forever.

"Hey, Faith!"

She looked to where Winnie was swinging. "Yeah?"

"How deep is a frog pond?"

Faith grinned. "How deep?"

"Knee-deep! Knee-deep!"

Winnie was trying to sound like a frog, but she sounded more like a goat strangling on a tin can. Even so, it made Faith laugh. She went to sit on the swing next to Winnie, but before she reached it, another girl pushed past her, grabbed the swing, and plunked down on it.

Trista Jennings. She always did things like stealing swings. Mean things.

Winnie frowned. "That's Faith's swing."

Trista wrinkled her nose and made a face at Winnie. "These swings are for big girls, not babies."

Faith put her hands on her hips. Who was Trista calling a baby? She was the same age as Faith. "I'm not a baby!"

Trista pushed off, swinging, barely missing Faith with her feet. "Yes, you are. That's why your *mommy* has to bring you to school."

"Faith's mom is nice."

Faith smiled at Winnie. She said things real quiet, but she said them real firm, too. Faith liked that.

Winnie went on. "I *like* Faith's mom. I think it's neat she walks Faith to school."

"Yeah, well, who cares what *you* like?" Trista kicked her feet out, sending the swing higher. "*You're* a baby, too. And you're stupid."

With that, Trista jumped off the swing. She landed with a thud right in front of Faith, then crossed her arms and pushed her face into Faith's. "Go ahead, take the swing. I don't want to be around you babies anyway."

Faith felt the mad deep inside. She wanted to yell at Trista, to tell her to stop saying mean things. But she didn't. Trista might get mad at her. The other kids listened to Trista. They kind of looked up to her because she did things other kids were afraid to do. They liked the people Trista said to like—and didn't like the people Trista said not to like.

People like babies.

Whose mothers had to walk them to school.

"Come swing, Faith."

Faith crossed her arms and turned to frown at Winnie. "I don't *want* to swing." She grabbed the swing and flung it away from her. "Swinging's for babies."

The hurt on Winnie's face made Faith's tummy hurt, but she didn't say sorry. She turned and walked away. And that made the icky feeling in her tummy even worse.

Stupid playground. Stupid swings. Stupid Winnie.

She kicked at the ground. *Ring, you stupid bell.* She rubbed a fist at her stinging eyes. *It's no fun out here anymore.*

Anne sipped her tea, savoring the momentary quiet in the kitchen. Faith had gulped down her breakfast, then raced from the room to gather her things.

"You all ready for Faith's second day of third grade?"

Anne smiled at Jared, watching him fill his travel mug with steaming coffee. "Well, I'm ready, but I don't know about Faith." She glanced toward the hallway leading to Faith's room.

"She gulped down her oatmeal then disappeared into her room."

Jared set his mug on the counter and moved to the hallway. "Faith, honey, come on, time to go. Your mommy's waiting."

Anne expected their daughter to come bounding out of her room, but all that met Jared's words was silence. They looked at each other and frowned.

"Maybe she fell asleep again?"

Anne shook her head, starting down the hallway. "I don't think so. She was all dressed—" She jerked to a halt near the stairs. Faith's coat, which had hung there moments ago, was gone. A shiver of panic sliced through Anne as she angled a look back into the kitchen. The lunch she'd just finished packing for Faith was gone as well. Then she noticed the front door was slightly ajar.

The shiver exploded into full-blown alarm.

"Jared!"

He came to meet her. "Her things are gone and the door's open. You don't think someone came in the house?" She couldn't finish the horrible thought.

Jared took in the hallway and the front door. "I don't think anyone came in, hon. If I had to guess, I'd say Faith decided to head to school on her own."

"Why on earth would she do that? We've been walking to school together since she started kindergarten."

Jared reached for his coat and Anne's. "Let's go ask her."

When Anne spotted Faith on the school playground, swinging and laughing, it was one of the most welcome sights she'd ever seen. Relief tore through her, making her knees weak. If Jared hadn't been standing with his arm around her, Anne was sure she would have collapsed into a heap on the ground.

"Thank God she's all right."

Anne swallowed, managing a nod at Jared's low comment.

He angled a look at her and gave her a fortifying squeeze. "Shall we?"

Grateful her legs were regaining their ability to support

her, Anne straightened. "Absolutely."

She followed Jared to the playground. They had just reached the swings when Faith looked up. Her eyes went wide, and she brought her swing to an abrupt halt. Anne and Jared didn't have to say a word. Faith slid from the swing and came to stand in front of them.

"Faith Adelle—" Thank heaven, her tone was even and calm. If that wasn't a miracle, she didn't know what was! "Why did you leave the house alone?"

If Anne had expected remorse, she was in for disappointment. Faith's only reply was a shrug.

Anne stiffened, then felt Jared's hand on her shoulder. She turned to see the caution in his eyes. His message came through loud and clear: *Don't let your anger get the better of you.*

He knelt so he was on eye-level with their daughter. "Faith, you need to answer your mother."

Her father's gentle prodding was Faith's undoing. Tears suddenly perched on the edges of her eyelids, and she swallowed hard.

Anne knelt, too, taking Faith's hand. "Sweetie, it scared us when we didn't know where you were."

Faith nodded, looking down, then away.

"Honey, look at me."

Faith complied, but only for a moment. Her gaze darted from Anne's face to look over her shoulder.

"Faith."

She jerked her gaze back to Anne. "I'm sorry, Mommy. I just—"

"Is Faith in trouble?"

Anne looked over Faith's shoulder. Two little girls stood there, watching. One was Winnie, Faith's little friend. Her furrowed brow showed how worried she was. Anne didn't recognize the other girl.

Jared answered Winnie's question. "We need to talk with Faith for a few minutes, girls. She'll come play with you as soon as we're done."

"Okay. Good." Winnie gave a small wave at Faith and turned to leave. The other girl didn't budge. Anne frowned.

Was she afraid they were going to hurt Faith? "It's okay…"

"Trista," Faith supplied.

Anne glanced at her daughter, wondering at the odd tone in her voice. Then she focused on Trista. "It's okay, Trista. Faith will come play in a minute."

The girl looked about to say something, then her shoulders lifted and she turned to head back to the swings.

Anne watched her go, a vague sense of disquiet crawling through her. So that was where Faith got that shrug. "Is Trista new?"

Faith nodded. "She started last year. Just before school got over."

Anne wanted to ask more, but now was not the time to get distracted. "We're still waiting for an answer. Why did you leave the house this morning?"

Faith's lower lip stuck out. "I can walk to school by myself."

Hurt came, quick and sharp, slicing Anne's heart into tiny, pain-ridden pieces. *See? She doesn't want you.*

"No, you can't."

"Yes, I can, Daddy. I'm not a baby."

"A baby? Who said you were a baby?" Anne glanced back at Faith's friends. "Did one of those girls call you a baby?"

Faith didn't answer. She just dug in, crossing her arms and standing there like a little stump.

I will not get angry. I will not. "You're right, Faith, you're not a baby. But you're still too young to walk to school by yourself. Or to walk home."

Faith opened her mouth as though to argue, but Jared held up a hand, stopping her. "Your mother is right." He gave her a firm look. "You are not to walk to school by yourself, understood?"

She looked down at the ground and nodded. "Yes, Daddy."

Anne put her hand on Faith's shoulder. "I'll be here when school is over. I expect you to wait for me, even if I'm a little late, do you understand?"

She kept staring at the ground and kicked a rock.

"Faith?"

With a heavy sigh that spoke volumes, Faith gave one curt nod.

Try not to be so excited about walking with me. "Fine, then I'll see you later today."

The bell rang then, and Jared laid his hand on top of Faith's head for a moment. "I'm glad you're all right, punkin'. Now go on, before the tardy bell rings."

Anne watched as her daughter turned and stomped back to join the other kids who were lining up. Winnie called to Faith, signaling for her to join Trista and her in the line. Faith did so, and the two little girls leaned over and whispered to Faith. Like the sun breaking through storm clouds, Faith suddenly transformed from a sulky, frowning rebel into a smiling, laughing playmate.

Jared's arm slipped around Anne's shoulders. "Let's go home, hon."

She turned, falling into step beside him, then hesitated. Someone was watching her. She could feel it in the raised hairs on the back of her neck. She cast one final glance back toward her daughter.

Trista was standing there, staring at Anne. And though she couldn't explain it, a shiver skittered down her back.

"Hey, you okay?"

Anne met Jared's concerned gaze and managed a smile. "I'm fine. Just…recovering."

He nodded, tightening his hold on her. As always, the contact warmed and uplifted her. And almost dispelled the unease Trista's stare had planted in Anne's gut.

Almost.

eight

"The best learning occurs in the context of a shared experience."
KENNY LUCK

THE FALL SPED BY, WARM DAYS TURNING COOL, sunshine easing into overcast days and nights where stars had to peek from behind thick blankets of clouds. Almost before Anne knew it, winter was upon them, complete with visits from the thick fog that fell over the valley, covering their world in a moist mist that gave sounds an odd, muted tone.

Anne loved the fog. Always had. Loved the way it enveloped her when she walked, the way it shrouded the familiar in a cloak of mystery, of hidden wonder. Faith liked the fog almost as much as her mother. Determined to nurture this bit of common ground, Anne made a point of taking Faith for walks when the fog came out to play.

This year had been especially fun. Though it was more of a struggle than in past years for Anne to walk for long—the diabetes had caused ever-worsening nerve damage in her feet—she and Faith went out a number of times, hand in hand, to enjoy their friend. Walking in the fog was one place where even the ever-ebullient Faith was quiet, thoughtful. She talked in a hushed voice, telling Anne what had happened at school or—in those rare moments—sharing her hopes and dreams.

Faith might be a little girl still, but her dreams were big.

"I want to help people. I'm gonna be a doctor."

"I want to write books for little kids, to make them smile."

"I'm gonna be an artist. Then I can paint beautiful pictures that will make people happy."

Yesterday, on their walk in the fog, Faith nestled her hand in Anne's and announced, "I want to work in a zoo."

"A zoo?"

She nodded. "Yup. And I'll take care of the tigers."

Anne squeezed Faith's small hand. Her little girl loved tigers more than almost anything. "So, you're not going to be a doctor, huh?"

"Oh, sure. I'll be a doctor, too. But I'll work in the zoo on weekends."

"Ah. And how about writing kids' books or painting?"

She thought about that, then smiled. "Easy. I'll write books about tigers and then paint the pictures to go with them!"

Anne slid her arm around her little dreamer. "That sounds perfect to me, sweetie."

Faith grinned. "Me, too!"

Anne could hardly believe it was already December. The month had gone by in a blur of fun and preparation as the Christmas season unfolded. She'd started playing Christmas albums the day after Thanksgiving, much to Jared's chagrin.

"A little early, isn't it?"

She'd shot him a grin, dropping the needle onto the next album. "Hey, be thankful I didn't start when I wanted to."

"And when—" he raised his voice to be heard over Nat King Cole crooning about chestnuts and open fires—"pray tell, was that?"

"The day after Halloween."

Though he painted his features with pained tolerance, she knew he loved the holidays as much as she. There was something magical about this time of year. Every event held special meaning.

This year was no different than previous years. They'd

started out, the first weekend of December, with the hunt for the perfect Christmas tree. The three of them—each cocooned in coats, knit caps, scarves, and mittens—piled into the car, thermoses of hot chocolate and handsaws at the ready. They headed up into the mountains, bouncing along rutted logging roads, fingers crossed against meeting a logging truck on its way *down*, accompanying the protests of their car with spirited renditions of every Christmas carol to which they could recall words. Those songs they couldn't remember joined the ranks of "Make It Up as You Go," Jared's favorite pastime. He kept Faith and Anne in stitches as he lifted his beautiful baritone voice to sing opera in Italian—or more accurately, his version of what *sounded* Italian.

Once they found just the right spot—which was entirely intuitive, of course—they parked the car and began the trek, studying each magnificent tree, deciding which one was begging to go home with them. Anne didn't know how Jared managed it, but he always led them to the most wonderful trees. Proud evergreens with thick, sturdy trunks and full branches reaching out as though anticipating the ornaments soon to adorn them.

With the tree for the living room chosen, it was Faith's turn to pick out a small tree for her room. Her excitement was contagious as she went from one little tree to another, fingering its needles, inhaling its fragrance, leaning her head close to talk to it.

"It has to be a friendly tree. A really friendly tree. One that smiles."

Jared's brow creased. "A…friendly tree. One that—smiles."

But Anne took her daughter's hand, tossing a nod over her shoulder at her husband. "Makes perfect sense to me."

And the wonderful thing was that it did! She and Faith were in perfect sync in December. No wonder Anne considered it a season of miracles.

Even Jared had to admit, once they had the trees home and decorated, that it did seem as though Faith's tree was grinning behind the glittering lights fastened to its branches. And who could blame it? When one is the object of such fervent adoration, smiling is an infinitely sensible thing to do.

Though Jared's long hours at the YMCA often left him weary, he always found the energy to spend evenings and weekends with them, decorating the house, putting up the tree, baking Christmas cookies, and going shopping.

And on those nights when they didn't have things to do, they relaxed in front of the TV, watching all the sappy, silly Christmas specials. Warming their hands on cups of cocoa with tiny marshmallows bobbing on top, they laughed at the old favorites: *How the Grinch Stole Christmas*, *Rudolf the Red-Nosed Reindeer*, *Little Drummer Boy*, and *A Charlie Brown Christmas*. And by special request, the Carpenters' Christmas special.

Anne had enjoyed The Carpenters for years. She loved the lead singer's low, rich voice. Faith, in all her eight-year-old wisdom, grimaced every time Anne played one of their records.

"Ugh! The Carpenters. They're *boring*!"

"Just because they don't wiggle their hips around—" Anne cast a pointed look at the Elvis poster adorning the wall in her daughter's room—"doesn't make them boring."

"Mother! Elvis doesn't *wiggle*!"

"Ah." Anne let her tone show how unconvinced she was. "My mistake. Ever so sorry, sweetie."

As much as Anne teased her daughter about her adoration of the singer, she'd spent weeks last August finding Elvis-themed party supplies for Faith's eighth birthday. Elvis plates and napkins, Elvis cups, Elvis posters, Elvis buttons, Elvis on the record player welcoming Faith's friends with "You Ain't Nothin' but a Hounddog." Everywhere you turned in their house, you were met with that famous smile. It was all worth it when, after everyone left, Faith threw her arms around her mom's neck and gave her cheek a sloppy smack.

"This was the best birthday, ever!"

Anne was especially glad she'd gone to all that effort when, just eleven days later, the TV broadcast the shocking news that Elvis had been found dead. When she heard, Faith burst into tears. Anne held her and consoled her, but the girl moped around for days. A week or so later, Anne went into Faith's room and found the Elvis posters gone. Faith's Elvis records from the shelf near her record player were gone, too.

When Anne asked where they were, Faith looked away. "I put them in a box, in my closet. It…it makes me too sad to listen to them."

Her daughter's tender heart never ceased to amaze her. But what amazed her even more came a month or so later. Anne was listening to one of her Carpenters' albums while she cleaned. When Faith came into the room, Anne steeled herself for an insult. Instead, Faith sat on the couch and listened.

"Can I borrow this record?"

Anne paused in the act of dusting a bookshelf. Had she heard correctly?

Faith stretched out on the couch, plopping her feet on one of Anne's best decorative pillows. "Can I borrow it?"

"*May* I borrow it?" Anne eyed the flattened pillow.

"You don't need to. It's your record."

Her kid was *such* a comedienne. Anne put her hands on her hips, her gaze fixed on Faith's offending feet.

Faith sighed—though Anne wasn't sure if it was at the grammar lesson or the daggers Anne was shooting at her daughter's feet. The answer came when Faith lifted her feet and swung them back onto the floor as she sat up. She tapped her toes on the carpet. "Happy?"

Anne gave the fruit of her loins a sweet smile. "Ecstatic."

"So can—*may*—I borrow this record?"

"Only if you promise not to burn it." Anne took the record off the player and slipped it back into its sleeve.

"Not to worry, Mom. I actually kind of like it."

What do you know? Miracles do *happen*, Anne thought as she handed it over.

Before long, Faith was an avid fan. So, of course, when she saw there was going to be a Carpenters' Christmas special this year, she was thrilled.

"We're going to watch it, right?"

Jared gave an exaggerated yawn. "I don't know…the Carpenters? Aren't they kind of *boring*?"

Anne shook her head. It was pretty clear where Faith got

her comic abilities. But Faith knew they'd give in. And they did. They watched the show together, a huge bowl of popcorn sitting between them, enjoying every minute.

Christmas cards afforded another holiday tradition. As soon as they arrived in the mail, they were placed in a festive basket sitting on the hallway table. Then, each evening, after dinner and before their Christmas devotions, the three of them would sit and read the cards together, making a prayer list.

Devotions came next, where they lit the candles on the Advent wreath, opened the day's "door" on the Advent calendar, then read a section from the Bible. As much as Faith and Jared enjoyed the whole Santa aspect of Christmas, they made sure Faith knew what the season was really about. And Faith, in turn, delighted in asking every department store or Salvation Army Santa, "Aren't you glad you get to bring presents for Jesus' birthday?"

They closed their nightly devotions with prayer, and Jared, Anne, and Faith each prayed for one of the "card people," as Faith loved to call them. Faith always prayed last, so she could add her most frequent and fervent prayer: "Please, God, can You give us snow for Christmas?"

Anne echoed the prayer. She loved it when it snowed for Christmas. But Jared always reminded her that snow seldom fell on the valley floor. "That's one of the nice things about this area," he'd say. "If we want to play in the snow, we just drive up into the mountains a half hour away. But we don't have to deal with it during the week."

Even so, nothing made Christmas Eve quite so enchanted as those fluffy white flakes floating out of an inky sky, landing with soft, almost imperceptible *plops* on the ground. And nothing made Christmas Day quite so perfect as a fresh blanket of snow, coating the world in glistening newness.

By the time Christmas Eve rolled around, though, Anne had to admit it didn't look good. The forecast called for a high of forty-two on Christmas Day. So much for a white Christmas.

Anne sighed as she taped a shiny bow to the final gift. As usual, she'd waited until Faith was in bed and asleep to finish wrapping gifts and put them out under the tree. Jared had pulled out the card table and set it up so Anne could "play Santa," as he put it. He'd helped wrap for a while, but fatigue got the better of him, and he headed for bed nearly an hour ago. Anne slid the gift under the tree, folded up the card table, and turned off all but the Christmas tree lights. She sank into her recliner, feet folded under her, and smiled.

This was her favorite time. When it was still, silent, and she could sit in the warm darkness watching the tree lights sparkle and reflect on the ornaments and the large plateglass window beside the tree.

But as much as she enjoyed this time, she found her eyelids growing increasingly heavy. After starting awake for the third time, she finally surrendered and went to turn off the tree lights. As she leaned down reaching for the plug, something outside the window caught her eye.

Was that…? Could it be?

She unplugged the tree lights so she could see out the window better.

It was! She clapped her hands together. It was snowing! Huge, white flakes cascaded from the sky, burying the sidewalk and lawn with icy abandon.

"Thanks, God." Anne smiled in the darkness. "You're the best."

Anticipation sang through her as she made her way upstairs, opened Faith's door, and sat on the side of her sleeping daughter's bed. She lay a gentle hand on Faith's cheek and leaned close to her ear, speaking in a whisper. "Faith. Sweetie, wake up."

Faith's eyes flickered, then eased open. "Mom?" She blinked a couple of times. "Is it Christmas already?"

Anne smiled. "Not quite, but I've got something I want to show you."

Sitting up with a yawn, Faith stretched her arms over her head. Anne stood and held her hand out. Faith took it and slid from the bed, pushed her feet into her slippers, and pulled on her thick robe. Hand in hand, mother and daughter went downstairs to the front door.

"Close your eyes."

Faith did as her mother asked. Anne pulled the front door open and led Faith out onto the porch.

"Okay, open them."

Faith's lids flicked up—and she stared. Anne watched realization wash over her daughter's features and wonder light her eyes. Faith turned to her mother. "It's snowing!"

"It certainly is."

"Oh, Mommy!"

Anne's throat constricted. Faith seldom called her that anymore. It had been her favorite name for Anne when she was maybe four or five. But in the last few years Anne had become *Mom*. She hadn't realized how much she missed being *Mommy*.

"God *heard* me!" Faith hugged Anne so tight she almost couldn't breathe.

"He always does, sweetie." She squeezed Faith close. "Because He loves you."

"I'm glad, Mommy."

The joy in her daughter's words resonated deep within Anne's heart. "So am I, Faith. So am I."

They stood there, joined by their arms and their delight, watching the snow sparkle as though it were a million miniature diamonds—but knowing what lay on the ground and what they held in their arms were even more precious gifts from a loving God.

As she looked out at the winter night, feeling her daughter's warmth and delight, Anne sent a prayer heavenward: *Please, God, don't let this change. Don't ever let us lose this connection.*

A sudden chill hit Anne, gripping her with frozen fingers.

"You okay, Mom?"

"I'm fine, sweetie. That blast of cold wind just got to me."

Faith frowned. "What wind?"

Anne looked at her daughter, then out at the night. Faith was right. There wasn't any wind at all. The snow was falling straight to the ground.

Odd. Even as Anne thought that, she felt a twinge of fear. It drove deep into her, making her catch her breath.

"You need to go inside, Mom?"

Anne shook her head. "I'm fine, sweetie." And she was. No matter what her foolish heart was trying to tell her. She was fine. Faith was fine. And, occasional mini skirmishes aside, *they* were fine together.

Nothing was going to change that.

Not now.

Not ever.

nine

"My temptation is quiet."

WILLIAM BUTLER YEATS

ANNE GLANCED AT THE CLOCK. SHE SHOULD HAVE left ten minutes ago.

"You in a hurry to leave us today, Anne?"

She turned back to Susan, who was balancing on a step stool and putting up the last of the spring decorations, and batted her eyes. "Of course not. I love my job. No place I'd rather be. Why, I cherish the time I spend here in this bastion of education, being at the beck and call of these precious minds. Why, it gives my life meaning."

"Ha ha." Susan climbed down, brushing her hands together. "All done!"

Anne took in the cheerful flowers, butterflies, and bees they'd crafted out of bright construction paper. Winnie, Faith's friend, had brought Anne construction paper in wild colors when she heard what Anne wanted to do in the way of decorations.

"Winnie, the school has paper."

"I know, but not in these colors. The kids will love these colors!" Winnie's excitement shone on her face.

Anne had taken the offering with a grateful smile. "Of course they will. Who wouldn't?"

Looking at the display now, Anne knew Winnie was right. The colors were perfect. But then, Anne should have known they would be. Winnie had such a knack for doing and saying the right thing at the right time.

Anne helped Susan put away the scraps, tacks, and tape they'd been using. Actually, though she'd been teasing Susan, she really did love her job. Teaching was in her blood, though she had to admit she preferred the role of teacher's aide to that of teacher. She got to do more of the fun stuff as the aide.

"So, enriching the minds of elementary school children gives your life meaning?"

Anne laughed. "Well, it sounds good."

"Better than saying the little darlings give you a headache."

Anne knew Susan was kidding. Well, mostly. It did get a little crazy nowadays with the increased number of students in their classes. Back when Faith started grade school, Anne never dreamed the classes would be so full. But the eighties were different. Better, in many ways, than the seventies. But harder, too. Life seemed to get more and more stressed.

Which was why Anne was so grateful to have a job she enjoyed. She'd started working at Lincoln Elementary three years ago in 1979, when Faith was still a student there. Susan, who'd attended the same church as the Bennetts, recommended Anne for the job.

The only challenge was that Anne had to work with several of the teachers, helping them however they needed her. The good news? Her days were varied and interesting. The bad news? She had to get to know one new person after another. Susan helped her during those first challenging months, and now, three years later, Anne knew all the teachers well and was comfortable working with them.

Except for those rare days when one asked her to stay later than usual. Days like today. Anne glanced at the clock again.

"Don't worry, Anne. Seventh-grade classes won't be out for another half hour."

Susan knew her so well. "I promised Faith I'd have cookies ready when she got home today. Just want to make sure I get home in time to keep that promise."

"Mmm, gonna make enough to bring some to work tomorrow?"

Anne laughed. "I think that can be arranged."

"Well, then—" Susan fluttered her hands at her—"get yourself home, woman! Time's a'wastin'!"

The oven timer went off, and Anne pulled the oven door open. A steamy cloud burst free of the oven, surrounding her with mouth-watering fragrances as she slid out the sheet of cookies.

What was it about fresh-baked chocolate chip cookies that made you feel like a kid again?

Keeping a firm hold on the large pan of golden brown treats, she popped the oven door shut with her hip, then she grinned. Faith had tried to teach her how to…what was it she called it? Oh yes, *boogie*. Much to her chagrin and her teenage daughter's amusement, Anne had been an utter failure at boogying—all except for the hip sway. Years in the kitchen had refined Anne's hip action to a near art form.

She chuckled, sliding the spatula under the cookies and easing them onto the brown paper bags spread over the counter. Faith could never understand why Anne used paper bags this way.

"You've got cookie racks, Mom," she'd say, her tone of voice communicating how silly she thought her mother was.

Obviously, contrary to Faith's own opinion, her almost-thirteen-year-old *didn't* know everything. "My mother used brown paper bags, and I use brown paper bags. Besides—" Anne always added a wink here, for good measure—"it makes the cookies taste better."

Faith stopped arguing that point. She loved the soft, gooey, fresh-from-the-oven cookies as much as Anne did. And she always said Anne's cookies tasted better than any other mother's.

Anne smiled. It had to be the brown paper bags.

She scooped more dough onto the cookie sheets, glancing at the clock again. With any luck, she'd timed it just right, and this last batch would come out of the oven right before Faith got home.

Sure enough, no sooner had Anne filled a plate with the hot cookies and set it and a glass of milk on the table, than the door flew open and Faith breezed in, all knees and elbows and grins. "Hi ya, Mom!"

Anne straightened and returned Faith's grin. "Hi yourself, Daughter."

Dumping her schoolbooks on the table, Faith lifted her face and sniffed the air. Her eyes lit up, and she leaped over to throw her arms around Anne and give her a bear hug. "Yum! Home always smells so *good*!"

Anne laughed and tousled her daughter's hair. "Put your things away in your room, hon."

"I will." Faith grabbed a handful of cookies and her glass of milk, then hopped up onto the kitchen counter. Anne sat at the table; dunking a cookie into her glass of milk; listening as Faith rattled on, giving a running account of her day; and doing her best to follow it all. She knew she should remind Faith about not sitting on the counter, but she just couldn't make herself do it. It might not be sanitary, but Anne loved these times when Faith couldn't seem to get enough of sharing her day with her.

"Better not have too many of those, Momster."

Anne's cookie paused in middunk, and she shot her daughter a sideways glance, feeling the heat rush into her cheeks. She never had to monitor her eating habits. Faith could earn honorary vulture status when it came to hovering over her mother, making sure she ate the right things.

Hopping off the counter, Faith snagged her mother's cookie and popped it into her own mouth.

"Faith!"

Utterly unrepentant, Faith washed the cookie down with a swig of milk. "I'm just saving you from yourself, Mother mine. Your sugars have been way too high lately. Gotta get 'em down."

"Hmph." Anne pushed back her chair and went to ease the lid off the stew she was simmering for dinner. "Remind me, will you—" she stirred the savory stew—"who's the child and who's the mother around here?"

Faith shot her a cheeky smile. "Oooh, '*Flashdance*'!" She ran to the radio to turn the volume higher. "I *love* this song. It hit number two on the top forty."

"That's good, huh?"

Faith laughed. "Yeah, Mom. That's good." The music filled the room. Faith grinned. "And *that's* good."

As her daughter lifted her hands over her head and moved to the music, Anne could only watch and wonder, *How did a woman with two left feet ever produce this graceful creature?* She and Faith were clear proof of God's sense of irony.

Or His sense of humor.

"Whaddya say, Mom? Feel like dancing?"

Anne sniffed. "Maybe. Unless you think I'm too fat."

Her daughter's low laugh tugged at her, drawing a smile from her. Faith danced over to her, taking her hands. Anne giggled and tried to mimic her daughter's movements.

Like a whale trying to imitate a porpoise.

She ignored the chagrined thought and focused on enjoying herself. And her daughter.

When the song was done, they collapsed against each other, breathless and laughing.

"That was fun." Faith hugged her mom. "You've still got it, Mom."

"Yes, well, if only I could figure out what to do with it."

Faith gave her another hug, then leaned past her to sniff at the stew. "Beef?"

"Beef," Anne confirmed. Before Anne could stop her, Faith snagged the saltshaker and tapped some into the pot. "You never put in enough salt."

Anne grabbed the wooden spoon she'd used to mix the cookie dough and swatted at the salt shaker. "I put in plenty, young lady."

Faith dodged the spoon to tap in another dash. "*Now* it's plenty."

The ringing of the doorbell cut off Anne's laughing retort. She glanced toward the front door. "Who on earth—?"

"Oops!" Faith dropped the saltshaker back on the shelf. "I forgot to tell you. Winnie and Trista are coming over."

Anne held back a sigh. "Sounds as though they're here."

"Right as always, Mom!" With that, Faith raced for the door. Where *did* that child get her energy?

A trio of squeals split the air, and Anne jumped, then went to toss her daughter a look.

Faith put one hand to her chest and waved at Anne with the other. "Sorry, Mom. We got carried away."

"Hey, Mrs. B!"

"Hey, Winnie."

Faith grabbed the girls by the arm and hustled them down the hallway. Her giggling voice drifted to Anne. "Oh, Trista! He did *what*?" They disappeared into Faith's room, but Anne could hear them chattering away, like magpies on uppers.

Amazing. You'd think it had been days rather than, what? A half hour since those three had been together? If they weren't at each other's houses, they were talking on the phone non-stop. Good thing Jared found an extra long cord for the kitchen phone. More often than not Anne found that cord snaking its way through the house as Faith went from room to room, giggling and talking a mile a minute.

Turning back to the stew, Anne took a pinch of seasoning and sprinkled it over the liquid. The Three Musketeers. That's what she called Faith and her two bosom buddies. Winnie was an especially good match for Faith. But Trista?

Anne put the lid back on the pot. It was evident how much Faith liked Trista, but they were so different. From what the other mothers had told Anne, Trista's father had a temper problem, one made worse by his fondness for anything alcoholic.

No one knew for sure that the man's anger had turned on his daughter, but there had been an abundance of speculation. Speculation Anne considered well founded, considering how…well, *hard* Trista was becoming. Oh, not in an obvious way, which to Anne's way of thinking would actually have been better. If she had something solid to hang her concerns on, she could lay down the law, tell Faith she couldn't see Trista any longer.

No, Trista wasn't that obvious. Her rebellion was subtle,

her disdain for everything cloaked in seemingly courteous words and actions.

The ringing timer pulled Anne from her deliberations, and she pulled out the last sheet of golden cookies. She slid several of the still-hot cookies from the sheet onto the ready and waiting plate, then placed the plate on a tray. Three glasses of milk joined the cookies, and Anne hefted the tray, heading for Faith's room.

Fortunately, the door to her daughter's room was cracked open. She leaned close to push it all the way open when Trista's disbelieving voice floated through the opening—and jabbed its way into Anne's chest.

"You're going to the movies. With your *parents*."

There was nothing overtly offensive in the words. It was what lay beneath them—a hint of something derisive—that troubled Anne. Kept her poised outside the door. Listening.

Apparently Winnie heard the undertone as well. "Something wrong with that?"

Anne smiled. *Go, Winnie.*

"Nothing." Trista's breezy response spoke volumes. "Hey, go with your parents. I mean, if you really want to."

Tell her, Faith. Tell her how much fun we have. How we laugh and teas—

"Well, I mean, it's not like I'd rather be with them than with you guys."

Anne pulled back. *Ouch.*

"But," Faith went on, though her voice was less confident, "they're okay. You know, for parents."

Anne tried to let the words encourage her. So it wasn't exactly a rousing endorsement. It was better than a poke in the eye with a sharp stick.

Kind of.

But Trista wasn't done. "Hey, fine. Whatever. But don't they…? I don't know. Never mind."

Hook baited and cast. Would Faith bite?

"What? Never mind what?"

Oh yeah. Solid hit. And as Anne expected, Trista set the hook—big-time—and reeled Faith in.

"Well, no offense, but gosh! Don't they have friends of their own? Why drag you to the movies with them?"

"They don't *drag* me."

Yeah. Anne nodded. *So there.*

"It sounds like fun to me."

Winnie again. Anne really liked that girl.

"Of course it would. To you. You'd be happy to have *anyone* want to spend time with you. Even if they were relics." Trista's tone was light, the words spoken as though in jest, but Anne knew better. Darts were flying. And striking home.

The room fell silent, and Anne held her breath. Should she back away? But they'd hear her, wouldn't they?

Thankfully, Faith broke the stillness.

"Come on, Trista. You don't have to be mean."

"Mean? I was kidding. Gosh, Winnie, I didn't hurt your feelings, did I? I mean, you *can* tell kidding from being serious, can't you?"

Good heavens. Trista's veiled insults would have done any actress proud. Sound like you're apologizing when you're really pushing the knife even further into the back. Anne had heard enough. Balancing the tray on one arm, she gave the door a sharp rap. "Girls?"

No response, as though the three inside suddenly lost their voices. Then Faith pulled the door open. "Uh...hi, Mom." She glanced back over her shoulder, then turned to her mother again. "What's up?"

Anne took in her daughter's wide eyes. Clearly she was hoping against hope her mother hadn't heard their little discussion. Anne painted a smile on her face and stepped into the room, lifting the tray a fraction. "Cookies, fresh from the oven. And some milk to wash them down."

Her smile slipped a bit when she looked at Winnie. The girl was staring at the carpet, misery in her posture, as she gnawed on one ragged fingernail. Obviously Trista's barbed comments hit their mark.

Irritation simmered deep inside Anne as she met Trista's wide-eyed, Gee-I-can't-imagine-what-upset-poor-Winnie gaze. "Gee, Mrs. B. Cookies! *And* milk. Thanks!"

Giving the girl her best don't-even-try-to-mess-with-me-you-infant-or-you'll-see-just-how-far-out-of-your-league-you-are look, she set the tray down on Faith's desk. "Everyone up for cookies?" She turned back to the girls. "If you'd rather, I've got some nice—" her gaze swiveled to Trista—"*aged* cheddar cheese and crackers."

Something flickered behind Trista's eyes, and Anne let herself feel the tiniest bit smug. Message sent and received: *You don't fool me, kid. Not one little bit.*

A slow smile spread across Trista's fine features—the girl would be such a beauty if she replaced that bored look with a smile—and she tipped her head, eyes still wide and innocent. "You use such neat words, Mrs. B." She batted her eyes. "*Aged.* Does that mean it's old and smelly?"

Anne pursed her lips. Trista's message sent and received as well: *And you don't scare me, you old bat.*

Several retorts came to Anne's mind, but before they could break free, Faith slipped her arm around Anne, giving her a squeeze. "Cookies are great, Mom. Thanks."

"Yeah, Mrs. B." Winnie roused herself from her contemplation of the rug. "Your cookies always taste great."

"Don't eat too many, Win." Trista's laughing caution was accompanied by a jab to Winnie's midsection. "You're roly-poly enough."

"Never you mind." Anne's words came as quick as the red in Winnie's cheeks. "You look just right to me, Winnie. Honestly. Some girls today are so skinny, if they turned sideways and stuck out their tongues, you'd mistake them for a zipper."

The red faded a fraction as Winnie giggled. "Thanks, Mrs. B."

"Actually, I need to thank you, Winnie. That paper you gave me was perfect. The decorations look great."

The girl's smile was beautiful, as was the glow that lit her face. "I'm glad."

As Anne walked from her daughter's room, she heard Faith's animated voice. "That's so cool you helped Mom like that, Win. We'll have to go take a look at the decorations later."

"Go to the grade school? Oh boy, *there's* excitement."

Trista's comment caught Anne, had her turning back to the room to tell the girl what she thought of her attitude, but Winnie's speedy rejoinder halted her in her tracks.

"You're right, Trista. You'd be bored silly. Faith and I will just go by ourselves. Right, Faith?"

"Sure." Faith's agreement sounded as though it was spoken around a half-chewed cookie. "You don't have to go Trista. We'll be fine."

Anne smiled and continued back to the kitchen. Faith was right. Trista or no Trista, she and Winnie *would* be fine.

Back in the kitchen, Anne found the lid dancing atop the pot of stew. She lowered the heat, then pulled a large spoon out of the drawer, dipped it into the stew, and took a sip to check the flavor. "Oh, dear..." She set the spoon down, grimacing. Too much salt. Someday she'd get through to Faith that it doesn't take much of the wrong kind of seasoning to affect the whole taste.

Kind of like rebellion. Doesn't take a lot to affect the whole person.

Pulling a potato from the pantry, Anne washed it, then sliced it into the stew. That should help absorb some of the excess salt. Too bad she didn't know any ways to temper Trista's attitude as effectively.

Setting the knife down, she turned to where the cookies were cooling on the counter.

Almost without thinking, she picked up a cookie and took a bite, chewing it the way she was chewing her worry.

For all that Trista liked to act tough, something was sad about her. Maybe, Anne thought as she chose another cookie, Trista was so hard on Winnie because she actually wanted to be more like her. But then, why didn't she get after Faith, too? Faith was a sweet, funny, loving kid who adored her daddy and seemed to enjoy being with her mom.

Thank You for that, God.

Even as the prayer slipped through her mind, Anne's gaze flitted past the cooling cookies and screeched to a halt. Good heavens! She hadn't really eaten that many, had she? Counting in her mind how many she'd taken the girls, her heart dropped.

Yup. She'd eaten five. Five cookies. Well, so much for the diet she started on Monday. *Oh, well*—she reached for cookie number six—*I've already blown it.*

She could only pray that she didn't blow it as easily with Faith. Or, for that matter, with Trista. It was easy to treat Winnie well—to smile at and welcome her into their home. Anne had to work at those things where Trista was concerned. And yet, didn't that mean Trista needed to be liked and welcomed most of all? Had the girl ever known love—real love? From things Trista had let slip, it sounded as though her mother was tired and bitter and spent most of her time talking Trista's father down.

Stop worrying, she scolded herself as she brushed cookie crumbs from her hands. *Faith isn't like that. Our home isn't like that. We've raised Faith right. There's no need to worry.*

She moved to the sink to wash her hands, but apprehension gnawed at her, setting her nerves on edge. Shutting off the faucet, she reached for the towel and caught her reflection in the window over the sink. Took in the furrow on her brow. The tight lips.

"Relax. There's nothing to be afraid of."

The only response to her whispered statement was a renewed stirring of anxiety—an uneasy confidence that she was wrong. She couldn't pinpoint why, exactly, but deep inside, certainty grew. There was something to be afraid of.

Something dark and determined.

Something that wanted her daughter.

Ten

"And we are put on earth a little space,

that we may learn to bear the beams of love."

William Blake

FAITH STARED AT HER MOTHER, SURE SHE'D HEARD her wrong. "You...want to do what?"

"I want to invite Trista over for dinner."

"But—" Faith stopped. Should she say it? She didn't want to hurt Mom's feelings.

"But I don't like Trista?"

Relief was a sweet release. "Yeah."

"And she's not particularly crazy about me."

Wow. Mom understood more than Faith realized. "I don't know that she isn't crazy about you, Mom. She just doesn't get you."

"Well, that's okay, sweetie, because I don't get her, either. I don't understand why Winnie is over here all the time, but Trista hardly ever visits. And when she does, you two hole up in your room."

Faith didn't want to sound defensive, but she couldn't help it. "We have stuff to talk about. Private stuff."

Her mom sat next to her at the kitchen table. "I realize that, Faith. But your father and I like to know your friends. And we like for them to know us. To know they can trust us. And it's evident Trista doesn't."

Faith decided to go for broke. "She thinks you and Dad are a little, you know, *out* there."

Her mom's forehead creased. "Out where?"

Faith waved her hands. "There. You know, far away from reality. She says our family is totally weird because we like to spend time together and talk and stuff."

For a moment Faith was afraid her mom was angry, but the storm that seemed to gather in her features vanished. Instead, her mom looked sad. Really sad.

"Honey, I'm sorry Trista feels that way. I'm sorry she doesn't have a better time with her parents."

Nobody could have a good time with Trista's parents. Her dad was a total nutcase; her mom a nag. Of course, Faith didn't say any of that to her mom. She knew better than to talk down other adults. But she'd been to Trista's house. She heard the screaming and swearing.

Trista's home was no fun.

So *maybe* it would help to have her come here. Maybe seeing that Faith's family wasn't nuts or fake, that they really did get along, would give Trista some hope that life could be better.

More likely it will confirm in her mind that you're a total dweeb.

"It was just an idea, but if you think it's not a good one—"

"I'll ask her, Mom."

"Oh." She blinked, kind of like Faith did early in the mornings when her dad turned on her bedroom light and told her to get up. "Well…good."

Why was her mom looking so unsure? It was her idea in the first place. "If, I mean, do you want me to?"

The smile her mom gave her was almost convincing. "Yes, of course."

"Okay, I'll let you know what she says." Faith rose from the table, glancing at her mom.

"Good." Mom almost looked a little green. "Fine." She waved a hand at Faith. "Go call her, then let me know."

Faith frowned as she left the kitchen. Sometimes Mom didn't make a whole lot of sense.

This was a bad idea.

Anne felt the dread deep within her, confirming the knowledge. But it was too late. She'd issued the invitation, and it had been accepted.

Lord, why did You ever let me get into this?

"Love your enemies."

A snort escaped her. Love Trista? Well, she'd do her best. But the girl certainly wasn't making it easy. Faith had called her, told her they wanted her to come over for dinner. Though Faith tried to muffle the phone against her chest, Anne heard the hoot coming through the lines.

"Trista, knock it off!" Faith hissed into the receiver.

When Faith hung up, she turned back to Anne with a pained smile. "She said yes."

Now it was Anne's turn to look pained. "She did? Oh. Great. That's great."

If only she believed it. The idea had sounded good when it first came to Anne while she was doing her morning devotions. Like a loving whisper spoken close to her ear, it had drifted into her mind.

Ask Trista to come for dinner.

She hadn't even hesitated. She'd gotten up right then and there and gone to find Faith in the kitchen.

That was probably her mistake. She should have thought it through.

Now she stood, staring at the set table, trying to push back the dread that had picked at her all day. She should have found out what Trista liked to eat. Should have asked about her preferences for drink and dessert. Instead, she asked Jared to cook hamburgers on the grill. Faith loved burgers on the grill. And there were brownies for dessert—another of Faith's all-time favorites.

Trista would probably hate everything.

At least you're trying.

No, *Trista* was trying. That was the problem.

The sound of the doorbell jolted through Anne, but Faith beat her to the punch. She dashed from her bedroom. "I'll get it!"

Firm hands circled Anne's waist. "You ready for this?"

Anne looked over her shoulder. "I wish."

"I think it's nice that you're doing this, hon." Jared snatched a black olive from the tray on the table. "Reaching out to Trista like this. She seems like a very unhappy girl."

Unhappy? Anne pondered that. She'd never thought of Trista in those terms. Difficult. Rebellious. A little devious, even. But unhappy? Never.

Now, thinking about it, Anne wondered if Jared's observation wasn't the more accurate one. Before she had time to really think that through, though, Faith sailed into the room, Trista in her wake. Anne put on her best smile, then promptly almost lost it when she took in Trista's outfit: a fluorescent pink T-shirt, hung off to the side, baring one slim shoulder. The ragged, torn bottom of the shirt almost reached Trista's belly button.

If her miniskirt were any tighter, it would qualify as a second skin. Fishnet hose made their incongruous way down her legs, ending in a pair of ratty army boots.

The girl's hair, which was teased to within an inch of its life, was tied with a gaudy bow. And Anne was fairly sure the girl's primary tool for applying her makeup had to be a trowel.

"Mom?"

Anne glanced at Faith, and her daughter's fierce scowl pulled her from her dazed stare at their guest. "Hi, Trista. Glad you could make it."

Trista nodded. *Like she's the Queen Mother bestowing a blessing on the peasants.*

Faith shifted, clearly uncomfortable. "So, are the burgers ready?"

"Burgers?" Trista's question was accompanied by a continuous popping of her gum. "Oh, man. You should have said something, Mrs. B., I don't eat meat."

Faith stared at her friend. "Since when?"

Pop. Chomp. Pop. "Since forever."

Anne could tell Faith was about to argue the point. "That's not a problem, girls. We have plenty of other things for Trista to eat." She indicated the table, and Trista went to peer at the array of baked beans, chips, three-bean salad, potato salad, deviled eggs, and Jell-O.

She shrugged, turning back to Faith and Trista. "Jell-O works."

"Jell-O?" Anne stared at her. "Is that the only thing here you can eat?"

"Not to worry, Mrs. B." Trista's smile was pure sweetness. "I can get something good at home later."

The evening went downhill from there. Trista refused to hold hands or close her eyes for prayer.

"I don't believe in God."

She sat there, steeped in defiance, as though expecting them to jump up from the table in shock. Instead, Jared smiled.

"That's okay, Trista. He believes in you."

Anne had prided herself on Faith's table manners. She'd taught her from an early age that elbows didn't belong on the table, to chew with her mouth closed, and not to interrupt when others were talking. It was as though Trista had found out all of those things and did her level best to do the opposite. Her elbows planted on the table, she slumped there, chin resting in her hand, poking at her Jell-O with a spoon. Anytime Jared or Anne tried to draw her into the conversation, she stared at them as though they spoke a foreign language.

I suppose courtesy could be considered a foreign language to some.

Shame scurried through Anne on the heels of that uncharitable thought, and she grabbed the bowl in front of her, holding it out to Trista.

"More?"

Trista looked from the bowl to Anne. "Gee, thanks. But no. I think I've about had all I can handle."

That makes two of us.

The girl couldn't have made it more plain if she spray painted it on the wall. She was bored out of her teenage skull.

At first, Anne was angry. But after the third or fourth snub, she started to realize something.

Trista was afraid.

She was putting on a good act, pretending it was all beneath her. But then something happened. Faith and her father were talking about the virtues of cooking hamburger rare as opposed to well done.

"That's not a hamburger!" Faith looked down her nose at Jared's plate. "It's shoe leather with bumps!"

"Yeah, well at least mine doesn't moo when I bite into it."

"No, it just breaks your tooth."

The two teased and laughed, as they usually did at mealtime. Anne watched them, enjoying the interaction. But when she looked to see what Trista though of it, she was shocked to see something unexpected on the girl's face.

Longing.

Stark, raw longing.

It didn't last more than a few seconds. Then the veil of boredom slipped back into place. But it had been there long enough.

Unhappy, Jared had called her. Suddenly Anne knew that wasn't the half of it. Trista wasn't just unhappy. She was miserable. Heartwrenchingly so. What could have happened to make such a young girl's eyes so haunted, so pained? *Lord, help her. Help Trista. She seems lost—*

Suddenly, Trista's eyes narrowed, and she glared at Anne. Then she dropped her spoon onto her plate, the loud clatter making Faith jump.

"Trista?"

The other girl shoved her chair back and stood. "This is stupid."

"What is?"

Anne looked at her husband. How could he sound so calm in the face of Trista's disdain?

Trista's slim hands spread. "This is! This little *Leave It to Beaver* act you're putting on."

"Act? What's that supposed to mea—?"

Jared lay his hand on Faith's arm, stilling her heated question. "Trista, I'm sorry if we're bothering you, but this isn't an act." He held the girl's gaze, and Anne saw nothing but compassion on his face. "This is who we are as a family."

Trista looked from Anne to Jared. Then at Faith. When she spoke, it was through gritted teeth. "You *think* it's who you are, but it's not. No one is like this. Not really. And if you don't know that, well...just wait."

Anne knew the words stemmed from a hurting heart, that it was simply a teenage girl striking out at something that made her painfully aware of the lack in her own life. And yet...those two words struck Anne, deep inside, planting a seed of dread.

"Just wait."

Anne swallowed. For what? Was something coming? Did Trista know something about Faith that they didn't know?

"Trista, please, sit down. You're welcome at our table."

She stepped away from Jared's kind tone and shook her head. "I don't belong here." She headed for the door, grabbing her purse where she'd let it fall on the floor.

Faith looked from one parent to the other, eyes pleading. "*Say* something! Stop her!"

Anne put her hand over Faith's. "Sweetie, there's not much we can say."

Faith shoved her chair back, jumping up. "She's my friend! You can't let her leave like this."

The front door slammed, and Jared tilted his head, looking after Trista. "Actually, Faith, I don't think we could stop her."

"Fine!" Faith crossed her arms. "May I be excused?"

Jared held her gaze. "Are you sure you want to be done?"

Anne watched her daughter waver, saw how the warmth and kindness in her father's question tugged at her—then watched her shove them aside, making room for her hurt.

"I lost my appetite."

After a moment's silence, Jared nodded. "You're excused."

Faith stomped from the room.

Anne and Jared sat there, staring at each other. Finally,

Jared reached a hand out to Anne. She lay her hand in his, letting his warmth flow through her.

"I think we've got some praying to do."

Anne nodded at her husband, but as she stood and followed him to the living room, the seed of dread that had been planted within her took root, sending out fingers that gripped and clawed through her.

"Just wait…just wait…"

Lowering herself onto the sofa, Anne had the powerful, albeit unwelcome, sense that they wouldn't have to wait long.

eleven

"We seek the comfort of another… Someone to help us through the never-ending attempt to understand ourselves."

MARTIN FINCH LUPUS

I WISH THEY LIKED ME.

Faith leaned back against her favorite tree, the one at the back of the high school that she ate under most lunch periods, watching Trista and her friends congregate. Junior high had been so much easier. In the seventh grade, she and Winnie and Trista had all gotten along. Well, for the most part. Winnie and Trista never really got along.

Now, they were all juniors in high school. But while they were in the same grade in the same school, it was as though Trista had starting living in an entirely different world.

Faith took a bite of her sandwich, listening to Trista and her clique talk and laugh as they lit their cigarettes and hopped up to sit on the hoods of parked cars. Faith glanced around. Everyone knew it was against school rules to smoke on school property. And everyone knew these kids broke that rule every day. So why, Faith wondered as she'd done hundreds of times before, didn't the teachers or principal ever come back here and make them stop?

I guess they're all as afraid of them as the kids are.

It was true. Trista's crowd wasn't like any other crowd. They weren't the popular cheerleader types. They weren't into school sports or the drama club. They weren't studious bookworm types. Faith grinned at that. Studious? Bookworms? Not by a long shot.

No, they were a breed all their own. Hard. Rebellious. Defiant.

And totally, totally cool.

In other words, they were everything Faith wasn't. She was about as far away from cool as you could get. Not that she was a geek. She was just...well, normal. Stupid old normal. She sang in the choir. Made good grades. Worked on the school newspaper. Even took over classes for her teachers sometimes when they needed to leave the room for a few minutes.

Face it. People liked and trusted her. She was, they often told her, cute and playful. Her lip curled. *A dumb ol' golden retriever, that's me.*

Utterly, totally harmless.

So why on earth did Trista—who no one since grade school had ever called *harmless*—like her?

Faith had never been able to figure that one out. Though they didn't travel in the same circles any longer, Trista was still her friend. And she made sure everyone knew it. Faith might not be a true part of Trista's crowd, but everyone—Trista's buddies included—knew not to bother Faith. Because if they did, they'd have Trista to answer to.

And no one wanted that.

Sometimes Faith got the impression she was some kind of project for Trista, like a stray puppy she'd picked up and decided to raise. But every time she thought that, guilt stabbed at her. Faith wished she had someone to talk to about it all. But who? Winnie? No way? Her mom? Get real.

Her mom was majorly down on Trista. Every chance she got, she asked Faith about Trista. About what she was doing. And what she was getting Faith to do.

Like Faith didn't have a mind of her own.

Her appetite suddenly gone, Faith grabbed the plastic wrap from her lunch bag and stuffed the sandwich inside. If her mother told her one more time to be careful, to be hesitant about trusting Trista too much, Faith was going to…to…

Well, she didn't know what, but she was going to do something.

Okay, so her mom was concerned. So she worried. Fine. But it was starting to irritate her. Faith got the point years ago. She didn't need to keep hearing it over and over.

The last time Mom started in on Trista, Faith lost it. "Why can't you ever say something nice about my friends?"

Her mom's wide-eyed stare hadn't fooled Faith. She knew exactly what Faith was talking about. "I do—"

"No, you don't. All you can do is rag on Trista and tell me how awful she is. But I like her, Mom, and that should count for something."

Her mother started to say something, but Faith had had it. "You know what? When you talk about her the way you do, it's not only Trista you cut down; you cut me down, too. You won't be happy, will you, until you're the one choosing my friends instead of trusting me to do it."

Yeah, that had been a bad fight. Her mother got all upset and sent her to her room. But Faith was right and she knew it. She figured her mom knew it, too.

Then there was the way Mom compared Trista to Winnie. Boy, when it came to Winnie, Mom was all praise, which was hardly a surprise. Winnie was quiet and polite and always had a sweet smile on her face—the perfect Christian girl.

Unlike Trista. And, truth be told, unlike Faith.

Trista always had something to say about Winnie. When they were kids, it used to be about Winnie's looks. But she'd grown out of that ugly, chubby stage. Winnie was actually kind of pretty. Not a stunner, like Trista. But she was okay. So without that to harp on, Trista had moved to Winnie's behavior.

"Goody Two-Shoes? Not hardly. Winnie's so stinkin' good she's more like Goody-Twelve-Shoes."

Boy, would Faith's mom have a fit if she heard Trista say things like that. Faith didn't care much for it either—she liked Winnie most of the time—but she'd learned long ago not to listen when Trista was on a rant.

Too bad her mom couldn't just let things fly once in a while. She took everything so seriously. Especially everything Trista said.

Faith had made the mistake of telling her mom something funny Trista said about one of her friends. Her mom just stared at her.

"She said this about a friend?"

"Well, yeah, but she was kidding."

Her mom gave that little snort that said she didn't buy it. "I'd hate to hear what she has to say about her enemies, Faith. You certainly don't hear *Winnie* talking about people that way."

Faith grimaced. If her mother told her one more time what a gem Winnie was, she would scream!

So Winnie acted like a saint. Did that make her better than Trista? Faith didn't think so. In fact, lately Winnie had been getting on her nerves. She was too nice. She let Trista walk all over her. She never talked back when Trista said rotten things or stood up to Trista when she called Winnie a wimp.

Winnie the Wimp, to be precise. Faith couldn't recall when Trista started calling Winnie that, but she remembered the hurt on Winnie's face when Faith didn't stand up for her, didn't call Trista on being so mean.

Faith pulled her knees to her chest, circling them with her arms. So what was she? Winnie's guard dog? If Win didn't like the name, she could stand up to Trista herself. What good would it do for Faith to get in the middle? She wasn't going to change Trista, and she'd probably make Trista mad at both of them.

And if there was one thing Faith didn't want, it was Trista mad at her. While she wasn't the same as Trista and her friends, she couldn't deny she liked the way it felt when they let her hang around with them. Oh, they didn't do that all the time. But every once in a while Trista would call her over. And the others would step back, making room for her as if she belonged.

Which she didn't. Faith wasn't as pretty as they were. Or as skinny. And she sure wasn't as fearless. And the most fearless of them all was Trista. She'd do and say anything, no matter who she ticked off.

"You gotta say your piece," she told Faith over and over. "And if someone doesn't like it—" she'd snap her long-nailed fingers in the air—"too bad for them."

The girls who hung around with Trista were as outspoken as she was. They did and said and wore what they wanted. And they got what they wanted, too.

Which, most of the time, was boys.

Not nice boys, but rough ones. Boys with cigarettes hanging from their sneering mouths. Boys who walked and talked as if they not only knew how to fight, but enjoyed it. Looked for opportunities to do it.

Boys who looked at a girl with a certain flash in their eyes, who made you aware, and not in a good way, that you were a girl and they were…well, *aware*. Even with Trista and her friends hanging on them, they scanned every female in sight, watching, speculating. It made Faith's skin crawl when she walked past them.

Well, when she walked past most of them, that was. There was one boy Faith wouldn't mind looking at her.

Dustin Grant was the most handsome boy Faith had ever seen. He looked like a rugged Rob Lowe. Though he was a senior, he was older than most of the kids in his grade. Trista said he'd been held back a year, though she never said why. And Faith didn't care to ask. She kind of liked that he was older, liked the way he seemed more…mature.

Of course, it didn't hurt that he had that lean, mean look of an athlete ready to take on any competition. His shock of thick blond hair was as unruly as he was, going whatever way it pleased. But that made it suit him that much more. And those eyes…those ice blue eyes that seemed to look right through you.

At least, that's what Faith figured it would be like if he ever looked at her. Which he never did. She was willing to bet he didn't even know she was alive.

She'd looked at him, though. A lot. She liked the way he moved, like a tiger, restless but in control. He didn't slouch like some of the other guys in their group. He stood tall and straight, as if he could carry the weight of two worlds on those broad shoulders. The others looked to him as a kind of leader. And who could blame them? One look at him was all it took to know he was full of confidence—and a dash of danger.

Okay, maybe more than a dash. But for some reason, that drew Faith to him as much as anything else.

Winnie told her once that she should steer clear of Dustin. She'd laughed at her friend. "Like I have a choice, Win. The guy's never said a word to me."

"That's a good thing, Faith. I mean, why would you even think of getting mixed up with a guy like that?"

"Oh, I don't know." Faith smiled and nudged her friend. "Haven't you ever wanted to pet a tiger?"

Winnie thought about that. Faith chuckled at the memory. Winnie always took things so seriously! Finally, she nodded. "Okay, maybe. But only if the tiger was caged first."

No one was going to cage Dustin; that was for sure.

Faith peered at Dustin, watching him now with Trista and the others. He pulled a cigarette from his jacket pocket, flipped a lighter open, and took a long, deep drag. With anyone else, Faith would have thought that looked stupid. But with Dustin, that action was like every other.

Tough.

Not bad tough or even mean tough. But good tough. Cool tough.

She couldn't explain, but something about Dustin Grant made Faith ache, deep in her gut. Like there was something missing, something only he could fill.

Heat flooded her face at the thought. She was being an idiot. *Dustin is always surrounded by beautiful girls. No way he's ever going to notice me, let alone fill some "missing part" of me.*

As though to confirm the thought, Trista broke away from the group of girls, sauntered up to Dustin, and trailed one long finger down his chest. A spark of something hot and angry flashed behind Faith's chest. What was Trista doing? She knew how Faith felt about Dustin!

Trista's every move gave a clear invitation. Faith had seen the other girl turn on the charm before, and it always worked. Tall and slim, Trista was one of the few who really looked good in the cropped tops and tight skirts everyone wore nowadays. Everyone, of course, but Faith.

And Winnie. Winnie wouldn't be caught dead in those kinds of outfits. She actually called them *shameful* the other day.

Faith laughed to herself. Shameful. That Winnie was from another century. Besides, when you looked like Trista, with her shape and that long, feathered hair that reminded everyone of Farah Fawcett, what was there to be ashamed of? Trista looked good. And she knew it.

Same way she knew how to get the guys she wanted.

If only I knew how to move like that. If only I could get Dustin to look at me like...like...

Wait a minute. How *was* Dustin looking at Trista? Though she couldn't be sure from this distance, Faith had the clear sense that Dustin wasn't the least bit impressed—or interested. He didn't react. Just stood there, looking down at Trista, taking long, deep draws on his cigarette.

Never one to dwell on rejection, Trista turned with a toss of her hair and plied her charms on Jim, a big, muscular mountain of kid. Faith's attention, though, stayed riveted on Dustin. She peered closer. He didn't look at all upset that Trista had walked away from him. If anything, he looked glad.

And though she didn't fully understand it, that thought made Faith happy deep inside.

She sighed and was about to look away, when her whole world came to a screeching halt. As though sensing her attention, Dustin Grant turned his head—and looked right at her. Despite the distance between them, something like an electrical jolt shot through Faith when their gazes brushed, then locked.

A lazy smile worked its way across Dustin's mouth, and a shiver spidered across Faith's skin, making her breath catch in her throat. She wasn't sure how long his gaze held hers, or how long they would have gone on staring, if not for an abrupt interruption.

"Faith, I've been looking for you."

With a start, she tore her attention from Dustin, her pent-up breath escaping in a heavy *whoosh*. She turned to blink at Winnie, standing beside her.

"I…you…huh?"

Winnie frowned. "Are you okay?"

Faith shook off the dazed feeling that had cloaked her and nodded. "I'm fine." She didn't dare look at him again. She grabbed her things and stood.

"Are you sure you're okay?" Winnie peered at her. "You look kinda flushed."

Faith shrugged, trying to evade both Winnie's question and the irritation it sparked. "So, you were looking for me?" In spite of her best efforts, her gaze drifted past Winnie back to the cars.

Dustin was talking to Jim, laughing.

"Faith, be careful."

Faith's attention jerked back to Winnie. "Excuse me?"

Winnie nodded her head toward Trista, Dustin, and the others. "Those guys. I know Trista hangs with them, but…" She frowned. "I don't know; I don't trust them." She cocked her head. "And I'm not sure you should either."

"I don't think it's any of your business who I trust." Faith hadn't meant to be sharp or mean, but the words came out both.

Color swept into Winnie's cheeks, then fled, leaving her pale. Hurt peeked out of her brown doe eyes as she looked at Faith. The irritation she'd felt fanned to life again. Fine! First Winnie butts in, then she makes Faith feel guilty for being honest.

She shrugged again. "Never mind. Just forget it, okay?" She spun on her heel and started walking, leaving Winnie to catch up or not.

When Winnie came alongside her, Faith kept her focus on the ground, refusing to look at her friend. If she met Winnie's gaze, saw that hurt again, she'd end up apologizing.

So instead, she concentrated on something far more enjoyable. She kept pace with her steps, repeating the same thing over and over…

Dustin Grant looked at me. Dustin Grant looked at me.

Even more than that, he'd seen her. Really *seen* her. She was sure of it.

And if his smile was any evidence, he'd liked what he'd seen.

A lot.

Dustin took a long drag on his cigarette, letting the smoke fill his lungs, then ease out on a slow exhalation.

He watched the feather of smoke drift away, lips pursed, as he rolled one name around in his mind.

Faith Bennett.

He allowed himself a small smile as he pictured her face, the startled expression in those wide eyes, the red that rushed her cheeks when he caught her looking at him.

At him.

His smile widened. Faith Bennett. He never would have guessed.

Sure, he'd heard Trista talk about her, how she came from another world, how she wanted to be like Trista but "didn't have the guts." But even as she sneered about Faith, Dustin saw the truth. Saw the jealousy, heard the longing.

It wasn't Faith who wanted to be like Trista. It was the other way around.

And who could blame Trista? Faith was…sweet. Dustin chuckled as he flicked the cigarette away. Yeah, sweet. He'd first noticed her a couple of years ago. That thick coppery hair was something else. And she was pretty, in a clean-cut kind of way. Real different from the girls he hung with. Trashy girls.

Girls like Trista.

Normally he wouldn't give someone like Faith a second glance. Her parents were still married! Jesus Freaks, Trista said. That was enough to turn anyone off. But the more Trista ragged on Faith's oh-so-perfect-*Leave-It-to-Beaver* life, the more Dustin watched her. And the more he watched her, the more interested he got.

Getting girls like Trista was easy. But a girl like Faith? Now that would be a challenge. He'd gone over it in his mind, thinking it through. He'd have to play it right. You didn't pull a girl like that away from Daddy Dearest and Home Sweet Home without careful planning.

Of course, he'd only toyed with the idea until a few weeks ago, when Trista caught him watching Faith.

"Forget it, Dustin. Faith ain't your type." She sneered. "She's a *church* girl."

He gave her the look. The one that warned her she was pushing her luck. "If I wanted her, I could get her."

Trista hooted. "Right! Trust me, she'd run away from you like a freaked-out rabbit."

"Trust *me*—" Trista stopped laughing. Smart move. "If I wanted her, I'd *get* her."

Trista didn't comment. She shrugged, flipped her hair, and sauntered away.

But today, when Faith looked at him that way, he knew.

She wanted him. Almost as much as he'd come to want her.

Which meant he was right. He *could* get her.

He pulled the pack of cigarettes from his pocket and tapped out another smoke. A quick flick of his wrist opened the lighter, and he closed his eyes as he drew in the heat.

Faith Bennett.

He leaned back against the brick building. This would be fun.

Anne couldn't relax. She wasn't sure why. All she knew was that every time she sat down, every time she tried to read a book or write a letter, something pulled at her. Her inner anxiety was like a mosquito buzzing around in the dark—utterly irritating but impossible to pinpoint.

What is it, Father? What's wrong?

She moved to the kitchen window and stood there, staring out at the backyard.

What was wrong?

Letting out a deep sigh, she picked up a dust rag and moved from the kitchen to the living room. She tried to concentrate on cleaning, but it was no use. She glanced at her Bible, lying open where she'd left it this morning on the coffee table next to the sofa. Ezekiel. Not exactly easy reading. She'd only made it through a few lines this morning.

The inner urging grew stronger. Tossing the dust rag on the table, Anne plopped down on the sofa, leaned over, and read the words in front of her.

> "Stand up, son of man," said the voice. "I want to speak with you." The Spirit came into me as he spoke and set me on my feet. I listened carefully to his words. "Son of man," he said, "I am sending you to the nation of Israel, a nation that is rebelling against me. Their ancestors have rebelled against me from the beginning, and they are still in revolt to this very day. They are a hard-hearted and stubborn people. But I am sending you to say to them, 'This is what the Sovereign Lord says!' And whether they listen or not—for remember, they are rebels—at least they will know they have had a prophet among them."

Anne caught her breath, trembling. Every word seemed to come alive, to slice through her, going directly to the core of her heart. She was overwhelmed by a powerful conviction.

God was speaking to her.

More than that. He was warning her.

Father, what's happening? She hesitated. Something stirred in her heart, in her mind. An understanding.

No, that wasn't right. It wasn't happening. Not yet.

God, please...what's going *to happen*?

She didn't really expect an answer, but she got one. A sudden certainty settled over her like a water-soaked woolen cloak, weighing her down, pressing in on her. One need pressed in on her with such force she almost cried out.

Keep reading. She had to keep reading.

Shaken, Anne opened her eyes and read on. But rather than follow the passage line by line, her gaze was drawn from one section to another.

> "Son of man, do not fear them. Don't be afraid even though their threats are sharp as thorns and barbed like briers, and they sting like scorpions. Do not be dismayed by their dark scowls. For remember, they are rebels!... the whole lot of them are hard-hearted and stubborn. But look, I have made you as hard and stubborn as they are. I have made you as hard as rock!"... Then he added, "Son of man, let all my words sink deep into your own heart first. Listen to them carefully for yourself. Then go to your people in exile and say to them, 'This is what the Sovereign Lord says!' Do this whether they listen to you or not...."
>
> Then the Spirit lifted me up and took me away. I went in bitterness and turmoil, but the Lord's hold on me was strong."

Anne stood, arms wrapped about herself. Unable to sit a moment longer, she paced the floor.

"I went in bitterness and turmoil..."

These words she understood. Far better than she'd ever wanted to. Bitterness and turmoil. Exactly what she'd felt for days. Like a kid facing a big test for which she hadn't prepared. It was driving Anne crazy, because she didn't understand it. She had talked with Jared about it.

"I didn't seek these emotions out, and yet it's like they've become my constant companions."

He sat on the edge of the bed. "And you don't know where they're coming from."

"No!" Anne stopped, took a deep breath. "I'm sorry. I don't mean to get so worked up. But it's as though these awful feelings are...are dwelling with me—no, dwelling *within* me—coloring my thoughts and words. Coloring the very fabric of who I am."

She'd worried a little about telling Jared, afraid he'd think she was being fanciful, foolish. She should have known better.

He held his hand out to her. She came to sit beside him, letting him put an arm around her and draw her into the shelter of his embrace. He leaned his head against hers.

"Sounds like it's something we need to be praying about."

And so they prayed. And she'd continued praying. Almost nonstop.

"But the Lord's hold on me was strong."

She blinked away the wetness blurring her vision, letting hope breeze through her. *Please, God, let it be true. I need Your hold on me.*

"I want to speak with you."

Anne froze. The message was as clear as if it had been spoken aloud. So there was still more. She turned back to the couch, swallowing. "Lord, please—"

"I want to speak with you... The Lord's hold on me was strong."

With a slow nod, Anne moved back to the couch. Placing her hands on either side of the open Bible, she lowered her gaze to the pages.

> "Son of man, I have appointed you as a watchman for Israel. Whenever you receive a message from me, pass it on to the people immediately.... If you warn them and they keep on sinning and refuse to repent, they will die in their sins. But you will have saved your life because you did what you were told to do. If good people turn bad and don't listen to my warning, they will die. If you did not warn them of the consequences, then they will die in their sins...and I will hold you responsible, demanding your blood for theirs. But if you warn them and they repent, they will live, and you will have saved your own life, too."

Though the chapter went on, Anne felt a sense of release and stopped reading. She leaned back against the couch, letting the words go over and over in her mind.

"If you warn them and they repent, they will live, and you will have saved your own life, too."

She didn't understand it all. Not yet. But she wasn't worried. It would be clear to her when it needed to be. She knew that because right now, one fact was crystal clear in her mind: Whatever was coming, whatever she was being prepared for, it had to do with Faith.

And as much as she hated to admit it, she was almost certain she wasn't being prepared to save Faith, but to confront her. Warn her.

And, if it came to that, let her go.

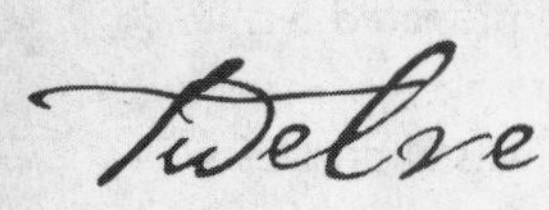

Twelve

"Evil is near. Sometimes late at night the air grows strongly clammy and cold around me. I feel it brushing me. All that the Devil asks is acquiescence— not struggle, not conflict. Acquiescence."

SUZANNE MASSIE

WHEN THE BELL SOUNDED SETTING FAITH FREE FROM her last class of the day, she looked up, checking the time. Usually the last half of the school day crawled by, but this one had come and gone in a heartbeat.

She stood and gathered her books, smiling. Amazing how fast time went by when you had something wonderful to concentrate on.

All day long she'd relived that moment when Dustin had looked at her. She replayed it as it happened, then went back and let her imagination have a field day. Now, as she made her way through the crowded hall to her locker, she went through the scenarios again. He'd not only looked at her, he'd come over to her. No, more than that, he reached down to take her hand, pull her up, and say—

"Hey."

Faith's books went flying, and she almost jumped out of her

skin. When she turned to see who had uttered that low greeting so close to her ear, she gasped.

Ice blue eyes. A lazy smile. And all right there, next to her.

"D-Dustin?"

His smile widened at the way his name squeaked out of her. "Yeah. You're…Faith, right?"

He knew her name? She was going to faint! Right here, in the middle of the school hallway.

"Yeah…I mean, yes. Right." She nodded. "Faith, that's me. I'm…uh, I'm Faith." She clamped her mouth shut to halt the babbling and knelt so she could pick up her books.

Okay, maybe she wasn't going to faint. Maybe she'd just die. Of total embarrassment.

Dustin knelt beside her, gathering her books before she could. He held them in one arm and put his free hand under her elbow, drawing her up.

Faith stared at him. *Like in my daydream…*

But this was way better. This was real.

He put her books in her locker and turned back to her. "So, Faith, you want a ride home?"

It took a second before she could answer, but finally she got the words out. "A ride? You've got a car?"

His grin as he pushed the door open and they walked outside made her shiver. "Better than that." He nodded toward the street. "I've got a hog."

Faith followed his gesture and stared. A motorcycle. He was going to give her a ride home on a motorcycle.

A sudden image filled her mind, and she saw herself seated behind Dustin, her arms wrapped around his waist, her face pressed to his back as they raced down the street, the wind whipping their hair, making them laugh.

"So what do you say?"

At his low, coaxing tone, Faith met Dustin's blue eyes, and another shiver hit her again, deep in her gut. What did she say? There was only one possible answer.

"Sure!"

Good grief, she was squeaking again. Dustin's slow smile didn't help, either. "We'll take a little ride up into the hills first."

He put his arm around her, walking her away from the building.

Faith swallowed, trying to think. But it was really hard with him looking at her like that. "A ride?"

"Yeah, to let you get the feel of real freedom." He coaxed her with that smile.

She swallowed again. She was going to get home late. Mom would be worried. She should probably call first. She looked around, hunting for a pay phone.

Dustin stopped. "Hey, you have someplace else you want to be?"

She started and stared at him. "What? *No!*"

Clearly, he enjoyed her heated denial. "Good. I'm glad."

Well, so much for making a phone call. But she couldn't take the chance that he'd leave without her. It wasn't every day the coolest guy in school asked you to go for a ride with him! Mom would understand.

Besides, with Dustin smiling at her like that, she could hardly form a word, let alone a sentence. And with his arm around her, she was afraid she might even faint right here.

"Hey, relax." He gave a deep chuckle. "It's only a ride on my bike. I'm not askin' you to marry me."

Faith laughed. It was either that or go into hysterics.

Dustin's arm tightened around her, and he directed a long look down at her. Faith's breath caught in her throat at the expression in those eyes. Then he broke the contact and held his hand out to her.

"Well...not yet, anyway."

Anne glanced up at the clock again.

Five minutes later than the last time she looked. So now Faith was an hour and five minutes late. Anne chewed the inside of her lip. Where could Faith be? It wasn't like her to be late like this, not without calling.

She went toward the phone, then stopped herself. For the last half hour, she'd gone back and forth, debating on whether or not to start calling Faith's friends. It was like that cartoon, where the devil sat on one shoulder and an angel on the other, was acting itself out in her mind.

You're being overprotective.

Overprotective, my foot! She could be lying in a ditch someplace, hurt, calling for you...

Now you're getting hysterical.

I am not hysterical. I'm a mother.

A hysterical mother.

Oh, shut up!

Now that's *mature. Yessiree. No hysterics going on here—*

Shaking the maddening dialogue from her mind, Anne gave in to the angel—or was it the devil? She wasn't sure—and picked up the receiver. She'd start with Trista. If Faith was with Winnie, they surely would have called. Even if Faith hadn't thought of it, Winnie would have.

As she started to dial the number, she heard a rumbling. It took a moment to identify the sound—a motorcycle. A big one. And it sounded like it was right out front.

Anne hung up and moved to the plateglass window at the front of the house. Her mouth tightened. Some leather-jacketed, Fonzie wannabe was pulling his monster motorcycle up to their curb. No helmet, of course, not on him or the passenger glued to his back.

The boy lowered one tightly jean-clad, booted leg, propping the bike up, and leaned his head back to talk into his passenger's ear. She leaned forward, her head touching his, her arms still clinging to his midsection. Some girls were so shameless!

Anne was about to go back to the phone when the girl slid from the bike and stood on the curb, waving as the boy gunned his bike up a couple of decibels and roared off. Narrowing her eyes, Anne peered closer. Who was this girl? Which poor neighbor would have to deal with this bad boy?

"What on *earth*?"

Anne couldn't believe her eyes. The shameless girl was Faith!

She watched her daughter all but float up the front walkway. Anne turned as the front door opened, then slammed shut.

"I'm home!"

Anne stared, taking in her daughter's appearance. Her hair was blown every which way, her radiant smile bordered by wind-roughened cheeks. But it was Faith's eyes that caught Anne's attention. They were positively glowing.

"Mom! You'll never *believe* it!"

Anne tipped her head up, breathing deeply to keep her anger from seeping out. She would welcome her daughter home. Tell her how glad Anne was that she was all right. Then she'd ask, in as innocent a way as possible, who her new friend was.

That's what she would do.

She opened her mouth. "Do you know what time it is, young lady?"

Even as the scolding words escaped her, she wanted to snatch them back.

Too late. The glow in Faith's eyes dimmed, her smile trembled, died.

"I...uh, no." Faith glanced at the clock, then looked back at her mother. "I'm sorry I'm late, Mom."

Well, she started down this road. She had to finish, didn't she? "You're late, and you didn't call. You know the rules. If you're going to be late—"

"I know; I have to call. I meant to. I looked for a phone. But—" her eyes pled for understanding—"but Mom, something amazing happened—"

Anne held up a silencing hand. "I don't care what happened. There's no excuse for not calling. Go to your room. After your father gets home, he and I will be in to talk with you."

Delight had danced in Faith's features when she got home. Now those same features were drawn with stark disappointment. She didn't say another word. She turned and walked away.

But Anne heard her daughter's flat whisper as she left the room. "I thought you'd understand."

Anne's heart longed to call her back, to ask her what had happened. But she couldn't let herself waver. She had to be firm. For Faith's sake.

If only being firm didn't feel so much like being mean.

thirteen

"Who overcomes by force has overcome but half his foe."

MILTON

FAITH WAS IN TROUBLE. BIG TROUBLE.

Her parents had told her it was time for a family conference. The last time they'd done that was when Faith was eight, and she swiped money from her mother's purse. The sadness and disappointment on her father's face that day had imprinted itself on Faith's heart. She'd promised herself she would never do anything that would make him look that way again.

So much for promises.

After her head-to-head with Mom over Dustin a couple of days ago, things had been tense. More tense than Faith ever remembered. Even church today hadn't seemed to ease the heaviness Faith felt in her chest. Several times she almost broke, almost went to tell her mother she was sorry. But each time, a voice inside her would stop her.

Why should you apologize? You're not the one who went off the deep end.

Now Faith wished she'd ignored the voice. Maybe that would have avoided this little get-together.

She looked up from the couch as her parents came into the living room. "Hi."

They both smiled at her. That was a good sign. Maybe things weren't going to be so bad after all.

Her dad sat in his chair, next to the couch, her mom sat next to Faith on the couch. Dad didn't waste any time.

"Punkin', do you know why we wanted to talk with you?"

She eyed her mom but didn't see any anger there. "Umm, because of Dustin?"

"That's the boy who brought you home on Friday?"

Faith nodded, then jumped a little when her mom put her hand over Faith's.

"Sweetie, I'm sorry I got so angry. I was worried when you didn't come home on time."

Sudden emotion choked Faith. She didn't want to scare her mom. "I know, Mom. I'm sorry too."

"We're a little concerned, that's all."

Faith nodded at her dad.

"You've always been good about letting us know if you're going to be late, punkin'. And we don't worry too much when we know you're with your friends, because we know your friends."

"But we don't know this boy." Faith's mom squeezed her hand. "You want to tell us about him?"

Heart pounding, Faith did so. At least, she told them what really mattered. That Dustin was a senior, that he was a nice guy who offered to give her a ride home.

"Have you known him long?"

She studied her father. "A couple of years." It was kind of true. She'd seen him at school for that long. So they hadn't talked until Friday. She'd known who he was long ago.

"Does he date much?"

Heat rushed into Faith's cheeks at her mother's question. She looked down at the floor. "Umm, I don't know." She didn't. Not really. Trista said Dustin had lots of girlfriends, but Faith had never seen him with one. Hey! She could say that, and it was honest. She met her parents' gazes. "I've never seen him with a girlfriend."

"So you like him?"

Good grief! Her own gaze dove for the floor again. Her face must look like a tomato by now! "Yeah." Yikes! She was squeaking again! This was ridiculous.

Her father's chuckle brought her head up. She felt his understanding, his patience, and suddenly the words rushed out. She poured her heart out, telling them how much she liked Dustin, how cool he was, how thrilled she was that he'd offered to give her a ride.

"I should have called, I know. I just..."

"You didn't want to chance missing this opportunity."

Faith smiled her gratitude at her mother. So she really was young once! "Yeah. That."

"Faith, I want you to know we love you and we trust you." Her mom's eyes were serious. "But we also need to know you'll be careful."

She frowned. Careful? "About what?"

"About Dustin. About boys. We've always said you can start dating in high school—" Faith had to grin. Her dad sounded like he really regretted ever saying that!—"so we knew this was coming. It caught us a bit off-guard."

Faith nodded. "Me, too."

Her mom scooted closer and slid her arm around Faith's shoulders. Faith leaned her head against her.

"We've talked with you before about boys and dating."

She giggled. She couldn't help it. "Oh, no! Not another birds and bees talk!"

Her mom's laughter melted the bits of hurt that were still holding on inside Faith. Why hadn't she come and talked to her mom? She always felt so much better when she did so.

"No, not another talk. We want to be sure you're clear on the rules."

She sat up straight, putting her hands on her knees and recited: "'No being alone with boys after dark or in dark rooms. No alcohol.'" She wrinkled her nose. "Ick! Like I'd drink the stuff. 'No kissing unless I've gone out with the boy for at least six months. When we do kiss—'" she grimaced, still grossed out by this one—"'no tongues. Sex belongs in marriage.'" She looked from one parent to the other. "For the record, I've always planned to save it for that."

Dad's lips quirked. "Glad to hear it."

Faith finished with a flair. "'And any boy who isn't willing to abide by these rules doesn't deserve to take me out!'" Her parents' laughter drifting around her, Faith sat back with a smile.

Her mom nudged her. "Any questions that you have, we want you to feel free to come ask us."

"I will, Mom." She meant it, too. Sort of. There were some things you just didn't ask you parents about. She had Trista for that.

"And you need to be prepared, Faith. Because any boy who wants to date you will have to come meet us first."

No way! "Aw, Dad—"

"Nonnegotiable, punkin'. I don't like the way this boy dropped you off without coming in the house."

Faith bit her lip. "I asked Dustin to come in to meet you guys."

"And?"

She shrugged. "He said he was late…for something."

Her dad's eyes grew firm. "Next time, late or not, he comes inside."

Faith nodded, but she knew it wouldn't happen. It would take time to get Dustin to come inside to meet her parents. She'd seen the resistance when she made the offer on Friday, the way his eyes swept her house, then got that cool, removed look. But his explanation had seemed fair enough.

"You know I would if I had time, babe. But I gotta go."

She hadn't pressed. Of course she hadn't! But she would keep working on him. Mom and Dad wouldn't understand that, though. So she'd make sure that, from now on, Dustin dropped her off around the corner. Where they couldn't see them. Just for a little while. Until he was ready to come in and meet them. And when he finally did so, she knew he'd love them.

Faith smiled at her parents.

Everything was going to work out just perfect!

"I can't believe you used to go to church all the time, Faith. I mean, you're so smart and everything."

Dustin watched Faith, gauging how Trista's comment affected her. Clearly, she didn't like it. But she didn't argue, either.

That was promising.

He leaned against the hood of Trista's car. Faith was stretched out on it, propped up on her elbows. Lifting the fall of auburn hair from her neck, Dustin caressed Faith's shoulder. "That's when she was young and foolish."

Faith leaned into his hand. "There's nothing wrong with going to church, you guys—"

"Sure, if you're a total loser."

Trista's snide comment hit home. Faith pushed herself up to a sitting position. "That's not true."

Dustin narrowed his eyes just enough to show dismay, but not to be threatening. "So what are you saying, Faith? You like church?" That's it. Confusion. Concern. But not anger.

"Well, no. Of course not."

Dustin smiled.

"But, some people do. And that doesn't make them losers."

"Well, what does it make them?" Trista flicked her long nails. "They sit in those uncomfortable benches—"

"Pews."

She ignored Faith's correction. "—and listen to some old guy go on and on about what they should do and say and what they can't do and say."

Go, Trista. She was on a roll.

"And then, to top it off, they *pray*! I mean, like, to who? It's not like God is real."

Alarms went off in Dustin's head. Oops. That was going too far too soon. Sure enough, Faith reacted.

"What?"

Trista stared at her, blinking at the force in Faith's astonishment. "What?"

"You–you don't believe in God?"

"Why would I? It's not like I've ever seen Him or heard Him." She pinned Faith with a glare. "Have you?"

Dustin leaned back, studying Faith's features. This should be an interesting response.

"I–well, if you mean actually *heard* Him—"

"Yeah, heard Him." Sarcasm dripped from Trista's words. "You know, with your ears?"

Faith shook her head, albeit slowly. "No. No, I've never heard Him. But I've felt Him."

"Felt Him?"

She slid from the hood to stand in front of Trista. "Yeah, when I pray sometimes. I...I don't know...I feel Him. In my heart."

So how was Trista going to get around this one? Dustin watched as she pursed her red lips. "You—felt Him." She made a point of seeming to think about that, then crossed her arms. "So how do you know it was Him?"

Faith's mouth opened, then closed.

Trista, you're a genius!

"I mean—" Trista glanced at Dustin, and the glitter in her eyes told him how much she was enjoying this—"so maybe you did feel something. But how do you know it was God?"

"What else could it have been?"

Trista's hands waved the question away. "Who knows? There's a bazillion gods out there, aren't there? I mean, you hear about them all the time. For that matter, maybe it was just indigestion!"

Faith was getting upset, and that wasn't good. She had to stay relaxed enough to keep listening. Time to step in. "Well, you've seen Him, though, right?" Dustin made sure he sounded like he wanted her to say yes. "I mean, you prayed and everything when you were young. He must have answered your prayers or something."

Pink tinged Faith's cheeks as she frowned, and Dustin almost burst out laughing. *Give it up, girl. Just admit it.*

"I don't know. I think He did."

"You think?" Trista hooted. "Man, if He was God, if He was real, don't you think you'd *know*?"

Faith's pleading eyes turned to Dustin, and he shrugged. "I don't know, babe. She's got a point. I mean, if God is really there, and if He answered your prayers, you should know it, right?" He laid his hand over her heart, letting the warmth of his fingers burn through her flimsy top, dropping his voice to that low, growling level that made Faith forget where she was. "In here? Where you know what's real."

He allowed himself a small victory smile when she struggled to swallow. He slid his hand up to cup her neck, then leaned toward her. She still hadn't let him kiss her, but she was getting close. He could feel it in the way she responded whenever he tried. It was getting harder and harder for her to turn so that his lips met her cheek and not her mouth.

He held her eyes with his, looking deep, coaxing her, promising everything as he leaned in. For a heartbeat he was sure he'd finally won. But then, just as his lips tried to claim hers, she uttered a small gasp and turned away.

His lips tensed as they pressed against her cheek, but he didn't let the irritation show. He just let the kiss linger, then pulled away.

Trista caught his gaze, and he saw the mocking laughter in her eyes. Then she focused on Faith again. "I'm not trying to be mean, Faith."

Yeah. Right.

"I just think you should be honest with yourself. God is a story, like the Boogey Man. He's what people use to make you do what they want you to do." She tipped her head. "So, I mean, what's the point of praying to something that isn't there?"

Faith stared at the ground. When she finally answered, her voice was low and troubled. "No point. No point at all."

Bingo. Dustin looked away so Faith wouldn't see his smile. Score one for the home team. He glanced back at Faith's miserable features, the sagging shoulders.

A big one.

Wiping all trace of the smile from his face, he drew Faith close. "It's okay, babe. Don't worry about it. You believe whatever you want to believe."

As she slid her arms around his waist, he savored the taste of pending victory.

It was sweet.

But not as sweet as it was going to be.

"I'm too young to feel this old."

Anne straightened, trying to work the ache from the small of her back. She brushed at her forehead, letting her gardening glove soak up some of the perspiration beaded there.

What was she doing working so hard on a day off? The teachers had training today, so she didn't have to go in. She should be sitting on the couch, relaxing.

That's the last thing you should be doing.

Anne nodded. Sad, but true. She turned her face to the sun's warmth. Hard to believe it was only spring. It felt more like summer. But the weatherman said the unusual heat wouldn't last through the weekend. Good. She could use a cooling down.

She should be wearing a hat. How often had Jared scolded her, telling her to put on a hat when she did the gardening? But she hated wearing hats. They flattened her hair and made her already round face seem that much rounder.

Fatter. They make your face fatter, not rounder. At least be honest when you're talking to yourself.

She shook the thought away and leaned over to stab the trowel into the stubborn ground. She loved gardening, but oh, how she hated digging in the rocky Oregon soil. Every time she planted a garden she swore it was the last time. "I'm going to buy silk plants next year!" she'd threatened more than once.

Jared always responded with a serene smile. "Whatever makes you happy, dear."

The rat. He knew she wouldn't be content with silk flowers. She needed the real thing. Roses and pansies. An abundance of them. Which meant an abundance of work.

Oh, well. She jabbed the trowel into the hard ground again. At least she was burning calories. That should make her doctor happy. He'd scolded her again at her last checkup, telling her the diabetes was getting worse. She knew he was right, could feel the effects in her body.

The constant weight gain was bad enough. She was heavier than she'd ever been before. A hundred and seventy pounds—it was far too much. If Anne hadn't known it in her head, her body would have told her so. She hurt all the time. Her back ached, her ankles throbbed, her knees felt like they were going to fall off.

But that wasn't the end of it. Diabetes seemed to taint everything. She couldn't sleep well, so she went through the day fighting overwhelming fatigue. It was so bad lately it got in the way of her relationship with Faith and Jared. Only last week Faith asked her to play a game of cribbage. Anne's response? "I'm too tired, sweetie. Maybe tomorrow."

Two days ago Faith asked her to go for a walk, and though Anne knew her daughter was trying to help her exercise, she shook her head. "I can't, Faith. I need to rest."

The hurt on her daughter's face still made Anne's throat ache.

She'd stomped out of the living room, where Anne was lying on the couch, into the kitchen. Jared, who'd seen their interaction, followed their daughter. They thought she couldn't hear them, but she could. Her hearing was one of the few things that still worked well.

Too well.

"Faith, you need to give your mom a break. She doesn't feel good."

"Come on, Dad! She *never* feels good anymore. She doesn't go anywhere other than work, and she doesn't do half the stuff we do. She sits here at home and says she's too tired? It's not fair."

"She's sick—"

"Tell *her* that! She still eats cookies and ice cream and cake. It's stupid!"

"Faith."

But the warning in Jared's tone didn't stop her.

"It's like she loves that stuff more than she loves us."

"Stop it."

"It's true, Dad. She's killing herself by eating that stuff. It's like she's having some kind of—of affair with food!"

Anne had turned her face into the soft cushions of the couch, letting them catch her tears. And she'd resolved to do better. To fight the pull food had for her, the hunger that always gnawed at her. She would lose weight. She would get healthy.

And so, here she was. Working in the garden. Sweating.

Faith's angry words had actually helped her. They'd motivated her, making her examine why she struggled so with eating what she knew she shouldn't.

Comfort food. That's what drew her. Cookies, brownies, bread, potatoes—anger and depression didn't stand a chance in the face of such things. So what if they were pure poison for her body? At least they made life seem better for a while.

Life isn't the problem, and you know it.

Another jab in the dirt, this one actually penetrating more than a fraction of an inch. No, life wasn't the problem. For the most part, life was good. She and Jared had never been closer. Her faith was growing deeper every day. She knew she had some things to work on—who didn't? But those things weren't what drove her nuts lately.

No, that job seemed to be the sole responsibility of a slim, talented, increasingly beautiful young lady, who, in the last year, had turned the act of eye rolling into a profession.

She'd known hard times with Faith were coming. That was clear last year when God sent her to those passages in Ezekiel. But Anne had been sure they'd be fighting external forces.

Not Faith herself.

The skirmishes started over little things. Faith announced one Sunday morning at the breakfast table that she wasn't going to church.

The memory still got Anne worked up, which actually helped. Amazing how a little adrenaline helped one dig holes for planting flowers.

As she pulled a plant from its cardboard holder and settled it in the hole, she went over that first battle again.

After his daughter's announcement, Jared looked at her

over the Sunday paper. "You not feeling well?"

Faith shrugged. "I feel fine. I don't want to go."

Laying the paper down, Jared glanced at Anne, who had to fight off yet another pang of guilt. Was this because she had such a hard time getting herself to church lately? But she thought Faith had always enjoyed church.

She looked at her daughter. "Care to tell us why?"

Another shrug, this one a bit more impatient than the last. "I don't enjoy it. It's the same thing, week after week. It's just, I don't know. Boring."

"You don't go to church to be entertained, Faith. You go to worship God."

"I can worship Him at home, Daddy. In my room. Or on a walk. I don't have to be in church."

Anne was glad to hear Faith saying she at least wanted to worship God. She poured creamer into her tea, then added a spoonful of sugar. "That's all true. But we're also warned about not giving up on getting together as a community."

Faith directed a pointed look at Anne's cup of tea, then at the spoon she held. Anne looked down at the traces of sugar on the spoon, then back up at her daughter. The message she was sending Anne was clear: *Who are you to tell me what's right and wrong, when you do things you shouldn't all the time?*

But Faith wasn't finished. She arched her brows. "So it's okay when Mom gives up on it, but not when I do?"

"Faith, this isn't about your mom. It's about you."

"Look—" Faith stood, dumping her cereal in the sink, then tossing the bowl in with an impatient flick of the wrist—"forget it! Forget I said anything. I'll go. I'll be bored out of my mind, but I'll go."

My child, the martyr.

Anne could laugh about it now, though her chuckle held a definite wry note. She slid another plant into its hole. Gardening was so therapeutic, so calming. No wonder she'd been doing it so much lately. After the church debate, the conflicts came more often and seemed to hit on every aspect of their lives: The shows they watched. The car they drove. Where they went for vacation. Their clothes. Their house.

Nothing seemed to suit Faith anymore. It was as though she'd suddenly decided she hated everything. Most especially her mother.

And most especially when her mother tried to talk to her about her hair. No matter how much Anne begged, Faith wouldn't keep it out of her face. As much as Anne loved her daughter's hair, she hated it hanging in her face, cloaking her features.

She had a hard enough time reading her daughter these days without having to deal with camouflage.

Then came the makeup melee. Faith wanted to wear it; Anne and Jared thought she was too young.

"I'm seventeen!" She'd blazed at them more than once. "I'm old enough to have babies, for cryin' out loud. What's it gonna hurt if I wear makeup?"

And so the battle had raged, day after day. Anne and Jared stood firm, and after a while Faith gave up.

Good thing, too. Anne had been starting to wear down.

She wiped perspiration from her face and stood with a groan. It had to be close to lunchtime. Even if it wasn't, she needed something to eat. She went inside, pulled her gardening gloves off, and turned on the faucet, letting the warm water run over her aching hands.

Everything hurt. All the time.

Stop feeling sorry for yourself! She slapped the faucet off and glanced toward the clock on the oven. But her gaze was waylaid by the lunch bag sitting on the counter. Faith forgot her lunch. Again.

Sighing, Anne dried her hands, took the bag, and went to find her purse. Good thing the high school was close by.

"I'm sorry, Mrs. Bennett, but Faith isn't in class."

Anne heard the words, but it was as though her brain couldn't process them. "Excuse me?"

The woman behind the desk spoke again, more slowly this time. "Your daughter isn't in class. I called the teacher, and she said Faith didn't show up today."

"Well, where is she?"

Casting a glance over her shoulder, the woman leaned closer so she could whisper. "I'm not supposed to say this, but I'm betting she's out back."

"Out back?" Anne dropped her voice to match the woman's. "Out back where?"

The woman pulled out a map of the high school campus and made a quick mark, then slid the map to Anne. "There. It's where the kids…congregate."

Though a bit dazed at this turn of events, Anne followed the map, walking past the buildings until she reached a back parking lot. Sure enough, a group of kids were there.

Anne stared, then shook her head. Faith couldn't be out here. These were rough-looking kids. Boys with long, shaggy hair, torn jeans, and cigarettes hanging from their mouths. Girls with teased hair, clothes that were too tight, and makeup you could scrape off with a spatula.

Where are these kids' parents? Well, it couldn't hurt to ask if they knew where Faith was. Anne walked toward them. *Thank heaven Faith isn't like these girls—*

Anne stopped in her tracks. Of course. Trista. Anne should have known she'd be with a group of kids like this. The girl arched a plucked brow when she saw Anne, and when Anne start walking toward them again, Trista smiled. But it wasn't a nice smile.

Not wanting to look at Trista any longer, Anne let her gaze travel over the other girls in the group. She frowned. One of them seemed familiar. The one sitting on the car, leaning into a boy whose leather-clad arm hugged her close.

Maybe it was another of Faith's less-than-desirable friends.

But something inside Anne knew that was wrong. She stared at the girl, and the way she sat there, the way she moved as she talked whispered through Anne, breathing an inner spark of apprehension to life.

Her steps slowed, and her gaze met Trista's.

"Oh, look Faith." Trista flicked the ashes from the tip of her cigarette. "Your mommy's here."

The girl on the car spun around, and Anne stared into her

daughter's face. At least, she *thought* it was her daughter. It was a little hard to tell with all the makeup.

Anne stared, speechless.

"Mom! What are you doing here?"

The accusation in Faith's tone brought Anne back to life. She held up the lunch bag, not even trying to keep the censure from her tone. "I brought you your lunch."

Red climbed up Faith's slim neck, washing into her painted cheeks.

"Isn't that sweet, Faith?"

Anne pinned Trista with a glare. "Keep out of this, please."

Trista made an exaggerated bow. "Of course, your highness. Whatever you say, your worship."

Fingers clenching the paper of the bag into a wad, Anne walked to her daughter's side. "Let's go."

"Mom!" Faith's whispered wail had no effect.

Anne reached out and took hold of Faith's arm. "I *said*, let's go!"

Tears sparkling in her wide, disbelieving eyes, Faith tried to pull free, but Anne kept her grip on her daughter's arm.

Until, that was, the boy who'd had his arm around Faith stepped in.

He sat on the hood of the car during the altercation, a small smile on his face, watching the two of them through the wisps of smoke he exhaled from his cigarette. But the minute Anne grabbed Faith, he slid from the car. Until that moment, Anne hadn't realized how tall the boy was.

Or how imposing.

He pried her hand from Faith's arm, his fingers like steel on Anne's wrist. "I don't think she wants to go with you, lady."

A shiver scuttled across Anne's nerves as he stared down at her. There was solid ice in those eyes and raw strength in the grip he still had on her wrist. Before Anne could form a reply to him, though, Faith stepped between them, putting a hand on his chest.

"It's okay, Dustin."

Dustin? The boy on the motorcycle? But Faith said she wasn't seeing him anymore—

"I'll go with her." Pure disgust looked out at Anne from her daughter's narrowed eyes. "For now."

"You don't have to go, babe."

Anne jerked. The boy's tone of voice when he talked to Faith alarmed Anne more than any of the horrible things that had happened so far. That low, seductive, clearly proprietary growl told Anne more than she wanted to know.

This wasn't just some boy. This was someone who thought he had a right to Faith. To her daughter.

Lord...what's going on here?

Anne turned, and Faith fell into step beside her. Neither of them spoke a word on the entire drive home.

When they reached the house, Faith slammed out of the car and raced inside.

Oh no you don't. Anne was right on her heels. She put her hand out, stopping Faith's door as she tried to slam it.

"This is *my* room."

Anne squared off with her daughter. "Which happens to be in *my* house."

"Fine! Do what you want. You always do!" Faith flopped onto her bed, arms crossed, staring up at the ceiling.

After looking at her daughter for a moment, Anne went to the bathroom, jerked a washcloth off the towel rack, and wet it down with hot water. She took it and tossed it to Faith. "Clean your face. You look like a clown."

Faith snatched the washcloth and threw it across the room. "At least I don't look like a pig!"

Anne's stomach surged, as though reviling the hateful words her daughter had thrown at her. Pushing her way through the nausea, Anne glared at her daughter. "I thought you told us you weren't seeing Dustin anymore."

Faith clamped her lips shut.

Anne clenched her hands, but she couldn't stop the agonized cry from slipping free. "How could you do this? Sneaking around. Lying—"

"I only did what I had to!" Faith sat up, eyes burning. "If you and Daddy weren't such prudes—"

Anne didn't remember raising her hand. But suddenly she

realized it was there, poised for the strike. She wasn't sure who was more shocked. She or Faith.

The color drained from Faith's face as she sat there, staring at her mother. Anne's hand fell to her side, and she turned away. Walked to the doorway. There, she spoke without turning.

"This isn't over, Faith. But I can't talk to you now. I'm too angry." The words caught in her throat, choking her. "Too hurt. It will have to wait until your father comes home."

Pulling the door closed behind her, Anne left her daughter's room. Back straight, she walked outside to her garden. She knelt, took up the trowel, and dug. And dug. And dug.

All the while her tears fell, bathing the hard soil with her fear and sorrow.

"I can't believe this is happening."

Anne pressed her face into Jared's solid chest. "Neither can I."

He'd come home an hour ago, and Anne told him all that had happened. His usually relaxed, smiling face grew pale, pinched. He hadn't cried, but Anne knew it was only because he held a tight rein on the emotions churning inside of him.

Pulling away from his embrace, Anne rubbed her hands over her temples. "How did this happen? What have we done wrong?"

"Anne—"

"No." She stood, pacing back and forth on the rug by their bed. "Jared, God called us to be parents, remember? We begged and begged for a child. For *Faith*. And He gave her to us. I thought we were good parents, that we were being loving and encouraging, but if that were true, then how could this have happened?"

Jared shook his head. "I don't know, hon. I don't know." He stood and took her hands in his own. "All I do know is that we need to pray together." He squeezed her hands. "And then we have to go talk with Faith."

Anne let him pull her close and buried her face against

him. "You pray." He hesitated. "Please. I…I can't."

She gripped her husband's shirt, balling it into wads in her fists, as his choked voice enveloped her.

"God, help us. We don't know what's happening, but we know it's not good. That something has pulled our daughter away from what's right and true. Be with us as we talk with her. Grant us Your peace and calm. And show us where we've been wrong. Just…help us, Lord. Amen."

"Amen," Anne muttered into Jared's shirt.

His hands gripped her shoulders, and he set her away from him. "Let's go."

"How far have things gone between you and Dustin?"

Faith stared at her father, defiance wrapped around her like a suit of armor. "Is that all you're worried about? Have I had sex with this guy."

"Faith, please—"

"Well, I haven't, okay? I *wouldn't*." The hurt in her voice cut at Anne's heart. "Daddy, how can you even ask me that?"

The tears he'd been keeping under such tight rein escaped down his cheeks. "You've lied to us. Done what we expressly asked you not to. What you said you wouldn't." The words came out in a hoarse whisper. "How can I *not* ask it?"

Faith's sobs were heart-wrenching. "You don't even know Dustin. How can you act like he's some kind of creep?"

"Because we don't know him." Anne hugged herself. "Don't you see? If we don't know him, we can't trust him—"

"So, what? You pick my friends? The boys I date? You tell me who I can like and spend time with?"

"Faith Adelle—"

She shook her head, stopping Anne's words. "What am I supposed to do, Mom? Just sit around by myself? Dad's gone at work all day, and *you* sure don't want to be around me."

Jared had heard enough. "Faith!"

A wretchedness of soul she'd never known before gripped Anne, a choking vise around her heart. "What are you talking about?"

Faith's hand cut through the air between them. "It's *true*." She looked at Jared. "It's true and you know it, Daddy." Her wounded gaze came back to Anne. "You never want to spend time with me anymore. I ask you to go for walks, to come play a game, but all you want to do is sit like a lump on the couch and watch TV. Or sleep. *That's* what matters most to you."

Heat surged into Anne's face. "That's not fair! You know how hard it is for me—"

"Forget it!" Tears streamed down Faith's pale cheeks, and she looked from Anne to Jared. "I'm sorry. I'm sorry I'm not the perfect little daughter who does everything right. I'm sorry I don't have the perfect Christian friends who do nothing but pray and praise God all day."

She folded her arms, making a physical barrier to match the emotional one between them. "You guys would be happier if I disappeared, wouldn't you? That'd make you happy, if I was gone!"

"Stop it!"

Even Anne jumped at Jared's bellow.

"Stop it this instant. I won't have you saying such things to your mother, or to me." He went to take hold of their daughter, pulling her into his arms. "We love you, Faith. God in heaven, don't you know that by now?"

She stiffened, then suddenly collapsed against him, her weeping joining his in a heartbreaking harmony of grief.

"I'm sorry, Daddy, I'm sorry…"

Anne lowered herself to Faith's bed, sitting there, numb, as though wrapped in a cocoon of anguish. Shame warmed her cheeks as she thought about the awful things she'd said to her daughter, how she'd very nearly struck her.

God, forgive me. I just…I don't understand! How did this happen? What did I do wrong? Help us. Please, help us.

Jared looked at Anne over Faith's head and held a hand out to Anne. She took it and let him pull her into the circle of his arms alongside their daughter.

She slid a tentative arm around Faith, so afraid she would pull away, but Faith turned to her, burying her face in Anne's neck.

"It's okay, sweetie," Anne crooned, rocking her weeping girl. "It's going to be okay."

But even as she spoke the words, Anne couldn't help but wonder if she was the one who was lying now.

Shallow Soil

"Other seeds fell on shallow soil with underlying rock.
The plants sprang up quickly,
but they soon wilted beneath the hot sun
and died because the roots had no
nourishment in the shallow soil....
The rocky soil represents those who
hear the message and receive it with joy.
But like young plants in such soil,
their roots don't go very deep.
At first they get along fine,
but they wilt as soon as they have problems
or are persecuted because they believe the word."

MATTHEW 13:5–7, 20–21

fourteen

"Don't fight forces, use them."
RICHARD BUCKMINSTER FULLER

WHY DID THEY MAKE PEWS SO UNCOMFORTABLE? Would it kill someone to make the seats soft?

Faith shifted in her seat. Fidgeted. Glanced at her father—and bit her lip.

Fatigue showed in the line of his jaw, the fixed stare he kept on the pastor. Faith had never seen him so weighted by weariness.

Guilt dug in its spurs, riding her. It was her fights with Mom that had him so worn out. In the months since her mom came to school and found her with Dustin, Faith had tried to do better. She really had. But almost before she knew it, something Mom said or did would set her off.

It helped a little that they'd agreed she could see Dustin—after, of course, they met him. Knowing how hard it would be to get Dustin to come to her house, she'd set up a meeting on neutral ground, at Denny's. Mom had been less than thrilled to see Dustin again. Faith had the distinct impression Mom was a little afraid of him. As for Dad…

Faith could still see the way her dad and Dustin faced off. Dustin was shorter than her dad by about an inch, but from

Dustin's posture, you'd think he was Andre the Giant. He stood there, holding Dad's gaze, that little smirk on his face. Dad extended his hand, and for one horrible moment, Faith thought Dustin would refuse to take it. But then his hand made a slow rise to shake hands.

"I'm glad to meet you, Dustin."

There was no hint of a smile when her dad said the words. Dustin's only response was a grunt.

The meal went as well as could be expected, and though her parents hadn't exactly been overjoyed, they abided by their agreement. Dustin came to meet them. Faith could continue seeing him.

Of course, every time she came home from being with Dustin, her mom gave her the fifth degree. Where did they go? Who did they see? What did they do?

It was enough to make her scream.

Faith stared at the back of the pew in front, chewing her lip. Yeah, Mom drove her nuts. But she'd never wanted their conflicts to hurt Dad. Though far from convinced prayer did that much good, Faith looked down at her folded hands. *God, please, be with Daddy. Help him to feel better.*

So praying might not help much. At least it couldn't hurt. Faith was willing to do whatever it took to make things better. She'd been spending more and more time away from home, just to avoid the fights. But that was okay. It wasn't so bad leaving home early and coming in before dinner. Then as soon as dinner was over, she could head for her room and her records and headphones.

A huge knot formed in her chest, lodging there, making her ache.

Who was she kidding? She missed being home. She missed laughing with her parents, having fun with them.

She missed them.

"Please turn to hymn number 532, 'Wonderful Grace of Jesus,' and stand as we sing this for our closing hymn."

Her dad pulled the hymnal from the holder in front of them, opened it, and pushed himself to his feet. Faith stood beside him, leaning against his solid arm, her hand holding the hymnal as well. The swell of music rose and bounded around them, and for a moment Faith gave herself over to singing.

Her dad's voice was so beautiful, so rich and strong. All Faith had to do was focus on his voice and let it carry her. When she did that, she could fly through harmonies.

When the song was over, Dad turned to her with a weak imitation of his regular smile. "So, home?"

Faith started to nod, then stopped. "Dad?"

He turned to make his way to the aisle. "Hmm?"

"Can we go for a drive?"

The request surprised her dad—almost as much as it surprised her. But then, when she thought about it, what was so surprising? When she was little, they used to go for drives all the time on Sunday. Faith hadn't realized how much she missed that.

He glanced back at her. "A drive? Where?"

"The Applegate?"

For a moment Faith thought he was going to refuse, but then his smile gained a little of its old spirit. "Sure, why not? Your mother is sleeping and doesn't expect us home until after we eat." Her dad flopped an arm across her shoulders as they walked down the aisle, heading for the exit. "The Applegate it is."

It was a beautiful day for a drive. The sun was shining, and though it was summer, the scorching heat hadn't hit yet. Faith tuned the radio to the oldies station, and the two of them sang along as they drove.

When they came to the river, Faith had the car door open almost in the same second her dad shut off the engine. "Race you!"

She ran across the rocky ground, laughing, not the least surprised when her long-legged father caught up with her. At the river's edge, they sorted through the rocks covering the sandy ground, plucking out those that were round and flat. Dad was a master at skipping stones. Once, when Faith was about six, her dad had thrown a rock that skipped twenty times! Faith and her mother had cheered as if he won the Super Bowl. The closest Faith ever came to that record was nine times.

I'll have to bring Dustin here.

The thought of him made Faith's heart pound, her pulse skip. They were fast becoming an item. Oddly enough, she'd been faithful to the rules her parents gave her about dating. Mom would never believe that, but it was true.

Dustin had been shocked the first time Faith told him she wouldn't kiss him. But he hadn't pushed her, which made it that much harder to stick to her guns.

Faith leaned down to choose another rock. "When did you know you loved Mom?"

He tossed another rock. "First time I saw her."

"Tell me about it."

He tipped his head. "You've heard this before."

She skipped her rock—four times. She was losing her touch. Faith went to perch on a huge boulder at the river's edge. "I know, but I want to hear it again."

Dad thought for a minute, then came to lean against the boulder. "It was during the winter of my first year in college. I happened to see a beautiful auburn-haired girl walking across the college campus with the college football fullback."

Faith nodded. "Woody."

Her dad grimaced. "Woody."

"So what happened?"

He drew in a deep breath, then looked out over the river. "Well, one look at her and my heart beat a rapid tune. Your mom was the prettiest girl I'd ever seen. And I wondered what she was doing with that silly fullback."

Faith circled her knees with her arms. "Instead of with you?"

"Exactly. But in my heart I knew a slightly older, shy guy from Idaho could never get to know, let alone date, such a beautiful girl." He shrugged. "I figured she'd never even notice me. I could forget her being interested in me."

"But she was." Faith loved this story.

Her dad grinned. "Eventually. But first, that next spring, she and the football fullback invited me to go to a movie with them."

Faith shook her head. "That must have floored you."

"I thought they were being nice to a lonely guy who spent much of his time alone. Later I found out they invited me to go with them because I had a car to drive us to the movie theater."

"Brats."

Her dad chuckled. "I saw your mom going across the campus now and then, and each time I spotted her my heart did that pounding thing again."

Faith nudged his shoulder. "You were in loooove."

"I was at that. Good thing she and Woody broke up when he fell for another girl."

"A girl you just happened to introduce him to?"

Her dad's laughter rang out. "Hey, you do what you have to do." He looked around, then nudged her. "Want to walk for a while?"

"Sure." She slid off the boulder and fell in step with him. "So what then?"

He gave her a sidelong glance. "You really want to hear all this again?"

"Yup."

"Well—" he slipped his hands into his pockets—"that next fall, I went on a college gospel-team trip to a nearby church." His brows waggled. "Guess who else went?"

Faith grinned. "Mom!"

"Since I had a car, I drove. And it just so happened that your mother sat beside me. And since there were three of us in the front seat, your mom and I were really close together." His face almost glowed as he remembered. "And that same heart pounding went on all during the trip."

"You should have seen a doctor."

He shoved at Faith with his elbow. "You want to hear this or not?"

She held up her hands. "Okay, okay. Go on."

"Well, wonder of wonders, we got to know one another on that trip. We started dating. But I was one of three guys your mom was interested in."

This was Faith's favorite part. "And you didn't like that."

"Not even a little. I finally told your mom how I felt, and we broke up for about a week and a half."

"And neither of you wanted to go to the dining hall because you were afraid of running into one another."

He laughed, shaking his head. "What days those were."

"So? How'd you get back together?"

"A mutual friend talked us into sitting together in the college chapel during a service. Both our stomachs started making strange noises from lack of food." His words were punctuated with laughter. "We were sure everyone there could hear the noise."

"And you've been together ever since."

"Every wonderful day."

They walked in a companionable silence, until Faith's dad looked at his watch. "We'd better head back, punkin'."

With a reluctant nod, she turned and followed him back toward the car. When they reached it and slid inside, Dad started to put the key in the ignition, then hesitated.

"Faith, are you in love with Dustin?"

She stared at the dashboard. "I...I don't know."

He looked out the windshield. "You know, your mom and I have had an incredible journey together. We're good friends as well as spouses. You hear so much about how opposites attract, how they make the best marriages. But for your mom and me, well, it's different. We're so much alike in our personalities and feelings about things that we knew from the first that God made us to be together for life."

Faith looked out the window. What would that be like, to be so in tune with someone that you knew you were meant for each other?

Did she feel that way with Dustin?

No. If she was honest, no. But she wanted to.

"I know you and your mom have had a hard time these last few months, but don't ever kid yourself, Faith. Anne is an amazing person. She's got things that she struggles with, but you'll never find someone with a deeper faith, a kinder heart."

Faith nodded. "I know, Daddy."

"Your mom is—"

At the choked sound he made, Faith turned to look at

him. The tears sparkling in his eyes sent a shiver of shock through Faith. Her dad hardly ever cried.

"Loving your mom, having her love me, it's helped me grow into a better person as a husband and a father. That's what I pray for you. That you'll find a man who will love and cherish you the way I love and cherish your mother."

Faith took her dad's hand and squeezed it. "I want that, too, Daddy." And she did. More than anything in the world.

"I don't want to go!"

Jared and Anne sat on the couch, watching their daughter pace the floor, arms crossed, eyes blazing. They didn't respond. Didn't argue. There was no point. Faith wouldn't have listened.

Besides, their minds were made up. And nothing Faith said was going to change that.

When she realized they were sitting there, silent, Faith clamped her mouth shut and flopped onto the overstuffed chair opposite them. "So what is this? The silent treatment?"

Anne watched Jared study their daughter. "No, Faith. I'm waiting for an opening."

It was actually a relief to see red tingeing Faith's cheeks at her father's quiet chiding. Thank heaven *something* still got to her!

"It's really quite simple, Faith. You agreed last summer to go to camp this summer. You signed up to act as a helper in one of the cabins. Your mother and I already paid your fees."

"But I forgot!"

Anne let a sigh slip free. "Forgetting doesn't release you from your obligations. There's no time to find someone to take your place."

"And heaven forbid you guys lose your money."

"Faith."

She fell silent at the firm word from her dad.

"You used to love camp—"

Faith groaned. "I was a child then, Mother."

Anne resisted the urge to say, "Which means you'll still have fun, considering how often you act like a child!"

Barely.

"You are going to camp. You are going to fulfill your obligations. End of discussion."

"Are you kidding me?" Faith sat rigid in the chair. "You think you can tell me what to do? That's not fair!"

"Fair doesn't enter into it, Faith. This is about what's right, not what's fair." Jared's words were weighed down with a raw weariness.

Anne took his hand, studying him. The conflicts over the last few months were taking a toll. It was evident in the wrinkles creasing his usually smooth forehead, the dark circles under his eyes. And yet, Anne knew he believed, with all his heart, that God had His hand on Faith, that He'd bring her out of this angry, combative stage—that one day soon He would restore their little girl to them.

Anne wished she was as certain.

Several weeks ago, when Faith and her father came back from a drive up to the Applegate River, Jared had been so excited. Almost his old self. He told Anne how they'd talked. "I think maybe I got through to her, Annie."

But within days, the battles raged again. For all Anne's efforts to get along, Faith had grown more and more withdrawn. The sole mercy was that she still treated her father well, spending time with him—though not nearly as much as she used to. And though Faith didn't often agree with what he said to her, at least she didn't lambaste him.

No, she saved that precious gift for Anne.

She'd always known her daughter was intelligent, that she had an excellent vocabulary for her age. Her daughter had excelled in debate in school. But she hadn't had any idea how vicious all that intelligence, that eloquence, could be. Words weren't simply a way for Faith to express herself. They were tactical weapons, wielded with great skill and precision to cause the most damage possible.

She learned that from Trista, I'll bet. Faith's rebellious friend had only grown wilder and more disdainful of anything good. But the time of Faith listening to Anne's concerns about Trista and her gang was long gone. Anne didn't dare breathe Trista's name in Faith's earshot, or she got an earful herself about being a self-righteous witch.

The first time Faith called her that, Anne stood there, mouth hanging open. She couldn't believe she'd heard right. As though sensing that, Faith repeated it, then smirked when tears ran down Anne's cheeks.

"Watch it, Mom. Water melts wicked witches."

Then her daughter spun on her heel and left the room. Of course, Anne was hot on her heels, ordering her to her room for the rest of the evening. But while Faith complied, it was a hollow victory.

When Anne told Jared about it that evening, he sat there, staring at the floor. Finally he looked up at her. "We have to do something. Now. Before we lose her for good."

They talked. And prayed. And talked some more. And they both felt God leading them to the same conclusion—they needed to talk with their pastor. They set up the appointment and met with him that next week.

It was in the course of their prayer and discussion that Pastor Fred remarked, "Maybe being at camp next week will be a good thing."

Anne and Jared stared.

"Camp?" Anne finally managed.

Pastor reminded them about Faith's commitment, pointing out that reminders had gone out in the mail several weeks earlier. Anne put a hand to her face.

"Oh my goodness! I thought that was a fund-raising letter. I—" she gave Jared and the pastor a look of abject apology—"I threw it out without even opening it."

Leaning back in his chair, Pastor Fred thought for a moment. "You know, I think God's hand may be in this. If Faith had remembered this sooner, she might have backed out. As it is, we don't have time to find a replacement for her."

"She could still refuse to go."

"No." Jared's tone was quiet. Confident. "She won't."

Anne looked at him, and he took her hand. "Faith is a lot of things, Anne. I admit that. But she doesn't let down people who are counting on her."

"And if she decides now is the time to start?" Anne hated saying it, but she needed to voice her fear.

"Then we tell her she hasn't got a choice. And we see what happens."

Pastor Fred leaned forward, placing his elbows on his knees. His crew-cut black hair was liberally sprinkled with white. His eyes crinkled at the edges, clear evidence to the man's propensity for laughter. "Do you mind if I call some of the others in the church? Those who've known Faith for a long time and ask them to pray for her while she's at camp?"

A wave of gratitude swept through Anne. "That would be wonderful."

"Absolutely." Jared nodded.

"I'll pray as well that God uses this time to recapture Faith's heart. Maybe once she's there, talking with the kids she used to hang out with at church, she'll remember what's really important. Maybe her hardened heart will break and open, and God can get hold of her again. Now—" he reached for the phone—"there's someone I'd like you to talk with, if you don't mind."

"Whoever you think will help."

Pastor Fred's face creased in a mischievous grin. "Oh, she'll help all right." He turned his attention to the phone. "Sarah, good! I was hoping you were still around. Can you come in here for a moment, please?"

Mere moments later, a knock sounded on the door. Pastor Fred went to open it, admitting a young woman.

"Anne, Jared, I'd like you to meet Sarah McMannis, the head counselor at the church camp."

They shook hands, and Sarah took the chair Pastor Fred indicated. "What's up?"

The pastor brought Sarah up to date, with Anne and Jared filling in here and there. When they finished, Sarah looked at Anne, compassion in her gaze.

"I'm so sorry for all you've been through." She looked at Jared. "Both of you. How can I help?"

Pastor Fred crossed one leg over the other, sitting back in his chair. "I'd like to assign Faith to you. As your assistant." He tossed a grin to Anne and Jared. "Believe me, no matter how tough Faith may be, she's no match for Sarah."

It only took talking with Sarah for an hour for Anne to believe Pastor Fred was right.

Tall and athletic, Sarah was the epitome of the girl next door. But her freckled face belied a graduation from the school of hard knocks.

As hard, it turned out, as they came.

"I understand girls like Faith" She stood and went to perch on the corner of Pastor's desk. "I was a girl like Faith. Raised in a Christian home, given all the love and breaks possible—and I hated it. Felt like my life was decided before I was born. I wanted excitement, challenges, danger."

She glanced at the pastor, then brought her steady gaze back to Anne and Jared. "And I got it all, and then some. I learned the hard way that turning your back on your family, your values, and God doesn't set you free. It turns the key in the prison door, locking you inside yourself with nothing but desperation and fear."

Anne's fingers tightened on Jared's. That was what she was afraid of. She knew Faith was drifting, testing forbidden waters and liking the sense of danger in the rapids. But what she didn't see were the rocks waiting for her at the end of the ride. Rocks that would shatter her, destroying her life and heart.

"But God can get hold of you, Mr. and Mrs. Bennett, no matter how far away you run." Sarah's face lit up. "If He could catch me and bring me back, then He can reach Faith."

"I believe that."

Anne could tell from the conviction in her husband's voice that he meant what he said. She could only hope and pray they were right. For her part, Anne was glad being at camp would get Faith away from Trista.

And Dustin.

Anne didn't know how far things had gone between Faith and that boy. But she was worried. More than she'd ever admit to Jared. Especially after last week, when she went to gather Faith's laundry. When she lifted a jacket from Faith's bed, something fell onto the floor. Anne reached down to pick it up, and her hand halted midair.

A pack of cigarettes. It fell out of her daughter's jacket pocket. Were they Faith's? For months Anne smelled the smoke on Faith's clothes, in her hair, but she'd always assumed it was from hanging around with Trista and Dustin. Faith knew better than to smoke. Her father hated smoking. Both of his parents had smoked, and they'd lost his mother to lung cancer when Faith was ten.

She'd adored Gramma Irene. After the funeral, she became an outspoken opponent of smoking. Every time someone lit up anywhere near her, Faith would tip her little nose in the air, glare at the person, and announce, "That's a smelly, ugly habit. And it kills people."

Anne looked at the pack. Was it possible? Had Faith really changed so much that she started doing something she'd once despised? Anne contemplated confronting her daughter, asking her if the pack was hers or not, but it wouldn't do any good. Faith would never admit they were hers. She'd say she was holding them for a friend.

Scooping the offending pack off the floor, Anne set it on Faith's dresser. Then she felt in the jacket pocket. Sure enough, there was a lighter as well. Anne pulled it free, and her heart sank.

Faith might be able to explain away the cigarettes, but it wasn't near as easy to deny a silver, rhinestone-studded lighter with the name "Faith" engraved on it. Probably a gift, and Anne could guess who it was from.

"Dustin Grant," she whispered. Oh, how she was starting to hate that name.

Anne set the lighter next to the cigarettes. Let Faith see them there. Let her see she's found out Faith was smoking.

When she told Jared about the incident, he absorbed it in silence. Anne understood. It was one more thing that convinced him they were doing the right thing.

So here they were, facing Faith—and her wrath—delivering news guaranteed to set her off.

"You don't care about me anymore, do you?"

Faith's ice-tipped question pulled Anne's focus back to the matters at hand.

"Actually, we care a great deal. Which is why we want you to live up to your agreements. You asked to go camp, Faith. We didn't make this decision, you did."

"A year ago!"

"A year ago or a day ago, it doesn't matter. You chose to go." Jared's tone was equal parts gentle care and firm conviction. "And go you will. I understand your reaction, but you must understand this—we are your parents, and we can make you go. And we will make you go. So you may as well reconcile yourself to the fact: You're going to church camp for the summer."

Faith's mouth compressed—a thin line daring them to cross—and her arms folded in front of her. "Fine. When do I leave?"

Jared and Anne looked at each other. This was the tricky part. For all Jared had said they would make Faith go, they both knew Faith could take off. But either they believed she was in God's hands, or they didn't.

"This Saturday."

"That's in three days!"

"Yes, we know. But we just found out about this last night, when we talked with Pastor Fred."

Faith pushed out of the chair. "I can't leave in three days!"

"Why not?"

Faith spun on her father. "Because...well, because..." She waved her hands in the air. "I can't!"

Jared went to stand before his daughter. She looked up at him, and Anne's heart jumped when she saw the adoration there. Yes, it was peeking out from layer upon layer of defiance.

But it was there.

"Faith, Sarah McMillian will be here to pick you up at seven Saturday morning." He reached out, cupped her chin, and tipped her face with gentle pressure until their eyes met. "I know you can leave if you want to. I know you could disappear and not show up again until after Sarah leaves. But I'm asking you, punkin'...please. Do what you said you would. Be ready when Sarah comes."

Faith stared at her father for what seemed an eternity, then gave one, curt nod. She stepped back, then walked from the room.

Anne's gaze met Jared's, and he shrugged. "It's in God's hands."

Indeed. Anne only hoped they were truly big enough to hold her little girl and protect her from all that was working against her.

Most of all, herself.

Saturday morning dawned bright and early, and Anne walked from her bedroom, heart in her throat. True, Faith had packed yesterday. But that didn't mean she was going.

Anne refused to play security guard, though. Rather than knock on Faith's door and check if she was there, she went on down to the kitchen. Jared joined her a few minutes later, starting the coffee.

Anne was in the middle of preparing an eggs and bacon breakfast when Faith entered. "I want mine scrambled."

Her heart singing, Anne could only nod. If Faith had wanted her eggs dipped in gold and served on a bed of peacock feathers, Anne would have found a way to do it for her. That's how relieved and grateful she was to see her daughter standing there.

The rest of the morning held a kind of surreal air. The three of them sat and ate, talking and even joking. The way they used to, what felt like a lifetime ago.

When the doorbell rang, Faith pushed back her chair. "I'll get it."

Anne and Jared followed her as she went to grab her suitcase, then open the door. Sarah stood there, her face beaming. "Hey. You must be Faith."

Faith's mouth quirked, and she looked down at her suitcase. "Wow. Keen sense of the obvious, eh?"

"The keenest." Sarah's eyes sparkled. "Want me to prove it? I bet that's your bag."

"Ooo, I am impressed." Faith peeked out the doorway. "So where's your car?"

Sarah tossed a wink at Jared and Anne, then pulled her keys from her pocket. "Right this way, your highness."

"'Bout time someone got that right."

Though Anne was sure Faith meant her response to be smart, she couldn't help smiling. Because something Anne hadn't heard in a very long time accompanied the words: Faith's laughter. It bubbled and tinkled, wrapping around Anne's heart, bringing quick tears to her eyes.

Jared's hands stroked her arms, and she leaned back against him.

"This is going to work, Annie."

She could only pray he was right.

Horseback riding. Swimming. Hikes in the mountains. Ping-Pong. Volleyball. Basketball. And yes, even the singing during worship time.

Faith had found herself not only participating in these things, but even enjoying them. She hadn't thought it possible. Hadn't thought she'd be able to endure a week, let alone a whole summer, away from Dustin.

She still wasn't sure what to think of his reaction when she had told him what was happening. She expected him to be angry. But he just looked at her, those blue eyes thoughtful.

"The whole summer, huh?"

She nodded.

"You could always not go, you know."

Faith straddled his motorcycle. "Yeah, right. If I don't go with this Sarah when she shows up, Dad will pile me in the car and drive me there himself."

"You could always leave."

She frowned. "Yeah, I am. On Saturday."

Dustin's eyes had an odd gleam in them as he gave a slow shake of his head. "No, babe. *Leave.* Home. Come here, stay with me. Then you could do what you wanted."

Faith's mouth opened, but nothing came out. She sat there, mouth gaping, speechless.

"Tryin' to catch flies?"

His soft, playful taunt made her clamp her lips together. "Are you?" Was he serious? "Do you really want me to…to…"

He moved them, coming to slip his arms around her and lift her from the bike. He held her close, brushing her hair back from her face. "Babe, I'd love having you here, with me." He smiled down at her.

Faith felt as though her head were spinning. Words didn't make sense when he looked at her that way. "I…you…"

Dustin's deep laughter enveloped her, and he lowered his head. But before his lips could find hers, she turned so that the kiss landed on her cheek. He stiffened, then relaxed, letting his lips trail down her cheek to her neck. Then, when she could hardly breathe, he let her go and walked away.

Faith stood there, shaking, swaying like tall grass in the wind. He'd always told her he understood her feelings about kissing. Even thought it was cool she wanted to wait until it meant something. Until it was real.

Now she wondered if he was getting tired of waiting.

Dustin pulled a cigarette out and lit it. "So, hey, go to camp. We'll make the best of the next few days, then have a celebration when you get back."

"You—" Faith's mind really was spinning now. Go, stay. What did he want? "You want me to go?"

He took a long drag on his cigarette. "Hey, of course not. But you don't have much choice, right?"

"R-right." That was right, wasn't it?

He shrugged. "Well, then, there you have it."

Remembering the odd exchange, Faith kicked a toe into the dust. Why didn't boys come with some kind of instruction manual?

"Hey, you goof. Time for swim lessons!"

Sarah was coming toward her, beach towel over her arm, customary grin on her face.

Faith would never have admitted it to her folks, but she

liked Sarah. The older girl stuck pretty close to Faith those first few days. Faith finally let her have it, telling her she didn't need a prison warden. "Relax. I'm not going to run away."

"I know that, Faith." Sarah hadn't been angry at her at all. She kept that smile on her face. "I'm not worried about you taking off." She indicated the woods all around them. "After all, we're a gazillion miles from the nearest bus station, and I can't see you walking the hundred miles back to the valley."

"Ha ha. So why are you dogging me, then?"

Sarah tipped her head. "I'm not. I just happen to enjoy your company."

That shut Faith up but good. Sarah enjoyed her company? Why?

Of course, Faith hadn't let on how much that surprised her. She tried to come up with some snappy retort, but only managed a lame comment that she figured Sarah saw right through.

For the next few days, Faith and Sarah spent a lot of time talking. When Sarah wasn't working, that was. As head counselor, rather than having a cabin of her own to watch over, Sarah managed the other counselors. She helped them deal with problems, anything from homesick or problem kids to the best way to build a campfire. Faith followed Sarah around, doing what was needed when it was needed, helping first one counselor and then another.

It was actually kind of fun.

Faith stayed in one of the cabins, and her counselor, Tammy, was okay. Faith discovered she didn't mind the other girls, either. She remembered a couple of them from Sunday school and church camp when she was little. But since the kids at camp came from churches all over the western region, there were plenty of strangers. Even so, they all kind of seemed to fit together. Faith thought that was kind of cool.

Tammy worked them hard, but once their chores were done, she let them play a lot, too. And she had a way of making work time almost as much fun as rec time. But what Faith liked most—and what surprised her most—was the way Tammy and Sarah and the other counselors treated them like adults. They didn't talk down to them. Didn't lecture them. Didn't even preach at them. Just talked to them like they talked to each other.

Every morning they read the Bible together and prayed for the day. Then, when they started their chores, Tammy would ask them all a question, and they'd get all caught up in the discussion. Before they knew it, chores were done and it was time to have fun.

Almost every day, right after chores, Sarah showed up at Faith's cabin. "Wanna go for a hike?" she'd ask, or "Lake is nice and calm today. How about we canoe to the other side?" Whatever they did, they always talked. About life. Friends. Family.

And God. Always God.

Faith and Sarah had talked late into the night last night, so Faith had a hard time crawling from bed this morning. Tammy teased her about doing her chores in her sleep, and Faith stuck her tongue out at her. "I was talking to your boss, Miss Counselor. So there."

Tammy laughed, then handed Faith the broom. "Think you can handle sweeping the floor?"

"Do I have to be awake to do it?"

"Nah. Why should today be different from any other day?"

"Ha ha." Faith pulled a face and got to work. Tammy kind of reminded Faith of her mom. They used to laugh and tease like this. A long time ago.

Tammy jumped in to the day's question-and-answer bit. "Okay, everyone look at Faith."

"Please," someone quipped. "I just ate."

Tammy threw a sock at the comedienne, then went on. "So what does it matter if you sweep the floor or not?"

Faith rolled her eyes and slapped a palm to her forehead. "Duh, Tammy. To keep it clean."

The other girls laughed, as did Tammy. "Okay, so why does that matter?"

"'Cuz you can't walk on a floor that's covered with crud." This from Billie, a chubby girl, who had a great sense of humor.

"Yeah, you'll trip and fall over," another girl added.

Billie held up a rotting banana peel she'd found under one of the bunks. "Or get stuck and not be able to move."

"Ewwww!" the other girls chorused.

"All right." Tammy held out a garbage sack for Billie to toss in the peel. "So take it deeper. Why is sweeping a room out like confessing our sins?"

"'Cuz God can't live in a heart that's covered in crud."

Tammy and the girls turned to Faith, eyes wide. It was the first time Faith had spoken up during their question-and-answer times.

"Go with that, Faith."

It felt funny to have all the girls' eyes on her, but Faith figured she'd opened her mouth, she might as well have her say. "Well, God's holy, right? He's clean and pure. And He won't stay in a place that's full of garbage, of sin. Either the sin has to go, or He does."

"Then let the sin go, baby."

Faith looked at Billie. For all that she liked Billie, she got the sense the other girl said things she thought Tammy wanted to hear. And if there was one thing that irritated Faith, it was a brownnoser. *Let's see how you hold up when you get pushed.* "Yeah? Why?"

If she expected Billie to falter, she was disappointed. The girl shoved her hands into the pockets of her shorts and met Faith's challenge without flinching. "'Cuz I've been without God, and it stinks. Sin's fun while it lasts, but it never lasts long enough. And when it's done, you're all alone. Just you—" Billie held Faith's gaze—"and the bad you've done."

Faith felt her cheeks go warm. For a minute she wondered if it was a setup, if Billie had been coached, told exactly the right thing to say so Faith would feel guilty. But the thought left as quickly as it came.

No way. Billie was saying hard things, and they were from her gut. Faith could tell.

"You did bad, Billie?"

The quiet question from one of the other girls brought a grin to Billie's face. "Oh, I did bad, all right. Baddest of the bad.

But that's not what's cool. What's cool is that it didn't matter."

Faith narrowed her eyes. "What do you mean?"

"To God."

Faith stared. Billie's smile was so happy it made her almost pretty.

"Once I asked Him for help, once I told Him everything I'd done and asked Him to forgive me, it was like none of it happened."

Faith snorted. "You telling me people weren't mad at you anymore?"

"Oh, they were still mad, but I wasn't. I didn't expect them to stop being mad, not right away. I mean, I worked hard to get them mad, you know?"

Faith knew. Too well.

"But I kinda figured I deserved their mad stuff, so instead of resenting it, I asked God to help me deal with it. And He did. And after a while, the mad stuff was over, and good stuff was starting. And it's still going, 'cuz I've got God."

Faith sat on her bunk. "So get God and everything's perfect?"

Billie shook her head. "Girl, what world are you livin' in? Nothin' here is perfect." She turned to tug her sleeping bag into place, smoothing out the wrinkles. "But it's a whole lot better with God than without Him."

Billie's words had stuck with Faith for days. Weeks, in fact. She'd discussed them with Tammy, often late into the night, while they lay in their beds, serenaded by the sound of frogs and crickets outside and the soft snores of the girls inside.

She talked about it with Sarah, too, when they took a walk together. Both told her Billie was right. They'd learned that lesson themselves the hard way. Life was definitely better with God on your side.

Faith supposed it was true. But she couldn't buy it. Not entirely. Still, the idea kind of pulled at her.

Then, the second to the last week of camp, something happened.

Everyone was gathered around a large bonfire, singing, toasting marshmallows, and talking about God. Everyone talked about God in this place. But it wasn't like they were talking about some invisible guy in the sky. They talked about Him like He was real, like He was right there with them. And as Faith sat there next to Sarah, listening to her new friends talk and sing, a kind of ache started inside her. It was like the ache she'd felt when she used to watch Dustin, but this went deeper.

Before she knew it, Faith was crying. Big ol' fat tears ran down her face. Nothing she did could stop them. She tried not to let anyone see. Kind of bent her head down, hiding behind her hair. But she didn't have any Kleenexes, and after about the fourth sniff, Sarah's arm came around her shoulders.

The sobs got serious then. Sarah asked her why she was crying, and Faith told her she didn't know. "It hurts—" she pressed her hand over her heart—"here."

"Faith, God's been calling you for a long time."

She nodded. "I know."

"He loves you."

A hiccupping sob escaped her. "I…I know. But I've been so rotten…"

"It doesn't matter, honey. God loves you, warts and all. He wants you to open your heart to Him, let Him come inside and love you. But it's got to be your choice. You can't get to God because your parents know and love Him. It's you and Him, right here, right now. He's ready to listen if you're ready to talk." She squeezed Faith's shoulders. "Do you want to do that?"

Faith wiped her nose on her sleeve. Did she? Did she want that? The answer rang sure and true deep within.

Yes.

She wanted it more than she'd ever wanted anything in her life.

When Faith nodded, Sarah's smile was like the sun breaking through the clouds. "Okay, then, go ahead and talk with Him."

Faith bowed her head, but nothing came. What could she say? Sure, she'd heard people talk about confessing their sins and all that. And she heard her mom and dad pray all the time.

But she'd never talked to God herself before. Not like this. And sure not out loud.

"Faith?"

She blinked her eyes open, surprised to find tears on her eyelids. "I don't know what to say…"

"I can help you. Or you can talk to Him yourself."

Faith grabbed Sarah's hand, clutching at it like she was lost in the ocean and it was a lifeline. "Help." The word came out in a ragged whisper.

With slow, tender words, Sarah led Faith in a prayer, a prayer of confession, of surrender, of acceptance. And as Faith repeated Sarah's soft words, as she told God how sorry she was for hurting Him and others, how much she needed Him, how much she needed Jesus, how much she loved them and wanted them in her life, it was as though something inside of her—something hard and brittle—cracked, then shattered.

Faith lifted her face to the night sky as shivers traveled through her. She had the oddest sensation…like she was being set free. Like she was a jar that had been crammed full of garbage, and suddenly everything was flowing out of her. And then something else—something wonderful and warm and light, something that made her feel as if she could fly—flowed in, filling her until it overflowed, escaping her in peals of laughter.

So this was what it was like to meet God.

So Jesus really was there.

Oh, she was glad! Gladder than she'd ever been in her life.

She opened her eyes and turned to Sarah, who was crying, too. She threw her arms around her. "Thank you! Thank you so much!"

They laughed and hugged, and then Tammy and the girls from Faith's cabin came to find out what was going on. When they heard about Faith, they squealed and danced around, and there were more hugs and more laughter.

Later that night, as Faith lay in her sleeping bag, she heard someone whisper her name. It was Billie.

"I was right, wasn't I?"

Faith didn't have to ask what she meant. She knew. "Yeah,

you were right. Life with God is a lot better than without him."

"See?" Billie yawned. "I don't care what the others say about you, you're a smart girl."

Faith laughed, snuggling down in her sleeping bag. Her mom had told her over and over how much she needed God, how wonderful His love was. And as she drifted off to sleep, she wasn't sure which amazed her more—how good she felt, or the fact that her mother had actually been right.

"[God] comes to us in brokenness..."

ROBERT FARRAR CAPON

NIGHTTIME.

Faith was learning to love the nights. The darkness made it easy to sit alone and think, and looking up at the stars reminded her of the One who'd put them there. Tonight the sky seemed so full of stars that Faith almost expected them to start spilling out onto the ground.

Hey, God was into miracles. He could make that happen if He wanted to.

"Faith, what are you doing out here?"

She turned. Winnie was walking toward her. Faith shrugged. "I don't know. I got kind of tired of youth group."

"Yeah." Winnie hopped up to sit beside Faith where she perched on the brick wall bordering the walk. "It went kind of long tonight."

Faith leaned her head back, looking up at the sky again. "No, it's not that. I just...do you ever get tired of hearing the same ol' Bible stories over and over?"

Win considered this. "Well, not really. I mean, I see new things in them each time I hear them."

"Oh, yeah? Like what?"

"Well, take tonight's discussion."

Faith shook her head. "I'd like to. Take it and toss it out, that is." At Winnie's silence, Faith turned to her friend. "What?"

"I wondered how you'd feel about the talk tonight. I mean…with you seeing Dustin and everything."

Suddenly anxious to escape this whole topic, Faith pointed to the sky. "Look, there's Orion. And the Big Dipper—"

"Faith—"

"And I think that could be Mars, though I'm not sure."

"Faith!"

"Okay, fine! What? What do you want me to say?"

"Just what you think."

Faith arched a brow. So Winnie wanted to know what she thought? Okay, she asked for it. "I think it's pretty sad when people talk about loving others, but then make judgments like you can't date someone because he doesn't believe the way you do. I mean, what's loving about that?"

Winnie swung her legs back and forth. "It's not that you can't love someone who isn't a believer, Faith. You just aren't supposed to let yourself fall in love with them. That's about obedience."

"To who? The almighty church?"

"No. To God."

"Well, then—" Faith jumped off the wall—"I think God's being kind of stupid."

"Faith!"

She planted her hands on her hips, facing Winnie. "No, I mean it. What does it matter what Dust—I mean, what the guy you love believes? It's not like he takes God's place. You're just marrying him. You're not worshipping him."

Faith waited for the reprimand, but it didn't come. Instead, Winnie sat there, an odd look on her face.

Faith cocked her head. "What?"

"Do you really love Dustin?"

First her dad, now Winnie. Why were people so interested in who she loved? Faith stuck her hands in her jeans pockets and shrugged. "I don't know." She looked up at the stars again. If only she could travel there, millions of light-years away. To a place where it was just her and God and the night.

Where life was simple.

Faith sighed. "All I know is that it seems mean, that's all." She pointed in front of her. "No, you can't like him. Yes, he's okay. He's wearing a cross and carrying a Bible. Oh no! Definitely not him! His hair's too long!"

Winnie giggled, and Faith smiled in response. Winnie jumped down and put her arm around Faith. "I'm glad you're coming to youth group again. And to church. I've missed you."

Faith nodded but didn't say anything. Believing was so much easier when she was at camp. Since she'd come home, things had gotten…weird. Complicated.

Irritating.

"I'm dying to know, Faith. What did your mom say when you told her?"

She pulled back. "About what?"

Winnie punched her shoulder. "About accepting Jesus, you dope! I mean, your mom must have been so excited."

Leave it to Winnie to think of Faith's mom. "I haven't told her."

"What?"

Faith squared off with her friend. "Good grief, Winnie. You don't have to sound like I robbed a bank or kicked a kitten."

Winnie's eyes were wide, and she halted. "How could you not tell your mom? Don't you know how much this will mean to her?"

Faith stared down at the ground. Yes, she knew. And she'd fully intended to tell her mother as soon as she got home. But then…

Well. She didn't.

She'd simply come home.

"Faith?"

She let her confusion slip out on a sigh. "I don't know, Win. I meant to tell her. But then every time I started to, something stopped me."

"What?"

Faith tried to sort it out. "I don't know. I guess…I guess I want Mom to come to me. To ask what's different." Yes. That was it. Even as she talked about it, she realized it was true. "I know you think Mom is just this side of a saint, Win, but you don't live with her. She was always so quick to point out the bad stuff I did, to be mad at me. Now…"

She bit the side of her lip, feelings chasing through her heart. Disappointment. Disillusionment. Hurt. They all seemed to crowd together inside her until she thought her chest might burst.

"Now?"

Winnie's gentle prod seemed to break free the logjam of thoughts. "Now, I wish she'd say what I'm doing right. Because I am doing things right. I'm following what it says in the Bible, being obedient, not talking back. Not swearing. All that stuff. I'm doing it all right." She blinked away the wetness stabbing at her eyes. "And what do I get from Mom? Nothing. Not a word."

She shrugged. "It's like she's waiting for me to mess up again."

"Oh, Faith, I'm sure that's not what she's thinking." She touched Faith's arm, her fingers gentle. "I wish you'd talk to her. Your mom, well, she's a good listener."

Faith stared at the girl standing beside her. "You've talked with my mom?"

"Sure, lots of times."

"When?"

They'd reached the door to go inside, and Winnie pulled it open. "Well, we used to talk once in a while when I saw her in the yard, on my way home from school." Winnie lived a few houses down from Faith. "But we talked the most this summer, while you were gone. I'd stop by to see how she was doing. She'd make me iced tea, and we'd sit and talk and laugh. She tells the greatest stories." Winnie shrugged. "It was nice."

"*It was nice.*"

Faith didn't say a word as she walked past Winnie into the building. She smiled and nodded and went back to the youth group gathering. But deep inside she was screaming.

"*It was nice.*"

Her mother was a good listener.

To Winnie.

She made iced tea.

For Winnie.

She talked and laughed and shared "great" stories.

With Winnie.

"*It was nice.*"

Yeah, Faith supposed it would be. But she doubted she'd ever find out for herself. Because now she understood. Her mom liked everyone and everything.

Except her.

Anne was slipping her key into the front door when she heard the phone ringing. Scrambling to get inside without dropping any of her packages, she shoved the door open and rushed to the kitchen.

"Keep ringing..."

She dumped her packages on the table, muttering to herself when one of them slid off the edge and fell to the floor. She grabbed for the phone. "Hello?"

"Hi, Mrs. Bennett. It's Sarah McMannis. Is Faith home yet?"

As battling emotions swept her, Anne went to pick up the bag that had fallen on the floor. Faith returned from camp several weeks ago so different, at least in the way she treated Anne. The anger and rebellion seemed to have disappeared. Though Faith didn't talk about it, Anne knew the change was due, in large part, to Sarah.

Anne told herself over and over she should be grateful to Sarah; instead she'd finally admitted she was jealous. Jealous of the fact that Sarah had been able to reach Faith when Anne couldn't. Jealous Faith was far more interested in talking with Sarah than in talking with her own mother.

Ever since that revelation, Anne was careful to use a neutral tone of voice with Sarah, a tone that gave away nothing of her inner struggle. "No, Faith's not home yet. She said she'd be late because she was helping tutor a couple of kids in English."

"Tutoring, huh? That's great. I guess it really took, didn't it?"

Anne frowned. "What took?"

"You know, Faith's conversion. At camp."

Anne's mouth went dry. Her heart pounded. She put her hand on the back of a chair and lowered herself into it. "Her…her conversion?"

There was a moment's silence. "Didn't Faith tell you what happened at camp?"

All Anne could manage was a ragged whisper. "No."

"Mrs. Bennett, Faith accepted Christ at camp."

Anne's eyes drifted shut. She should be thrilled. Ecstatic. Instead, she was almost shaking from the pain screaming through her. Faith had accepted Christ? She'd made the most important, wonderful decision of her life…and she hadn't breathed a word of the experience to Anne.

Surely Faith knew how much it would mean to her to hear what had happened. Surely Faith realized how important God and faith in Christ were to Anne. Hadn't she talked about it from the time Faith was a baby? Hadn't she read Faith Bible stories, sung her songs and hymns? Hadn't they prayed together from the time Faith was old enough to understand talking to God?

A sob caught in Anne's throat.

Hadn't she begged Faith, these last few years, to let God in? And now, when she'd finally done exactly that, she did it in silence. Without telling her mother.

Or her father, Anne realized. If Faith had told Jared about it, he would have said something.

"Mrs. Bennett, I'm sorry."

Sarah's quiet compassion almost freed the tears Anne was holding back. But she shored up her resistance and straightened. "It's okay, Sarah. I'm glad to know this happened—"

You're lying. You're angry. Hurt. Far from glad.

"—and thank you for your part in helping my daughter. I appreciate you."

Liar. You resent her.

"Okay…you're welcome."

Anne didn't give Sarah a chance to ask anything further. She told her she'd have Faith call when she got home and hung up.

She didn't tell me. Anne sat there, staring at the table, her hand still on the receiver. *My own daughter didn't tell me about accepting Christ.* Her eyes closed, but that didn't hold back the hot tears, the wracking sobs.

For Faith to have kept this from her could only mean one thing.

She must hate me. All these times she's said so, I thought it was words, teenage angst. Confusing emotions tormented her, tore at her heart. *But God…she must really mean it.*

My daughter hates me.

Images flooded Anne's mind, snapshots of their family through the years accompanied a by vivid, crystal-clear soundtrack. She didn't know how long she sat there, but it was long enough. For as she watched the replay in her mind, she could no longer deny the truth.

She'd done something no mother should ever do. Something *her* mother had never done. Wouldn't have done. *Couldn't* have done.

She'd let her daughter down.

Not intentionally. Never intentionally. But that didn't make it any better. Intentional or not, the end result was the same. Time after time, she hadn't been the kind of mother—no, the kind of *person*—she needed to be. As though they'd lodged in some dark corner of her mind, waiting for this moment, Faith's complaints against her came rushing back, and Anne considered them, one by one.

"You never want to spend time with me anymore. All you want to do is sit like a lump and watch TV. Or sleep. That's what matters most to you."

For once, Anne didn't try to defend herself. She took in the words, absorbed them, and acknowledged the facts. Faith was right. And Anne was…

Guilty.

"You want me to be like you, not like me."

Guilty.

"You want to choose my friends instead of trusting me to do it."

Guilty.

"You tell me I have to go to church, but half the time you don't go anymore."

Guilty.

"You never listen to me. You don't care what I think. You want to tell me what you think is right."

Guilty on all charges, and more besides. Anne leaned her elbows on the table, folded her hands, and pressed her knuckles to her stinging eyes. *God...God, forgive me.*

She slipped from the chair, going to her knees beside it. And there, in the kitchen, where she and Faith as a toddler had so often laughed and delighted in each other's company...there, where Faith as a budding preteen had perched on the counter to share her day...there, where her angry almost-stranger daughter and she so often waged war...

There, in the quiet of the room, Anne laid her heart out before her Lord.

"Jesus, all these years. All this time, I thought I was serving You. Living for You. And now...now I see I was living for me. I'm so sorry. For the anger. The jealousy. The resentment—even toward the woman You sent to bring my baby to Your side!—God, forgive me."

She opened her hands, holding them out in front of her. "Help me, Lord. Release me from the prison of self, and let me walk in Your freedom, Your grace. Help me change, Father. Help me let go of what I want and look to You, to live for what You want. Let me be the kind of mother Faith deserves. She's such a precious, tender girl. And I've been so wrong—"

Emotion stole the words from her, trapping them in her tight throat. But she prayed on, in her heart, begging God to touch her, to show her how to love others as He loved her—unconditionally.

And most of all, she prayed it wasn't too late.

Faith had settled at her desk in her room, her Bible out in front of her, when she heard a light knock on the door. She leaned back in the chair. "Come in."

The door opened, and her mother peeked around it. "May I come in?"

"Oh. Sure."

Mom made her way to Faith's bed and sat down. She folded her hands in her lap, and Faith had the distinct feeling she was nervous.

Great. What did I do now?

"Faith, sweetie, I need to talk with you—"

Faith swallowed. *Whatever it was, God. I didn't mean to do it. I mean, how could I? I don't even remember it.*

"To apologize."

The words hung there, suspended in silence, as Faith stared at her mother. "I—you...excuse me?"

Stains of scarlet appeared on her mother's cheeks. "Oh, sweetie, I'm so sorry. Most of all that I haven't said that more." Mom looked down at her hands. "I've been doing a lot of thinking. Praying. And I've...God has shown me some things. Most of all that I haven't been the kind of mother I should have been."

Faith sat there, too stunned to do more than nod. Then, realizing that might seem as though she were agreeing with her mom, she shook her head. "No, wait. I wasn't agreeing. I mean, well, I do, kind of. But not really."

Her mother's laughter eased Faith's tension, and she chuckled. She rose to sit on the bed beside her mother. "I'm sorry, Mom. I just...you caught me by surprise. That's all."

"I know, honey." She took Faith's hand. "There's a lot I need to say to you, but it's going to take time. Mostly I wanted to tell you I love you." Then she cupped Faith's cheek. "I always have, even when things were hard. You're precious to me, sweetie."

The words washed over Faith like an anointing oil, seeping deep into her heart, filling the places that had felt empty for so long. She gripped her mother's hand. "I love you, too, Mommy."

Her mom pulled her close and held her. Faith wasn't sure how long they sat there, but she didn't care. She would have been happy if it had gone on forever.

After a while her mom kissed Faith's forehead and stood. "Well, I'd better leave you to your study." She glanced at the desk. Faith waited for the raised brows, the exclamation of surprise and excitement. But instead, her mom smiled.

"Romans. It's a good book."

Her mom was full of surprises tonight. "Yeah, I think it is. I mean, I haven't read much of it, but I like what I've read."

Her mom was almost out the door when she hesitated. "Hey, you know I go to a women's Bible study every week with some of the gals from church?"

"Yeah."

"Would you like to come with me?"

Faith tried to answer, but her throat was too crowded with the emotions surging through her. She managed a nod.

"Great. Thursday night, okay?"

"Okay."

Long after her mom left, Faith sat there, basking in the warmth of the smile that had covered her mother's face.

A smile of pure love.

sixteen

"Anyone complaining he was led astray by others is admitting he has no mind of his own."

VERNON HOWARD

FAITH PULLED HER LOCKER OPEN, STRUGGLING TO balance the pile of books in one hand. She almost made it, too. Almost. But the books teetered one way, then another, and finally cascaded to the floor with a crash that drew curious looks from the kids rushing by in the hallway.

"Great. Just great." Faith knelt to gather her things together, biting her lip against the frustrated tears that wanted to take over. "The perfect crummy end to a perfectly crummy day."

She paused in midreach. "Oh man..." Her breath came out on a heavy sigh. Her old friend was back. Sarcasm. She hadn't let it out to play in months.

That was one of the first things Sarah urged her to give up. "You know what sarcasm is, don't you?" she'd said one afternoon as they were hiking.

Faith plucked several pine needles from a tree as she passed it, crushing them between her fingers and setting the pungent fragrance free. "Sure, it's being funny."

"No, it's not. Sarcasm isn't funny at all. It's anger disguised as humor, and it's a tool for hurting." Sarah planted her hands on a fallen tree in the path and vaulted over it, landing with a light plop on the ground. She waited for Faith to do the same. "Problem is, you're too good at it."

Faith cocked her head. "At sarcasm?"

"Absolutely." Sarah hitched up her pack as they started walking again. "You've got a quick wit—which is good—and a quick tongue—which isn't. Not when it comes to sarcasm, anyway. I've seen you use words to cut someone off at the knees." She angled a look at Faith. "And believe me, that old bit about sticks and stones and words not hurting? It's bogus. Words hurt plenty."

It took a while for Faith to see Sarah's point, but finally she did. By the end of the summer, she'd done it. Sarcasm was a thing of the past. It hadn't been easy, not by a long shot. But she'd made a concerted effort to clamp her mouth shut whenever she was about to say something sarcastic. At first, she was shutting her mouth every few minutes. But soon it became a habit to keep her sarcastic thoughts to herself. And then, much to Faith's surprise, even the thoughts hadn't come nearly so often.

Until today. A steady stream of sarcastic thoughts had run through her mind since first period. And now they'd escaped into their favorite tool: words.

Faith waited for the surge of guilt she was sure would come. And waited.

Nothing.

No, that wasn't quite true. She did feel a slight nudge. A niggling that she was doing something she shouldn't.

And she felt something else, too. Something far stronger.

Good. She felt good. Letting her frustration out like that plain felt good.

Faith grabbed another book and slammed it on the pile she was making. Sarah would be disappointed in her. But what was she supposed to do? It had been a truly rotten day.

"I tried, Sarah. I really did."

She shook her head at the whispered comment. Talking to someone who wasn't there. She was really losing it. But it was true. She'd been trying all week to follow Sarah's lead, to do things the way Sarah wanted her to do them. But every time she sat down to read her Bible, she'd look up and find Trista and her group watching her. She'd shoved another book over the Bible, so they couldn't know what she was reading.

Still, it bugged her.

Then there was Dustin. Since she got back from camp, things had been far from great between the two of them. Dustin didn't like the changes she was making. Every time Faith tried to tell him about the summer, about Sarah and all Faith had learned from her, he shrugged her off. Changed the subject. Threw his arm around her shoulders and tugged her close.

"I don't care what you did there, sweet thing. All I care is that you're finally back *here*. Where you belong." He smiled down at her. "With me."

She'd wanted to say more, to make him understand. Instead, each time she let it drop. She still wasn't quite sure why.

Sure you are. You didn't want him getting mad at you. Or thinking you're some kind of religious freak.

It was true. She could still see the look in Dustin's eyes when she started talking about Sarah and God. He hadn't wanted to hear it. Not then...and not today.

Stupid, stupid, stupid!

She slammed another book on top of the pile. She still couldn't believe she'd been so stupid today. After lunch, she'd gone out to the back of the school, looking for Dustin. He was there with his buddies, smoking and talking. Taking a deep breath, Faith went to slip her arm in his.

He looked down at her, but he didn't smile. "Hey."

That was it. "Hey." Not even his usual "Hey, babe." Just..."Hey." Faith had never been all that crazy about being called *babe*, but suddenly she wanted him to do so. Wanted it more than she'd wanted anything in a long time.

If he called her *babe*, that would mean he still liked her.

She stared down at the toes of her shoes. "So...can we talk?"

"Sure." Dustin took a drag on his cigarette and blew a stream of smoke. "Go for it."

She glanced at the other boys. "Privately."

Dustin stared straight ahead, not saying anything. With each passing second, Faith felt smaller and smaller. Just when she thought she couldn't stand it another second, he shot his pals a look and jerked his head toward the school. They got the message.

As they walked away, Faith tried to sort through what she wanted to say. *Please...please, let this go well.* Surely God would listen. Surely He wanted Dustin to understand. Maybe even wanted to use her to help Dustin accept Him.

Faith's eyes widened at the thought. *That would be so great, God.* Then they could be together, and her mom couldn't complai—

"So?"

She jumped a little, then looked at Dustin. "Well, I wanted to tell you...to talk with you about...you know, this summer."

"You already told me."

Faith shook her head. "No. Not really. Dustin, something happened to me this summer. Something...really cool."

Unfortunately, those last two words came out all shaky and tense. Dustin's sideways glance told her it wasn't the most convincing she'd ever sounded. She wiped her sweaty palms on her skirt.

"Does this have to do with that God-stuff again?"

She hadn't expected him to go on the offensive. She blinked, her mouth suddenly dry. "Well, yeah. Kinda. I mean, yeah..." She was so dry her lips were sticking to her teeth. She ran her tongue over her teeth, forcing a quick swallow.

"You telling me you got religion this summer?"

Searing heat filled Faith's face, then drained away, leaving her cold. Shivering. "No, Dustin. Come on. I'm not talking about *religion*—"

He flicked his cigarette away, watching it arc into the air. "Good. One thing I don't need is a preacher." He pulled a new cigarette from his pocket and lit it, then held the pack out to her. She looked down at it.

She could use a smoke. Man, she could use one. But she'd promised Sarah she would give them up. Along with the sarcasm. And swearing. And all the stuff that used to feel so good—

Faith pulled her eyes from the cigarettes and shook her head.

Dustin's eyes narrowed. "You suddenly too good to smoke with me, babe?"

"No, it's not that." Faith looked away. She wanted to cry. Why wasn't God making this easier? "I promised someone—"

"Someone more important than me?"

"Well, yes." Faith's eyes widened at what she said. Her heart sank at the sudden color surging into Dustin's face. "I mean—no! Of course not."

The conversation went straight downhill from there. They'd ended up arguing. Yelling. Finally Dustin told her to get lost. How did he say it? "Take your religious garbage and go find someone who cares."

Yeah. That was it. And the memory of the words hurt almost as much as when he'd said them.

Gritting her teeth against new tears, Faith let out a muttered oath. She picked up another book and plunked it down, accompanying the action with another choice obscenity.

Amazing how good some words felt when you were really, royally steamed.

She grabbed the armful of books and stood, carried them to her still-open locker, and jammed them inside. They fell into a pile, and one slid out onto the floor. Faith muttered under her breath, grabbed it, and flung it back inside.

"Now that's what I call hitting the books."

She spun to find Trista and two of her buddies standing behind her. "Oh, hi."

Trista's finely plucked brows arched. "Don't sound so excited." Before Faith could reply, she looked at the floor. "You missed one."

Faith looked down and almost swallowed her teeth. *Oh no...don't let her notice. Don't let her—*

"Well, well, looky here." Trista leaned down and grabbed

Faith's Bible off the floor. She held it between her forefinger and thumb, the way Faith's mom held limp, dead lettuce she was tossing out. "A Bible?" Trista's smirking gaze drifted from the Bible to Faith. "You carry a *Bible* to school?"

"It's for a class."

Faith couldn't believe she'd said that. Couldn't believe she'd lied.

Oh yeah, Sarah would be really proud now.

Trista wasn't buying it. "Ain't no class in this school that teaches Bible, and you know it."

Faith snatched the book from Trista and tossed it into her locker, slamming the door shut. "Yeah. Whatever." She turned to leave, but Trista stood there, blocking her way.

"So what? You gonna be on TV?" She glanced at the two girls flanking her and grinned. "You gonna start asking us for money to feed orphans?"

As the girls giggled, Faith blinked back the tears burning her eyes. She wasn't going to cry. No way. Trista would nail her to the wall if she cried. Calling on all her reserves, she pulled herself to her full height, crossed her arms in front on her, and put on her best smirk.

"Ask you? For money? Get real, Trista. All I need to do is look at your clothes to know you can't afford to feed yourself, let alone a bunch of orphans."

The giggling stopped, and Trista's friends stared at Faith, mouths agape. For a moment, Trista looked as if she was going to let Faith have it. Faith braced herself, waiting.

But what came wasn't a punch. It was a slow smile, easing its way across Trista's face. "So, you haven't gone all Goody Two-shoes on us, huh?"

Faith didn't have to fake the snort. It rushed out of her, a mixture of relief and self-denigration.

Goody Two-shoes? Hardly.

She'd thought she was. Thought she could be like Sarah. Now she knew better. She wasn't anything like Sarah. Not a bit.

Trista reached out to link her arm with Faith's. "Glad to hear it." Her gaze bored into Faith, as though she was trying to read her soul. "Dustin said you were…being weird."

Faith fell into step with Trista, heading for the exit. "Yeah, well, not anymore." Something deep inside her ached as she said the words. For one horrifying moment Faith thought she would start bawling right there, but she tossed her head and forced herself to keep walking.

Away from her locker.

Away from the book it hid.

And no matter how much that ache inside tugged at her, crying out for her to turn around, to stop, she refused to give in.

She was done with that book. Done with Sarah and all her talk about God. It had sounded good at camp, but this wasn't camp. It was real life.

And in real life, what you needed wasn't God.

It was friends. The right kind of friends. Friends who kept you from getting hurt. And from doing stupid things.

Like thinking you could change.

Anne leaned in the doorway of the living room.

"You remember tonight is my Bible study night?"

Jared lowered the paper and winked. "I remember." He put on a sad puppy dog face. "Tonight is the night you abandon me."

"Poor baby." Anne crooned her insincerity. "It's terrible how I make you order in pizza once a week."

"Nope." Jared snapped the paper. "Tonight's going to be Chinese."

"Yum. Save me an egg roll. And save Faith some sweet-and-sour chicken." But Anne didn't have time to talk longer. She and Faith were going to be late if they didn't hurry. She went to tap on Faith's door. "Faith?"

No response.

She tapped again. "Faith? Come on, sweetie."

"She's gone, Annie."

Anne turned a questioning look to Jared. "Gone?" The sympathetic regret on his features made her heart plummet.

"Gone." She looked down at the floor. "When?"

"About fifteen minutes ago."

Well, maybe she was going to meet Anne—

"She said she and Trista were going to a movie."

Ah.

Jared lay his hand on her arm. "I'm sorry, hon."

The hurt crawling through her was enough to make her want to stay home, but she was taking the refreshments. With a quick nod to Jared, she gathered her things and hurried out the door.

Chattering women's voices, reminding Anne of an aviary full of birds at feeding time, filled Marge Clark's living room.

Normally, she joined in the Bible study's conversations. Tonight...she didn't have the heart. Or the energy.

Actually, she was exhausted.

All evening something had been nudging her to ask the women for prayer. To tell them what was happening with Faith, to seek their counsel and guidance. But every time she tried to open her mouth, the words caught in her throat.

What would they *think* of her?

Many of them knew, of course, that there had been problems. Anne had asked for prayer a few times over the last few years. No specifics, of course, just, "Please pray for my family. We're having a little trouble with Faith."

A little trouble. Talk about putting a spin on something!

Marge Clark and her sister-in-law, Anita, had never been fooled. They'd known Anne for nearly twenty years. They'd watched Faith grow from infancy. Their children had gone to Sunday school together, played together, had birthday parties together. They'd cornered Anne, asking her what was really going on. And she told them. It had been such a relief to tell someone.

So why couldn't she do that tonight?

Because they've prayed for us already. They *had* to be sick of hearing about Anne's problems, listening to her litany of misery. So Anne sat through the study, pushing down the urge when it popped up again. And again. And again.

Now, thankfully, the Bible study was over. While the others gathered their things, talking away as they readied to leave, Anne slipped into the kitchen to wash coffee mugs. Let the gang clear out, then she'd grab her cookie plate and go home.

She heard the front door close and seized the hand towel. Time to make her escape. But suddenly she was flanked on one side by Marge, and on the other by Anita. The two women stood there, arms crossed, pinning Anne with insistent looks.

"Okay, Anne. Time's up. Spill."

She felt like a prison escapee caught with a shovel in the tunnel! She should have known she couldn't keep her pain from these two. She folded and hung up the hand towel.

Anita shooed her hands away. "For heaven's sake, forget the towel! What's up?"

No more stalling. *Okay, Lord. You win.* "It's Faith."

Marge nodded. "Well, we figured that. So what happened?"

"First—" Anita took Anne's arm and ushered her toward the living room—"let's get comfortable." She studied Anne's face as they sat. "I have a feeling this is going to take a while."

Anne settled in the middle of the couch; Anita and Marge sat on either side of her. Grabbing one of the soft, decorative pillows, Anne hugged it to her.

Marge eyed the pillow. "I have one of the kid's old security blankets in a trunk, if you'd like it."

"Hush!" Anita patted Anne's arm. "Ignore her. Now, start talking."

The laughter at the two women's teasing died, and Anne finally gave in. She told them everything. All the struggles. Her battle with the diabetes. Her fatigue. Her hurt when she found out Faith had accepted Christ and not told her. Her jealousy. How God confronted her, revealing her own failures and weaknesses. Her hope after the wonderful talk with Faith.

And then, tonight.

"I wish I understood what was going on in her mind. One minute she seems to be back on the right track, then boom!

She does something like this." Anne gripped the pillow. "What am I doing wrong?"

"Maybe it's not about you."

Anne frowned at Anita's soft words. But Marge was nodding. "I think that's true. I think it's more about Faith herself than about you, Anne."

"I'm not sure I understand."

Anita took Anne's hand. "I've known Faith all her life. And I'd be willing to bet she's feeling some of the same things you are. Confused. Rejected. Even like she does everything wrong."

"Insecure," Marge added, and Anne sat back.

Insecure? Faith? "But she's so confident! Faith isn't afraid of anything."

"Actually—" Anita's words came out slow and thoughtful—"I get the sense she's afraid of lots of things. Especially not being liked."

Her daughter? The social butterfly? Not liked? "By *whom*?"

"By anyone," Marge said, "and everyone. The kids at school. The teachers. The cool crowd."

"You. And Jared."

Marge built on Anita's comments. "Maybe even God."

Anne let their words roll around in her mind and heart. Let them penetrate deep, testing them. And like the beam of a flashlight cutting through the night, understanding dawned.

They were right. And that realization brought a wave of regret and sorrow crashing down on her. Tears sprang to her eyes, overflowing. Anita grabbed a tissue and handed it to her.

"So what do I do?" Anne crumpled the tissue in her hand. "I've told Faith how much I love her, but if she doesn't believe me, what can I do?"

"You go ahead and cry." Anita handed her another tissue. "And then we fix what's wrong."

Anne blew her nose. "How on earth do we do *that*?"

Marge patted her arm, her lips lifting in a small, warm smile. "You know, Anne, you're a wise lady most of the time. But when it comes to your daughter, you seem to forget the basics."

The basics? Anne looked from one woman to the other, then her eyes widened.

Oh.

The basics.

She shook her head. What a fool she could be sometimes. “We pray.”

“See there?” Anita looked around Anne to grin at Marge. “I *told* you she was smarter than she looked.”

Anne lifted the pillow and delivered a light, albeit much-deserved, swat to the back of Anita’s head.

The women laughed, and Anne gripped their hands. “Thank you.”

They smiled.

“That’s what friends are for, Anne.”

Marge’s words sunk deep into her heart. That’s exactly what friends were for. And she would take extra time tonight thanking God for these two friends in particular.

And for not letting her escape as she’d planned. He really did know best, after all.

Among Thorns

"Other seed fell among thorns that shot up and choked out the tender blades so that it produced no grain.... The thorny ground represents those who hear and accept the Good News, but all too quickly the message is crowded out by the cares of this life, the lure of wealth, and the desire for nice things, so no crop is produced."

MARK 4:7, 18–19

seventeen

"God...plants his footsteps in the sea and rides upon the storm."

WILLIAM COWPER

"WOULD YOU GET OUT OF MY WAY, YOU MORON?"

The kid in front of Trista scrambled to comply.

"Freshmen. What a waste of space."

Faith laughed as they made their way down the steps, heading for the buses. "Hey, they gotta be someplace."

"So long as it's not around me." Trista tossed her hair back, gave a smug smile, and planted one hand on her hip. "That particular place is reserved only for the most deserving."

"Hmm." Faith had seen Trista's *most deserving*, and she wasn't impressed. Why was it Trista always gravitated toward losers?

"So we going to your place tonight?"

Faith shrugged, falling into the line forming at the bus stop. "I don't know. My mom's being a pain about you coming over all the time."

"So tell her to take a pill."

Faith snorted. "Believe me, I have. But—oh *crud*!"

"What?" Trista pulled a bottle of nail polish from her purse and started touching up her nails.

"I left my jacket in my locker."

Trista shrugged. "So? It's an ugly jacket."

Faith made a face at her. "It's not ugly, and it's got my keys in it. Save me a seat, okay?" Without waiting for Trista's response, she made a dash back down the sidewalk, up the concrete stairs, and into the school.

In her rush, she had to work her locker combination three times. When she finally pulled her locker open, it was with a muffled obscenity.

"Faith?"

She hesitated, her hand on her jacket, and closed her eyes. Wonderful. Just what she needed. Winnie the Saint to catch her swearing. She'd probably run to tell Faith's mom what a slug Faith was.

She grabbed her jacket and slammed the locker. Spinning on her heel, she made to push past Winnie as though she hadn't heard her speak. But Winnie's hand shot out and grabbed Faith's arm, stopping her cold. Faith looked down at Winnie's hand, then up into her face. "What are you doing?"

"Actually, that's what I was wondering. What are *you* doing?"

She looked down at Winnie's hand again. "Waiting for you to get your hand off me?" The sarcasm was back in full force now, more honed than ever.

Winnie's hand slid away. "I wanted to talk with you for a minute, okay?"

"Fine." Faith cast a glance to the ceiling. "Whatever." She put on her best say-what-you-gotta-say-and-make-it-fast face.

Winnie didn't seem to notice. She studied Faith for a moment. "You've really changed."

Another shrug. "People change, Win. That's life."

She gave a slow nod. "You ever think about what you're doing?"

Faith narrowed her eyes. What was *this* about? "Meaning?"

"The way you treat some of the kids, the way you talk about your mom—"

Faith crossed her arms. "You got a point, *Winola*?"

She'd expected Winnie to back off, to recoil from the force

in her tone. But the other girl didn't budge. She met her glare with an expression Faith couldn't quite understand.

Compassion. It touched Winnie's features, reaching out to Faith with an offer of cooling water on a hot, scorching day.

"I want to help you, Faith."

She stepped back. "Help me what? Miss my bus? I don't have time for this—"

"For me, you mean."

Faith stopped. She met Winnie's gaze, and images flitted through her mind—Winnie in grade school on the playground...Winnie laughing and teasing her...Winnie encouraging her when Trista hurt her feelings...

"You don't have time for me. Not anymore."

An unfamiliar emotion twisted in Faith's gut. She bit her lip and looked away. "Look, Win—"

"No, it's okay. I understand."

Faith looked back at her—and she had the oddest feeling Winnie did understand. Everything.

"You're hanging out with Trista, and that's your choice."

"Listen, just because you don't like Trista—"

Winnie held up a hand, halting the words, leaving them crowded on the tip of Faith's tongue. "This isn't about Trista and me. It's about you. You came back from the summer...different. Happy. You found what really mattered."

Faith swallowed hard. *Don't let her see she's getting to you.* "What *you* think mattered. Not me."

This time it was Winnie who shrugged. "I'm telling you what I saw. And it was good. Like you were finding out who you really are instead of who Trista says you should be."

"Lay off Trista. Good night, Win. What makes you think you need to fix everything and everyone? Trista's my friend. I like her. As she is."

Winnie glanced down, then sighed and met Faith's gaze. "Fair enough. I won't say anything else about her. I wanted you to know I'm still here. I care about you. And if you ever need to talk, well...I'm here."

Faith stood there, staring. She tried to say something, but her usually glib tongue couldn't find any words.

Winnie smiled, and though it seemed kind of sad, it was clearly sincere. "Take care of yourself. Thanks for being my friend for so many years." With that, she turned and walked away, shoulders straight, head held high.

Two words came to Faith's mind, words she'd never used in her life, words her mother used...words that suddenly made sense.

Class act.

Suddenly uncomfortable, Faith made her way to the bus stop, slipping into line behind Trista. The boy behind her started to protest, but one glare from Trista shut him up.

"*Thanks for being my friend for so many years...*"

Faith gripped her jacket. Why would Winnie say that?

"What did *she* want?"

Faith started. "Who?"

"Winnie the Wimp." Trista smirked. "I saw her talking to you. Talk about a total loser—"

Trista went on, ragging on Winnie, her words caustic and crass. But Faith wasn't listening, not really. Not to Trista. No, the voice she heard was entirely different.

"*Thanks for being my friend for so many years... Thanks for being my friend for so many years...*"

But what got to Faith wasn't *what* Winnie said. It was the way she said it. There'd been no resentment, no anger.

No, Faith heard only one thing in Winnie's tone as she spoke those words, one thing that made no sense whatsoever.

One thing that shook her to the core.

Love.

"Hey, hon. If you need me, I'll be in my shop."

Anne looked up from the sink full of dishes she was washing, stretching her aching back. Jared saw the movement and pressed his warm palm to the base of her spine.

"Hurting again?"

"Always."

"Did you talk with the doctor about it?"

Anne plopped her hand in the fluffy soapsuds. "He said it's

the extra weight. It makes me stand wrong, and that makes my back hurt."

Jared slid his arms around her. "I'm sorry, hon. I wish I could help."

She leaned back against him, batting her eyes at him. "You could always take over washing dishes."

He chuckled and gave her a peck on the tip of her nose. "Keep dreamin', Annie. Keep dreamin'."

"Fine, leave me in my misery." She infused her tone with as much woe-is-me as she could muster. "I slave all day, working at the junior high, making sure kids get a good education, and then I come home and slave all night…" She glanced at him to see if it was working.

No such luck.

He just stood there, pretending he was playing a violin.

She flicked soapsuds at him. "You're all heart, Bennett. You said you're going to work in the shop?"

"For a while." He grinned. "I've got a slave driver of a wife who expects me to fix stuff around this place."

She shooed him away, smiling as he closed the kitchen door behind him. No sooner had he left than the front door slammed.

Faith was home. Oh, joy. And only a half hour late.

Anne steeled herself, hating that she felt the need to do so with her own daughter. Ever since the night a couple of months ago when Faith left rather than attend Bible study with Anne, she'd grown increasingly hostile. Anne wasn't sure why.

She had spent hours talking with Jared about it. Had talked with Susan, who also worked at the junior high now and had years of experience dealing with problem kids. Had prayed with Marge and Anita, asking God for wisdom. Always, the answer was the same.

"*A soft answer turns away wrath.*"

And so Anne did her best to be soft. Understanding. Patient. She figured, as hard as it was, it had to be refining her.

If it didn't kill her first.

Faith came breezing into the kitchen a few seconds later, and Anne turned to face her. "Hi, sweetheart."

Faith didn't even look at her. She went to pull the fridge open and rummage.

"So, no friends with you today?"

"Do you *see* any friends with me?"

Anne's fingers drew into a fist. "Faith—"

She emerged from the fridge, chomping on a carrot stick. "Well, then, unless they've turned invisible—" Faith swept an exaggerated looked from side to side—"which isn't going to happen, no matter how much you want it to, they're not with me today. That okay with you?"

Anne's jaw ached from grinding her teeth. "Enough with the sarcasm, Faith. I asked a simple question—"

"Oh, so now *simple* is a synonym for *stupid*?"

That almost undid Anne. Faith had never been this out-and-out hateful before. *Soft answer, my Aunt Fanny!* She opened her mouth to let Faith have it, but she didn't get the chance.

"That's *enough*!"

Anne and her daughter both spun to look behind them. Jared stood there, red creeping up his neck, a storm cloud brewing on his brow. Anne glanced back at Faith. The girl's features were pale as she stared at her father.

"Daddy. Where—?"

"I was outside the door, young lady." Jared met Anne's questioning gaze. "I remembered I'd bought some more duct tape and left it on the counter." Anne glanced at the counter. A bag from the hardware store lay there. "I was coming in the door when I heard what Faith said." He pinned his daughter with a glare. "Every rotten thing you said to your mother."

Faith scowled. "Of course, you don't say anything about the way she rides me. Gives me the fifth degree anytime I come in the house."

Before Anne could deny the accusation, Jared stepped forward. "Because that's not true. I heard the whole thing, Faith. Your mother was making conversation, trying to be nice. To which you responded with undeserved insults. And that, young lady will *not* happen again. Underst—"

Jared stopped and stared at his daughter. Anne followed his gaze, and her mouth dropped open. She'd been so focused on Faith's words, on her face, that she hadn't realized what Faith was wearing. Where were the jeans and T-shirt she'd had on when she left that morning? And where on *earth* did she find that getup? A cropped, filmy top over a black bra? A miniskirt that majored on mini and minored on skirt?

"*What* in the bald-headed dog snot are you wearing?"

Anne couldn't have put it better.

The sullen expression that washed over their daughter's face was all too familiar to Anne—and sent a chill raging through her. She'd seen that same look before. Time after miserable time. On Trista's face.

"They're called clothes."

Jared's brows shot up, and he took a step toward Faith. "I beg your pardon?"

She backtracked, clearly realizing she'd used the wrong tone on the wrong parent. "It's nothing, Daddy." She was all sweetness and sugar now. The adoring little girl. Anne wanted to throw something at her. "It's the style." She went up on her tiptoes to kiss her father's cheek—a ploy that never failed, when she was little, to turn Jared into putty—but the kiss missed its mark. Didn't even get close.

Jared held her away from him like a viper about to sink its fangs into his throat.

Hurt sparked in Faith's eyes, and Anne ached for her. She and Jared had always shared such a special relationship. Didn't she realize her actions, her poisonous words, were slowly destroying it?

Jared looked at Anne, and the anguish in his eyes made her want to weep. He clenched his jaw, then nodded and let his hands fall away from their daughter.

Anne turned to Faith. "We're concerned, sweetie. We've never seen you wearing anything like—like this."

"If I had," Jared ground out, "you never would have been allowed out of the house."

Faith trembled, rubbing her arms. "*Everyone's* wearing this! What do you want me to dress like? Some kind of nerd?"

"Nerd?" Jared's hands clenched at his sides. "Is that what this is about? Being popular?"

Faith's chin lifted. "Is there something wrong with that?"

"There is if you make popularity your god."

"Oh, come on, Daddy. That's not true!"

"No? I think you need to take another look at yourself, Faith. You used to be a beautiful girl, a *sweet* girl. You used to want to honor God with your actions and words." He cast a scathing look at her outfit. "But there's no honor in what you're wearing right now. You're telling everyone who sees you that you couldn't care less about God, about your family. About yourself."

Faith hugged herself, as though her arms could protect her from her father's hard words. "People like the way I look."

"*What* people?"

"The *right* people!"

"Faith, don't you see what you're doing to yourself?" Jared sounded desperate. "How can you sell your self-respect for something as empty and meaningless as being accepted by the in crowd?"

"I'm not selling myself to anyone!"

Anne held out her hands. "But you are. Dressing that way, it's wrong, Faith. There's no way we could like the way those clothes make you look."

She glared at Anne. "Then don't look."

"You will *not* take that tone with your mother."

Anne had always thought Jared's patience was unending. Now she knew better. He was clearly about to lose it.

"You speak to her with *respect*."

"Right!" Faith threw the carrot she'd been holding at the sink. It bounced off the counter and spun onto the floor. "I have to *show* respect, but I don't *get* it."

"Faith!"

Anne heard the warning in Jared's tone, but Faith was on a roll. "Faith, fix your hair. Faith, change your clothes. Faith, do the dishes. Do this, do that!" She stomped around the kitchen. "Why am I the only one around here who does any work?"

She pointed at Anne. "*She* comes home from work and falls asleep in her chair or on the couch." She crossed her arms over her heaving chest. "I'm not your daughter, I'm your *slave*.

At least you could have had more kids so I'd have someone to help me!"

Anne had had enough. More than enough. Ten times more than enough. "You need to take a break and calm down."

Faith made an exaggerated bow. "Yes, Master. Whatever you say, Master."

"Faith Adelle, I swear—"

A harsh laugh cut through the room. "No, you don't. You never do. You're too *holy*."

"That's *it*!"

Faith shrank back against the wall, staring at her father. Anne understood the sudden alarm on her daughter's face. Faith had never seen her father so angry—but then, neither had Anne. Suddenly the rebel vanished as acute remorse washed over the girl's features. Anne had the fleeting impression even Faith was shocked at how far she'd gone this time.

And suddenly, there, standing in front of them, was their little girl, the Faith they used to know, a daughter who adored her father and was brokenhearted at a harsh word from him.

Anne's heart constricted, and she put her arms around her daughter. "Faith…"

"Daddy, I'm sor—"

Jared put up a hand, halting both Faith and Anne. "Go to your room, Faith."

"But Daddy—"

The cold, cutting glare he gave their daughter sent shock fluttering through Anne. As did the tone of his voice. Hard. Rigid. Utterly void of warmth. "I don't want to hear it. Right now, all I want is for you to go to your room before I say something we'll both regret."

Faith looked from her father to Anne, tears balancing on her lashes, lips trembling. "Mom…"

Anne's heart shattered. She started toward Faith again, but Jared caught her arm, gave one abrupt shake of his head. "To your room. Now."

The young girl's tears flowed in earnest now. She pushed away from the wall and raced down the hallway. When the door slammed shut, Jared turned to take Anne in his arms. She felt the shuddering breath that seemed to come from the depths of his heart.

Anne couldn't speak. Could only hold him close, her face buried in his chest.

His bewilderment flowed in low, hoarse words. "She seemed so much happier after camp. Wasn't she better?"

Anne nodded.

"I thought...I thought things were better. *She* was better." His arms convulsed around Anne. This was tearing him apart.

"She was better, for a while. But something happened."

He leaned his head against the top of her head. "We're losing her, Annie." His broken, ragged voice was choked with tears. "We're losing our little girl, and I don't even know why."

Anne squeezed her eyes shut, as though to close out the reality of what was happening. *Help us, Lord.* She drew in her breath on a sob. *You're the only One who can.*

eighteen

"Defend me from my friends!"

CLAUDE LOUISE HECTOR

"I DON'T KNOW WHY YOU LET THAT WITCH GET TO YOU."

Trista flicked the ashes from her cigarette, the sparks dancing in the darkness.

Faith dug the toe of her shoe into the dirt, her hands gripping the thick metal chains on the swing. Though Lincoln Elementary had closed down several years ago, the city kept the playground open, making it into a park.

Faith was glad. She loved these swings. They reminded her of being little. Of being happy.

Of being liked. By her mom.

Yeah, she'd be crazy about you if she knew where you were right now.

Faith clenched her jaw and stared into the darkness. So what? So she'd snuck out. So it was almost two in the morning. Big deal. She'd been doing it for months now, and her parents were none the wiser. She'd been so nervous at first, so sure she'd get caught. But it was easy. No need to battle with her parents, to do the screaming fits. Just come and go as she pleased.

And times like today, when they sent her to her room? No

problem. She shut the lights off, put pillows under the covers to look like she was sleeping, and out the window she went. A step off the half roof to the big tree beside it, and within seconds she was on the ground, ready to go.

And I'm not gonna feel guilty about it anymore, either.

She'd never admitted it to Trista or Dustin, but as much as she figured she had the right to do what she wanted, she couldn't help feeling a little guilty. Until today. After the way Mom and Dad talked to her…

Hurt lodged in her chest, right behind the breastbone, as she remembered their voices, their anger.

Their disappointment.

"So?"

Faith turned at Trista's demand. "So…what?"

Trista rolled her eyes. "So why do you let her get to you?"

Faith wished she knew. But she didn't. She didn't understand it at all. "She just does, okay?"

With a flip of her long, blonde hair back over one slim shoulder, Trista shrugged. "I'm just sayin', it's stupid, you know? Your mom should accept you for who you are, not keep trying to make you something different." She shifted in her swing. "And all that talk about God and church. I mean, what's up with that?"

Faith looked away. "Nothing's *up* with it. She talks about it because she believes it."

"Yeah? So why isn't she living it? I mean, isn't she supposed to love you…what's that word they use all the time?" She waved her hands in the air. "Unconditionally. So, why doesn't she love you like that?"

Faith opened her mouth to argue, to tell Trista she was way off base, then she shut it. How could she argue? Her parents *didn't* love her that way. Not that Faith could see.

"*I* accept you that way." Trista's cajoling voice wrapped itself around Faith, spreading fingers of resentment through her heart, her soul. "And so does he."

He? Faith followed Trista's gaze, and in the glow of the streetlight saw Dustin walking toward them with that long-legged stride of his. His bike sat on the street. Man. She'd been so inside her head she hadn't even heard him drive up.

"Yeah...from the expression on his face, I'd say he likes you *fine* the way you are."

Trista's slow grin—and the gleam in Dustin's electric eyes as he drew close, his smile all for Faith—brought a quick surge of heat to Faith's cheeks. Her heart constricted. Trista was right. *She* accepted Faith. So did Dustin. It was her stupid parents who were self-righteous and judgmental.

"Hey, babe." Dustin leaned down, weaving his fingers in her hair, and brushed his lips against her cheek.

Faith reached up. Caught his face with her hands. He hesitated, his eyes locked with hers.

No kissing? It made sense when she was young and stupid.

Now she knew better.

She slid her hands across Dustin's cheeks, linked her fingers at the back of his head. Urged him forward.

His gaze slid to her mouth, and a smile crept across his lips. He cupped her face, his thumb caressing the line of her jaw, and his mouth covered hers with a hunger that made her tremble.

She gave herself freely to the passion of the long, delicious kiss, losing herself in the rush of heady emotion coursing through her.

Who needed rules? *This* was all that mattered. Feeling this way. Being held. Being cherished.

Being Dustin's.

When he raised his head, Faith caught Trista's look. She didn't need to say a word for Faith to understand.

See? I told you so.

Faith punched Trista in the arm, and she chuckled.

"Hey, is that any way to treat your best friend?" Dustin leaned against the swing frame, watching them with a half smile as he pulled his cigarettes from the pocket of his jacket.

"It is when she's bugging me."

One brow rose, and he looked at Faith over the flame touching the tip of his cigarette. "Bugging you?"

Trista pushed off, sending her swing soaring. "You talk to

her, Dustin. I'm not getting anywhere."

He took a long drag and lifted his face to the sky, blowing a stream of smoke into the air, watching it rise like wispy fingers reaching to the sky. Then he lowered his head to meet Faith's gaze, and his half-lidded expression made her fidget. "Let me guess. We're talking about the nag again?"

Trista's giggle drifted around them, and Faith looked away.

"You got it." Trista's voice grew louder then fainter as she swung past Faith. "I've been saying Faith's mom should accept her the way you and I do, as she is. If she really loved her."

A pang sliced through Faith. "Of *course* she loves me. She's my mom."

Oh, yeah. That was lame. A glance at Trista and Dustin told Faith they thought so, too.

Trista's long, slim fingers waggled at her as she swung by, waving the stupid words away. "Yeah…okay. Whatever. Your mommy loves you, as you are." The mockery in Trista's tone drew Faith's fingers into fists on the chain of the swing.

"Hey, Dustin, you gonna share?"

He pushed away from the swing set, tapped a cigarette out of the pack, then held it and the lighter high. Trista snatched them as she went past. Faith watched her light the cigarette on the fly, then toss the lighter back to Dustin.

"You're welcome."

She stuck her tongue out at him, then looked at Faith again. "It just, you know, seems like a total waste of time to let her get to you. I mean, so she's your mom. So what? They get pregnant and have you, so they think they own you?" She took a long drag on her cigarette, then blew out the smoke, leaving a trail in the air as she swung.

Like those ice crystal trails a jet leaves behind as it slices through the air, way up in the sky…

Dustin snorted. "Like anyone wants to own you, Trista."

"Hey!" She flicked ashes at him. "Doesn't matter what they want. Nobody owns me."

Faith shook her head at her friends and pushed off, swinging high into the sky, staring up at the stars. If only she could really fly, really soar away, free…

Like Trista. She was free to do what she wanted, when she wanted. No one gave her the third degree about where she was going, who she'd be with, when she'd be home.

Faith closed her eyes, face turned up to the night. Why couldn't her parents be more like Trista's? She kicked the dirt again as she swung by. *Why can't they leave me alone?*

A wicked laugh coaxed Faith's eyes open. Trista had stopped swinging, and the grin on her face was pure trouble.

Faith braked her own swing and came to a stop beside her friend. "What?"

"Your mom." Trista waggled her perfectly plucked brows at Faith. "Wouldn't she have a cow if you didn't come home tonight?"

Didn't come…?

Dustin came to stand behind Faith, one hand smoothing her hair, caressing the side of her neck. "I like the sound of that."

Trista's smile grew. "Yeah. Think about it. No phone calls. No asking permission. You don't show."

Dustin let out a whoop. "Perfect! Let her sit there and wonder where you are."

Faith started to comment, but Trista cut her off. "Will she ever see you again? Will the last words you said to each other be angry ones? And the longer you're gone, the higher her fear gets—" she flicked her cigarette into the air, watching it arc and fall, leaving a trail of red sparks in the darkness—"until she turns into a little puddle of panic."

Trista clutched her hands in front of her, filling her features and tone with an exaggerated sorrow. "Oh, what have I done? How could I have been so mean to my poor, sweet little girl?"

Dustin's appreciative chuckle surrounded Faith. When he laughed like that, deep in his throat, it did funny things to her. Made her feel good and worried all at the same time.

His hands lifted her hair off her neck, and she felt him letting it fall through his fingers. "This could be great."

"Yeah." Trista nodded and pushed off, setting her swing in motion again. "That'd teach her good. Leave you alone or lose you." She grinned at Faith. "Bet she'd keep her mouth shut then."

Faith liked the sound of that.

Dustin's hands covered hers on the swing, the strength of his fingers making her feel protected, cared for.

Loved.

His hands slid down, gripping the swing near the seat. He pulled her, swing and all, back and up, holding her there, suspended in the air for a moment. She felt his breath, warm and tantalizing, as he whispered in her ear. "Ready to fly, baby?"

She leaned against him, felt his smile against her neck, then nodded. He gave her a push, and she sailed up, up into the sky.

Leave me alone or lose me…

The birds were free.

Trista was free.

Leave me alone or lose me…

Faith closed her eyes. That's what she wanted. To be free.

Leave me alone or lose me…

And that's what she was going to get.

She turned to Trista as she swung past. "You're a genius!"

"Yeah—" her half-lidded expression was almost as smug as her tone—"I am."

The three of them laughed, and the sound rose on the night wind, a symphony of pure delight. Faith didn't even try to hold back the grin.

This was gonna be great.

Two days.

Anne couldn't believe it had only been two days. It felt like ten. Twenty.

A lifetime.

But it was only two days. Two days with no word from Faith.

Anne and Jared had awakened on Saturday morning, hoping against hope for a new day with Faith. A new start. They'd let her sleep in without calling up the stairs, like they usually did on Saturdays, telling her to get up before it was dinnertime. Amazing how that girl could sleep the day away. But when the clock struck one in the afternoon, Jared made his way up the stairs to rouse Faith.

What he found was an empty room. Her bed was made, clearly not slept in. Her window was open, the curtains flapping in the breeze as though waving good-bye.

Anne had scarcely been able to take it all in. Grim determination written in his features, Jared made his way down the stairs and to the phone. They'd called everyone they knew to call. The school. Winnie. Even Trista and that boy, Dustin, neither of whom had been any help at all. In fact, Trista only added to Anne's worry when she commented, "So Faith finally bailed, huh? Can't exactly blame her, can you?"

Anne frowned. What was the girl talking about? But before she could ask, Trista breezed on. "Maybe you'll think twice before you treat her like a prisoner again."

With that, the girl hung up.

After two hours of calling, the answer was still the same: No one knew where Faith was.

Their next call was to the police. Twenty-four hours, they said. Faith had to be gone for twenty-four hours before they could file a report.

Desperation grew, spreading through Anne with tendrils that surrounded and squeezed her heart. She followed Jared back up the stairs to Faith's room, watching, her arms wrapped around her middle, as he turned the room upside down, looking for some kind of clue as to where she'd gone.

He flipped her mattress up and frowned. Reaching down, he lifted a leather-bound book. Faith's journal. He met Anne's eyes, and she knew what he was thinking. They'd always sworn they would never invade their daughter's privacy, never read her diary or journal without permission.

But she'd left them no choice.

Fear goading her forward, Anne took the journal from her husband's hand. They stood together as she opened the cover. Read the flowing script. And gasped.

Page after page of poison had poured from their daughter's

heart onto the pages. Angry, hateful words written to and about them. At first, the tirades focused on Anne. But the last few pages added Jared to the mix, bemoaning the fact that he'd turned against her.

Their shocked eyes read account after account of Faith sneaking out and going to meet Trista or Dustin. The details turned Anne's blood cold.

Her daughter was utterly, totally out of control.

That was two days ago. They still hadn't recovered. And they still didn't know where Faith was. They'd called the police yesterday, then gone down to file the report.

Now, all they could do was wait.

Anne stood, though she'd only sat a few moments earlier, and went back to stare out the window. *Faith...where are you?*

"Hon, you've got to get some rest."

She turned to meet Jared's worn concern. Did she look as haggard as he? Probably more so. At least he slept some last night. She'd been up all night, praying, weeping, worrying.

"I can't rest." She muttered the words almost as much to herself as to him. "Not with her out there...somewhere." She looked out the window again, and her hand lifted as though of its own accord, the palm pressing to the cold glass, as if she could somehow reach through it, draw her daughter home.

She closed her eyes. *Faith...*

Jared's hands closed on her shoulders, his touch as familiar to her as her own.

"She's all right, Annie."

The fury that grabbed her, shaking her like a crazed terrier with a rag doll, almost stunned her. She gritted her teeth, her words hissing out. "You don't know that."

His hands tightened, and he didn't reply. Not right away. When he did, she kicked herself for the heaviness in his voice. "No...I don't. But I do know that God is watching over her—"

"Bad things happen all the time. Even with God watching."

No emotion in her voice. As though she'd gone dead inside. Well, maybe she had. How could she be alive when her child was missing?

Jared turned her, cupped her face with his hands, and forced her to meet his gaze. And Anne knew she hadn't gone dead. Not by a long shot. Rather, every painful emotion conceivable coursed through her veins like molten magma from the very core of her being. Fear, rage, helplessness, despair, agony, grief—they shredded her defenses and poured out of her on a sob.

Suddenly, the front door opened and slammed. They both bolted for the entryway.

"Faith!"

She turned at Anne's gasping exclamation. "Oh. Hi."

There was a moment of stunned silence. Then... "Hi?"

Jared's barely contained rage stunned Anne. Almost as much as it did Faith. Anne watched her daughter's eyes widen as the color drained from her cheeks.

"*Hi?* That's all you have to say?" Jared took a step forward.

"Jared, wait—"

"You put us through two days of pure terror—" the words ground out between his clenched teeth—"of not knowing if you're dead or alive, and all you can say when you come in is *hi*?"

Faith didn't reply, though Anne wasn't sure if her silence stemmed from defiance or fear.

"Well?"

Faith flinched at Jared's angry demand. "Well what?"

"Faith, so help me—"

Anne stepped between them. "Where were you?"

"Nowhere."

This time Anne and Jared exploded in unison. "*Faith*!"

She shrugged, waving one hand in the air. "I was out, that's all. I needed time to think. I mean—" the sulk seeped back into her eyes, her tone—"it's not like you two want me around."

"Of course we want you around—"

Jared's hard tone cut her question short. "Faith, I'm asking you one more time." There was a wealth of restraint in his slow, measured tone. "I don't want any dramatics, excuses, or sidesteps. I want an answer." He pinned her with a look that brooked no opposition. "Where have you been for the past two days?"

She stared at him for a moment, and Anne had the distinct feeling her daughter was sizing Jared up, determining how serious he was. Apparently she realized he was serious as a heart attack, because she lowered her eyes and muttered, "With Trista. And Dustin."

"What?" Anne wanted to hit something. "They said they didn't know where you were."

Faith rolled her eyes. "They lied."

"And these are the kind of people you choose as friends? Liars?"

Faith met her father's eyes, glare for glare. "At least they love me!"

"Is that right?"

Apparently Faith didn't hear the warning in Jared's whispered words. "Yes! They accept me as I am!"

"And what, exactly, is that, Faith?"

She crossed her arms, a well-practiced woundedness in her features and stance. "You shouldn't have to ask! Of all people, *you* should know who I am, Daddy."

Jared stared at her, and for a moment silence reigned. Then he dragged in a breath, the sound so ragged and harsh it almost hurt to hear it. "I used to know you, Faith. I saw it every time I looked at you, that tender, sweet little girl who could make my heart smile. That little kid I used to love to spend time with, to talk and laugh with."

Faith bit her lip, and the sudden longing that filled her features made Anne want to weep.

"Daddy—"

The choked word was barely past Faith's lips when Jared lifted a hand, stopping her. "That's who you used to be. My little girl." His eyes narrowed and his tone hardened. "But as for knowing who you are now?" Laughter, harsh and humorless, escaped him. "I haven't got a clue. Because all I see when I look at you is a stranger."

The words struck their mark, and Faith's lip trembled.

"We found your journal."

At her father's words, the color drained from Faith's face. "You…you read my journal?"

Jared's jaw tightened. "You didn't give us much choi—"

"You had no right!" Faith's hands clenched into fists. "Those were my private thoughts! You had no—"

"We are your parents, and that gives us every right!"

Anne stepped in. "Faith, we were desperate to find out where you were."

"Desperate? You're not desperate; you're pathetic!"

The words slapped her, and Anne pulled back, fighting the mixture of anger and hurt that swept through her. Jared's steadying hand on her shoulder was a blessed relief. She reached up and put her hand over his.

"If that's true, Faith, then it's you who made us so."

Faith flinched, but her father wasn't finished.

"The day you were born, we almost lost you. I don't know if we've ever told you that, but you almost died during the delivery. When I found out you were okay, I went down on my knees and thanked God. I knew then He had His hand on you. I knew you were going to be a true blessing in our lives."

Anne hadn't thought it possible, but Faith's features grew even whiter as she listened to her father talk.

"W-what are you saying, Daddy? That you wish I'd died?"

"No!" He swung away from Faith, his hands clenched at his sides. "God in heaven, Faith, do you hate us so much that you could ask something like that?"

There was such pain in Jared's voice that Anne almost couldn't stand it.

Faith made no reply. From the haggard look on her face, Anne was convinced she couldn't. That any attempt at words would only get choked off in her throat.

Jared turned back to Faith, his eyes searching her features. When he spoke again, it was in a hard whisper. "Who *are* you?"

Anne wanted to stop him, to keep him from saying things he'd regret, but she might as well not even have been there. For so long Anne had been almost envious of the bond her husband and daughter shared, of the way they always seemed to understand each other, to get along. Now…

Now that very bond had become a weapon—a razor honed and wielded by Faith's actions, slicing her father's heart with cruel, careless strokes.

"You want me to accept you as you are? How do I do that when your actions and words show me a spoiled brat who runs away when she doesn't get her way? A selfish, mean-spirited girl who hurts people because she can, the very people trying to take care of her, trying to do what's right for her."

Tears slid from Faith's wide eyes, coursing down her cheeks. "What's right for me?" Her voice trembled. "You don't care what's right for me!"

Jared straightened. "No, Faith. It's you who doesn't care. Not about what's right. All you care about is you. Getting what you want. When you want it. Well, I'm telling you, here and now, it's going to stop."

Faith's chin lifted. "Meaning?"

"Meaning you are going to change. You're going to stop acting like a two-year-old out of control and start taking responsibility for your actions."

"And if I don't?"

Anne wanted to scream. She knew what was coming but didn't know how to stop it. *God, please.*

Jared's own chin lifted at his daughter's defiant tone. "It's simple, Faith. If you want to continue living under our roof, then you will abide by our rules."

Faith blinked. Once. Twice. Then a dull red seeped into her skin, blooming in her cheeks. When she spoke, it was in whispered disbelief. "You'd throw me out?"

No, no. Anne's mind begged. *Tell her you got carried away, that you were angry. Tell her you didn't mean it.*

But he did. She knew it. And she knew something else.

He was right.

"No, I wouldn't throw you out. You'd be choosing to leave." Jared's tone softened then, but only a fraction. "I don't want that. Neither does your mother. But we can't go on this way, Faith. We're your parents. We love you. But you have to understand, we won't be abused by you." Jared looked at

Anne, and she saw in the pain ravaging his features what his words were costing him. "We've had enough."

Faith stared at them for a heartbeat, then spun on her heel and ran up the stairs, slamming the door to her room.

Anne stood beside her husband, words flowing through her mind and heart—but her tongue seemed paralyzed. She couldn't speak, couldn't make a sound. His arm eased around her shoulders and drew her close.

She closed her eyes, resting her forehead against that broad chest, listening to his broken heart beat as they held one another, joined in their sorrow, trapped in the silence of inevitability.

nineteen

"The strongest of all warriors are these two:
Time and Patience."

LEO TOLSTOY

THE NEXT MORNING ANNE ROSE EARLY AND MADE her way to the kitchen. As restless as she'd been those nights Faith was missing, last night had been even worse. Yes, she knew where Faith was. Physically. But as Anne lay there last night, staring at the ceiling in the darkness, she realized what she didn't know was far more important.

Where was Faith emotionally? Spiritually? Was she as lost to them as she seemed? Was there any way to bring her back?

And the most troubling question of all: How did they end up in this terrible place?

Anne stood in the kitchen, longing for those long-ago days when Faith was little and used to sit in the kitchen, chattering away as she worked. Well, she might not be able to bring those days back, but she could at least bring a small taste of them to Faith.

She would fix her favorite breakfast.

Anne opened the cupboards, pulling out ingredients, working in silence. On the outside, that is. Inside, a Mardi Gras of questions cavorted through her mind, tormenting her.

She pulled out mixing bowls and frying pans, unable to dislodge the stab of guilt that lay buried deep in her chest. She flipped pancakes and filled the plates to the echo of despair in her spirit. She'd wanted to be the perfect mother, to have the perfect family, but she'd made so many mistakes.

If only she'd been more patient, more understanding…

On and on the litany went, following her as she lifted the breakfast tray. But before she made it out of the kitchen, the phone rang. Anne set the tray down and went to answer it.

"Anne? I saw Faith."

She gripped the phone. Anita and others from the church had been praying for Faith's safe return. "It's okay. Faith came home last night."

"She…? But Anne, I saw her this morning. Just a few minutes ago."

Alarm tore through her, making her knees weak. "What? Where?"

"She was walking down the sidewalk when that boy she's been seeing came up on his motorcycle. That's what caught my attention, the noise so early in the morning. She got on the back of his bike, and they took off."

Anne sagged against the wall. "Thanks for letting us know. I'll—I'll talk with you later."

"Is there anything I can do?"

The concern in her friend's question warmed the frozen lump that was her heart. "Pray. Please. Just pray."

Anne hung up the phone and turned. Jared stood there looking at her. He didn't even need to ask.

"She's gone again."

Anne nodded.

Though they knew it was so, they went to Faith's room and pushed the door open.

Empty.

There, in the middle of Faith's bed, was Anne's purse, its contents strewn across the quilt. The heirloom quilt her great-grandmother made. The quilt passed from generation to generation of women in Anne's family.

Faith had been so excited when Anne gave her the quilt

on her thirteenth birthday. She'd wrapped it around herself, all smiles, and promised to take care of it—

A sudden realization jolted Anne back to the present. One thing was missing from her purse's contents. "My wallet..."

Anne expected Jared to be angry, to rail and vent, but instead it was as though quiet confidence cloaked him. "Hon, Faith left us long before this. I don't know why. I don't understand what we did wrong. But there's nothing we can do at this point. Nothing but trust God to bring her home."

She wanted to argue, to scream at him to go find their daughter, but she knew it was no use. Even if they could find her, even if they could bring her back, they couldn't watch her twenty-four hours a day. Eventually, she'd leave again.

"Come on." Jared led her to sit on Faith's bed, and there, on the quilt Anne's mother made for Faith, she and Jared prayed for their little girl. They begged God to watch over her, to keep her safe.

To bring her home.

When the sound of their amens faded away, Anne opened her eyes. She looked at Jared, and he squeezed her hand.

"Okay. We've got phone calls to make."

She fingered her purse. "Phone calls?"

"To cancel the cards."

Anne started to protest, to say Faith would need money, then realized how crazy that would be. *God, please...help us get through this.*

Her prayers continued, a steady stream. Because she knew it was only through God's strength that she'd be able to survive what was ahead.

Days. Weeks. Years.

She shuddered. Maybe the rest of her life.

Without her daughter.

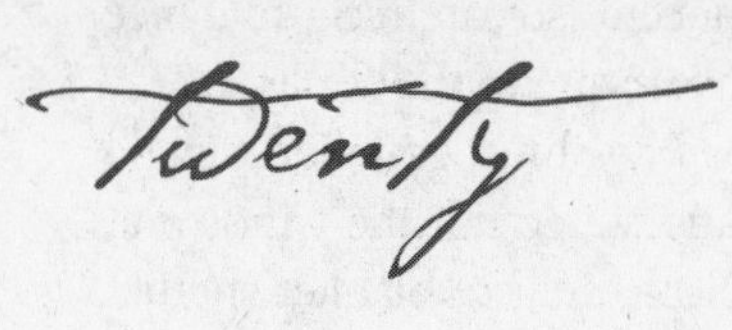

Twenty

"We need to find God, and he cannot be found in noise and restlessness. God is the friend of silence."

MOTHER TERESA

ONE YEAR LATER

IT WAS DARK OUTSIDE.

Anne rubbed her eyes to rid them of the gritty feel, but to no avail. The pain wouldn't go away.

Not from her eyes.

Nor from her heart.

She rose from the bedroom floor, feeling far more than her knees protesting, and eased into the large overstuffed chair. This had been her mother's chair. It had been such a haven when she was younger. She'd crawl into this chair and let it surround her with a sense of peace, of safety. And it had been there for her when Faith was little, too. So often she'd sat there feeding Faith, coaxing her to sleep, or holding her after a bad dream, singing to her.

The memories engulfed her as completely as the chair. Her fingers caressed the worn fabric. So familiar. So comforting. She felt like a child again. Small and innocent.

Oh, if only that were true! If only she were small again, able to go through each day so innocent, so carefree—to dance and sing and play—and leave the worrying to the adults.

But she wasn't a child. She was fifty-three, going on ninety.

She leaned back in the chair and stared out the window at the moonlit sky. So beautiful—a black, velvety blanket spotted with shimmering dots of light. Clouds drifted across the moon, misty shadows dancing through the black expanse, obscuring the golden light for a heartbeat before slipping away.

Anne used to love the night. Used to love sitting like this, watching the subtle changes in the sky, the way the shadows seemed to come to life. The darkness was so comforting, almost a friend. A place of quiet and peace. A place to drink in the silence and be restored.

Even that had been taken from her.

The darkness no longer brought her delight and beauty. Instead, it bore sorrow and laid it at her feet. The night mocked her, reminding her that her little girl was gone, that she didn't know where Faith was or what was happening to her—that she couldn't protect her own child.

Her once-welcome companion had been twisted into a dreaded foe.

The loss went deep.

Anne rested her head against the chair's soft cushion, her eyelids lowering. She drew air in, feeling it fill her lungs, then let it ease out through barely parted lips. She focused on each slow, deliberate breath. In. Out. In. Out… The cadence of life, flowing through her, easing the tension that had become so familiar she almost didn't notice it anymore.

A low, resonant chime sounded, and Anne opened her eyes. She glanced at the clock on the wall, but the darkness hid the face from her. How long had she been here? All she had to do was count the chimes as they sounded, but that was too much work for her weary mind. The last year had drained every ounce of energy she had.

An entire year of waiting. Worrying. Twelve long months of listening for the front door to open, for the sound of her daughter's voice as she said those precious words: "I'm home!"

A year of utter silence.

Anne shifted. She'd been in this room several hours, at least. The ache in her knees bore clear testimony to that fact. She'd come here after noon, collapsing beside the bed. She couldn't fight any longer. Couldn't keep up the front of "everything's fine" one more second.

Anne clenched her teeth against the frustration.

No. Time to be honest.

She wasn't frustrated. Mere frustration didn't burn this way, like a forest fire raging out of control, ravaging her heart. No, only one thing fueled this kind of consuming blaze.

Anger.

Pure, gut-churning anger.

Annie's fingers clenched into a fist, and her gaze drifted to the wall, to the picture of Faith hanging there. Jared had snapped that shot months before Faith left. He caught Faith in an unaware moment, sitting out in the backyard, staring up at the sky.

Anne took in her daughter's beauty, those clear emerald eyes that could shine with such joy or burn with such disdain. Looking at those eyes now, she saw so clearly her daughter's rebellion, her willfulness. Her jaw was set and stubborn, and Anne half expected the photo to come to life and turn to her, that mocking smile on its lips. She could hear the caustic things Faith would say if she were here, if she could see Anne's pain.

"Who are you trying to kid, Mom? Acting all sad and sorry. Get real! You didn't want me around any more than I wanted to be here."

Words boiled up inside Anne. Words that had been there for so long, begging for release, but she'd always pushed them away, consigning them to some inner prison. Well, she couldn't stop them any longer. The cell door had been eaten away by the acid of her anger, and the words broke free, tearing through her.

She pushed herself from her chair, was at the wall in two steps, and before she realized what she was doing, snatched down the photo. Her fingers dug into the frame as the words tumbled from her lips in a low, hoarse whisper.

"How could you do this to me?" She shook the picture, teeth gritted. "How could you be so selfish?"

Unable to bear the sight of her daughter one moment longer, she flung the picture away. It slammed into the floor, the glass shattering, the frame breaking apart. Anne leaned against the wall, her angry questions hanging in the darkness, the silence punctuated only by her ragged breathing.

As she stared down at her daughter's ruined picture, sorrow gripped her. She moved as though in a dream, lifting the photo, brushing away the shards of glass, pressing it against her chest.

I'm sorry... I'm sorry...

With legs barely able to support her, she made her way back to her chair, wrapping the quilt around her and the photo like a downy shield. Hot tears anointed the tiny stitches on the quilt formed generations ago by a mother's patient, loving hands.

Words wouldn't come. Prayers caught in her throat and floundered. All she could do was weep. Deep, wrenching sobs that came from some place within her she hadn't even known existed. She'd given herself over to the sorrow, not trying any longer to deny it, to restrain it. Letting it run its agonizing course, and then...

Silence.

Stillness.

Peace.

Long-forgotten words drifted up from some inner repository where they'd been waiting until she could hear them—really hear them—again.

Shepherd of Love, You knew I had lost my way.
Shepherd of Love, You cared that I'd gone astray.
You sought and found me,
placed around me strong arms that carried me home.
No foe can harm me or alarm me,
never again will I roam...
Shepherd of Love, my Savior and Lord and Guide.
Shepherd of Love, forever I'll stay by Your side.

Anne rested her damp cheek against the chair back. She'd known she was as lost as Faith. God showed her that so clearly the day she found out Faith had accepted Him—and hadn't told her about it. Anne learned so much that day. And even more since.

But now—now God was teaching her something else. Something even more difficult to accept.

She had to let go.

Give up. Let go, as the saying went, and let God.

Verses came to her, filling her mind. She'd read them over and over in the last months, so many times she memorized them. But she had not really understood them. Not until this very moment.

"I wait quietly before God, for my salvation comes from him."

From Him, not from her. She'd tried. Tried everything she knew. But all her efforts, all her carefully-thought-out strategies, had failed. She hadn't been the perfect mother. Hadn't produced the perfect daughter.

"He alone is my rock and my salvation, my fortress where I will never be shaken..."

He alone. No one else could hold off the enemy that had torn their home apart. Torn them apart.

"My salvation and my honor come from God alone. He is my refuge, a rock where no enemy can reach me."

No enemy. Not even her own stubborn heart. And what an enemy that had been. She hadn't realized it until now. But her heart had been working against her, against Faith.

Now she saw clearly the many times she'd grown angry with Faith for not acting the way her daughter should act. Saw how she'd reacted to her daughter not with patience and peace, but out of disappointment and frustration.

How she'd based the way she treated Faith on the way Faith treated her.

Now, at last, Anne understood. Her heart was as rebellious, in its own way, as Faith's had been. All that time, all those years, she'd been looking at Faith when what she should have been looking to was God. To His Word. To His example of love. Love that didn't waver, no matter what His children did. Love that held on, even when those He loved let go.

Love that never failed.

That was the love she should have had with Faith. A God-centered love. Love that treated Faith as God commanded, not as Faith's actions deserved.

God, God, forgive me.

Anne bent her head, hugging Faith's picture to her. She heard the paper crumple and laid it in her lap, smoothing it out. As she gazed down at her daughter's face, regret formed a cocoon around Anne's heart. How could she have been so mistaken? What shone in Faith's eyes wasn't rebellion at all.

It was longing.

Longing to be accepted. Loved. Affirmed. A longing Anne had never really fulfilled. Not without expectation of something in return.

Anne spread her fingers over her daughter's photo. If only Faith were here…if only she could hold her daughter's face, look into her eyes, and tell her how sorry she was.

"O my people, trust in Him at all times, pour out your heart to Him, for God is our refuge."

The words brought her head up, and she gasped. Here, again, was that unfailing love. Even as Anne finally saw herself for who she was, even as she realized how far short she'd fallen, God was opening His arms. Her Father was reaching for her, wrapping her close to His heart, inviting her to pour out her heart, her desperate longings. And leave them to Him.

But it was even more than that. She'd already given Him her longings. What she hadn't done was give Him Faith's. And so she bowed her head, thanking Him, and laying in His mighty hands her precious daughter's dreams and hopes. Her longing to be loved and accepted. Her fears.

Everything.

Please, Father. Let her find You.

He could bring about the healing, the restoration they so desperately needed. He could save Faith. Could save them.

Yet, even as her heart bent in obedience, even as she finally let go and surrendered to the Father's will, Anne knew it wasn't going to be easy. But like Mary watching her beloved son, bruised and beaten, carry the cross that would take His life, Anne knew she had no choice. She would walk this path her daughter had chosen—this path that Anne as well as Faith had put them all on—bathing every painful step in prayer. But she did not walk it alone.

The Shepherd of truest love, who knew in His own eternal heart the unending pain of losing a child, walked beside her.

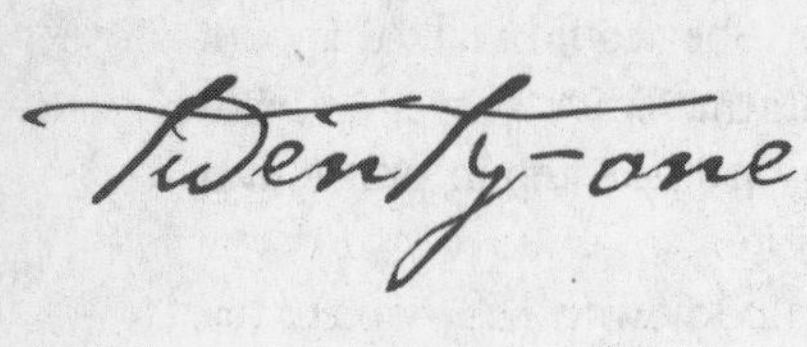

Twenty-one

"There are two kinds of people:
those who say to God, 'Thy will be done,'
and those to whom God says,
'All right, then, have it your way.'"

C.S. LEWIS

IT WAS COLD. SO COLD.

Faith pulled her coat around her and shivered.

Miserable weather. Was any place more miserable in the winter than Illinois? Nothing but miles and miles of snow and ice. Why had she ever come here?

Because Dustin wanted to live in Chicago. No rhyme. No reason. Just, "It's where I want to be," and that was it. He spoke; I followed.

Dustin. Faith still couldn't believe what a fool she'd been. She'd trusted him with everything. Believed he meant it when he said he loved her, would take care of her. She walked away from her home, her family, because he promised her something better.

That night—that horrible night a year ago—she'd gone up to her room, angrier than she'd ever been. A knock on her window told her Dustin was there, and she rushed to open it and let him in. Trista slid in after him. When she told them what happened, Dustin put his arms around her.

"You deserve better than this, babe."

"We all do," Trista agreed.

Faith stepped back. "Yeah, well, good luck."

"You gotta make your own luck, girl." Trista folded her arms, giving Faith a hard look. "No one hands it to you."

Faith looked from one to the other, understanding dawning. "You're running away. Both of you."

Dustin grinned. "Nah, we're running to, darlin'. To life and freedom. And we want you to come with us."

One look at Trista told Faith the *we* was an exaggeration. Clearly, Trista preferred Dustin to herself. Jealousy streaked through her. Dustin was her boyfriend! What did Trista think she was—?

Dustin's hand taking hers stopped her thoughts. His thumb moved over her palm, coaxing. "Come on, Faith. There's nothing holding you here." He tugged her into his arms, whispering in her hair. "Come with me."

He didn't have to ask twice. It had taken all of fifteen minutes to make their plans. Faith would pack her things, then slip out the window and meet Dustin just down the road.

It had worked perfectly. He'd been there, waiting, on his hog. A quick ride to Trista's, and they had all their things packed up in her old beater of a car. She got in the car, and Dustin slid onto the bike, holding his hand out to Faith. "Let's get outta here."

She took his hand without looking back.

Dustin promised her heaven.

Instead, he brought her hell on earth.

Four months with the two of them was more than enough to know she'd made a mistake. They wanted to try anything and everything. Faith didn't. Each time she opted out of their plans, something shifted in Dustin's eyes, in the way he looked at her. Still, she convinced herself it would work out. That Dustin loved her. Nothing could come between them.

She'd been an idiot.

That had been painfully clear the day she'd come back early from trying to find a job. It was another day of disappointment, and she was tired and frustrated. She climbed the twelve flights to their dingy apartment—the elevator never worked—and shoved her key in the lock, ready for a hot bath. Maybe even a nap.

She'd pushed the door open, started to close it behind her, then stopped. Cocked her head. Listened.

What *was* that noise?

She listened again, and sudden, horrified understanding slammed into her, stealing her breath, almost knocking her flat.

Heart pounding, she flung her purse down and went to throw open the bedroom door. Her bedroom. Hers alone.

No matter how Dustin pleaded and cajoled, Faith hadn't slept with him.

"Sex is for marriage."

Yes, Faith gave up on the other rules. But that one, she kept. She wasn't quite sure why, but she did. She was tempted, of course. Dustin could be very persuasive. But every time they got close, she'd stop, push him away.

Finally, he'd quit asking. Faith was relieved. And touched. How many guys would be so understanding?

As the door to her bedroom swung open, and she took in the scene before her, Faith knew the real answer.

None.

Absolutely none.

Dustin had quit asking Faith for sex because he'd found it elsewhere. With Trista.

Remembering that scene now—the way they'd been wrapped in the sheets, so engrossed they didn't even realize she was there until she screamed at them—sent a wave of nausea coursing through Faith.

She blinked dry eyes, refusing the tears that wanted to come. *Stop it! He's not worth one single tear!* Even so, it hurt when she thought about him—about the way he'd betrayed her. Then, a few days later, abandoned her.

He hadn't even had the guts to tell her he was leaving. She woke up two mornings later to find Dustin and Trista gone. Along with all of Faith's clothes and money.

She'd stayed in the ratty apartment as long as she could.

But the manager was big and ugly, and he stomped his way up the stairs to tell her it was either get out or start paying for the room. And since he knew she didn't have any money, he said she'd have to use "whatever you got."

No contest. She got out.

The streets were home for a while. She'd done okay, taking what handouts she could scrounge. But too many people offered to "help" her in ways even she wouldn't accept. She had to get out. So she started walking.

She'd made it as far as a deserted rest stop on the tollway that night, then bad weather hit. Unable to walk in the fierce wind and snow, she huddled against a building.

Desperation, as heavy as the snow covering the ground, cloaked her. Hunger gnawed at her gut. Shivering so bad she could hardly stand it, Faith pressed her face to the frigid concrete and did what she'd sworn she'd never do.

God, help me.

That was it. No big, wordy prayer. Just, *Come on, give me a break.* Not that it would help. Still, she had to admit she felt a little better. She was about to doze off when things went dark. She jumped up, fists ready, but her heart plunged to her shoes when she saw what had caused the massive shadow to fall across her.

A huge man. One of the biggest she'd ever seen.

He glared down at her through a beard and glasses, and she clenched her hands. She didn't have a prayer. The thought almost made her laugh. That's what she got for asking God for help.

"Child, what you doin' out here in the cold?"

Faith could only stare. For all the gruffness in his words, there was such kindness in his tone that she was speechless. Finally, she forced words through her shivering lips. "I-I was looking for a-a j-job—" She sounded like a nitwit! But she couldn't keep her mouth from shaking. "And a p–place to stay. But then the st–storm hit..." She looked down, biting back tears. They'd probably turn into ice cubes on her cheeks. "I n-needed a place to wait out the s-storm."

He buried his hand in his beard, scratching at the chin

that had to be in there somewhere, and tipped his head. "Tell you what. I know a place 'bout two hours from here. It's in the middle of nowhere, but they're lookin' for a waitress." He eyed her. "You willin' to work hard?"

She nodded. Anything to get away from this crummy city.

"Well then, come on."

With that he led her to his truck and opened the door. "Name's Gus."

Faith climbed inside the cab. What choice did she have? If she didn't go with this guy, she'd sit there and freeze to death.

She settled on the hard seat—and found herself facing a plastic Jesus on the dashboard.

Gus noticed her looking at it and gave a short nod. "Don't go nowhere without Him." He fired up the truck and put it into gear. "'Course, I'm talking 'bout the real thing, not that plastic one. Reminds me the Big Guy is with me, holdin' me 'countable."

Faith didn't talk much during the ride. Gus didn't give her a chance. He talked pretty much nonstop. About God. And Jesus. And how they'd saved his worthless hide when no one else gave a spit, so he'd promised to spend his life paying them back by helping others in need.

Usually, Faith couldn't stand that kind of talk. It grated on her nerves, making her jumpy and restless and just this side of angry. She didn't need God or His bunch of stupid rules in her life.

But this time, she listened. And she liked it. There was something about the way Gus talked about God. Something pure and honest. It was clear he believed with his whole heart.

Faith found herself wishing she could do the same.

True to his word, Gus took her to the café—which really was in the middle of nowhere—and introduced her to the owner. The woman, who introduced herself as Ethelda—"But you call me Ethel"—eyed Faith like she was a piece of fruit gone bad.

Faith was about to tell the woman to forget the whole thing when Ethel looked at Gus.

"You standing for her, Gustel?"

The huge man gave a solemn nod.

Ethel pursed her lips and looked back at Faith. "Well then, that's good enough for me. You're hired, young lady."

Faith wasn't sure what it meant to "stand" for her, but she did understand that she owed Gus. Big-time. She walked with him out to his truck.

"Thanks, Gus."

He studied her for a moment, then reached out one big bear paw to pat her on the cheek. "You're welcome, Missy. Make me proud."

The words rang in her ears long after his truck had disappeared in a swirl of driving snow.

Months later, it still made Faith smile to think about it. She shivered again and pulled her coat closer around her. She should know better than to go walking at night this time of year. Too darned cold. But the tiny TV she had only got two channels. She'd complained about that once to Ethel, and the woman gave her one of those pointed looks.

"Two channels or two hundred, it don't matter. Ain't nothin' worthwhile on anyway. You need to feed your mind on better than that, girl."

That had started a lively debate that was still raging. Faith would describe the shows she used to love to watch when she was at home, like *Cheers* and *The Cosby Show*; Ethel would tell her about books she'd read, then tell Faith why they were better than "any ol' TV show."

Truth be told, their debates *were* more fun than watching TV. Sometimes Faith dropped by Ethel's home in the evenings so they could continue what they'd been talking about during the day. Invariably, Ethel would work a suggestion that Faith call home into the conversation, but she never pushed.

That was one of the things Faith liked best about her.

Too bad Ethel wasn't home tonight. What's more, there wasn't anything worth watching on TV. The thought of spending another night alone in her small apartment had been more than she could bear. Since the tiny town all but closed up by six every evening, that left few options for nightlife. Bingo. Church. Taking a walk.

So Faith was taking a walk.

You should have gone with Ethel.

Faith shook the thought away. She liked Ethel. A lot. The woman reminded her of—well, anyway, she liked her. Tonight, as they shut down the diner, Ethel had asked her—for the kazillionth time—if she wanted to go to church with her. It wasn't even Sunday, and the woman was going to church. Again. Faith's answer was always the same: "God hasn't had any use for me in a long time. Or me for Him. Pass."

The first time she'd said that to Ethel, she'd braced herself for a lecture. Instead, the big woman busted into laughter. "Got no use for you. Now there's one I haven't heard." She shook her head, her hairnet dancing to keep the woman's wild curls contained. "You keep tellin' yourself that, hon, if it helps."

Now when she asked Faith to go to church, she'd say, "Got any use for Him yet?" When Faith said no, she'd grin. Her parting shot was always the same: "The day's comin', child. I can feel it."

Faith couldn't hold back a grin of her own. Ethel was tough as nails on the outside, but inside, she was a big ol' marshmallow.

A blast of cold wind slapped Faith in the face, snatching her breath. She hunched her shoulders to her ears and shoved her hands even deeper into her pockets. She'd been in Illinois for a year, and she still couldn't get used to it being cold for so long. It was almost Easter, for cryin' out loud!

At home, the fruit trees would be blooming, and temperatures would be easing their way past the sixties and into the seventies—maybe even the eighties. If she closed her eyes, she could almost see the blue sky, the clouds drifting past the mountains on all sides of the valley. She could even hear her mom and dad tease each other as they worked in the flower garden.

The sudden tightness in her throat took Faith by surprise. She had to swallow several times to dislodge the tears hanging there. She shook her head at the unfamiliar sensation. She hadn't cried in a long time. Not since that morning she woke up to find Dustin gone.

Great. It wasn't bad enough she had to think about home, about Mom and Dad, now she was thinking about Dustin again. Why was it that everyone who mattered in her life couldn't stand to be around…around…?

She frowned. What *was* that sound?

Cocking her head, she could just make out the strains of piano music. She looked up and down the street, finally spotting a glow of light at the north end. She walked toward it, her steps slowing when she realized what stood there.

A church. Ethel's church, to be exact.

Faith hesitated. The piano music tugged at her, coaxing her to come closer. She gave in, at least until she was at the bottom of the outside steps. But that was it. The thought of going up those stairs, in that open door…

She shivered again, and it had nothing to do with the cold. She'd walked away from all of this a long time ago. Long before she left home. No way she was going back now, because she was a little homesick and lonely.

Is that the only reason?

"Shut up." Faith started, looking around to see if anyone overheard her fierce whisper. Good. She was alone. Better get out of here before someone saw her. But as she turned to walk away, someone started singing. A young girl, from the sound of it. But the voice, as pretty as it was, wasn't what stopped Faith cold.

It was the words. The words of the song, drifting to her on the night breeze.

She knew this song.

Knew it as well as she knew anything. And suddenly, listening to those words she once loved, the tightness was back in her throat. Her heart pounded, and before she could stop herself, she turned and made her way up the stairs. Walked in the doorway. Through the small entryway.

Right into the main church area, where people sat in the pews, listening as a teenager stood up front, singing the song through again. A girl not much younger than she was.

A girl who sang the words as though she really truly meant them.

"Shepherd of Love, You knew that I'd lost my way. Shepherd of Love, You cared that I'd gone astray."

Faith had to swallow hard and fast now. No way she was going to cry all over herself, and in a church no less! She wanted to run from the building, but her feet wouldn't budge. It was as though the song had her riveted in place.

"You sought and found me, placed around me, strong arms that carried me home."

Faith closed her eyes and could almost feel those strong arms. No amount of swallowing worked at the thought, and tears seeped past her lids, down her face.

"No foe can harm me or alarm me, never again will I roam."

What would that be like? To stop roaming? Stop wandering, looking for someplace to belong? What would it be like to find a place where they really accepted you? Loved you?

The ache in Faith's heart was so sharp she almost cried out. *I want that. God, please, I want that.*

"Shepherd of Love, Savior and Lord and Guide..."

Each word struck her heart, taking away her breath.

Savior. She'd accepted Him as such when she was small. Then again that summer at camp. She'd known it was real, that He was real. So what had happened?

Lord. Ah, that was it. She knew Him as Savior, but Lord? No one had been her Lord. Not ever. No one told her what to do. She was her own boss, her own lord—

"And that's working for you, is it?"

Ethel's question struck home, and she reached out to grab the pew beside her, steadying herself. Working for her? Images of Trista and Dustin flitted through her mind. Of those months on the street. Of sleeping in the cold, always half awake so you could hear if someone came toward you—

No. No, it wasn't working. Not at all.

And Guide.

A sob escaped her. She was so tired. She wanted someone else to make the decisions. To tell her how to get where she wanted to go.

Where do you want to go, Faith?

The question resonated within her, full of tenderness,

understanding. She suddenly knew the answer. Without a doubt. "I want to go home."

"Well, it's about time."

Faith's eyes flew open. Ethel stood there, that grin on her face. She took Faith by the shoulders, pulling her into a soft, comforting embrace. Faith buried her face in the woman's ample bosom.

"The day come, didn't it, girl?"

Faith could only nod.

Murmurs of "Praise God," and applause sounded around them, and Faith peeked out over Ethel's arms. They were surrounded by the people who'd been seated in the pews. Even the young singer was there, smiling at them.

Faith blinked and pulled back, then fixed Ethel with a pointed stare. "Did you plan this?"

Ethel's laughter boomed though the room. "Oh, no, honey. That was God's doin'. I was sitting here, minding my own business, when you came walking in." Her eyes softened, and she cupped Faith's cheek. "I could tell by the look on your face that the Holy Spirit was working on you something fierce."

The smile Faith managed was shaky but genuine, nonetheless. "Yeah, He was."

"And haven't we all been prayin' for that?" Ethel's nod took in the people standing around them.

Faith's mouth fell open. "You...you've all been praying for me?"

"At every service." This from the girl who'd sung the song.

Faith turned to her. "How did you know?" At the girl's slight frown, she waved toward the front of the church. "How did you know to sing that song?"

"'Shepherd of Love'?" The girl smiled. "I sing it every year at the Ash Wednesday service." She reached out and took the hand of a woman standing beside her. "It's my mom's favorite."

Faith's laughter was tinged with tears. God didn't miss a trick. "Yeah...my mom's, too."

"So what do you say, Faith?" Ethel took her hand. "You ready to make a phone call?"

"Yes. I'm ready."

The people around them broke into cheers. Ethel's grin broadened as she slid her arm around Faith's shoulders. "You'll have to forgive them, kiddo. They just love seeing miracles up close and personal." She nudged Faith. "Better'n anything on that ol' TV any day!"

"About ready for bed, hon?"

Anne looked up from her reading and smiled at Jared. "Just about. You go on. I'll be there in a minute."

He leaned down to kiss her, then paused, his gaze holding hers. "I love you, Annie."

She touched his cheek. "I love you, too."

He was on his way out of the room when the phone rang. Frowning, he glanced at the clock. "Who'd be calling this late?"

Anne shrugged and reached for the phone. "Hello?"

When silence met her greeting, Anne looked at Jared. He came toward her.

"Hello? Is anyone there?"

Jared held out his hand. "Probably some kids. Let me take it."

Anne held the receiver out to him, just as someone spoke.

She froze. That voice! It *couldn't* be.

Eyes fixed on Jared, Anne jerked the receiver back to her ear. When she spoke again, her voice was hushed. "Hello?"

"Mom? I–Mom, it's Faith."

She wanted to say something, to tell Faith how much she loved her, but no words would form on her frozen tongue.

"Annie?"

She held out a trembling hand, and Jared took it.

"Mom? Are you there?"

"Yes!" The word almost exploded, and Anne half laughed, half sobbed. "Oh, yes, Faith. I'm here." Jared's eyes widened, and he sat next to her. Anne held the receiver between them. "So is your father."

With that, Faith started to cry. Wrenching sobs came across the lines, and Anne and Jared poured out their love, their forgiveness. Anne wanted to ask questions, to know where Faith was, if she was all right, but now wasn't the time. All she wanted to do right now was tell her daughter she loved her.

When Faith was able to speak again, she asked a question that made Annie's heart sing: "Mom, do you…do you think I could…?"

"Come home, sweetheart."

"I'll see you soon. I love you." The joy in Faith's voice almost sang through the telephone lines.

"We love you, too."

Jared took the receiver from Anne and hung up. Then he opened his arms and Anne fell into them. They held each other, weeping and praising the One who had found their little girl.

And was, at long last, sending her home.

Twenty-Two

"I am prepared to go anywhere,
provided it be forward."
DAVID LIVINGSTONE

FAITH PULLED HER CAR INTO THE DRIVEWAY AND threw it into park. Shoving the door open, she raced through the garage, into the house.

"Mom!" She tossed her purse on the couch as she flew through the living room. *"Mom!"*

"Outside, sweetie."

She hurried through the kitchen, pulling open the sliding glass door, and flinging herself out into the garden where her mother was on her knees. "I got a job!"

Faith grabbed her mom's hands and pulled her to her feet. She danced her around in circles. "I got a job! I got a job!"

Mom's laughter came in gasps, and Faith stopped their dance of joy, sudden alarm tingling inside her. "You okay, Mom?"

"I will be, once I catch my breath."

Faith ran to grab a lawn chair and brought it over for her mom. Her mom lowered herself into it, smiling up at Faith as she did so. "Now, tell me all about it."

Plopping down on the ground, Faith leaned against her mom's

knee. "It's as a lifeguard at the YMCA. Dad told me about an opening there, and I got it! I work during the day, teaching swim classes, then on the weekends during the free swims. And this fall when I start college, I can work my schedule around my classes." She hugged her mom's knees. "It's going to be so much fun. Even if I will be older than all the other freshmen."

Her mom stroked Faith's hair. "Not that much older, sweetie. Twenty-one is hardly ancient. So you're only two or three years older."

"Yeah, it just *feels* like ten years."

Mom understood. "That's the wonderful thing about second chances, Faith. What you learned in the hard times makes you stronger. And wiser."

"I hope so, Mom. I really hope so."

"I'm proud of you, sweetie. I know you'll be wonderful."

Faith smiled. God was so good! In the year since she'd come home, He'd walked with her through so many changes. He'd helped her get her GED, so she could go to college. And he'd helped her relationship with her parents grow stronger than ever. It felt so good to be able to talk and laugh with them.

And to pray with them.

If there was one thing her mother was good at, it was praying.

When Faith had commented on it, Anne said, "That's because I had so much practice while you were gone." The fact that her mom could say such a thing with a warm smile was even more proof that God was real and at work.

Faith jumped to her feet. "I'll be back in a while."

Her mom looked up at her. "You're leaving?"

Faith grinned as she headed back into the house. "I've got to go shopping! I'll need at least a couple of new swimsuits."

"Of course you will." Her mom's lips twitched. "And a new towel or two."

"Exactly." Faith winked. "Who says you and I don't think alike?" She slid the door shut and headed for the garage, the sweet sound of her mother's laughter ringing in her ears.

Faith finished swimming her laps and pulled herself out of the water in one smooth motion. Grabbing her towel, she looked to see what time it was. Good. She had fifteen minutes before the pool opened and the first wave of kids showed up.

After two weeks, she felt as if she was really getting the swing of her job. She liked swim classes best, because she got to spend one-on-one time with the kids. Open swim was fun, but with the heat this summer, the kids flocked to the pool in record numbers. Linda, her boss, was great to work for. She was witty and good at her job.

If only she'd quit telling Faith she needed a boyfriend. "I'm not ready to date," she'd told Linda over and over.

"Ah, you haven't met the right guy yet. You need someone to sweep you off your feet."

"Been there. Done that." Faith grimaced. "Had my T-shirts stolen from me."

Undaunted, Linda delighted in stopping by during open swim to point out likely candidates. The last one she'd chosen had been a particularly hairy man of indeterminate age—who could see wrinkles under all that hair?—and a potbelly hanging over his Speedo.

Faith thanked her for her concern and told her to get lost.

Yesterday, Linda stopped by early in the morning to let Faith know she'd hired a second lifeguard. "Open swims are too full for one lifeguard. So your cohort starts tomorrow."

Faith didn't mind. She'd like having a coworker.

She gathered up the float rope, which divided the shallow end of the pool from the deep, and started toward the hooks to fasten it in place for open swim. She should have thought to ask Linda the new girl's name, but she'd know it soon enough. She was supposed to be here any min—

"Hey."

Faith spun at the deep voice right behind her—and suddenly her feet slipped off the edge of the pool. "Eep!"

The float rope went flying when her arms pinwheeled in a

frantic effort to regain her balance. But just as she was about to fall backward into the pool, strong hands grabbed her wrists and jerked her forward. Before she knew what was happening, Faith found her nose smashed against a broad chest, her arms pinned at her sides in a bear hug.

"Fanks," she muttered into the chest, then pushed away—and almost fell into the pool out of pure shock.

A tall, trim, sandy-haired Adonis stood there. Faith looked up, up, up—he was at least as tall as her dad, and he was six-foot-one—and found bright blue eyes smiling at her.

"Don't mention it." With that, he leaned down and picked up the float rope. Watching him, Faith realized he was wearing swim trunks.

"Here—" she reached for the rope—"I'll take that. Open swim doesn't start for another ten minutes."

"I know." He didn't surrender the rope. "I'll help you with this."

She frowned. She didn't care how tall, blond, and handsome he was, she could get into trouble for letting him in early. But before she could point that out, he stuck out a hand.

"I'm Zeke Galine. Your new partner."

"My..." Ooooh, she was going to get Linda for this!

He held out one end of the float rope to her. "I'll head to the other side, and we can fasten it in place."

Faith nodded. She let the rope out as Zeke headed around the pool, his long, lean strides eating up the distance in record time. This guy was definitely in shape. Very, *very* good shape. A tug on the rope drew her attention, and she realized with a start that Zeke was standing there, watching her watch him.

The smile that eased across his face sent heat surging into her cheeks. She knelt down, fastened the rope, then went to the lifeguard stand. But as she got there, a muscular arm reached from behind her, plucked her whistle off the hook, and held it out to her. She peeked over her shoulder.

Zeke's grin met her.

The least she could do was grin back.

So she did.

Jared had just settled in his recliner after a long day at work when the front door opened.

"I'm home!"

He glanced up to greet his daughter, but the words died on his lips.

Who on earth was that?

"Daddy?" Faith peeked from behind the tall, well-built young man, a sheepish grin on her face. "This is Zeke. He works with me at the Y, so he, uh, he gave me a ride home tonight. And, well, he wanted to come meet you and Mom."

"He did, eh?" Jared stood and held out his hand. Zeke came forward and took it in a firm grip, meeting Jared's eyes without hesitation.

"Mr. Bennet. I'm Ezekiel Galine. But please, call me Zeke."

"Ezekiel, eh? Good biblical name."

Zeke smiled. "The best. My mom was a firm believer and raised me the same way."

Jared held the boy's gaze for a moment—and what he saw there alarmed him. Then it made him smile. *Well, well*… "Nice to meet you, Zeke."

"Faith, you didn't tell me we had a visitor."

Jared put his hand on Zeke's shoulder and nodded to Anne. "Hon, this is Zeke. He works with Faith." He watched Anne's eyes widen as she came to shake Zeke's outstretched hand. "He drove Faith home and wanted to come in to meet us."

"Oh?"

Jared caught her eye and grinned. Yup. She'd seen it, too.

Anne linked her arm with Faith's. "Well, that was nice of you, Zeke. Would you like to stay for supper?"

The boy gave Anne a shy smile. "Thanks, Mrs. Bennett, but I've got to go home and study. I've got class Monday night."

"Class? During the summer?"

Zeke turned back to Jared and nodded. "I'm in the last year of my MBA in Entrepreneurship. I'm in the accelerated program, so we have class year round."

MBA? Entrepreneurship? That sounded promising. "Well, we'll have to talk about that sometime," Jared said, walking him to the door. "I'd like to know what kinds of plans you have."

Zeke got the message, loud and clear. And it didn't bother him at all. In fact, he looked past Jared at Faith, and a slow, easy smile worked its way across his features. "I'd like that."

"Good. See you soon then."

Zeke inclined his head. "Yes, sir."

As Jared closed the door behind him, Faith scampered to the plateglass window to watch Zeke leave.

Anne slid her arm around Jared's waist. He looked down at her. "So."

She looked at Faith. "So."

"You see what I did in that boy's eyes?"

She nodded. "As clear as the very straight nose on his handsome face."

"So." Jared looked at his daughter, a slight catch in his throat.

Anne nodded.

The sound of a car engine told Jared their visitor was gone. Heaving a heavy sigh, Faith pried herself from the window and came back to the living room.

Actually, *floated* to the living room would be more accurate. Jared wasn't sure her feet touched the ground.

"That's a nice young man."

Jared was amazed Anne managed to say this with such calm. He'd half expected her to start dancing around the room. He pursed his lips. "A little tall, don't you think?"

"*Da*-ddy! He's perfect!"

Jared chuckled, gave his wife a squeeze, then headed for the door. "I see. Perfect." He put his hand on the doorknob. "So, are you ready?"

Faith blinked. "Ready? For what?"

He held back the grin. It was hard, but he did it. "To go get your car. You drove to work today, remember?"

Faith's eyes widened, and red flooded her cheeks. "Oh my gosh!"

"Uh huh—" Jared pulled the door open—"Like you didn't know that when he offered you a ride."

Faith followed him out the door, then linked her arm in his. "You know what, Daddy?"

"What's that?"

She leaned her head against his arm. "I love you."

"I love you, too, punkin'." He slid his arm around her shoulders, and a twinge of sadness blended with his joy. It had been clear in the way Zeke looked at Faith.

And the way she looked at him.

Their time of having Faith at home would be over soon.

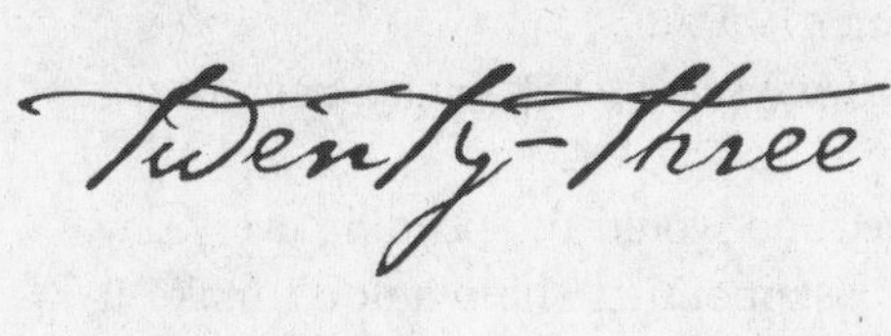

"I cannot make myself a refuge, but Jesus has provided it, His Father has given it, His Spirit has revealed it, and lo, again tonight I enter it, and am safe from every foe."

CHARLES SPURGEON

WHAT A DAY.

Faith slid from her car and trudged up the path, sliding the key in the door with a heavy sigh. Mom and Dad would be in bed asleep by now. She'd meant to be home earlier, had been looking forward to sitting and talking with them, but the prof's lecture had taken longer than usual. Yes, class was slated from eight to ten p.m. But this prof almost always had them out by nine. Nine-thirty at the latest.

Tonight, when he was still going strong at nine-forty-five, Faith slipped out to call her parents, let them know she'd be home late. Then she called Zeke to tell him she wouldn't be able to see him tonight.

Faith could hardly believe they'd been together for a year and a half. Of course, they'd been engaged for almost a year of that time. Talk about a whirlwind romance. Meet in June. Get engaged in November. At least they decided to wait a year to get married. As hard as that had been, Faith knew it was the right decision. Now,

December 21 was a mere two weeks away. Fourteen days, and she'd be Mrs. Ezekiel Galine.

She'd be entering the new year—1992—and a new life, all in the same month.

Though she and Zeke soon would be spending every day together, Faith was still disappointed she wouldn't make it home in time to see him tonight.

"I miss you," she pouted into the phone.

"I know, darlin'." Zeke's warm laughter flowed through the lines, folding her in a cloud of happiness. "It's been at least four hours since I've seen you. But I'll see you tomorrow. I promise. Oh, and the forecast is for fog later tonight, so be careful driving home. Love you."

"Love you, too."

Sure enough, Zeke's warning was right. By the time she came out of the building when class was over, a dense fog blanketed the valley. The drive back to town—normally a half-hour drive at the most—took over an hour.

Thank heaven she was finally home.

Slipping her shoes off so she wouldn't disturb her parents, she padded toward the stairs leading up to her room—when something caught at her, pulling her to a halt.

Brownies. Fresh baked, from the smell of it.

She leaned back and saw a dim light shining in the kitchen. What on earth?

When she peered in the doorway, the sight that met her eyes made up for the day. There, in front of her chair at the table, was a plate of brownies and a glass of milk. Her mom sat in her chair, head pillowed on her arms, sound asleep.

Faith came in, laying a gentle hand on her mom's shoulder.

She woke and looked up with a smile. "You're home."

Faith leaned down and kissed her on the top of the head. "I'm home." She slid into her chair and sniffed. "Thanks, Mom."

Her mother stretched. "From the sound of your voice when you called tonight, I figured you could use them."

The first bite was heaven. The second even better. Was

there anything more comforting than fresh-made brownies and milk?

Faith and Anne talked, their conversation warm and relaxed. As she watched her mother, Faith marveled yet again at the changes in her. She was so much softer, more accepting. She'd apologized to Faith for how she'd treated her as a child—and that fact alone told Faith she'd changed.

Of course, Faith knew she'd made more mistakes than anyone. But to hear her mother say she was sorry, tell her she loved her no matter what…well, that meant more to her than she could say.

Now, surrounded by the fragrance of her mother's care, Faith knew the time had come. "Mom?"

Anne tipped her head. "Yes, honey?"

"I want to tell you…about the year. When I was gone."

She'd never talked about it. And, thankfully, her parents had never asked. Never pushed her. She'd always been grateful for that. She needed the perspective of time and distance to be able to tell anyone about it.

Anne considered her. "Okay."

Warmth flooded Faith. Such simple acceptance. Such complete trust.

No wonder she loved her mom so much.

Anne listened as Faith talked, her mother's heart cringing and weeping as she heard for the first time all that had happened to her daughter when she'd been missing from them. Her heart pounded when she related about the man at the truck stop, then filled with praise when Faith told her about the man's love for God, the way he helped her.

God had indeed been watching out for her little girl. Why had she ever doubted Him?

She laughed at Faith's tales of Ethel and the diner.

"The woman drove me nuts half the time, had me in stitches the rest of the time." Faith grinned. "I felt at home with her right away—"

Anne knew the twinge of jealousy was understandable,

but she didn't let it take root. Instead, she just thanked God for this woman who'd been such a blessing to Faith.

"—and I finally figured out why. Her spirit. Her devotion to God. Her love of life. It all reminded me of you, Mom."

Anne blinked away the sting of grateful tears and took Faith's hand. She listened, awed at the way God kept her daughter safe, at the way He continually drew Faith to His side. And when Faith told about hearing the song, tears washed Anne's face.

They talked into the small hours of the morning, and when they at last walked toward the stairs, Faith linked her arm with her mother's. She tugged her mother to a stop at the bottom of the stairs and hugged her.

Anne sniffed. "I'm so glad you're home, Faith. That you've found such a wonderful young man to love." She smiled. "To marry."

Her daughter pulled back and gave her a watery smile. "Me, too, Mom."

Anne lay a hand on Faith's smooth cheek. "My little girl is all grown up. An old lady of twenty-two."

At the wistful sound of Anne's words, Faith lay her hand over her mother's. "Just don't let that make you think I don't still need you."

"Well, of course not! A girl always needs her mother."

Faith giggled. "Exactly right. God's been really good to us, hasn't He?"

"That He has."

They started up the stairs. "And I have a feeling," Faith whispered as they reached the top, "He's not done with us yet." She hugged Anne once more, then went to her room. "'Night, Mom."

"Good night, sweetie." As she headed for her room, she knew, deep inside, that Faith was right. God wasn't done with them.

More likely, He'd only just begun.

She took hold of the doorknob, then stopped. Frowned. Then pressed a hand to her chest, breathing deep until the discomfort eased.

Chest pains? She'd never had chest pains before.

It's just the darned diabetes.

Anne nodded. Of course. The disease had caused neuropathy in her feet, which sent stabbing, burning pains from the bottoms of her feet to her shins. And it had aggravated her arthritis as well.

She might only be fifty-six, but sometimes she felt ninety. Like right now. "Lord," she whispered. "Any chance you feel like coming back soon? If so, I won't argue. Those new, perfect bodies sound pretty good."

Cheer up. You've got a wedding coming.

A wedding. And one day, grandchildren.

Okay. So she'd stick around awhile longer.

"As long as you give me, Lord." She opened the bedroom door, heard Jared's soft snores. The sound made her smile—and as she crawled into bed and snuggled close to her husband, Anne had to admit she wasn't ready for eternity yet.

Take Your time, Lord. She lay her head on Jared's broad chest. *Just take Your time.*

PART TWO

"Anyone who listens to my teaching and obeys me is wise, like a person who builds a house on solid rock. Though the rain comes in torrents and the floodwaters rise and the winds beat against that house, it won't collapse, because it is built on rock."

MATTHEW 7:24–25

"The happiest moments of my life have been the few which I have passed at home in the bosom of my family."

THOMAS JEFFERSON

The Rain

"Though the rain comes in torrents..."

MATTHEW 7:25

Twenty-four

"Every tomorrow has two handles.
We can take hold of it with the handle
of anxiety or the handle of faith."
HENRY WARD BEECHER

WINTER WAS FINALLY OVER.

Okay, maybe not for the year, but at least for the last week.

Faith stretched out in her lawn chair. It was like the old folks always said, if you don't like the weather in Southern Oregon, give it a week. It'll change.

She held her arms out in front of her, letting the sun wash over her skin. She'd forgotten how good this felt. Was it only a few days ago she'd been grumbling to Zeke that the overcast sky would never be clear and blue again?

He chuckled at her, but she insisted it was true. She planted her hands on her hips. "Do you realize how long it's been since we've seen the sun?"

"About as long as it was last winter?"

"Ooohhh, you!" Faith turned and plopped a dirty dish into the sink, sending a dollop of warm, soapy water splashing over the edge and onto the tile floor.

"Avast, ye wench, watch yerself there, or you'll sink us for sure!"

She eyed Zeke, telling herself not to give in, not to grin at his pitiful pirate's accent or laugh at the way he morphed his face into a fairly passable leer.

But not even her sour mood could resist his playful efforts. Her lips twitched then lifted.

"Aaarrrhhh—" he swept her into his arms, and the grumble of his words vibrated deep in his chest, beneath her hands—"there be a comely smile, fer sure. What say you and me gets to know each other, eh, lass?"

She couldn't hold back a giggle as he waggled his brows at her. "You're a nut, you know that."

"Aaaarrrrhhh, but I'm yer nut, I am."

"Ooo, lucky me."

Faith smiled anew, remembering the exchange. Zeke could always make her smile. That was just one of the things she loved about him.

"Brought you some tea, darlin'."

She squinted up at her husband, accepting the tall glass with a grateful sigh. She took a sip.

"Good?" He settled into the chair opposite her.

"Absolutely. How'd you know exactly what I needed?"

He stretched his arms out, then folded them behind his head. "It's a gift."

Faith didn't argue. In the almost fourteen years they'd been married, he'd proven countless times that was true.

"I'm telling you, Zeke, 2005 is going to be a good year."

"Oh?" He let his fingers trail down her arm. "What makes you think so?"

"Look at it." She lifted her arms toward the sun, soaking in the warmth. "It's only February, but it feels almost as warm as summer."

"*Almost* being the operative word."

She made a face. "You're such a literalist."

"Ain't it da truth."

Faith closed her eyes. The weather forecasters were all talking about the unseasonable temperatures and how everyone had to be ready for them to plunge again. She didn't care. She planned on enjoying every minute of every beautiful day.

Her coffee group—a gathering of woman who met together every Thursday evening to talk and laugh—had even met outside a few nights ago. The Coffee Crew, they called themselves. Faith had never known such fun, thoughtful, down-to-earth women. They'd met at an area Christian women's conference six years ago and started coming together out of a need, one of them said, for "female companionship and hilarity." Well, they supplied that in abundance. They'd been through so much—from family crises to cancer to divorce—each struggle knitting them ever closer together.

They stayed in touch through the week via e-mail, sharing everything from jokes to prayer requests. What did the world do before e-mail?

They talked in person, came the dry rejoinder from within.

Maybe so, but with people's busy schedules nowadays, e-mail was a lifesaver. There was something so comforting about sending off your worries, knowing with a click of the mouse they were winging their way to friends who loved you and would do more than mouth platitudes. They'd pray.

Faith had always wanted a sister. Now she had nine. They ranged in age from late twenties to late forties, but there didn't seem to be any real age differences. They all were young at heart.

A breeze ruffled her hair, and Faith drew in a deep breath, savoring the tangy scent of newness that filled the air. Flowers were budding and starting to bloom, and the mix of fragrances tickled her nose.

What a beautiful day. And what a blessing that it came on the weekend when they could bask in it. She opened her eyes, studying the yard, the house, and a sense of gratitude swept over her. Never in a million years, when she was young and so angry, could she have imagined being as blessed as she was. But God had never let her go. In spite of herself, He worked His will and brought her from a place of despair to where she was now: married to a wonderful man, living in a home that they both enjoyed, and closer than ever to her parents.

She wasn't the only one close to them, either. Zeke loved them.

Faith turned her head, drinking in the sight of her husband of fourteen years. It had been so amazing to watch him connect with her folks. When the opportunity came for them to buy this house she didn't even have to convince Zeke. Of course, she'd had a speech all planned, one reminding him that her mother's health was only getting worse, that it would be good for them to live closer, and that it was a great neighborhood for raising a family, should God ever bless them with a child. But before she could open her mouth, Zeke came in after work one day and told her he'd contacted a Realtor.

"You what?"

Zeke grabbed an apple from the basket on the kitchen counter and took a bite. "I contacted a Realtor. If we're going to get that house a few blocks from your parents' place, I figured we'd better act on it fast."

"How did you—?"

His grin was pure delighted smugness. "Hey, I'm a contractor, remember? I build houses for a living?"

"Beautiful houses, thank you." Which they were. Zeke's homes were almost a work of art, built to suit the specific needs of those who would be living in them. Which was why he was in such high demand.

He inclined his head. "And you're not the only one who drives around that neighborhood watching for places to go on the market. I want to be closer to your parents, too."

She'd leapt into his arms with a squeal, not even caring that the apple flew out of his hand and landed with a *plop* on the floor.

They'd bought the house, and it all worked out even better than they'd hoped. Zeke and Faith's dad got along so well, they did yard and house work together. Faith walked to their house for visits several times a week.

That had been especially helpful as her mom's diabetes grew more severe. Mom had difficulty walking. Standing for more than ten or fifteen minutes was terribly painful for her. Faith and Zeke went to her parents' every other night for dinner, and Faith prepared meals for her folks because her mother couldn't cook any longer. And every other weekend she and Zeke went over to clean.

Faith knew it bothered Mom that she couldn't take care of the house and cooking, but she was working hard at accepting her limitations. She always told Faith how grateful she was for her help. And how guilty she felt that the help was necessary.

She'd said that again just yesterday. "I'm so mad at myself."

Faith looked at her. "Why, Mom?"

"Look what I've done to myself. If only I'd been more careful with what I ate, more determined to exercise."

"You did the best you could with what you knew, Mom."

"I wish the doctors had told me, but then, they didn't know yet, did they?"

Faith stroked her arm. "What?"

"That once you're diagnosed with diabetes, you have a window of about fifteen years to manage the disease well."

Yes, that would have been vital information. Might have made all the difference. If her mom had known that what she did in those fifteen years would impact how devastating the disease would be, the extent of the complications... But it didn't help to think that way. They *hadn't* known it then.

Mom sighed. "Back when you were young, I used to think you were the rebellious one in the family. But I've been rebellious all along, eating what I wanted when I wanted, even though I knew it wasn't right. Or healthy." She took Faith's hand. "I'm sorry, sweetie, that all this falls to you."

Faith hugged her tight. "I'm not! It gives me more time to spend with you."

She meant it, too. She loved being with her mom, talking and sharing. Her mother had been an invaluable sounding board when Faith and Zeke finally gave up actively trying to have a baby.

"The doctors have no explanation," Faith told her mom one day through tears. "They say we should be able to get pregnant, but we're not. So that's it."

"That's what?"

Faith put her elbows on the table and rested her chin in

her hands. "We're not going to keep trying. I mean, we won't do anything to keep it from happening, but no more counting days and taking temperatures and all of that."

"Well…that's good."

Faith sat back, staring at her mother. "It is?"

"Absolutely. That means you're going to trust God with it all."

Faith thought about that, then gave a slow nod. "Yes, I guess it does."

"Then it's not just a good thing—" her mother said as she refilled Faith's glass of tea—"it's a *very* good thing. Believe me, I know. I waited long enough for you."

"You had a hard time, didn't you?"

"Yes, but I knew God was calling me to be a mother. And I wasn't going to let diabetes keep me from that. Your dad and I prayed and prayed. And when the doctor told me it wasn't safe for me to become pregnant, we prayed some more. And here you are!"

Faith laughed. "Here I are! Was it worth the wait?"

Her mom's eyes shone. "Absolutely."

Faith let her hand rest on her flat abdomen. Waiting on God was definitely the best thing to do. But it was so hard! She longed for a child, longed to be a mother, longed especially to share with her daughter all the things her mother had shared with her. The idea that it might never happen made her heart ache.

But there was no denying that it was up to God. Faith would have to learn how to be content as she waited on Him.

"So—" Jared's sleepy voice drew her attention back to him—"are we going to your folks' for dinner tonight?"

Faith pulled her knees to her chest and circled her arms around them. "As far as I know. I told Daddy we'd pick up Chinese."

"Egg rolls?"

From the anticipation in his tone, Faith knew Zeke's mouth was already watering. "What good is Chinese without egg rolls?"

Zeke jumped up from his lawn chair and pulled her into a

tight hug. "See? I don't care what anyone else says. You're a smart little fortune cookie." He nuzzled her neck. "Mmmm, I *love* fortune cookies."

She poked his side, but before he could retaliate the phone rang.

"I'll get it." Zeke was off, covering the ground between them and the house easily with those long legs.

Faith lowered herself back into her chair. Life wasn't perfect. Not by any means. Her mom had suffered extensive neuropathy in her feet, which affected her balance. The doctor told them it made it hard for Mom to sense her connection with the ground. That was probably why she had fallen a couple of times. That was the hardest for Mom, falling like that. Faith could remember her mother scrambling over the rocks on their visits to the ocean when she was small. Her mother had always been so surefooted, so nimble. Now…

It took a long drink of cold tea to dislodge the lump in Faith's throat. No, life wasn't perfect. But it was good. Very good.

So quit worrying, will you?

Faith laughed softly. Jennifer, one of the coffee crew, had said that to her at coffee last Thursday. "Faith, stop worrying. Relax. God's in control! Either you trust that or you don't."

Before Faith could respond, the others chimed in.

"You know what you need? A hot bath." This from Deb, the tenderhearted dreamer in the group. "Light some scented candles, put on some soft music…"

"…and burn the house down." Patti's cheeky grin never failed to make Faith laugh.

Connie piped up. "But you'll be okay, 'cuz you're in the tub."

"You're terrible!" Deb would have been far more believable if she hadn't been laughing as she scolded Connie.

"Of course she is." Andi leaned back in her chair. "She's Connie."

"Ha ha." Connie met this scintillating repartee by sticking out her tongue.

Sandy, who was the Earth Mother of the group—she was

the first woman Faith had ever met who *enjoyed* elk hunting and wilderness camping—put her hand on Faith's arm. "You know, that's what I love about these women. Their spiritual maturity."

"We're mature."

Faith looked at Linda. She always seemed so steady, so grounded. Faith wished she could be more like that. "We are?"

"Sure." Linda's dimples peeked out. "*Mature* is another word for old, right? Well, we're definitely that!"

The table erupted into a free-for-all of laughter and playful insults, and even Lori, the quiet philosopher in the group, couldn't let Linda's cut go by without comment. "Old is a state of mind, nothing more."

"Yeah," Connie could hardly get the words out she was laughing so hard, "but the state of my mind is utter confusion!"

Faith chuckled anew at the memory. They had such fun together. What a rare combination to find friends who could laugh or be serious with equal ease.

She took another sip of tea, then stretched out. For once she would listen to Jennifer's wisdom and stop worrying. Overall, her mother seemed to be doing well. Dealing with her disease better than ever before.

The doctor was keeping a close eye on her and had even scheduled some tests for today, just to be sure everything was okay. Yes, Mom had to fight continual weight gain, but with the doctor's guidance and the probable adjustment he'd make in her medications after today's test, things should be fine.

Besides, wasn't Mom always telling her worry was a waste of time and energy?

She lifted her face to the sun's rays, letting the warmth caress her cheeks. Yup. For once, she would let worry take care of itself. Let those unfounded fears and apprehension drift off to some faraway place where they couldn't touch her.

Relax. Enjoy.

Always good counsel. Today she'd follow it.

And nothing was going to stop her.

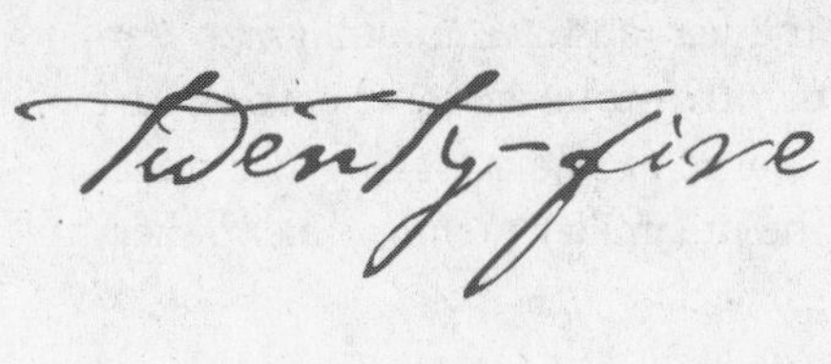

"Storms make trees take deeper roots."

DOLLY PARTON

"FAITH."

She started. She'd dozed off, and Zeke's voice shot through her like an electrical jolt. She turned, blinking away the drowsiness. He stood there beside her, holding out the phone. "It's your dad."

Something in his tone set her nerves on alert. Wide awake now, she sat up and swung her legs around so she was sitting on the edge of the lounger. Heart pounding, her gaze rested on her husband's face.

His expression was clear. She'd been wrong. Something was definitely going to ruin this day.

He handed her the receiver, capturing her hand between his as she took it. Their eyes met. "It's your mom. It's not good."

Worry cackled, slid from that faraway place where she'd banished it, and returned to gnaw at her. She felt it slither from there to settle on her brow, folding it into deep creases. She raised a hand to rub away the sudden throb behind her temples.

She lifted the receiver to her ear. "Dad?"

"Hi, punkin'."

Something was in her father's tone…something heavy. Like the feeling in her gut.

"Your mom's in the ER, hon."

Faith swallowed back the fear and sat up straighter, narrowing her eyes to focus, to make sure she took the information in around the waves of panic fogging her mind. She listened, honing in on the unfamiliar tremor in her father's voice.

God...help him. Please, help him...

"The doctor says your mother had pulmonary edema."

"Pulmonary edema." She nodded, as though she understood what that meant. She didn't. Didn't have a clue. All she knew was it sounded serious.

"From what I can understand, it's a severe form of congestive heart failure."

"Heart failure?" Faith almost choked on the words, and her gaze met Zeke's. He moved to sit beside her on the lounger. He didn't touch her, just let his presence support her.

"He said her lungs and heart were surrounded with fluid, and that made her heart work too hard. Less efficient." Her father hesitated, and Faith gripped the phone with both hands, wishing she were there beside him.

Please, God...

"It limited the amount of oxygen getting to her system, which made it really hard for her to breathe. She told the tech she couldn't lie on her back because she couldn't breathe, but he wouldn't listen. Told her the test had to be done that way. Had her lie flat anyway. And you know how anxious she was about this test."

"I know." Faith forced reassurance into her tone—which wasn't easy considering what she wanted to do was scream. She reached for Zeke's hand and clutched it in her own.

"Anyway, by the time she told them she had to get out of the machine, she was in pretty serious trouble. They rushed her to the ER and hooked her up to oxygen and started her on nitroglycerin and some other things—diuretics of some sort—to get rid of the liquid gathered around her lungs and heart."

O God... Faith closed her eyes. *God, please...*

"And they put in a catheter, too. Then they came and got me."

Faith's eyes jerked opened at that. "You…you weren't with her?"

"No." His voice cracked, and that told her more clearly than any words could how upset he'd been at that fact. "It all happened so fast. They had to get her to the ER right away. I was still sitting in the waiting room of the office where they'd been doing the test."

"Oh, Daddy…"

"I knew something was going on, though. The doctor said the test would only take twenty or thirty minutes. It was over an hour by the time they told me they'd taken your mother to the ER."

Faith realized her knuckles were turning white from her grip on the phone. She relaxed her fingers. "Are you there now, in the ER?"

"Yes."

"Okay, I'll be right there. And Daddy?"

"Yes."

She tried to speak, but the words wouldn't come. When she finally forced them out, they were thick with tears. "I love you."

"I love you, too."

As quickly as she could, Faith filled Zeke in. He listened, watching her face. Faith looked down at their linked hands. How often had she seen her parents hold hands like this? More times than she could count.

She stared at her hands. "This test wasn't supposed to be anything serious."

"Do you want me to go with you?"

She looked up at him. *Thank You, God, for a man like this to love me.* "No, it's okay. I'm sure…it's probably just a temporary setback."

His sky-blue eyes studied her. "It sounds pretty serious, darlin'."

Faith looked away. She wouldn't listen to that kind of talk. God wouldn't let anything happen to her mother. He couldn't. He knew how much she meant to Faith, to Faith's father…how much they needed her. Mom had spent her life serving God, being obedient and sacrificing for others to follow Him. Now, she and Dad had finally retired, were finally ready to start relaxing and maybe even traveling a bit.

No. God wouldn't let anything happen to her now.

She hugged Zeke and held on, soaking in his solid strength. "I'll run over to the ER so Dad's not there alone, so I'll know what the doctors have to say." She straightened and even managed to muster up a smile. "Why don't you start the church prayer chain going? And give the coffee gals a call for me, okay?"

Zeke hesitated, then gave a slow nod. "Okay, but call me if you need me."

"I will."

It was almost midnight when Faith sat at her computer. She knew she needed to go to bed, to get some rest. But she needed to do something else, first.

She turned on the computer, then pulled up her e-mail program. Her fingers rested on the keyboard as she went through all that had happened that day.

Reliving the tension, the fear, brought familiar words washing over her.

"The Lord is my shepherd..."

She'd been praying the same words over and over lately. This morning, when she woke up was the first time in days...weeks...it hadn't been running through her mind. She'd thought that was a good sign. That maybe she was learning to trust. That maybe things would be okay with her mom.

She should have known better.

"He maketh me to lie down in green pastures..."

She could use a nice, green pasture right now. Soft grass, the sun shining down... What she wouldn't give for a good, solid sleep. Lately that same nebulous apprehension worked its way into her unconscious nearly every night, wreaking havoc with troubling dreams that left her exhausted when she woke.

No wonder she'd dozed off so quickly this afternoon.

"He restoreth my soul..."

That's why she'd been so thankful to wake up free this morning. But that was over. The heaviness was back in full force, settling deep in the middle of her chest, ratcheting the muscles there until her chest felt so tight it was hard to breathe. Her pulse raced, then slowed as she deep-breathed her way to calm, then raced again as fear clawed its way to the surface.

Her gaze drifted to the computer.

"Yea, though I walk through the valley of the shadow of de—"

No. She wouldn't even think that. She'd write what she knew. Borrowing trouble never helped.

She started typing.

From: FaithinHim

To: TheCoffeeCrew

Sent: Sunday, February 6, 2005

Subject: Prayer request/my mom

You know you've had too many crises when the emergency room staff knows you by name.

The thought brought a weak smile to Faith's face as she typed.

Hi, friends. What a day this has been. Dad and I just got back from the hospital. As some of you already know, Mom is in the ICU, being monitored constantly. She had pulmonary edema. It all happened this morning during a chemical stress test on her heart. She tried to deal with the discomfort and breathing trouble, 'cuz, as she said, "I thought I was being a baby." Crazy lady. By the time she told them she had to get out of the machine they had her in, she was in bad shape.

When Dad called me, he was pretty shaken. He doesn't get like that too often, so I knew things were serious. When I got to the ER, her breathing was so labored it was scary to listen to her. Sounded like she was breathing through pudding. And she was about as white as the hospital sheets on her gurney.

They did test after test, and then the doctor came in and said they'd be admitting Mom to the ICU. Not just to the hospital, but to the ICU. She was as shocked to hear that as we were, and she reached out a trembling hand to Daddy. He cradled it between his two large, strong hands, and I could see the peace flow from him to her.

Such comfort in a single touch.

We were in the ER with her from about eleven-thirty to a little after two, when they got her into the room in ICU. Dad and I went back to visit her tonight, and before we saw Mom the nurse told us she'd already passed roughly thirteen pounds of fluid! Amazing. There's more to go, but overall she's doing much better now, breathing more easily and much pinker. When Dad and I got ready to leave, Mom was even teasing us a little, asking us if we wouldn't like to have cots brought in so we could sleep there with her.

They'll be doing more tests tomorrow, and the cardiologist will come up with some kind of game plan. I'll let you know what we learn tomorrow.

For now, please continue praying for Mom's healing and for Dad's peace of mind. I have to admit I'm scared. Mom's only sixty-nine! I keep praying it's not as serious as we're thinking. I told my dad that everything would be okay. I reminded him that Mom's been through rough things before and come out fine. She's a fighter—after all, she survived my rebellious years, and you all know how ugly *that* was—and she's got lots of years ahead of her.

But even as I was saying all that and sounding so confident, inside I was scared to death. This is my mom! And she looked so weak, so frightened. I wanted to have her turn to me, like she did all those years when I was a kid, and tell me everything's going to be okay. But she couldn't do that.

As we left, one of the nurses told us to try and get some rest. I must have looked at her like she was nuts, because she patted my arm and said, "Don't worry. The doctors here are the best." Of course, I trust that. But here's what scares me.

What if even the best doctors aren't going to be good enough?

So I'm coming to you guys for help. Please, keep us in your prayers. And, if you think of it, tell me everything's going to be okay.

I need to hear it.

Thanks. I really appreciate you.

Love ya,

Faith

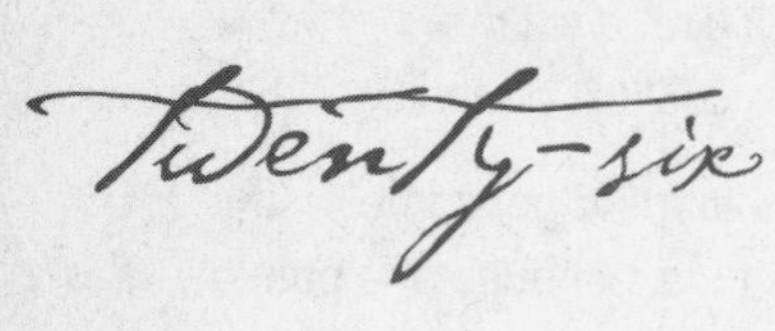

"We have to pray with our eyes on God, not on the difficulties."

OSWALD CHAMBERS

"WELL, WE'VE GOT SOME ANSWERS."

Faith watched the cardiologist page through the papers on his clipboard, afraid to say anything. Zeke stood next to Faith. Her father sat on the edge of her mom's bed, their hands entwined.

Jesus...be with us...

"The angiogram showed two, possibly three blockages."

Faith swallowed hard, wrestling the anxiety within her to the ground, not allowing it to push through and keep her from being able to listen, to take in what the surgeon was saying.

"In addition, we need to replace the aortic valve." He lifted his gaze from his clipboard to Faith's parents. "So Mrs. Bennett, we've got you scheduled for open-heart surgery in two days."

Faith stiffened, and Zeke's thumbs worked the muscles in her shoulders, doing his best to soothe her. She leaned back against him as the surgeon went on to explain the procedure. Faith did her best to absorb it all, but the moment he'd uttered those words—*open-heart surgery*—fear surged within her like a tide gone wild. Her heart raced, her head ached, her face felt hot and then cold.

Open-heart surgery. Her mother had to have open-heart surgery.

Jesus, where are You?

"I'm not going to lie to you, Mrs. Bennett—"

That comment brought Faith's focus zooming back to what the doctor was saying.

"The surgery won't be easy, but it will be far easier than your recovery. You have a lot working against you."

Faith looked at her mother, taking in the somber expression on her sweet face, the sudden lack of color in her cheeks, the way her fingers gripped her husband's hand.

She was frightened. And who could blame her? They'd been through this with Faith's father a few years ago. No one had to tell them how hard and long the recuperation could be. And Mom had a lot more working against her.

"What if we don't have the procedure done?"

Faith was surprised at how steady her father's voice was. She felt a surge of hope at his question. Maybe it would be okay. Maybe this was something they could work on, fix with diet. Maybe the threat of surgery was enough to scare Mom into walking agai—

"Of course, that's your option. But if this surgery isn't done, I'd guess she'd have a few months left at best."

A few months? Faith couldn't breathe. A few *months*? How was that possible?

From the expressions on her parents' faces, she could tell that had hit them as hard as it had her.

"And if it *is* done—" Faith squeezed the words out around the boulder-sized lump in her throat—"will it take care of the problems Mom's been having?"

The doctor looked at Faith. "It certainly should help a great deal." He turned back to Faith's mother. "You should find your mobility greatly restored, and you won't have nearly so much trouble breathing when you lie down and try to do things."

"Will I be able to exercise again?"

The tremor in her mother's words was almost Faith's undoing. But she wouldn't give in, wouldn't let herself dissolve. Not yet.

"I believe you will." The doctor's tone was kind, as though he sought to ease some of Mom's fear. "The good news is that this valve surgery is the safest of heart surgeries. And you really should feel a lot better after the recovery is over. The valve problem is what's been causing your shortness of breath and lack of circulation."

Hope sparked in her mother's eyes, and Faith drew every ounce of encouragement from it that she could.

"It will be slow at first—" the doctor leaned forward, putting his hand over Mom's where it rested on the bed—"but with the heart problems taken care of, you'll start feeling better and better as you recover."

Faith appreciated the way the doctor really thought through the questions before answering them. She had the sense he was doing his best to be encouraging, but to also give them a realistic picture of what they were up against. That was good. Faith didn't want pie-in-the-sky promises. She wanted to know the truth. How else could she prepare for what was to come?

If only she knew exactly what that was. If only she could find something to calm the anxiety chewing at her, leaving her ragged and raw inside. For no matter how encouraging the surgeon tried to be, no matter how encouraged her parents might be at promised improvements, as Faith listened to the doctor finish up explaining the procedure, she could no longer deny the truth.

She had a bad feeling about this.

You're overly tired. And you're letting fear have its way with your imagination. All you need is some sleep.

"When will you do the surgery?"

Zeke's question brought Faith's attention back to the doctor.

"The sooner the better. Probably Tuesday or Wednesday."

Two days. If they were moving that fast, it had to be even more serious than she'd thought.

The doctor stood, ready to leave. Faith tried to muster a smile, but her trembling lips didn't want to cooperate. "Thanks for all your help—"

She'd sworn she wouldn't cry, not in front of Mom and Dad, but her voice didn't seem to care.

Zeke's arm came around her shoulders. He held his hand out to the doctor. "Thanks for everything."

The surgeon nodded, and as he left the room, Faith went to hug her father and press a kiss to her mother's head. "It's going to be okay, Mom." Her mother nodded, and Faith put her hand on her dad's shoulder. "I need to go get something to eat, okay?"

"Sure, punkin'. You go ahead."

Her mother smiled at her. "I think I'll wait here."

Her teasing words accomplished what Faith was sure her mother intended—to make Faith laugh. She leaned over to give her mother a fierce hug. "I love you, Mom."

"I love you, sweetie." Her soft hand cupped Faith's cheek. "Now go get something to eat."

Faith nodded, and she and Zeke walked from the room. When they were out of sight, she turned to her husband. "Would you mind going down to the cafeteria alone? I'll be down in a few minutes, but I need to do something."

"I'll be downstairs. Take your time."

With slow, heavy steps she made her way to the hospital chapel. She peered in. Thank heaven. It was empty. Pulling the door closed behind her, Faith eased onto a pew, closed her eyes, and let the tears come.

Darkness could be comforting.

Faith liked sitting in her computer room with the lights off, letting the glow of the computer screen bring illumination. Okay, so it probably wasn't good for her eyes, but she didn't really care.

She'd slipped in here when she got home to read her e-mails. The words of care and encouragement from her friends were a balm to her hurting, frightened heart. Everyone in the Coffee Crew had responded, and to a person the message was the same:

"Everything's going to be okay. God's in control."

Of course, Jennifer added that she needed to relax, and Deb told her to take a hot bath. Sandy suggested a long walk in the woods, and Patti urged her to "go ahead and have a tantrum if you want, you're entitled." Lori sent her a heart-warming prayer, Linda sent her a moving devotion, and Connie sent her a joke that had her in stitches. Andi and Connie assured her they were with her. Every step of the way.

Faith sat there, grinning at her computer screen through her tears, more grateful than she could ever express for these crazy, heart-friends.

From: FaithinHim

To: TheCoffeeCrew

Sent: Monday, February 7, 2005

Subject: Mom's surgery

Okay, my mom's open-heart surgery is set for early Wednesday. Angiogram showed two, possibly three, blockages, so they'll be doing a double or triple bypass in addition to replacing the aortic valve. I can't explain it, but I'm nervous (I know, I know, relax, take a bath...☺).

What's hardest right now is that Mom is apprehensive, not just about the procedures, but about the recovery. Her diabetes can make it slow and potentially dangerous. But the good news is that this is a really safe surgery, and it should make Mom feel lots better. I hope so. It's been so hard on Mom, these last few years, to continue losing ground physically. She's been great, of course, always looking to God for strength and encouragement. But it still hurt her to not be able to walk, to move well, to do the things she loved. And it hurt us to see her struggle so.

Please be praying for God's hand on those caring for her in the hospital, for His touch on the surgeons and on Mom during the surgery, and for His healing and mercy on Mom as she recovers. And please keep Dad in your prayers as well, for peace and calm during all this. Mom means everything to him. I can't imagine what he'd do without her. She completes him, and he her.

Okay, I'm going to stop now before I make myself cry again. Thanks for your prayers. I love you guys!

Faith

The Floodwaters

"And the floodwaters rise..."

Matthew 7:25

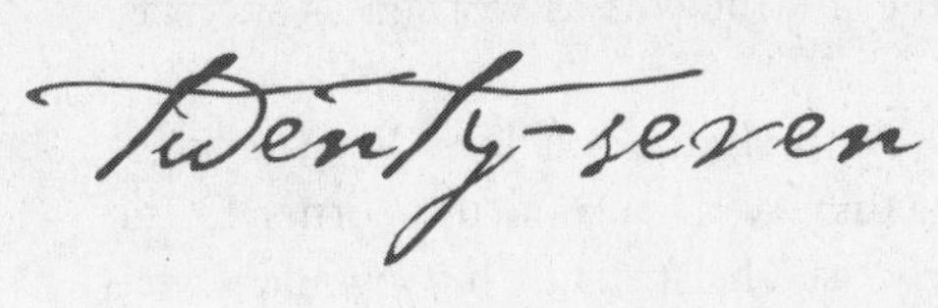

"The friend who can be silent with us in a moment of despair or confusion, who can stay with us in an hour of grief and bereavement, who can tolerate not knowing… not healing, not curing…that is a friend who cares."

HENRI NOUWEN

TWO DAYS HAD NEVER PASSED SO FAST.

And four hours had never passed so slowly.

Faith looked up from the magazine she'd been trying to read for three of those four hours. None of the words seemed to penetrate. All she saw when she stared at the page was her mother's face.

Why didn't the doctor call?

The surgery should have been finished over an hour ago.

"You want to take a walk?"

Faith mustered a smile for her husband. "That'd be nice." Good thing he had employees he trusted to oversee the company when he was gone. With all the time he'd spent with her at the hospital, he'd be in trouble if he didn't have good people to take the reins for him.

She stood, studying Dad's face as she did so. He looked so weary. "Dad, can we get you anything?"

"I'm fine, dear."

If only that were true. But he was as worried as she was, and she knew it.

"Zeke and I are going to stretch our legs. We'll be right back." He nodded, and they went around the corner to the desk where the Pink Lady sat. The sprightly little woman came hours ago to let them know that the surgery had begun.

"The next phone call will be to let you know she's off the bypass machine and the heart is working." Her smile had been confident and comforting, putting Faith more at ease.

Until now, that was, when Faith glanced at the clock and realized how long ago that first call had been.

The Pink Lady looked up as Faith and Zeke approached, answering the question before Faith could ask it. "No word, dear." She smiled. "But don't worry. I'm sure everything's fine."

Well, that makes one of us.

The phone rang. Faith froze, looking up when her father came to stand beside her. The Pink Lady spoke briefly, then turned to them with a bright smile. "Your wife is off the bypass machine, Mr. Bennett."

"Thank God!"

Faith hugged her father's waist. "How long until we can see her?"

The woman glanced up at the clock. "It shouldn't be long at all. The surgeon will come out to talk to you first."

Faith's father nodded, then went back to sit in the waiting area. Zeke rubbed Faith's back. "God's with your mom, darlin'. I know it."

The Pink Lady reached out and touched Faith's hand.

"I'm glad the surgery is going well."

Emotion welled up within Faith, making her words hoarse. "Me, too."

The surgeon came around the corner about an hour later. He shook Zeke's and Dad's hands and smiled. "She did great, Mr. Bennett. It was a hard procedure. Her weight complicated matters, but it all worked out fine. We did the valve replacement and a triple bypass. Your wife flew off the bypass machine like a champ—"

Way to go, Mom.

"—and within minutes we were using meds to lower her blood pressure when we usually have to use them to raise it. So that's all good. The next few days are critical, of course, but we're encouraged."

"Can we see her?"

At the eagerness in her father's voice, Faith slipped her hand in the crook of his arm.

"Give them about a half hour to get her settled, then call on the white phone and go on in."

Faith threw herself into Zeke's arms and hugged him.

"Whoa, darlin'. I need to breathe."

"She's going to be okay, Zeke. She's going to be okay."

He cradled her against his chest. "God's good, no doubt about it."

The phone on the Pink Lady's desk rang. She answered it, then turned toward Faith and Zeke. "Mr. Galine?"

Zeke nodded. She held the phone out to him, and he talked for a few minutes, then hung up.

"Trouble?"

"Looks like we've got a slight problem at one of our sites."

Faith's dad put his hand on Zeke's arm. "Go ahead and deal with your business, Zeke."

"Are you sure?"

Faith nodded. "Go ahead, sweetheart. I'll ride home with Dad."

Zeke gave Faith and her father a hug. "I'll keep praying."

Faith touched his cheek. "I know. Thank you."

Neither Faith nor her father could sit still for the next half hour. When the wait was finally over and they'd made the call, Faith's heart pounded as she followed her dad down the sterile hallway to the Cardiac Care Unit. The nurse met them as they came in.

"Faith, Mr. Bennett! I'm so glad to see you!"

Faith stared, then her mouth fell open. "Winnie?"

The nurse's grin was broad and warm. "I would have known you anywhere, Faith."

"I can't believe you work here." Faith looked around, then shook her head and took Winnie's hand in hers. "No, I take that back. I can't imagine you doing anything else."

Winnie squeezed her hand. "Well, you always said I wanted to fix people, and you were right." She waved her hand, indicating the unit. "Plenty of people here to fix." Her smile softened. "Some of them more special than others. You ready to see your mom?"

At Faith's nod, Winnie led them to Mom's room.

Her father hesitated at the doorway, closing his eyes for a moment. She knew he was praying, asking for strength. Then he straightened and walked into the room.

The doctor and the Pink Lady had warned Faith and her dad that Mom would look bad—kind of white and gray—after the surgery. But Faith looked at her, lying there—deep asleep, her soft salt-and-pepper hair framing her face on the pillow—and she knew they were wrong.

Her mom didn't look bad. She was beautiful.

Alive and breathing and utterly beautiful.

Winnie made a gentle adjustment to Mom's pillow. "Look at those pretty pink cheeks." She smoothed Mom's hair back. "She's got great color, and believe me, that's unusual. Patients of this kind of surgery don't usually look that good until a day or so into recovery." She smiled at Faith's dad. "You can tell Mrs. Bennett really wants to get better and go home soon."

"Not near as much as I want her there."

At the choked sound of his words, Faith had to blink to hold back the tears. She went to put her arm around her dad's shoulders.

After a moment of looking at Mom's face, he leaned down to kiss her forehead. Then he sighed and looked at Faith. "She's going to be okay."

"She's going to be great, Dad."

He gave her a weary smile as he took her arm, and they waved good-bye to Winnie and left the room. "She already is, hon. Always has been."

The next several days went by in a blur of visits to the CCU. Faith's mother progressed, though more slowly than the doctors had hoped. The first few days she'd been disoriented and frightened—which was even more upsetting for Faith than it was for her, because when it was over, her mom didn't remember it. But Winnie's calm presence kept Faith calm as well, and it was Winnie who finally discovered Mom was reacting badly to the pain medication. Once they got that changed, things were better.

Even so, Faith couldn't shake a heavy sense of dread. It had been five days since the surgery, and Mom still hadn't talked to anyone. Only that morning, while she and Zeke were visiting, Faith had to step out of the room to keep Mom from seeing how distressed she was.

"Faith?"

She turned to face Winnie. Her struggle must have been evident in her features, because Winnie took her by the arm and led her to the nurses' station. She sat Faith in a chair, then got her a cup of cold water to drink. Faith sipped at the liquid, letting it run down her throat.

Winnie stood there, compassion evident in her features, her stance.

When Faith could speak, she sighed. "I-I'm sorry, Winnie."

"Nothing to apologize for."

Faith stood. "It's just that she won't talk! I try and try to get her to say something, but she lies there, looking at me with those wide, hurting eyes." She swallowed back a sob. "I know she's in pain, Win. But why won't she talk?"

"Sometimes when patients have been through a great deal of struggle, not just with the surgery but even before that, their poor, weary brains need time to heal as well as their bodies."

Faith looked at Winnie, taking in the kindness wreathing her face, the gentle beauty she'd acquired as an adult. Or had it always been there, and Faith had been too full of herself to see it?

"Winnie, I'm really sorry."

She shook the apology away. "It's a normal reaction, Faith."

"No. I don't mean about today. I mean about...before." She wanted to hide her shame by looking at the floor, but she wouldn't let herself off the hook that easily. "I'm sorry for the way I treated you when we were kids. You were my friend, and I blew you off." She straightened, meeting Winnie's gaze without flinching. "You didn't deserve that, and I was wrong."

She waited for the change in Winnie's features, for the memory of those days to cloud her smile. But it didn't happen. If anything, the compassion and kindness in the other woman's smile only deepened.

"Thanks, Faith. I appreciate that. But it really is okay. And it's nice to see you've found a good man this time." She glanced to where Zeke was talking with Faith's mom, and she grinned. "And a particularly handsome one."

"He is, isn't he?"

"Much better than Dustin."

Faith laughed. It felt good to do so, and she gave Winnie a hug.

When she came back into Mom's room, Zeke was sitting, holding Mom's hand. Faith grinned. "Can't leave you alone with another woman for a second, and you're holding her hand."

"I always was a sucker for a pretty face." Zeke stood. "I need to get back to work, darlin'." Faith hugged him good-bye and went to sit beside her mother.

She spent the rest of the morning talking to her mom, brushing her hair, kissing her cheek. Her mom smiled and touched a gentle finger to Faith's face, but she stayed silent.

As much as she wanted to believe Winnie that this was normal, Faith couldn't relax. The heaviness returned, settling at the back of her mind. Her concern grew so strong that she finally asked Winnie to see if she could talk with Mom's doctor. Winnie made the appointment without hesitation.

"Two o'clock this afternoon. His office on the third floor."

A couple of hours later, as Faith sat in Dr. Campbell's office, waiting for him to come in, she wondered if she was doing the right thing. Was she being paranoid? Overly protective?

God, please, help me know what to say—

"Mrs. Galine?"

Faith started as her mom's heart surgeon came in the room. "Dr. Campbell." She smiled her gratitude. "Thanks for taking the time to talk with me."

He inclined his head, leaning back against his desk. "What can I do for you?"

Faith explained her fears as best she could, trying to keep the emotion from her tone. He was a doctor. A surgeon. He dealt in facts, not fears.

He listened, nodding from time to time. When she finished, he pursed his lips. "Well, the good news is that your mother's heart is working great."

Faith nodded. It was all true. She knew it.

"Her lungs are clear, and her blood pressure is right where it needs to be. So from the medical standpoint, she's doing well. However—" at the solemn look in his eyes, the heaviness in Faith's chest grew—"her muscles are beginning to atrophy from lack of movement. So in some ways you're right; your mother is still in crisis mode. The simple answer is that she has to want to get better."

"You don't think she does?"

The doctor considered her question. "I don't know, Mrs. Galine. You know your mother better than I. But I believe she's been struggling physically for quite some time?"

Faith nodded. For way too long.

"Surgery like this can take a great deal out of a person. Your mother needs to find the inner resources to start moving, standing, even taking steps to get the muscles working and to keep her heart and lungs going." He met her worried gaze. "As much as I hate to say it, if she doesn't start to move and work at getting better, we can still lose her."

The words hit her hard, especially because they held a ring of truth. She blinked, struggling with the emotions swarming through her. "Thank you, Doctor."

He started to turn away, then hesitated. "From what your father has said, I take it you're a religious family?"

Swallowing hard, Faith hugged her arms around herself. "We're Christians."

"Then it seems the best prescription I can give you for your mother is prayer. We can give her all the medicine in the world, but none of that can give her the will to live, to work at getting better. That can only come from one source."

Faith met his eyes, and the sincerity she saw there sparked a tiny ray of hope. "God."

"Indeed."

With that, he walked away. Faith watched him go, her heart full. She'd hoped for a word of encouragement when she talked with him. But she'd gotten far more.

He'd given her truth. And the firm reminder that her mother was in the best hands possible: the hands of the Great Physician.

twenty-eight

"Hope says to us constantly, 'Go on, go on."

Francoise d'Aubigne de Maintenon

From: FaithinHim

To: TheCoffeeCrew

Sent: Thursday, March 3, 2005

Subject: Progress!

Hello, dear sisters. Good news! Mom is finally out of CCU into a regular room! It's on the heart floor, of course, but it's a regular hospital room. I wondered if this day would ever come. Winnie, the friend I've told you all about, who I've known since grade school when I kicked her in the head with a ball (I know, I know, I was a terror), told me the CCU normal stay for a heart patient is a couple of days, sometimes three or four. Mom was there for a little over three weeks! Win said that's about the norm for someone as high-risk a patient as Mom.

But the CCU is definitely where Mom needed to be. You guys know my poor mom's endured one complication after another. First she had a hard time coming out of the anesthesia from the surgery, then it took longer than usual to get her off the oxygen, then her kidneys shut down. Zeke and I spent night after night praying, begging God for His intervention.

He answered, and none too soon. We came so close to losing Mom that I still shudder when I think about it.

But finally, thanks to the prayers of so many, she started doing better a few days ago. And then, this afternoon, her heart doctor came into Mom's room, planted his hands on his hips, and gave her a scolding look.

"Are you *still* here? I'm sick and tired of seeing you."

Mom and Dad stared at him. Zeke grabbed my arm because he knew I was about to launch at the guy. That's when the doc broke into a grin.

"So what say we move you out of here and into a regular room?"

We all broke into cheers. Almost made me cry.

I told Winnie I would miss seeing her every day, but that I felt like celebrating. She gave me the tightest hug ever.

So Mom's all settled in. You can even come visit her if you want.

Thanks again for your prayers. She still has a long way to go, but this is progress. And that's wonderful.

Love ya,

Faith

Faith raised her arms above her head and stretched.

"Did you have a good nap?"

She stood and went to take her mom's hand. "I thought *you* were supposed to be resting, not me."

Mom smiled from behind the oxygen tube. "I slept."

Faith eyed her, and her smile turned sheepish.

"A little."

"Hmm." Faith opened the bedside stand drawer, taking her mom's comb out. "How 'bout we get you all prettied up for Dad?"

"Okay."

Her response was made on a half gasp. Faith tried not to show that it bothered her. In some ways, her mom was doing well. In others, she worried Faith.

Faith had asked the nurses about Mom's shortness of breath, and they told her it was part of the healing process, that mom had to work hard to teach herself how to breathe right. They told Faith and her dad how they could help, by encouraging her to hold her heart pillow and cough, and to use her spirometer, a device she was supposed to blow into, moving an indicator to a certain point.

Faith had tried. So had dad. But the exercises were so painful, Mom had a hard time doing them as often as she needed to. Despite her mom's protests, Faith insisted. She knew it was the right thing to do. What she had to do.

Faith wished doing what was right didn't feel like being mean.

She sat on the bed beside her mother, drawing the comb through her mom's soft, salt-and-pepper curls.

Her mom leaned against her and sighed. "Do you remember when I used to comb your hair?"

Did she ever. "Yeah, but I hated it." Faith nudged her mom with her elbow. "You like this."

"I could squirm and complain, if it would make you feel more at home."

"Ha ha ha."

Faith was so glad her mom's sense of humor was coming back. It took nearly two weeks for Mom to start talking after her surgery, and even then it had only been to Dad at first. But bit by bit, Mom came back to them.

It helped, too, when Faith and Dad convinced the nurses

not to give Mom sleeping pills anymore. She and her mother might be different in a lot of ways, but they shared one peculiar trait—they couldn't handle medication.

Mom had really started gaining ground then. She was able to do more—to walk and do her breathing exercises more often. And though she battled frustration over her slow progress, she talked and smiled more.

Especially when Dad was there.

All he had to do was walk into the room, and her face bloomed into a beautiful smile. And looking at her, his eyes glowed with a special light. A light that made Faith's heart swell with joy.

She remembered thinking, as a little girl, that everyone's mom and dad were like hers. She knew better now. They were as rare as it got. And she was as grateful as could be that God had given them to her.

"Knock, knock!"

Faith and her mother looked toward the door. Winnie stood there, arms loaded down with bag upon bag of what looked to be silk pansies. Faith's mom *loved* pansies. Bright, cheerful helium balloons—a pansy, a Scooby Doo, a Smiley face—danced at the end of strings looped around Winnie's wrists.

"What in the world?" Faith giggled. "You moonlighting as a clown?"

Winnie arched her brow. "I'm here to help decorate your mother's room."

"Decorate it?" Mom managed in her gasping voice. She looked from Winnie to Faith. "A hospital room?"

Sweeping into the room, Winnie plunked the bags down on a chair and started pulling out silk flowers, beautiful vases, posters of the ocean, and stuffed animals. She winked at Faith. "Hey, it may *be* a hospital room, but it doesn't have to *look* like one."

"You're amazing."

Winnie grinned. "Yeah, I am."

Faith hopped off the bed and went to help. Winnie's enthusiasm was contagious, and soon she had Faith's mom pointing to tell them where to put things so she could see them best.

By the time they were done, every available space had something colorful and cheerful on it. The crowning touch came when Winnie pulled out what looked like markers, then removed the cap of one and turned to the window.

"Win—"

But Faith's caution came too late. Winnie starting writing a Scripture verse on the glass.

"I hope you know what you're doing."

Faith looked at her mom. "*I* hope she knows she's paying for the windows."

Winnie grinned at them as she went from the window to the mirror. She held up one of the markers. "Window chalk. Completely washable."

"Well then!" Faith took one of the markers from Winnie's hand.

"Hey! What are you doing?"

Faith grinned this time. "You forgot to draw butterflies."

A half hour later, Faith's dad walked into the room. Stopped. Looked around. Then stepped back outside to check the number on the door.

The three women laughed and called him back in. Faith went to link her arm in his, waving at the gaily adorned room. "Isn't it beautiful? It was Winnie's idea."

He offered her a smile. "Thank you."

"My pleasure." She turned to Faith. "My shift starts in a few minutes, so why don't you walk me to the unit."

Faith glanced at her dad, and he waved them on. "Go. Enjoy."

They no sooner got out into the hallway than Winnie took Faith's hand and dropped the window chalk markers into it. "Write new messages for your mom every day." Her smile held a depth of understanding and encouragement. "Remind her she's not alone in this." She closed Faith's fingers over the markers. "And neither are you."

Faith hugged her friend. "Thank you. I never would have survived all of this without you."

"Oh, you would have survived." Winnie winked again. "But you wouldn't have had anywhere near the fun."

During the rest of Mom's hospital stay, it became the norm for nurses to stop Faith and tell her how much they loved going into her mother's room, that they'd never seen a room done so beautifully in all the years they'd been working that floor. Faith just smiled. If it was that uplifting for the nurses, surely it would help her mom as well.

And it seemed to, Faith thought as she and her dad walked to her mom's room about a week and a half after Winnie's visit. Mom had been getting a little stronger each day.

They came into the room—and immediately knew something wasn't right. Mom's breathing was worse than ever.

Dad was at her side in half a heartbeat. "Annie?"

She looked up at him, and Faith could see she was near panic. "I'm calling the nurse."

The nurse, in turn, called the doctor. Who ordered her mother taken down for X-rays. Faith and her dad sat in the waiting room of the X-ray lab, paging through magazines more than three years old.

It didn't matter. Faith couldn't have concentrated enough to read anyway.

"Mr. Bennett?"

Faith and her dad looked up. Dr. Campbell signaled for them to come with him. At his somber features, Faith's heart plummeted. He took them to a room where the X-ray film was clipped over a light board.

"The X-rays show fluid gathering around Mrs. Bennett's lungs and heart again. It's to be expected, since she hasn't been moving as much as we'd like."

"So what do we do?"

Faith could tell her dad was struggling to stay calm.

"We drain the fluid."

"With diuretics, like they used in the ER?"

The doctor shook his head. "No, diuretics wouldn't be fast enough." He went on to explain the procedure, in which they would insert a needle to draw off the fluid. "We'll do it in Mrs.

Bennett's room, though you'll need to wait outside until we're done."

"Will it take long?"

"No." He hesitated. "But I'm afraid it may be painful."

Misery wormed its way into Faith's gut. More pain. Hadn't Mom been through enough?

Apparently not.

Faith and her dad stood in the hallway, outside Mom's room as they drained the fluid. Mom had asked the doctor if Dad could stay there, but he said it would only take a minute. She nodded, though Faith could tell she was afraid.

A few moments after they started the procedure, Faith heard her mom cry out.

At the sound, Dad leaned his head against the wall, his eyes closed.

Faith wanted to hit something.

She settled for putting her arms around her dad and hugging him tight.

God, help us. Help Mom.

It wasn't the most eloquent prayer, but it helped. Faith felt a calm settling over her, as though God reached down and placed His hand on her head, letting His strength pass into her.

Faith was grateful. She needed God's strength. And so did her dad.

Their own was fast being depleted.

Two days later, Faith walked into her mom's room. "Mornin', Mom."

No reply. Faith hesitated, studying her mom. She was sitting up, her head rolled to the side, her eyes half open.

"Mom?" She hurried to the bed, alarm grabbing her in a merciless vise. "Are you okay?" She shook her mother gently, then not so gently. But she didn't open her eyes. Just mumbled something incoherent.

Faith grabbed the nurse's call button.

"May I hel—"

"I need someone in here, now! Something's wrong!"

In seconds, two nurses were in the room. Faith stepped aside, her heart pounding, as they tried to rouse her mother. When they didn't have any more success than Faith, one of the nurses pulled her mother's chart.

"Well, no wonder."

Faith went to stand beside the nurse, following her pointing finger. "They gave your mom sleeping pills last night."

Faith frowned. "*Sleeping* pills? We asked you to take her off of those last week."

The young nurse shrugged. "It was on the orders."

"Then the orders—" Faith ground out—"are wrong."

The nurse's seemingly cavalier attitude irritated Faith. But when the girl rolled her eyes at Faith's words, she went straight from irritated to ballistic. Faith snatched the chart from the twit's hands and spun on her heel.

"Hey! You can't take that."

"Watch me."

Faith went to the nurses' station, plopping the chart on the desk. "May I please speak with the head nurse?"

A nurse Faith recognized stepped forward. She'd been working with Faith's mom for the last week. "Sure, Mrs. Galine. What can I do for you?"

When Faith explained what had happened, the nurse flipped Mom's chart open. As she read, the slight furrow in her brow became a canyon of incredulity. "I don't believe it."

"What?"

The nurse's lips thinned. "They not only gave her sleeping pills. They gave her a double dose!"

Faith fought her rising fury. "Can you explain this?"

The woman planted her hands on her hips. "No, but *someone* is going to."

When Faith's dad arrived a few hours later, her mom was still terribly groggy. But, as always, hearing his voice helped. It pulled her out of the stupor she'd been in enough to talk a little. At least, Faith thought, her jaw clenched, it was something.

It took Mom several days to recover from the effects of the pills. But after the sleeping pill fiasco, Faith allowed herself a satisfied smile when the same young nurse from a few days ago came in with a tray of medications. But before she administered them, she went to check the chart. Then double-checked it.

Apparently the head nurse read her staff the riot act.

Good.

From: FaithinHim

To: TheCoffeeCrew

Sent: Friday, March 18, 2005

Subject: Out of the hospital!

Finally, finally, finally!

The doctor gave the order we've been waiting for. Mom moved out of the hospital today and into the rehab wing of a nursing home. It was hard for Mom to hear she'd have to go to a nursing home rather than home. She almost burst into tears. But Dr. Campbell was adamant. Told her she's come a long way, but she isn't ready to be at home yet.

Mom asked how long she'd have to stay there. Dr. Campbell patted her arm. (He's really a nice guy.) "As long as it takes, but we're hoping that won't be more than a month or two. We'll see."

So, though we wish Mom was coming home, we're still encouraged.

She's doing so much better. Keep praying, ladies! Wouldn't it be cool if Mom could be home by Mother's Day?

Thanks!

Faith

"Faith, you're a nut."

She looked down at her mother and laughed. She couldn't help it. The sound of her mother's voice was the sweetest music in the world.

"Why? Because I challenged Mrs. Beamis to a wheelchair race with you?"

The weariness in her mother's eyes couldn't hold back the sparkle. "Faith, the poor woman is ninety-three years old!"

She grinned. "Okay, so we'll make her carry some weights from physical therapy to slow her down."

Mom shook her head, and Faith kissed the top of it as she leaned over to push open the door to the garden area, then eased her mom's wheelchair across the threshold. "See? I told you it was warm out here."

Her mom lifted her face to the sunshine. "I suppose I should learn to listen to you."

Faith jerked to a halt, pressing a hand to her chest. "Breakthrough! It's a breakthrough!"

"Ohh, you!"

Their laughter floated on the warm breeze as Faith wheeled her mother to the benches, her heart dancing at their playful banter. How she'd missed this! With every day, Mom seemed more and more her old self.

If only her physical condition would improve.

Faith adjusted the lap blanket over her mom's legs and set the brakes on her wheelchair. "My Cadillac," her mother called it. Still, in spite of her attempts at humor, Faith knew her mom was discouraged.

Though she'd hoped to be out of the nursing home in a matter of weeks, they were coming up on the two-month mark this week. At the beginning of Mom's stay, Faith was so sure each day would see her mother growing stronger. So many people were praying for Mom, she *had* to get better. Besides, God knew how much Dad needed Mom, how much Faith needed her. Which made it that much more frustrating that the series of ups and downs had continued. What made things even more upsetting was that, as often as not, the people running the nursing home didn't seem all that with it.

About three weeks after she was at the nursing home, Mom's difficulty breathing had returned. Faith called the nurses' attention to it, but it wasn't until two days later, when her mom's oxygen saturation levels dropped, that they sent her for X-rays. Sure enough, the fluid was back. They drained it again. At least it wasn't nearly as painful as the first time.

Faith tried not to be upset with the nurses on the rehab floor. She figured they had to deal with overly concerned family members all the time. Still, it bothered her that they hadn't taken her seriously enough to check things out sooner.

It was a good thing Zeke's construction company was doing so well that Faith didn't need to work. She spent most of her days at the nursing home, watching over her mother, encouraging her to do the exercises the physical therapists gave her, to do her deep breathing exercises, even to eat.

Her mom always used to say she'd never had a day when she wasn't hungry. But since the surgery, getting her to eat had been a battle. Nothing tasted right to her. And she had a terrible time swallowing.

The good news was that her mom had lost sixty pounds. The bad news was that she'd lost all her energy as well. She struggled to stay awake, and Faith found herself having to wake her so she would get up and try to walk down the hallway. Mom had to walk, or she'd never regain her strength! The most she'd made so far was forty steps.

Nowhere near enough for her to be discharged.

At least the weather was nicer now, and they could sit in the garden. Faith's mom loved being outside, especially with the flowers blooming. So Faith brought her here as often as she could.

Now, Faith looked up at the cloudless sky. *Father, I know You're with us. I've seen You over and over in the things that happen each day. And I know You're aware of everything happening with Mom. I believe You're working to heal her, to make her strong. But—*

She looked away. *But.* There was always that but. Faith shouldn't feel this way, but some days it felt as if God wasn't paying attention. As if He got distracted or looked away a fraction too long and suddenly her mom ended up in trouble again.

It wasn't true, of course, but fear had a way of making it seem true. *Father, help me trust You. I know You love Mom far more than I do. But she doesn't seem to be getting any better. Please help us.*

She glanced at her mother, who had dozed off in the sunshine. Laying her hand over her mother's, Faith squeezed. "Mom?"

Her mom's eyes fluttered open, and she gave Faith a drowsy smile. "Sorry about that."

Faith shook her head. "That's fine, Mom. You need to get rest. But I think it's time for lunch so we'd better head in."

Dad was there when they got to the room. "I wondered where you two ran away to."

Faith's mom held her hand out to him, and he took it, folding his large, strong fingers around her small hand.

"Your lunch tray is here."

Mom grimaced, and Faith couldn't blame her. The food at this place was terrible. Worse than that, it had been wrong.

"So did they get it right this time?"

The look on Dad's face was answer enough. Faith lifted the lid on the plate, and let her frustration out on a slow sigh. Starchy foods. Fruit. A dessert with whipped cream.

What was it going to take to get these people to put her mom on a diabetic diet? Faith and her dad had talked to everyone they could think of about the meals. She'd even gone to the kitchen and talked with the staff there. Everyone assured her they were fixing her mother diabetic meals.

And yet, here again was the wrong kind of food.

"What is *wrong* with these people?"

"Faith—"

"No, Dad. This is ridiculous. They're supposed to be the professionals. How can they keep messing up like this?"

"So, we'll call for another tray."

"I have a better idea." She took hold of the food tray. "I'll be right back."

"No hurry, sweetie."

Her mother's apathetic words only fueled Faith's frustration. She carried the tray down the hallway, into the kitchen, and straight to the head dietician's office. Enough was enough. She was going to the person in charge. Balancing the tray on one arm, she knocked on the door. A woman's muffled voice called for her to come in.

Faith did so, then plunked the tray down on the desk. The woman seated there was in her late fifties, and her bespectacled eyes blinked at Faith. She looked from the food tray to Faith then back again. "Yes?"

"Does this look to you like a diabetic meal?"

The woman studied the tray. "No—"

"Then can you explain to me why it's being sent to my mother, who is diabetic?"

The woman opened her mouth, but Faith's anger overflowed and words came tumbling out. "And then can you explain why I've have to fight for almost two months to get you people to serve my mom the kind of food she's supposed to have? Why she's had to battle blood sugars over four and five hundred because she's being given the wrong food? You're supposed to be helping her, not helping kill her!"

To the woman's credit, she didn't get defensive. She listened to Faith's tirade. Then when Faith ran out of steam, she turned and pulled a small box from the shelf. "I can't explain any of that. Not yet. But tell me your mother's name, and we'll take a look at her food card."

Faith gave the woman her mom's name, then sat in the chair beside her and waited. She'd learned several weeks ago that the food card held all the patient's vital information, and that it was what the staff used to prepare the patient's meals. The dietician frowned. "This doesn't show your mother as being diabetic."

Her fingers gripped the chair arms. "I was told it did. By three different people."

The woman pursed her lips. "Well, they were wrong."

The casual words almost brought Faith out of the chair and over the desk. She drew a deep breath, glancing down at the woman's nameplate on her desk. "Mrs. Wilfried, my mother has been here two months, and she has yet to receive the right kind of food." She fought to keep her voice steady. "I don't know about you, but from where I'm sitting, this is coming perilously close to neglect."

The woman stood with a nod. "I understand. I will take care of this immediately."

Faith stood as well, and for the first time in two months, she believed someone actually *would* take care of the problem. She hoped it wasn't too late.

Zeke sat in the quiet room, listening to his mother-in-law's shallow breathing as she dozed.

He hadn't been able to come see Anne often. Work was always crazy this time of year. The weather was warming up, and everyone wanted their projects started. Now. But he'd told the guys working for him that he would be out as much as he could in the next few days.

He wanted to be there for Faith and her parents. He offered to spell Faith and Jared, sitting with Anne. Something they'd needed more than ever today, after the fiasco with Anne's food.

"Ezekiel?"

He looked toward the bed. Anne was awake, watching him. He lay his hand over hers, where it rested on the bed. "Hello, beautiful."

Her smile was as sweet and loving as ever. "Thank you."

"For calling you beautiful?" He winked.

Her breathless laughter tugged at his heart. *Help her, Lord. Ease her pain.*

"No, though that was nice. Thank you for being there for Faith. For being the man you are." Her eyes misted. "For loving my little girl so well."

It was hard to talk around the emotion surging through him. "Thank you for raising her so well."

Anne gave a small shake of her head. "Oh, Zeke, I did so many things wrong, but God kept hold of Faith in spite of me. I'm so proud of her, of all she's made of her life, of the way she's living for Him." Tears glistened in her eyes. "I'm so grateful God never let her go."

Zeke stroked the back of her hand. "He's never let either of you go, Anne."

"No, He hasn't. Even now—" she looked around the room—"I know He's with me, watching over me." Her eyes shone with an inner confidence. "No matter what happens."

"You know what?"

"What?"

"You've always told me you and Faith were different."

She nodded.

"But you're not. Not really. Your daughter is just like you, Anne." He lifted her hand and pressed a soft kiss to the back of it. "She's easy to love."

When Faith got home that evening, Zeke met her at the door. He'd been doing that lately, standing there and opening his arms, letting her walk into them, holding her until she was ready to move away.

Usually that only took a few minutes. Tonight she might stay in those arms for good.

"Did your day go any better?"

With a sigh, she pulled away. "They actually brought the right kind of meal for Mom at dinner, but she was dozing again. Dad and I couldn't get her awake enough to eat. And when she was awake right before we left, her right shoulder, front *and* back, was hurting her like crazy."

Faith rubbed a trembling hand over her burning eyes. "It's probably muscles and tendons protesting at the use they're getting. You know, with the physical therapy. I rubbed some topical pain stuff on it, but Zeke, it hurt so much she was in tears. She couldn't even lift that hand to feed herself. Daddy had to feed her."

His touch, as he led her to the couch, communicated his sympathy. They sat, and she curled into the shielding circle of his arm.

"How's your dad holding up?"

Faith rolled her shoulders, trying to loosen the tense muscles. "He's so tired. He told me when I got to the nursing home this morning that Mom didn't want him to leave last night. So he stayed until they kicked him out, way after ten.

He was so tired when he got home, he didn't eat. Just went to bed. But he hardly slept."

She lay her head back, so weary she could hardly think straight. "I'm almost as worried about him as I am about her. His eyes are so full of sorrow." Her voice choked up, and she cleared her throat to continue. "It's so hard to see Mom the way she is now. And it's not only the physical stuff, though that's bad enough. There are so many indignities she has to endure, and they're as wearing as the constant physical struggle."

She pulled her knees to her chest. "I wish I could wave a magic wand and make her all better and strong."

"That's not your job, Faith." Zeke's quiet words held the ring of truth.

She nodded. "I know."

"You may not like the way things are going, but you have to believe God knows what's happening and what's coming. He's with your mom. And with you."

Tears trickled down Faith's face, and she turned to press into his shoulder. He held her while she cried. When she finally stilled, he smoothed back her hair.

"Speaking of eating, the church folks brought another meal."

She looked at him. "You're kidding."

Their church family had been amazing, visiting her mother in the nursing home, providing her father and them with meals for the whole time her mother had been ill. The food was almost as delicious as the fact that Faith hadn't had to even think about cooking.

He grinned. "Nope. I think it's spaghetti. And you need to eat to keep up your strength. So come on."

Zeke stood, holding out his hand. She took it and let him pull her up. They made their way to the kitchen, but as Faith prepared a plate of delicious-smelling food—as she sat at their kitchen table, so grateful to be in her own home—she couldn't help thinking of her mother.

Three months. That's how long her mother had been fighting this physical assault. That's how long since her mother had been in her own beloved home, the place she'd shared with

Dad for almost forty-nine years. Three months since she'd been able to walk well, to breathe without struggle. Three months of one crisis after another.

And if Faith was exhausted, she couldn't imagine how deep her mother's weariness and despair went.

The feel of Zeke's hand on hers pulled her from her dark thoughts. She met his gaze, and the love and tenderness she saw there warmed her suddenly cold heart.

"You want to pray for your mom and dad?"

She couldn't speak, so she nodded. As they bowed their heads, Faith knew she was blessed among women. Not only did she have the best mother and father in the world, she had the best husband as well.

Twenty-nine

"Peace is a journey of a thousand miles and it must be taken one step at a time."

LYNDON B. JOHNSON

IT ONLY TOOK TWO DAYS FOR DISASTER TO STRIKE.

Again.

Faith and her dad were at the nursing home with Mom. They'd gone with her to physical therapy, then come back to the room to sit and watch TV together. Mom's breathing grew more and more ragged as the day wore on. By the afternoon, she couldn't walk at all, could hardly stand. Faith asked the nurses about it, but they said her mother was fine.

Dad was worried, but both he and her mother didn't argue with nurses or doctors. They trusted them.

But when Mom's face turned pasty white, Faith was at the nurses' desk, demanding to see the administrator. One of the nurses Faith had asked about her mother earlier looked up from the paperwork she was filling out.

"What can we do for you, Mrs. Galine?"

"You can get the administrator."

"If you'll tell me what's wrong—" The woman's condescending tone and look of strained patience was more than Faith could bear.

"What's wrong is my mother can't breathe. What's wrong is I've asked you and two others to come check her oxygen levels, and no one has done so. What's wrong is my mother is in trouble, and all you seem to care about is your stupid paperwork!"

With that, Faith reached down and snatched the papers from beneath the nurse's pen. She crumpled the papers in her hand.

"Mrs. Galine!"

The woman was on her feet, but Faith didn't care. "I told you this morning Mom was acting the way she did before, when fluid was gathering around her lungs and heart."

"It would be extremely unusual for that to happen again so soon."

Faith fought back a scream. "Are you *listening* to me? My. Mother. Can't. *Breathe!*" She planted her hands on the desk. "Now either you get on the phone and call the doctor, or I'm taking her out of here. Now!"

"Fine!" The nurse didn't even try to hide her disgust. Faith didn't care. All she cared was that she was picking up the phone and dialing.

When the nurse described the symptoms Faith saw in her mother, the doctor ordered her sent immediately to the ER. He was there to meet them when they arrived. He listened to her breathe and ordered X-rays.

Two hours later, Faith's mom was back in the hospital. Fluid had, indeed, gathered around her heart and lungs again. More than ever before. The doctor said her lung capacity was down to about a quarter of normal.

No wonder she'd struggled so to breathe!

After Mom was settled in her room, Dr. Campbell took Faith and her dad aside. "I'm concerned this has happened three times now since Mrs. Bennett's heart surgery. Her heart is working well, so that's not the problem. Which means we have an underlying issue to deal with."

An underlying issue? Faith went cold. What did that mean?

Dr. Campbell slid his hands into the pockets of his white

coat. "We'll send Mrs. Bennett back to the nursing home tomorrow morning. I'd like to put her on increased doses of diuretic to try and get the fluid out from around the lungs. We'll do that through the weekend, then reevaluate."

"And if it doesn't work?"

The doctor looked at Faith's father, his gaze steady. "Then we're looking at lung surgery."

"Another surgery?" Faith's mind felt like it was going numb. How could her mother endure another surgery? "Is she strong enough?"

"We'll do everything we can to ensure she is."

Amazing what little comfort that was.

From: FaithinHim

To: TheCoffeeCrew

Sent: Wednesday, April 20, 2005

Subject: I'm afraid

Friends, Mom doesn't look good. It terrifies me to admit that, but she doesn't look good at all. Breathing is such a struggle for her.

When I look at her, this hard lump of dread sits in my gut. Tonight, my heart finally gave in and asked God the question I've been doing everything to avoid:

Are we losing her?

I don't want Him to answer. Because I'm afraid I know what the answer is.

And I don't want to hear it.

Please, be praying for Mom, for Daddy, and for me. Most of all, be praying that God's will is done. And that we're able to endure it if His will is not as we hope.

Love,

Faith

The phone call came early Friday morning.

It was Faith's dad.

As Dr. Campbell had directed, Mom returned to the nursing home. They'd started the regimen of diuretics, which seemed to be helping. Until this morning.

"Your mom went into respiratory distress." Dad's voice was trembling. "The nursing home called the EMTs to take her back to the hospital."

"I'll be right there, Dad."

She hung up and turned into Zeke's arms. Her breath catching on sobs, she told Zeke what was happening.

"I'm going with you to the hospital."

Faith didn't argue.

When they walked into her mother's hospital room, the sight of Mom's white face... *Jesus, please*... She steadied her voice. "Hey, Mom."

Her mother's smile trembled from behind the oxygen mask. The all-too-familiar sound of oxygen hissing from the tank whispered around them. Faith met her father's eyes.

"They've scheduled your mother for lung surgery today."

It was a good thing Zeke's arm was supporting Faith, because her knees went weak at this news.

Just then the nurse came into the room. "You ready for your epidural, Mrs. Bennett?"

Mom's smile was as sweet as ever. "Sure."

The nurse moved to place a hand on Mom's shoulder. "Hon, just so you know, with your breathing depressed the way it is, we can't give you much pain medication for putting the epidural in. I'm afraid this is going to hurt a bit." Her gaze lifted to Faith's father. "I'm afraid I'll have to ask you all to step outside."

Mom reached for Dad's hand. "I want Jared to stay."

The nurse's tone was kind but firm. "I know, Mrs. Bennett, but he can't. I promise, it will only take a minute. Then he can come back in."

Faith's dad kissed her mom, then Faith went to cup her

mother's face, to look into her deep green eyes. Eyes so like her own. Eyes filled with love.

"I love you, Mom."

Her mother smiled, and that gaspy voice replied, "I love you too, sweetheart. I always will."

Throat tight, Faith turned and walked with her father and Zeke from the room. Faith put her arm around her father's shoulders, leaning her head against his arm.

Her father had always seemed taller than anyone else, taller and straighter and stronger. A tall oak that never bent, no matter how fierce the gale. But when he spoke, Faith heard the tremor in his words. "She looked so afraid."

Faith nodded. "I know, Daddy. She's been through so much." She patted him on the shoulder. "It'll be over soon."

As though to prove her right, the door to her mother's room opened, and the nurse looked out. "She's asking for you, Mr. Bennett."

They started into the room, and the nurse halted them for a moment. "We'll be taking her to surgery as soon as she sees you."

Dad nodded, and they hurried into the room. He went to Mom's side, taking her trembling hand. Faith could tell her mom had been crying, and that was almost more than she could take.

"Hi there." Her dad's soft voice was so full of love. "You okay, hon?"

Mom looked up at him, eyes wide with love and trust, and managed a smile. Her breathless whisper was for Dad alone. "I am now that you're here."

Zeke tugged Faith's arm, and they walked from the room. He drew her into his strong embrace, and when he spoke, emotion roughened his voice. "If anyone ever wonders what real love is, all they have to do is look at those two."

Amen, Faith thought. *Amen.*

Unlike her mother's heart procedure, the lung surgery seemed to go by in a flash. The surgeon came to tell them that, during surgery, they'd drained another litre and a half of fluid from around each lung, but the procedure—inserting a fine talc that would seal areas where the fluids were gathering—was a success.

So why doesn't he look more encouraged? Faith couldn't make herself ask the question out loud.

The surgeon pulled off the cap covering his head. "She's still on a ventilator and may be through the night. She'll be in ICU for a few days, then will be moved into a regular hospital room. You should be able to see her in about a half hour."

"Thank you, Dr. Campbell." Faith's father held out his hand, and the doctor took it. "For everything."

The doctor's eyes seemed shadowed. "I wish I could do more."

"So do I," Dad said with a weary smile. "But God's with Anne, and He will work this out as is best."

Faith wanted to echo her father's words, wanted to feel confidence about them. But for once she couldn't.

What if God's idea of *best* wasn't the same as Faith's?

When Faith and her father went to the ICU the next day, the nurse didn't buzz them in as she had the day before. Instead, the doors opened and Winnie and the surgeon came out to meet them.

The look on Winnie's face told Faith all she needed to know.

The news wasn't good.

Winnie hugged Faith's father, then led them to the ICU waiting area. They sat, and Winnie took Faith's hand as Dr. Campbell explained the situation. "Mrs. Bennett had a bad night. Her blood pressure dropped. Her kidneys have shut down." He looked at Dad, his gaze level. "Your wife is in a fight for her life."

Faith couldn't take it in. She sat there, her hand gripping Winnie's hand. The doctor had to be mistaken. Had to be talking about someone else.

"What are her chances for recovery?"

Dad's quiet question startled Faith. She shot a look from him to the doctor. *Don't say it! Don't—*

"Fifty-fifty at best. We've got her on all the meds we can to help, but for now it's going to be a waiting game." He looked down, then back up at Dad. "I'm so sorry. Her body's been through so much…"

Faith's father nodded. "She's tired. It's time for her to rest."

"Dad!"

He lifted tearful eyes to Faith. "I haven't given up, punkin'. But the outcome is in God's hands. Not ours. And we have to be ready for whatever comes."

Faith closed her eyes. No. She would not be ready. Not for this.

Not ever.

Zeke sat in his bedroom chair, his Bible sitting closed in his lap, a steaming mug of coffee cupped in his hands. Faith was in the office room, writing e-mails to update friends on Anne's situation. So he'd taken the opportunity of these few moments to sit and pray.

To ask God for guidance.

It was so hard to see Faith and Jared going through what they were. Faith still wanted to believe her mom would rally, recover. But Zeke had a feeling that, no matter how they might want that, it wasn't going to happen.

He opened the Bible to 1 Thessalonians, which he'd been reading that week, and found his place in chapter four. Taking a sip of coffee, he started reading. His breath caught as he took in the words on the page in front of him.

> "And now, brothers and sisters, I want you to know what will happen to the Christians who have died so you will not be full of sorrow like people who have no hope."

Zeke closed his eyes, sorrow washing over him. He'd been so afraid of this. But then, maybe this didn't mean anything. Maybe it was just a coincidence that this was his reading for today. He read on.

> "For since we believe that Jesus died and was raised to life again, we also believe that when Jesus comes, God will bring back with Jesus all the Christians who have died. I can tell you this directly from the Lord: We who are still living when the Lord returns will not rise to meet him ahead of those who are in their graves. For the Lord himself will come down from heaven with a commanding shout, with the call of the archangel, and with the trumpet call of God. First, all the Christians who have died will rise from their graves. Then, together with them, we who are still alive and remain on the earth will be caught up in the clouds to meet the Lord in the air and remain with him forever."

Goose bumps skipped over Zeke's arms; shivers traveled across his neck and down his spine. It was as though he could see it happening. Hear the shout! The trumpet blast! And there, among those rising into the air, was Anne, her face glowing with the purest joy he'd ever seen as she went into the arms of her Savior and Lord.

Blinking back tears, Zeke read the last line: "So comfort and encourage each other with these words."

He bowed his head. The room was oddly still. Like it was packed in some kind of supernatural cotton. Certainty pressed down on Zeke like a sodden wool blanket—heavy, weighted, inescapable.

This was no coincidence.

Knowing that, he opened his heart, asking God to touch him, to prepare him for what was coming—and to equip him so he might help those he loved so dearly as they let go of the mother and wife they adored.

The Winds

"And the winds beat against that house..."

MATTHEW 7:25

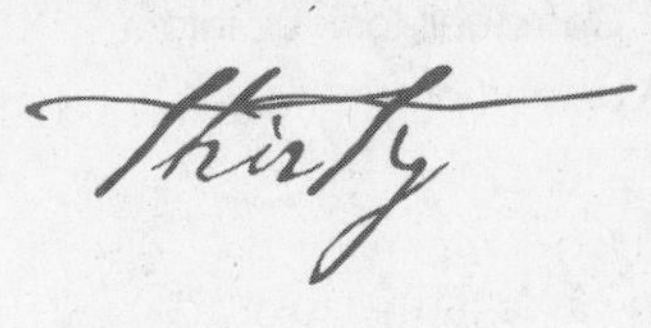

"Be kind, for everyone you meet
is fighting a hard battle."

PLATO

From: FaithinHim

To: TheCoffeeCrew

Sent: Saturday, April 23, 2005

Subject: Jesus is Lord

Dearest sisters, I've been sitting here, wondering what to title this post. I'm sad and weary, but so very aware of God's gracious love and presence. Then I glance at my desk, and there is an open hymnal, and this hymn, "Jesus Is Lord," is the one that met me. The lyrics seem so appropriate:

"All my tomorrows, all my past, Jesus is Lord of all

I've quit my struggles, contentment at last, Jesus is Lord of all."

Today, it seems, my sweet, wonderful mom has quit her struggles. Or at least her body has. She's in the ICU (they had her in a regular hospital room for a day), and the doctor talked with Dad, Zeke, and me yesterday, telling us Mom was in a fight for her life. When we arrived at the ICU this morning, Dr. Campbell took us into a small room next to the waiting room. A quiet room.

A room for bad news.

I'll never forget the sadness on his face as he turned to my dad. "Your wife has developed pneumonia on one side. Her blood pressure is dropping, her kidneys are slowing, she's unconscious. We've got the oxygen wide open, but it's not helping." He looked at us. That final kind of look that you know isn't going to change, no matter how much you cry and rant and rave. No matter how much you plead. "I'm sorry. She's not going to pull through this."

I sat there. Stunned. Broken. Angry. Desperate.

Helpless.

I wanted to crawl away somewhere and scream. Instead, we nodded. Said thank you. Then we went back to the waiting room. The doctor came in about fifteen minutes later and suggested we go home for a short time. That they had some further tests to do before we could see her and we'd be more comfortable at home.

"Can we see her before we go?"

I was glad Dad asked that. I'd wanted to but was afraid. Thankfully, Dr. Campbell let us go in. Just for a minute. Dad did get Mom to rouse slighty one time. Dad and I were holding her hands, and she squeezed our hands to say she heard him, but when we left, she was unresponsive.

The doctor walked us out of the ICU. "Come back in an hour."

So here I am, writing you because I can't think of what else to do. They can't say how much time Mom has left, or if she'll ever come to again, but we're losing her. Probably soon.

Once again, I'm not sure what to ask you to pray, other than for

God's will and mercy. Mom fought long and hard, but her body is so worn down...

I can't imagine life without her, but I am so very grateful that, if we do say good-bye in this life, it won't be forever. And I will long for eternity even more than I do now, because I know I'll see her glorious, sweet smile and feel her arms around me again. I can't wait for that day.

I can't write anymore, but I want to thank you for all your prayers and care. I love you.

Faith

The hour came and went.

Faith, Zeke, and her dad came back, and Winnie met them at the double doors leading to the ICU. "I'm really sorry, but it will be another hour or so until you can come in."

"She won't—" Faith couldn't make herself finish the question, but Winnie understood. Her eyes glistened as she shook her head. "No, she won't die before you see her."

Faith put her arm around her dad and led him to the ICU waiting room. She sat on the couch, staring but not seeing. Zeke sat beside her, silent, his arm firm and tight around her. Dad stood at the window of the waiting room, staring out at the hospital parking lot. Faith leaned into Zeke, wanting to say something to encourage and comfort her dad, but she couldn't.

There weren't any words.

Just a weary, sad silence.

A bustle of sound at the doorway jerked their attention that direction, but it wasn't the doctor. It was another family coming in—an older woman and what looked to be her two adult children. They sat on the couch across from Faith and Zeke, the woman between the other two. She shredded a tissue in her trembling hands, looking from one of her children to the other.

"He was doing so well! I don't understand..."

The man beside her shook his head. "Mom, there's no explanation. Dad took a bad turn."

"They were hitting him—"

"CPR, Mom." The daughter stroked her mom's arm. "They were doing CPR on him."

The older woman stared at her hands. "What will I do without him?"

Faith choked back a sob. *Father God, this could be us any time… Please, please help these people.*

The too-familiar sound of the ICU doors opening and closing came and then footsteps. A doctor entered the waiting room, and Faith was ashamed at her relief when she realized it wasn't Dr. Campbell.

The woman stood, going to him. "Is he…?"

The doctor took her outstretched hands, holding them. "I'm sorry. We worked on him for forty-five minutes, but he was gone."

The woman dissolved into tears, and her children came to support her, to lead her back to the couch. Faith gripped Zeke's hands, the doctor's words hitting her almost as hard as it did the poor woman sitting there.

Just then, another man entered the waiting area. He went to the weeping family, introducing himself as the hospital chaplain. Faith and her father exchanged a look of relief. Here was help and comfort. *Thank You, God. Give Him the right words.*

He sat beside the grieving woman, talking with her. But as he talked, he offered no comfort, no promise of eternity. Rather, the man made light conversation. Chitchat. He even attempted a joke.

Faith wanted to slap him.

Finally, he asked if the woman wanted him to call her pastor, and she gave him the phone number.

Faith watched the man leave, then caught sight of her father. His features were drawn and troubled. He looked at Faith, then moved to the weeping woman's side. Zeke and Faith stood and followed, and suddenly she understood.

Her father had wanted the chaplain to pray for the

woman. And since the man hadn't, her father—her introverted, usually reserved father—was stepping in. Tears stinging her eyes, Faith watched her dad kneel beside the weeping woman.

"Ma'am, forgive me if I'm intruding, but are you a believer? In Christ?"

She wiped her face and looked at him. "Yes. Yes, I am."

"Well, I'm not a pastor, but if it's okay with you, I'd like to pray for you." He looked at her son and daughter. "For your family."

"Oh, yes!" The woman reached for Dad's hands.

Without a word, Zeke and Faith knelt beside her father and placed their hands on the woman's. Faith listened with growing awe as her Dad prayed.

"Most holy God, precious Father, help us. Our hearts ache with sorrow, our souls feel wounded by grief and loss. You know, Lord, what has transpired here. You know how lives have been forever changed. And You know what it is to lose one You cherish, one who is part of You."

Faith struggled to hold back the sobs. *"One who is part of you."* That's what her mom was. Part of her. Part of her dad. How could they bear the loss?

"Please, Jesus, be with us, even now, in this very moment. Come to this woman and her family, loving God, and cloak them with Your peace, Your comfort. Speak healing to their broken hearts, hope to their sorrowing spirits. Help them to remember, God of eternity, that the good-bye is only temporary."

Her father's voice rang with such certainty that shivers skittered across Faith's skin. Grief and fear couldn't douse the truth. Indeed, as her father prayed, it was as though his words breathed the embers of her own shaken trust back to life. They shimmered, caught, and blazed through her, creating warmth and light that shone brighter than ever before, chasing the shadows from the dusty corners of Faith's weary heart.

"One day we *will* be reunited with You, Father, and with those we love who knew You."

Her dad's voice choked, but Faith knew it wasn't so much

from sorrow as from anticipation. For she felt the same thing surging through her. What a day that would be!

"But right now, that day seems so far away. Help us endure. Grant us grateful hearts for the many gifts You give, for the memories of the love we have shared—and especially for the promise of the life to come. And during the coming days, as these, Your children, walk through the valley of the shadow of death, let them know You are there, beside them, loving them, guiding them."

As You're beside us. Thank You, Lord...

"We place them in Your hands, Almighty God, knowing there is no better place for them to be. Amen."

Tears coursed down their faces when he finished, and Faith had never been quite so proud of her dad. There he was, in his own quiet way, reaching out in the midst of his own pain to minister to someone who was hurting.

If Faith had ever doubted her father had a heart governed by God's love, she would never do so again. Yes, she was still weary and afraid. Still painfully aware her mother was even in that very moment, slipping away from them. And yet...

Beneath it all, Faith sensed holy hands holding and comforting and guiding. God was there. He was with her mom. He was with them.

And that was sufficient.

thirty-one

"Why does it take a minute to say hello,
and forever to say good-bye?"
ANONYMOUS

"MR. BENNETT? FAITH?"

At the sound of Winnie's voice, Faith, Zeke, and her father looked up from where they were sitting on the couch with friends from church. Don and Anita Clark, and Von and Marge Clark, two couples who had known Faith's mom and dad since right after they were married. They'd been a part of Faith's life for so long, they were like extended family.

She'd been so grateful to see them walk into the waiting room. She went to embrace them, thanking them for coming.

"We couldn't be any place else," Anita said, her eyes glistening with unshed tears. They all sat together, talking, praying, waiting.

And, best of all, sharing memories of Faith's mom.

Faith had been so engrossed in the stories she hadn't heard Winnie come into the room. When she looked up and saw her there, Faith stood. As did her father.

Winnie smiled at them. "You can come see Mrs. Bennett now."

Faith turned to their friends.

Marge nodded. "Go ahead. We'll be right here when you come out."

Faith, her dad, and Zeke followed Winnie into the ICU, to her mother's room. The room was full of the sounds of machines. Blips and beeps, hissing oxygen. They had her mother on a machine that forced air into her lungs.

Faith went to one side of the bed, Dad to the other. Zeke stood beside Faith as she and her father each took one of her mother's hands.

"Anne?"

It took all Faith's strength not to break down and weep at the sound of her father's voice, calling her mother.

"Annie, open your eyes, hon."

Nothing.

Faith knew without a doubt if there had been any way her mother could do as her father asked, she would. She would never have refused that voice she adored.

But there was nothing. Not even a flicker of her eyelids.

"She's not in any pain," Winnie said. "She's in a deep sleep. Her breathing will slow more and more, until..."

"Until it stops."

Winnie nodded at Dad. "Yes." She put her hand on Faith's arm for a moment. "We'll be right outside if you need us. I'm praying for all of you."

Faith nodded her thanks, and when Winnie left, the room fell silent except for the sounds of the machines. After a moment, his gaze fixed on his wife's face, Dad said, "We should sing to her."

Faith bit her lip and nodded. Her mother loved to sing. Loved to hear Faith and her father sing. He opened his mouth, but nothing came out. *Jesus...Jesus, help us.*

Her eyes on his, Faith began to sing. All the old songs, the songs from her childhood. Songs they'd sung as a family for as long as she could remember. "This Little Light of Mine." "Every Day with Jesus." "Whisper a Prayer." "Everybody Ought to Know Who Jesus Is." "How Great Thou Art."

On and on they sang, the words flowing around them, soothing their ragged spirits, the sound filling Faith's ears and soul. She closed her eyes, focusing on the music, on singing the songs her mother loved.

On saying good-bye.

She didn't know how long they sang. It was as though she was transported from that place of pain to a place of quiet and peace. And in the stillness of that place, one more song came to her. The last song they would sing.

"Shepherd of Love..."

The words came halting at first, then they flowed more smoothly, as though God Himself poured them from heaven into her heart that she might anoint her mother with the sound of His love.

As the last of the words faded into silence, Faith looked at her father. "Do you want some time alone with her?"

His eyes stayed on her mother's face. "No. I already told her everything I needed to." He looked at Faith. "Do you?"

She bit her lip, and he nodded. "We'll be right outside."

Tears burning, Faith waited. Then, when she was alone, she touched her mother's face and poured out her heart. "I love you, Mom. I know you know that, but I wanted to tell you again. You were the best Mom in the world. You loved me the way no one else could. You fought for me, didn't give up on me. And you prayed me back to life when I was lost."

Her breath caught on a sob. "I'm so grateful you are my mom. Thank you for everything you taught me. Thank you for sharing your heart with me." She clenched her teeth, knowing what she needed to say, forcing the words out though it tore her apart to speak them. "I know you don't want to leave us. But it's okay, Mom."

Faith could scarcely talk through her tears. How was it possible to feel two years old and a hundred years old at the same time? "I love you, Mom. I'll miss you every day of my life." She squeezed her mother's hand, laid her head on her mother's chest, and let the tears flow.

When her tears were spent, she lifted her head and pressed a kiss to her mother's soft cheek, then walked from the room and into her husband's waiting arms.

It was time.

Faith and her dad stood there, holding her mom's hands. Zeke stood close by, watching. Praying. Winnie had come in and turned off the machine that had kept Mom's body breathing.

"What will happen now?"

She looked at Dad, answering his question in an even tone. "Her breathing will slow. You'll see the numbers drop on the oxygen monitor. When they get below sixty, it won't be long."

Faith's dad nodded.

They stood there, watching. Bit by bit, the movement of Mom's chest slowed. Faith's gaze went from her mom, to the monitors, then back to Mom again. The numbers on the oxygen monitor kept dropping.

75. 71. 66. 64...

"It's okay, Annie. My sweet Annie." Dad held her hand to his chest. "I love you. I'll always love you. It's okay to go..."

Faith's throat constricted. She wanted to cry out, to beg God to stop what was happening. But she couldn't.

62. 61. 59.

She reached trembling fingers to touch her mother's curls. Smooth them. Stroke them away from her sweet face. "Go to sleep, Mommy." Faith's whisper was ragged. "Rest now. I love you. Go to sleep."

With one final whoosh of air, it was over.

Faith's mom was gone.

Her father choked, tears streaming down his face. "Oh...oh..." He broke down, his sobs tearing at Faith's heart.

Faith laid her mom's hand on her still chest, and then she and Zeke moved as one to embrace her dad.

They stood there, weeping, until Dad took a gasping breath and straightened. "Let's go. I need to go home."

Faith nodded. She gripped his hand as they walked from the room, allowing herself one final glance back at the still form that used to house the center of her universe.

thirty-two

"Forsaking All I Trust Him. Now that is FAITH."

ANONYMOUS

From: FaithinHim

To: TheCoffeeCrew

Sent Saturday, April 23, 2005

Subject: Homecoming!

Surely, there is rejoicing in eternity tonight because one of the sweetest, funniest, kindest, most loving, most encouraging, most godly women who ever walked this earth has passed from mortality to immortality. Mom fell asleep in Jesus this evening, around six-thirty.

This whole day seems unreal, and yet I know it's true. Mom is gone. Even writing that makes me shake my head. I think I held out a sliver of hope that she would rally, that we'd all be looking back on this time saying, "Whoo, yeah. Remember how we thought we were going to lose you? Man, am I ever glad you made it through that." And yet…

God is good. He is faithful. And He has been with us through this horrible, wonderful day.

He was with us early this morning, when the doctor called and said we needed to come, that Mom was not doing well. He was with us when dear friends—friends who are like family—from the church came to sit and weep with us. He was there in the hearts and kind spirits of the nurses who cared for Mom and for us, in my friend, Winnie, who God used to bless me in both childhood and adulthood. He was with us when the doctor told us Mom wasn't going to make it. He was there when I couldn't hold back the tears any longer and wept.

He was there when Dad, Zeke, and I were in Mom's room in the ICU, holding her hands, and we started to sing her favorite choruses and hymns for her one last time.

And He was so clearly there in the way the last hour unfolded. As her breathing and heartbeat slowed, I stroked her hair and whispered, "Go to sleep, Mommy. It's okay. I love you. Go to sleep…" And she did, her hands held by those who cherished her, anointed by our tears, cradled in the arms of the One who called her His own.

Anne Marie Bennett may only have walked this earth for sixty-nine years, but she will be a part of us forever. And I will never stop thanking God for the gift of this woman, this mother, who was a blessing every day of my life. If ever I have done you a kindness, know that it was because of my mother. If ever I have been a blessing to you, know that it comes from all that my mother gave and taught me. She was one in a million. I'm so glad she was mine.

Thank you, dearest friends, for your prayers and notes. I will let you know when the memorial service will be held.

Until then, if you still have your mother in your life, go tell her how very precious she is to you. And give her a hug from me.

I love you.

Faith

The Solid Rock

"It won't collapse,
because it is built on rock..."
MATTHEW 7:25

thirty-three

"She was past weeping, wrapped in the ineffable solitude of grief."

LADY MABELL AIRLIE

THE NEXT FEW WEEKS WENT BY IN A BLUR. THE memorial service was held the Saturday before Mother's Day. Though it had meant waiting longer than usual, Faith and her father knew it was the right thing to do.

They needed the time to deal with details they'd never wanted to deal with. Faith had never imagined there was so much to be done when one passed from this world to eternity.

The passing happened in less than a heartbeat. No such luck with all that was left to do for those who remained. One decision after another had to be made. Decisions that reminded Faith and her dad, over and over, that Mom was gone. That this gaping hole in their hearts and lives would never be filled.

Not in this life.

Faith's emotions ran the gamut, from despair to hope, anger to gratitude. It was the anger she had the hardest time dealing with. Especially the anger with the nursing home and hospital. Yes, some in those places had been a great help. But others…

Others had done things, made decisions, that Faith was sure

had contributed to her mother's death. A death that she still felt shouldn't have happened.

Finally one day, she talked with her dad about it all. They were driving together, coming back from having chosen her mom's cremation niche.

"Dad, do you ever wonder if Mom shouldn't have died? That the mistakes people made in the nursing home, in the hospital—that those things made it impossible for Mom to recover?"

He kept his eyes on the road, thinking. "Sometimes."

Faith turned to face him at the admission. "Doesn't it make you mad? I mean, don't you want to make them pay for it?"

"You mean sue them." He sighed, glancing at her. "Sure, I've thought about it, but I keep coming back to the same questions. First, what would that accomplish? It wouldn't change anything. Your mother would still be dead—"

When his words choked off, Faith started to tell him to never mind, that she was sorry she'd brought it up. But he continued.

"—and I'm not convinced suing would be the right thing to do. But it's the other two questions that really stop me."

Faith waited. She needed something to stop her, to calm the bitterness within her.

"What would your mom want me to do?" His wistful smile tugged at Faith's heart. "Your mom was an amazing woman. She had such a capacity to love, to show God's love. Would she want me to immerse myself in anger, in bitterness, and making people pay for their mistakes?"

The answer was a no-brainer. "No."

He shook his head. "No. Your mom would want us to focus on the good, on the blessings, and on the last question. The one that matters most: What would God want me to do? What is He calling me to in this situation?"

"He sure couldn't want us to let people get away with killing someone."

"Faith, those people didn't kill your mother. They may not have helped her the way they should have, but your mom was sick. Her body was worn out. Yes, they made mistakes. But will suing them change that? No. Would it make things any better? I doubt it. The only thing I can imagine helping is to keep my eyes on God, on His word, on His call."

She closed her eyes at her dad's soft words. What *would* God want? He was a God of justice, but He also called them to love, to forgive. And when it came right down to it, He could have overcome all the mistakes, all the bad decisions, and brought Faith's mom through this. He was God. His was the final word.

And that ate at Faith as much as anything. Why didn't God heal her mother? "Are you mad at God?"

He hesitated. "Mad isn't the right word. I wish it hadn't happened. I'd give anything to have her still here, with me. With us. I feel like part of me has been torn away. But, punkin', God was the one who shared your mom with me. He brought us together. He kept and held us together for nearly fifty years." Dad blinked, but that didn't stop the tears from trickling down his face. "God didn't take your mom away. Diabetes did."

Faith had thought about their conversation many times since that day. And as she did so, she realized her father was right. Suing wouldn't accomplish anything. There were times when it was right, she supposed, but for them—for her—the right thing was to forgive. To let go of her anger and ask God to replace it with His peace.

That was the legacy her mom would want to leave.

So that was what Faith would do, with God's help. She'd face each day looking to the good, the blessings, the evidence of God's hand. And each time she saw those things, she'd praise Him for the mother who taught her how to open her eyes. And her heart.

The day of the memorial service dawned bright and sunny. The kind of day Faith's mom used to love. They'd decorated the room for the memorial with blankets of pansies, silk pansies and real ones. The room looked like a garden. And in the center of the flowers was a picture of her mother, laughing, eyes sparkling.

Friends and family came from all over the country, and the

room was full to overflowing. Teachers who had worked with Faith's mom. Students she'd taught and helped. Church members. Family members. And, much to Faith's utter delight, Sarah McMannis, from the summer at church camp. She'd moved away shortly after Faith came home from camp. Faith had no idea she'd even known about her mom.

"Pastor Fred let me know," she explained as she embraced Faith. "I knew I had to be here." She held Faith's gaze. "Your mom loved you, Faith. Deeply."

Faith could only nod and squeeze Sarah's hands.

When the time came to share memories of her mother, person after person stood and talked, relating stories that brought Faith's mother to life, even if only for a moment. For more than an hour the stories came and the room echoed with a sweet blend of laughter and weeping.

Afterward, the church held a luncheon, and everyone gathered there, talking, remembering, laughing. It was as though they all were loathe to leave, as though leaving would be the final chapter in Anne Marie Bennett's life. The final page turned, the book closed.

The end.

But Faith knew that wasn't so. It wasn't the end. It was only the beginning of the pain she would feel every time she looked at her mother's chair and didn't see her there, every time she saw pansies or smelled roses.

Zeke and Faith talked it over and asked Dad to come live with them. When he said he would, Faith was delighted. It was the first time in months she'd felt any joy.

Then came the task of sorting through her parents' possessions. Her mother's possessions. Her jewelry. Mom's letters from her mother. Her treasures.

And her clothes.

That was what did Faith in. Taking her mother's clothes out of her closet, placing them in boxes. Clothes that still had her mother's scent on them. Clothes that she could still see her mother wearing.

She'd held it together until she got the clothes to her house, to a back room where she planned to sort through them. That's where Zeke found her, sitting on the floor, surrounded by her mother's clothes, face pressed into her mother's favorite jacket.

"I—can't—*do*—this!" Faith gasped the words out when Zeke crouched beside her, placing a tender hand on her hair. She looked at him, begging him with her eyes to understand. "I can't *do* this without her. I don't know how to act, how to be... I don't know who I am without her."

"You're Faith Adelle." Zeke's quiet voice rang with love and conviction. "You're the baby she waited for, prayed for. The one she named *Faith* because God answered her prayers; the one she named *Adelle* because she knew you'd have a noble and kind spirit."

"But only because of her! How can I go on without her?"

"Because you're your mother's daughter. You're the thing that kept her going year after year. You're the one who brought her joy and delight. Just a day or so before she died, your mom and I talked. She told me how much she loved you. How proud she was of you. How grateful she was to see you living your life for God. Faith, your mom loved you! You meant the world to her. You and your dad were her world."

Each word flowed over her broken heart like a healing ointment, soothing the pain, warming the cold places.

Zeke took hold of her hand, drew her to her feet, then led her to a mirror. He stood behind her, his hands on her shoulders, as she looked at her reflection. He cupped her cheek.

"Your mom's not gone. You're the image of your mother. You have her smile, her hands, her laugh. And her faith. She lives on in you."

She leaned into him. "I miss her so much!"

"I know, darlin'. I know."

"Will it ever stop hurting? Does grief ever let you go once it gets hold of you?"

He was silent for a moment, and she met his gaze in the mirror. She saw the answer in this eyes.

"It won't, will it?"

He shook his head. "Not entirely. It will be better, but it's always going to hurt that your mom is gone." He turned her to face him, framed her face with his hands. "But we'll get through this. I promise."

Zeke looked at the piles of clothes. "But you know what? You don't have to get through this alone. I'm calling Winnie to come help you."

Faith didn't argue.

The next day she and Winnie sorted and folded. And though there were moments of tears, there were also times when they shared a memory that made them laugh.

"Your mom always wore this when she worked in the garden." Winnie held up the T-shirt with a lamb on the front and the saying, "I'm not fat, I'm fluffy!"

Faith grinned. "Mom loved that thing. She said she liked thinking of herself as fluffy."

"You know, Faith, your mom was a beautiful woman."

Winnie's words touched Faith's heart. She'd always considered her mom beautiful, but she knew others who looked at her, those who didn't know her, only saw a woman who was obese.

"Did you know—" Winnie folded the top and laid it in the box with gentle hands—"that the nurses were convinced your mom was younger than she was?"

Faith smiled. "She didn't look her age, that's true."

"One of the nurses I work with said your mom had the smoothest, prettiest skin she'd ever seen." Winnie's eyes twinkled. "I told them what your mom always used to say."

Faith almost choked on her laughter. "You didn't!" She knew exactly what Winnie was talking about.

Winnie nodded. "Oh, but I did. I told them your mom always said that was the nice thing about being fat..."

They finished it together: "There's no room for wrinkles!"

It felt so good to laugh. Faith had wondered these past weeks if she'd forgotten how.

She laid down the scarves she was folding and sat on the bed. "Thank you, Winnie."

Her friend glanced at her. "For what?"

Faith motioned at the clothes. "For this. For your help. For everything." She looked down. "I was so mean to you when we were in school, and you know what? I'm only starting to understand why."

Winnie came to sit beside her. "Faith, I forgave you long ago."

"I know, but I've been doing a lot of thinking since Mom..." She still had a hard time saying that. "Since Mom died. And I realized something." She gave Winnie a lopsided smile. "Did you know you're just like her?"

"Me?" Pink tinged Winnie's cheeks.

Faith nodded. "You. You have the same kind of heart and spirit she did. The kind that reaches out to people, wants to help them, to care for them." She folded her legs under her. "When I look at you, Win, I see so much of Mom."

Winnie blinked away tears. "I think that's the nicest thing anyone's ever said to me."

"Well, it's true. And it always has been, which is why I think I was such a brat to you back in school." Faith had been thinking this through for the last few days, and as she said it out loud, she knew it held the ring of truth. "You reminded me of Mom, and that made me mad." She met Winnie's surprised gaze. "Because I wanted to be like her. And I wasn't. I was jealous of you, Win. And I resented that you were more like my mom than I was. I'm so sorry for the way I acted."

Winnie hugged Faith. "It's okay. Really it is. And you know what? I think you're very much like your mom. I see her smile in you."

Faith sniffed and hugged Winnie. "That's what Zeke says."

"Well, you should listen to him." Winnie stood and grabbed the next pile of clothes. "Anyone who looks at you sees your mom, Faith. Her heart. Her kindness. Her faith." A smile of realization bloomed on Winnie's face. "You're her legacy!"

Faith stared at her friend, stunned. She'd never thought of it that way. But as she rolled the idea around in her head, it made sense. During these last few months, Faith had realized something. The very fabric of her life was made up of millions of tiny threads, many of which either came from her mother or bore her imprint. Faith always knew, even in the hard and angry days, that she and her mother were close, connected. But she'd never imagined what losing her mother would do, how devastating a separation that would be. How she would feel torn apart. Incomplete.

She'd always believed life would never be the same without her mom. Now she understood *she* would never be the same. What she didn't know, though, was what that meant. Only One could help her with that. And so, as her mother had always taught her, she went to Him, praying, seeking His peace and guidance. Reading His word.

And always, always, the word she received from Him was the same.

Wait.

Be patient. Be still.

Wait.

And so she did. She waited. Trusting with her mind, if not with her heart yet, that the answer would come.

In the meantime, she thought as she smiled at Winnie, she was grateful she didn't have to wait alone.

thirty-four

"Isolation has led me to reflection, reflection to doubt, doubt to a more sincere and intelligent love of God."

MARIE LENERU

From: FaithinHim

To: TheCoffeeCrew

Sent: Saturday, August 20, 2005

Subject: Thoughts about Mom

Hello, friends.

I'm sitting here, realizing it's been four months—just shy of four months actually—without Mom. Life goes on.

I don't know why or how, but it does. Doesn't matter whether it makes sense or seems all wrong. It goes on its merry way.

A part of my mind is relieved that things seem to be returning to some semblance of normal. But that thought no sooner comes than my heart rebels, screaming that I don't want life to go on. I don't want to return to normal, or any semblance thereof. How can life ever be even close to normal without Mom?

Sometimes I'm so scared I'll forget. Forget her sweet, beautiful smile. Forget the feel of her hand or the comfort of her hug. The sparkle in her eyes. The special look on her face when she saw my dad.

So many things I want to keep. Pieces of her. Tiny fragments that touch so many corners of my life. I miss her. So much. I don't want to get used to life without her, and yet, that's what's happening. During the day, as I'm caught up in everyday life, it's okay. But at night, as I lie in bed, surrounded by her absence, I HATE that I'm getting used to it. To her being gone.

I can't even imagine what Christmas will be like. I can only ask you all to be praying for us. This is going to be a year of firsts. Our first Thanksgiving without her. Our first Christmas. Our first…everything.

Please, ask God to help us. I don't know how else we're going to get through it.

Faith

thirty-five

"To live in hearts we leave behind is not to die."

THOMAS CAMPBELL

WHOEVER COINED THE TERM "THE DOG DAYS OF August" had to be an Oregonian. A southern Oregonian, to be exact. Faith was sure of it. Because few places were hotter than Southern Oregon in August.

Thank heaven for air-conditioning in cars!

Faith pushed her sunglasses back on her nose, wiping her face as she did so. She was nuts coming out here on a day this hot.

That's what you get for putting it off for so long.

Hmph. She glanced at the arrangement of silk pansies on her passenger seat. The cheery blossoms danced as the car raced along. What was it Mom always said about pansies? Ah, yes. They had the friendliest faces of any of the flowers.

The thought made Faith smile.

She turned her car up the long drive, taking in the tall evergreens lining the road. She'd say one thing for the memorial park. It was beautiful. You could see the mountains on all sides, and the numerous trees and lush shrubbery gave it the appearance of a park.

When she and her father had decided this was the place they would bury Mom—where they'd all be buried someday—Faith had commented on the fact that it had a great view. Her father's bland stare made her realize what she'd said, and for a moment she feared she'd added to his grief.

Instead, he burst into laughter.

Amazing how healing laughter could be, even in the most terrible moments.

Faith could use a little laughter right now. But she wasn't feeling terribly jovial. Maybe after she got this over with. She'd never liked feeling guilty. And though there was no good reason for her to feel that way—it wasn't like her mom was going to be upset with her for not coming sooner—that's exactly how she felt.

Guilty as all get-out.

She pulled the car into a parking place, took hold of the pansies, and slid from the car. Walking up the cobblestone path, she lifted her face to the slight breeze stirring the air. Cool fingers caressed her brow, her cheeks, ruffled her hair as though greeting her.

Faith's steps slowed as she approached the brick wall of cremation niches. She hadn't been here since the memorial. Couldn't make herself come. Couldn't stand the thought of seeing her mother's name there, on the small, square plaque. Gold letters standing out in stark relief on the polished black background.

Name. Date of birth. Date of death. Inadequate testimony to the woman her mother had been, the life she'd led.

But when Faith woke that morning, she'd known, deep inside, it was time.

Drawing a breath, she stepped to her mother's niche. It was on the top row, so that made it easy to put the flowers right above her plaque. Faith took her time, arranging the flowers, setting them just so.

Anything to avoid looking down. At the plaque.

But finally, she had to do it. She let her gaze travel down, and then stop. Read the name.

ANNE MARIE BENNETT
SEPTEMBER 14, 1935—APRIL 23, 2005
"Gone, but not forgotten."

The burning behind her eyes hit, and she grit her teeth. She'd sworn she wouldn't do this. Wouldn't cry again. But seeing her mother's name like that…

Made it real.

Faith knew that was silly. Her mother's death was as real as it got, plaque or no plaque. She was getting to the point where she could sleep regularly again. Well, somewhat regularly. But better than she had been. And now it was only once in a while that Zeke had to hold her while her sorrow worked its way through her.

Still…somewhere in the back of her mind, Faith had been able to convince herself her mother wasn't really gone. Not for good. She was *away*. On a really long trip. That's what she'd convinced her heart. Until now.

She lifted her fingers and traced the letters of her mother's name. Then she pressed her palm to the plaque and let out a shivery sigh. "Oh, Mom. You're really gone, aren't you?" Her mouth trembled. "You're not on a trip someplace. You're gone."

Faith rubbed the heel of her hand into her eyes, wishing she could rub the pain away as easily as she could the tears. *Father God, this hurts so much.*

After her mother's death, Faith had remembered all the times she talked with someone who lost a loved one. The stupid things she'd said. Things she wasn't sure would help, but that she felt she had to say. After all, one had to say something to fill the silences, didn't one?

Faith shook her head. Why didn't those poor souls tell her—tell everyone who spouted empty platitudes—to *shut up*. Now that people had said those things to Faith, she understood. Understood that many words of supposed comfort were salt on a raw, pulsating, bone-deep wound.

"She's in a much better place now."

"She's where she can watch over you."

And Faith's personal favorite: *"She's not hurting any longer. After all, you wouldn't want her back, would you? Not if it meant she was in pain again?"*

That's what a well-meaning person at the memorial service had said, and it had taken all of Faith's resources to keep from yelling, "Are you *stupid?* Of COURSE I want her back. On any terms. She's my mother! I'd take her any way I could get her. Don't you get it? Grief isn't about her, about her pain or freedom, but about *me.* About the fact that my mother is gone."

My mother is gone.

Faith let the words echo through her. *My mother is gone.* Faith would never see her smile again. Not in this life. Never feel her soft hands on her face. Never know the solid sensation of her hug or the sweet fragrance of her nearness as she pressed a kiss to Faith's cheek. Never hear that tender, loving voice telling her how treasured she was, how she didn't know what she'd do without Faith, how glad she was that Faith was there.

Wouldn't want her back?

Now, almost four months later, those words rang so false. No words could help or heal. What really helped was silence. And listening. And letting her talk and vent and weep and grieve. Sitting with her and holding her hand because her mom couldn't do that any longer. And letting her talk about Mom. Remember her. Laugh about her and all she was to Faith's family.

A family that would never, ever, this side of eternity, be the same.

Faith moved away from the wall. She walked to where she could look out over the valley. How her mom had loved this valley! Loved its rugged beauty, the mountains that cradled it in massive arms. She'd found such delight in the beauty all around them.

She'd found such delight in *life.*

She'd celebrated the blessings God gave them, savoring each moment—teaching Faith to do the same. And as Faith stood there, she grew more and more aware. Of silence. Of peace.

Of a presence, around her, within her.

From deep within her memory, words came rolling forward. Words she'd read long ago. Words of truth and life.

"The Spirit of the Sovereign LORD is upon me."

A tingling sensation began at the base of Faith's spine, working its way up, as the words continued.

"He has sent me to comfort the brokenhearted and to announce that captives will be released and prisoners *will be freed.*"

The last three words rang through her, filling her heart, overflowing her spirit.

Free. She was free. And suddenly Faith understood. Yes, losing her mother hurt. Of *course* it hurt. How could it not? Her mother was joy and celebration and love. Her mother was God's touch in Faith's life. Losing her had to hurt. Deeply. And it would take a long time to deal with such a loss.

And Faith realized something more.

It was okay.

Okay to cry, to grieve a year, two years, even ten years down the road. Okay to wish her mother was still with them. Okay to long for eternity, because it was there she would once again be with her mother.

And it was okay to enjoy life until then. To laugh. To find joy.

To live.

Because that was what her mother would want for her. She'd want her to embrace life. To delight in all God had for her.

Laughter, as pure and refreshing as water from a mountain stream, bubbled up from inside her and lifted on the warm, summer wind. Something was different. Something inside her had changed. Turning to walk back to the niche, she looked again at her mother's name—and smiled.

The heaviness was gone. Not the pain. That would be there for a long time. But the heaviness that had pressed down on her heart and spirit was finally, blessedly gone.

She was free.

She pressed a kiss into her hand, then put it over her mother's name. And then, smiling, Faith walked back to her car.

She was ready. Ready to do all that God had for her until she could be with her mother again. Ready to live. Really live.

"Bring it on," she said with a small laugh as she pulled the car door open. "Bring it all on."

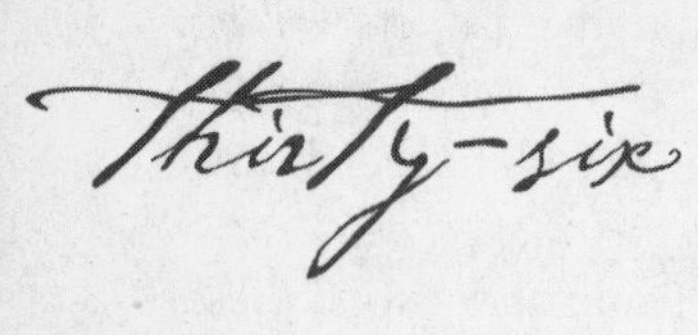

"Looking for peace is like looking for a turtle with a mustache: You won't be able to find it. But when your heart is ready, peace will come looking for you."

AJAHN CHAH

"HELLOOO... YOU READY FOR VISITORS?"

Faith looked up and grinned. "Connie, come on in!"

Connie glanced over her shoulder, looking like a kid about to break and run for the playground. "I'm not alone."

Faith laughed. "There's a big surprise."

With that, the Coffee Crew came through the door in a tumble of giggles and chatter. They sounded like a bunch of birds gone looney. They surrounded her bed, laying stuffed animals and helium balloons and bouquets of flowers from one end of the bed to the other.

One of the bouquets landed on Faith's face.

"Look out, you clod! You're going to smother her!"

Connie gave Andi a soulful look of utter woundedness. "It slipped."

Linda brushed her aside, pulling the flowers off of Faith's face. "Your brain slipped, you mean."

"Come on, guys, is that any way to talk in a hospital?" Deb

perched on the bed. "Especially around a livin', breathin' miracle."

"Speaking of which—" Jennifer peered over Linda's shoulder. "Where is it?"

"*It?*" Patti hooted. "We're not talking about a puppy, you know."

"Oh, I love puppies! That's what we should have brought, a puppy!"

Faith looked to the door, where Sandy and Lori were coming in. She waved at Faith. "I had to park the car, and *they*—" she tossed her head at them—"wouldn't wait for me. How's that for a bunch of brats?"

"We wanted to come see the miracle." Deb shot Faith a quick, apologetic look. "Not that we didn't come to see you—"

"Okay, okay!" Faith was laughing so hard tears ran down her face. "Zeke took the baby for a walk."

Lori came to give Faith a hug. "I bet he's so happy."

"Even though he didn't get a son?" Patti teased.

"Son, schmon, I got the most beautiful daughter in the world. Who needs a son?"

With a collective squeal, the women spun toward the doorway where Zeke stood holding their daughter.

He came into the room, handing the baby to Faith. The women gathered round, crooning and cooing.

"Have you decided on a name?"

Faith nodded, and Zeke answered Lori. "We're going to name her Annette." He met Faith's gaze. "It means 'little Anne.'"

"Little Anne!" Andi sighed, threw her arm around Connie, and hugged her. "That's perfect!"

Sandy touched Annette's downy crown of hair. She slanted a glance at Faith. "And you thought you couldn't get pregnant. I told you God was in control."

Jennifer piped up. "And it helped that you quit worrying about it."

"I'll bet the scented candles helped—"

"Okay, ladies." Linda cut Deb and the others off before they really got going. "I think we've tired Faith and the baby out enough." She shooed them toward the door.

"Yes, Mother." Connie pulled a face at Linda.

With waves and calls of good-bye, the women headed out the door. Zeke and Faith heard them giggling and talking all the way down the hall. They grinned at each other.

"Is it safe to come hold my granddaughter?"

Faith looked up. Her father was peering in the doorway. "I take it you're referring to my coffee friends."

He entered the room. "I think they all piled in the elevator, pinning one poor guy to the back wall."

"Was he young and handsome?"

Faith's dad nodded.

Zeke shook his head. "We'd better say a prayer for the poor kid!"

Dad came to the bed and held out his arms. "You plan to share?"

"Absolutely." Faith lifted Annette and watched her father's strong hands close over her baby with gentle care.

He looked down into her face, then beamed at Faith. "She's got your mother's eyes."

Faith nodded. "We noticed that too."

"Annette. Little Annie." He drew a finger down the baby's cheek."Oh, my, how she would have loved you."

Faith held a hand out to her father, and, supporting Annette with one arm, he gripped it. "Dad, I'll need you to help me tell her about Mom. I want her to know Mom."

His grip tightened. "I will. You know I will."

It wasn't as hard to talk about Mom as it had been in that first year after she died. Now, after a little over two years, the loss didn't overwhelm Faith every day. Just once in a while.

Like now.

Tears trickled down her cheeks. "I wish she could be here."

"I do, too, punkin'. I do, too." He looked down at Annette. "She would have considered this quite the birthday present."

"Almost birthday present."

"So your little one thought she was supposed to make her appearance on September fifteenth rather than the fourteenth. She was only off by a day." He let go of Faith's hand and cuddled his new granddaughter close. "That's pretty good, for a newborn."

Faith chuckled as her dad went to nudge Zeke with his elbow. "So, how about we go show this little beauty off?"

"Dad—"

But neither one of Faith's men was listening to her.

Zeke clapped his father-in-law on the back. "Sounds good to me!"

Before Faith could stop them, the two made their way out the door. Faith lay back against the pillows, chuckling.

"I heard there was a baby in here."

"Winnie!" Faith waved her friend into the room. "I wondered when you'd be able to stop by."

"I'm on break." She pulled the chair up. "And I actually saw your dad and hubby walking down the hall, showing that little girl to anyone passing by. *Proud* doesn't begin to cover what they are."

"How about *crazy?*"

Winnie patted Faith's hand. "So how are you feeling?"

"Sore." She shifted on the bed. "And grateful. More grateful than I've ever been in my life."

"You have a beautiful baby, Faith. And she has a wonderful name to grow into."

Faith held out her hand, and Winnie took it. "Will you help me tell her about Mom, Winnie? I want Annette to feel as though she knows Mom. Really knows her."

Winnie's eyes misted. "Of course, I'll help. I'll tell Annette how your mom waited for you like you waited for her. And how God answered your mom's prayers, and yours. But the best way for Annette to get to know your mom is for her to get to know you."

Faith squeezed her friend's hand. "I wish Mom were here."

"I know, Faith. But she's a part of you. I see her in you all the time. And the older you get—"

"Hey, you're just as old as I am! And I'm not old!"

Winnie ignored her. "The more I hear her in you. You sound like your mom more and more."

"That's a good thing."

"That's a very good thing." Winnie glanced at her watch, then rose. "Now, I'm going to go tell the nurse to chase down those two scamps of yours so that baby gets some rest. And you, too."

"That's what happens when you have a baby at the ripe old age of thirty-eight." Faith grimaced.

"I seem to recall someone saying we're not old..."

This time Winnie was the one who got ignored. "They make you stay two nights instead of letting you go home the next day."

"At least you don't have to fix your own meals here." Winnie gave Faith a hug and waved as she left the room.

Within minutes, Zeke was back in the room, Annette cradled in his arms. Faith looked over his shoulder, but no one followed him in. "Daddy go home?"

"Yup. He said he'd stop by to see you tomorrow morning. Tonight he just wanted to see Annette before he headed home to bed."

"Hmpf! Fine thing!"

At her mock outrage, Zeke wrapped his arms around her. "Hey, I love you."

She snuggled against them, then had to stifle a yawn. "Oops." She pulled away. "Sorry about that."

He took her hand as she settled back against her pillows. "No problem. Having a baby is hard work. Or so you keep telling me." He pulled the covers up to her chin. "Get some rest."

"You're not leaving, are you?"

"Not until you fall asleep."

She smiled, letting her eyes drift shut. "Zeke?"

"Hmm?"

"Are you worried?"

"About what?"

"The baby. I mean, so many things could happen. And kids can get into so much trouble—"

"Faith?"

"Hmm?" She pried her eyes open to look at him.

His eyes glowed with a warm, tender light. "Relax, hon. Go to sleep. God's in control."

Faith smiled. So He was. And with that truth cradling her, holding her tight, she drifted into a deep, peaceful sleep.

Dear Reader,

Novelists are odd ducks. We experience the same joys and trials as everyone else, but we do so with a mental notepad. Bad encounter in traffic? Hmm, better write that down. Fight with the spouse? Gotta remember how that felt, what we said. Sickness, job loss, parenting challenges, good or bad times with friends and family, sick dogs, laundry stains, gardening...

Doesn't matter what it is. We jot the details down. Because who knows? One day we just might use it in a book!

When I first started writing, I planned to have fun, to write entertaining, uplifting stories of adventure and romance (and a sprinkling of my love of animals). And that's what I did. Until two years ago.

That's when I finally quit telling God, "No, I can't."

He'd nudged me for years to write about my marriage; I'd resisted for years. I mean, it would be hard! The hardest book I'd ever write. After all, it was based on the hardest thing I'd ever experienced. But finally I knew the time had come, and so I wrote *The Breaking Point.*

I was right. It was the hardest book I'd ever written. But when I finished, oh, man! I felt great! This was the story God had been preparing me to write. And so I sent it off to my wonderful editor, Julee Schwarzburg, grateful for God's work in my life—and ready to go back to writing the easy stories.

Funny how our plans are so seldom God's plans, eh?

I'm glad He doesn't tell us that. I'm glad I didn't know then—in my "Praise God, the hard book is done!" glow—that the worst thing I'd ever face was just around the corner. It hit with savage force in 2002, when my mother, the center of our family's universe, fell seriously ill due to complications of diabetes.

Mom was diagnosed with diabetes more than thirty years ago. Back then, they didn't know that once you're diagnosed with diabetes, you've got, generally speaking, about fifteen years to manage the disease. What you do in those years has a huge impact on the kind—and severity—of complications you'll face. And believe me, the complications of diabetes can be horrific.

Sadly, because we didn't have this knowledge, Mom didn't manage her disease as well as she might have. So her complications were severe: eye disease; nerve damage to her feet, which limited her mobility; and heart and pulmonary disease.

It was those last two that hit Mom in early 2002. We went through run after run to the ER, a score of tests, unexpected heart surgery, weeks in the CCU, then the ICU, months of rehab, battles with medical professionals, and day after day of prayer and petition.

But on April 23, 2002, my sweet mom's body couldn't fight any longer, and she left us for eternity. I was stunned. It was as though someone had reached in and ripped out part of my heart. As much as I adored my mom, I hadn't realized how much of my identity was tied to her, how much I leaned and depended on her. Awash in grief, I went to the Christian bookstore, frantic to find something—anything—that would help make sense of what I was going through.

There was very little.

I found general books on grief, most about losing children or spouses. But there was nothing—not one book—about a woman losing her mother. Fortunately, God gave me wonderful friends and family, and talking with them helped. And showed me I was far from alone.

While men shared their losses, it was the women's stories that got to me. Women of all ages poured out their sorrow and pain. Losing a mother is hard for anyone, but I realized that for a woman, whether she's close to her mother or not, it's one of the most difficult, painful, and shattering things she'll ever face.

Good, bad, or indifferent, mothers mold us. They model womanhood, motherhood, and friendship. They impart physical, emotional, and relational threads that weave together to make up the very fabric of who we are. So much of our focus, as young girls and as adults, centers on our mothers. We want to be as much like them (or as different) as possible, to make them proud (or not embarrass or humiliate them), to do what they did (or didn't do) in their parenting, to make them smile (or stay out of the line of fire).

And when our mothers die, we often feel lost. Abandoned. Incomplete. It takes time to sort through all of that. To understand who we are without a mother-mirror reflecting the image we have of ourselves. To find our way as individuals rather than as daughters.

I'm still sorting it all out, and it's been just over two years since Mom died. But at least I can see a picture of my mom now, or share a memory of her, without falling apart. And I'm discovering, in some ways, she's still here. People tell me I have Mom's smile or her hands, that they hear her when I laugh. I love that. Part of my sweet, loving, godly mom lives on in me. And though I don't have children of my own, I share Mom and all she taught me with the young girls and women in my life.

Because she was amazing—the most wonderful mother, the most gracious woman.

And so, when my editor, Julee, came to me almost a year after Mom died and asked me to write a novel about a daughter losing her mother, I didn't run. I asked for time to pray, and when God made it clear He was asking me to do this, I said yes.

Writing *The Breaking Point* was hard; writing this book was devastating. When I got to the scenes about Anne's illness, and especially her death, I could hardly type for the tears and sobs. It was like losing Mom all over again. And yet...

God brought me great joy in sharing this story. Because in doing so, I get to let you all know what a remarkable woman my mom was. What a blessing she was to me. What a pure gift from God. I get to give you a glimpse of the woman who shaped and molded me, who taught me above all else that God is good, He is in control, and He is worth trusting.

If your mom is still living, I pray this book will help you appreciate and cherish her. If your mother is gone, I pray it will bring you a touch of comfort from someone who understands—really understands—that loss.

May the Master touch you today, may He grant you peace, and may He hold us all in His hands until that day when He comes again. And I don't know about you, but on that day, I know my mom will be there, waiting, her arms open wide. And I plan to run to her as fast as my legs will take me, throw my arms around her, and not let her go for a really, really long time.

I can hardly wait.

Peace,

Karen M. Ball

Discussion Questions

Part One

1. How would you describe your relationship with your mother? With your daughter(s)?

2. Did you think Anne and Jared handled Faith wisely? Why or why not? Did they contribute to the problem? Consider Job 28 and Proverbs 2. How can you, as a parent, avoid making matters worse when your children rebel?

3. If you have troubled relationships with your children or with your parents, do you feel free to share your struggles with your church family? Why or why not? Read Romans 1:12; 2 Corinthians 13:11; Philippians 2:1–2; Colossians 2:1–2, 3:12–15; 1 Thessalonians 5:11. In light of such Scriptures, what is our responsibility both as those struggling and as those seeking to help those who struggle?

4. Exodus 20:12 says: "Honor your father and mother. Then you will live a long, full life in the land the Lord your God will give you." Ephesians 6:3 tells us: "And this is the promise: If you honor your father and mother, 'you will live a long life, full of blessing.'" What does it mean to honor your mother? How can one honor a mother who was less than wonderful? Do you feel you've honored your mother? If so, how? If not, can you think of one thing you could do that would be honoring to your mother?

5. Proverbs 1:8 warns: "Don't neglect your mother's teaching." What is the most important truth you learned from your mother? What seeds of truth are you, as a mother, planting in your own children?

6. Faith struggled with wanting to be loved and accepted as she was. What kept her from seeing that love in her mother? In God? Are there things that keep you from seeing another's love for you? God's love for you? Read Proverbs 10:12; John 17:22–24; 1 John 3:16–17, 4:8, 17–19. What do these verses say to you about God's love for you? Can anything stand in the way of that love?

7. Both Faith and Anne realized they were in rebellion—Faith against her mother and God, Anne against her disease and its impact on her body. What was the result of each one's rebellion?

8. Read the following verses: Joshua 24:19; 1 Samuel 15:23; Psalm 39:7–9; Ezekiel 18:30. What is the cost of rebellion for a believer? Now read Psalm 32 and Ezekiel 18:31–32. What can we do when we realize we've given in to rebellion?

PART TWO

1. Serious illness and death are difficult issues for any of us to face. Often grief brings anger and doubt. Sadly, many in the church are afraid to talk honestly about illness, death, and grief. Do you feel free to be open and honest about these things in your church? What does Scripture say about sharing our struggles? (See Romans 12:12–13, 15.)

2. Have you had a family member or close friend who was seriously ill? How did you cope with the situation? How did you offer comfort and support to that person?

3. Proverbs 23:22 gives us all an interesting caution: "Don't despise your mother's experience when she is old." Our parents' generation has experienced so much. They hold a wealth of wisdom for us, if we'll only take the time to

listen. Why do we so often struggle with spending time with those who are older than we are? Why are we often uncomfortable in places like nursing homes?

4. Faith had to act as her mother's advocate with the medical world. Have you ever had to stand in the gap for someone when those who were the "professionals" weren't doing what you knew they should be doing? How do we know when it's time to step in for friends or family in such situations? How should we conduct ourselves when doing so? (See Proverbs 3:1–8, 13–26; 1 Corinthians 13.)

5. Have you offered fervent prayers for someone's healing, only to have that person die? How did that affect your trust in God? How do we reconcile Scriptures like Matthew 7:7–11; John 14:13; and James 4:2 with such unanswered prayer?

6. Even the firmest believer may be shaken when someone he or she loves deeply dies. Loss is never easy to endure. Grief can be debilitating. Is it a sin to doubt in the face of loss and death?

7. Read through the book of Job. What does this teach us about doubt? About grief? About false comfort? When her mother died, Faith was angry when people offered her empty comfort or careless platitudes. How can we truly help those dealing with grief? What are some practical things Faith's friends did for her?

8. Read Psalm 18; Matthew 4:15–16; Romans 5:21; 7:4–6; 8:34–36; 1 Corinthians 15:54–57; and 1 Thessalonians 4:13–18. What do these verses tell us about death and dying?

9. Read Psalm 42; 94:17–19, 22; and Romans 15:13. Where can we find hope, even in the darkest of times?

"Karen Ball has penned a modern classic and given us two unforgettable characters to root for. This is an author to watch!"

—ROBIN LEE HATCHER, bestselling author of *Firstborn* and *Promised to Me*

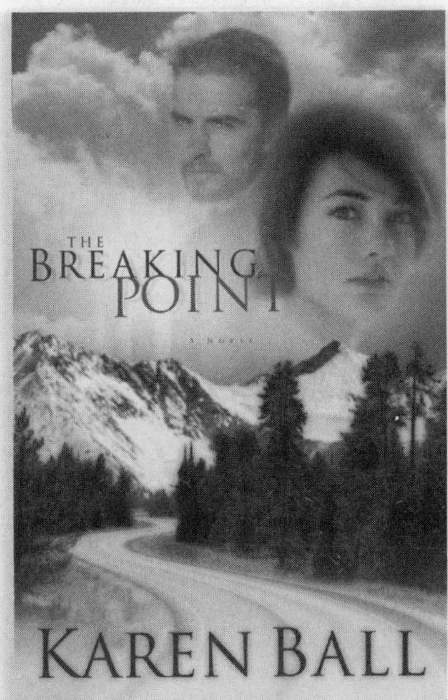

1-59052-033-5

Gabe and Renee Roman are on the edge—relationally and spiritually. But after years of struggling in their marriage, their greatest test comes in the most unexpected of forms: a blizzard in the Oregon wilderness. Their truck hurtles down the side of a mountain, and suddenly they are forced to fight for survival by relying on each other. But both must surrender their last defenses if they are to come home at last—to God and to each other. Only then will they learn the most important truths of all: God is sufficient, and only through obedience to His call can we find true joy. Can the Romans overcome their greatest obstacle—themselves—in time?

www.multnomahbooks.com

"A wonderful story of love, forgiveness, and stewardship over the world God has given us."

—FRANCINE RIVERS, bestselling author of *And the Shofar Blew* and *Redeeming Love*

1-57673-597-4

Taylor Sorensen has a secret: There are wolves on her ranch. Taylor's new ranch hand, Connor Alexander, has a secret, too: He's a wildlife biologist who's been sent to find out if, after sixty years, wolves have returned to Wyoming. Caught in a fierce battle against angry ranchers and centuries of superstition, Taylor and Connor are drawn together by their desire to protect these wild, majestic animals. What they don't know is that there's someone else out there who hates the wolves, someone who's determined to get rid of them—and Taylor and Connor if necessary—at any cost.